ENRAPTURED

ENRAPTURED

ELISABETH NAUGHTON

WITHDRAWN

sourcebooks
casablanca

Published by Sourcebooks Casablanca, an imprint of Sourcebooks, Inc.
P.O. Box 4410, Naperville, Illinois 60567-4410
(630) 961-3900
Fax: (630) 961-2168
www.sourcebooks.com

Printed and bound in Canada.
WC 10 9 8 7 6 5 4 3 2 1

For the Running Girls:

Connie, Stephani, and Sara.

Because you kick my butt into gear and make me run even when I don't want to,

Because you listen to me grumble about characters and plots and all things writing related while we're on those runs,

And because you're awesome friends who not only love me, but the crazy worlds I create.

For all these reasons and so many more too numerous to list,

You girls totally rock!

So mighty is the hidden power of truth…
For the one achieved high heaven,
And the other…on sounding wings hovered a
  conqueror in the fluent air.

—Ovid, *Metamorphoses* 4

Chapter 1

DEATH GROWLS, DEVIL HORNS, AND A MOSH PIT. NOT Orpheus's idea of a good time. Not by a long shot.

As he maneuvered through the metalheads in the crowd of outdoor concertgoers banging to the beat of the pounding bass, he couldn't help but be slightly amused by their stupidity. They had no idea what they were opening themselves up to with the satanic lyrics and black-magic worship. But Orpheus did.

Boy, did he ever.

He glanced around the crowd again, searching for the familiar darkness he knew was hovering somewhere close. His urgency ratchetted up about ten notches. After tracking her for the last three months, he'd finally found her at this outdoor concert in western Washington. What she was doing with a bunch of headbangers, he didn't know, but he wasn't about to lose her. Not to the chase, and definitely not to them.

A blur of black crossed his line of sight four people over, and his adrenaline amped. He pushed past a man wearing leather pants and a dog collar.

Beer sloshed over the man's T-shirt. He turned and glared Orpheus's way. "Hey, dickhead, watch it!"

Normally Orpheus would be right up in the guy's face, but not tonight. Tonight he had more important matters to deal with. He scanned the crowd again, searching for her. She was petite, and dressed all in black with that long dark hair, not easy to find, but he caught sight of her again when she looked back to see if he was still following. The whites of her eyes all but glowed in the darkness, and the recognition and fear on her pale face told him she knew just what he was.

Smart girl to run. In any other situation, that might amuse him. But he'd had it with playing cat and mouse.

She picked up her pace, maneuvered easily through the crowd as she headed away from the stage. Orpheus wasn't so lucky. His size kept him from weaving through the throng of people. He muscled his way past the pulsing fans, intent on not losing her.

She brushed by a woman with long blond hair. The blond turned to look after her, said something Orpheus couldn't hear, but his target didn't even slow. She disappeared again in the crowd. The blond, however, turned to look his way as if she sensed him. Their eyes held for the briefest of seconds.

Violet eyes. The color so startling, he faltered. Like polished amethyst. Déjà vu struck him square in the chest. He didn't know how or where, but he'd seen this human before.

Before he thought better of it, he took in the long hair that fell to the center of her back. She wasn't dressed outrageously, like some of the others in the crowd—no chains or dog collars, just a denim jacket that covered a fitted scoop-necked black shirt and slim black pants. But the clothes accentuated her curves in all the right places. And the knee-high black goth boots that propped her up a good four inches were sexier than hell.

She wasn't headbanging or jumping to the beat, but she was obviously here for the show. One corner of her glossed lips curled into a wicked smirk as she studied him back. As much as he would have liked to let her look her fill, the longer he distracted himself with this human the farther away his target would get.

And yet...where the hell had he seen her before?

He turned away from the blond, scanned the crowd again. Called himself ten kinds of stupid for being distracted by a measly human. He let his senses guide him. The darkness within his target he could stomach. It was the light that repelled him. That odd light that marked her as one of Zeus's own and told him exactly where she was located in the mass of people.

There.

His daemon surged forward. He moved to see past a couple with spiked purple hair and caught sight of the ends of her long black locks waving in the wind as she ran past the last concertgoers and dropped down over the other side of the hill.

Damn it.

He picked up his pace and finally reached the peak of the grassy incline. She was already at the fence some thirty yards below, nothing more than a shadow climbing up and over the chain link like a seasoned cat burglar. Where had this female trained? With the Argonauts themselves?

He shoved that thought aside and followed. Darkness pressed in, but the eerie orange lights spaced every so often across the vast parking lot made her easy to see. That and his heightened night vision, now that they were out of the chaos of the concert.

He was over the fence in moments, this time easily weaving through cars in the lot. She didn't look back, but his highly attuned hearing caught every pound of her heart and each push and pull of air in her lungs as she ran toward the trees.

The music faded to a dim thump. The crowd's screams died in the background. His boots crunched across the pavement, then turned quiet as he moved from asphalt to forest floor to mix with the scents of earth and moss wafting on the air. Did she think she could outrun him? Hide in the trees? It didn't matter that she could trace her roots back to Zeus himself. The female was about to learn there was no hiding from him. Not when she was the key to his getting what he needed most.

Douglas fir rose up around him. In the distance, the White River gurgled over rocks and downed limbs. He slowed when he saw her standing in filtered moonlight twenty yards away, still as stone and staring into the darkness as if she were nothing more than a statue.

For a second, he wondered if she'd been frozen in place by some sort of dark magic. His brother Gryphon possessed that gift—the ability to freeze those around him for miniscule seconds—but Gryphon was now dead, his soul rotting somewhere in Hades, all thanks to Orpheus. No way his brother had cast any kind of power from the other side, and not once in three hundred years had Orpheus come across another with the same gift. Which meant something else had stopped her. Or spooked her more than he had.

The familiar darkness he'd sensed earlier stirred his daemon within. Anxious to get to her before it did, he stepped cautiously toward her, was just about to tell her who he was so they could end this idiotic game of chase, when a voice at his back drew him to a stop.

"Step away from her, daemon."

He turned—as did his target—toward the blond in the goth boots, who stood near a cluster of trees.

His quarry gasped. He reached out and wrapped his hand around her upper arm before she could get away. The female was nothing but skin and bones. Though she was definitely quick.

She struggled, but he held her firm and dragged her toward his chest. To the blond he growled, "Go back to the concert, woman."

But before he could send the blond packing, Orpheus realized something besides him had spooked the female in his arms. *Sonofabitch*.

He whipped around, spotted the three massive males walking their way. His target tensed, sucked in a breath. Orpheus cursed his dumbass luck and pushed her behind him. He wanted to tell the blond to run, but there was nothing these dogs liked better than a chase. He'd take care of them, then her.

"Look what we have here," the one in the middle said. All three wore sunglasses, even though it was night. But Orpheus didn't need to see their eyes to know they were glowing. He could *feel* it. Just as he could feel his own eyes begin to glow in response.

Damn it. And damn his target for running straight for them.

"Looks to me like he has plenty to share," the one to the left said, the one with the shaved head and double gold hoop earrings. "We're hungry too, brother."

Oh, Orpheus didn't doubt these three daemons were hungry. Atalanta, their leader, may be trapped in the Fields of Asphodel, but her new breed of daemon— monsters who looked human but weren't—lived on.

And they needed to feed to regain the strength they were no longer getting from the Underworld. What Atalanta didn't know was that she couldn't control hybrids the way she could her army of ordinary daemons. They weren't brainless soldiers. They were part human, and as such retained that human characteristic that all the gods hated—free will.

Yeah, Orpheus knew that better than anyone, didn't he? Cursing his luck all over again, he scanned the trees, focused on his senses. Didn't pick up any other threat around them, which meant these three dickheads were alone.

"Look, guys. The chick and I were just about to get nice and friendly, so why don't you just turn right around and go find some unsuspecting sheep to toy with. I'm sure that's right up your alley."

"Come on, man. You don't need two. We'll take the blond." The leader licked his lips and stepped forward.

Skata. Stupid human with her stupid curiosity. Behind him he heard the female he'd been chasing shuffle backward. She obviously knew what they faced, but the human probably didn't. In a minute though— unless he figured a way out of this mess—she was going to discover just what kind of nightmare she'd wandered into.

Man, his day was heading right for the shitter.

He reached back for the blade he kept sheathed against his spine beneath his coat, the one as long as his forearm. The one that had belonged to his brother and bore the marking of their forefather on the handle. Then he whispered, "Run. Take the human and run."

"That," the male to the right growled, taking a step

away from the others and puffing up his chest, "is an unwise move, daemon."

Yeah, no shit, Sherlock. But Orpheus was out of options, as far as he could see. If his target died, he was screwed, and daemon hybrid himself or not, he didn't want to see the stupid human female get eaten either. Maybe because she was hot and he didn't like seeing hot chicks sliced and diced. Maybe because he still felt like he knew her from somewhere. Either way, it meant she was a burden he just didn't need. And the sooner she got gone, the sooner she'd be someone else's burden.

He gripped his blade with both hands. While he wasn't thrilled with his odds against three blood-starved beasts, he was pretty sure he could take them. If he shifted. He just hoped it didn't come to that.

"You boys have been warned," Orpheus said.

The leader chuckled and pulled his sunglasses from his face. His eyes were already glowing a blinding green that lit up the small clearing.

A whir echoed near Orpheus's ear before he could move. The leader gasped, his feet stilling midstep. His eyes flew wide. He looked down at the arrow protruding from the middle of his chest. With shaking hands he grasped it, pulled it free with a grunt. Blood gushed from the wound as he slumped to the forest floor.

Stunned, Orpheus glanced over his shoulder and saw the blond standing with her boots shoulder-width apart, a bow she'd pulled from somewhere in that obscenely tight getup poised at her shoulder, her hand already gripping and aiming the next arrow. "He told you to leave. I suggest you listen."

Growls echoed in unison. Clothing ripped, bones

cracked. The other two hybrids morphed and shifted, growing in size until they were at least seven and a half feet tall. Claws sprouted from their hands as their faces twisted and transformed. The human features disappeared until what stared back at Orpheus in the dark was a grotesque mix of cat and goat and dog, with protruding fangs.

Shit. Go time.

Blade in hand, Orpheus dropped back four steps and grasped the dark-haired female by the arm, shoving her in the direction of the amphitheater they'd just come from. "Run!"

He reached for the blond, tried to push her back too, but she stepped away from him, lined up another shot, and released a second arrow. It sailed through the air with a deafening whir, struck the beast on the left with a thwack. The daemon growled in response, stumbled, but then roared and found his footing.

"Sonofabitch," Orpheus muttered, lifting his weapon as the daemon charged. "Get back!"

Another whir sounded. This arrow embedded itself in the chest of the charging daemon. The blond released two more arrows in rapid succession as if she'd done it a thousand times. The daemon stumbled. The blond moved her weapon to the left and hit the third daemon near the shoulder.

Her expert marksmanship meant Orpheus might get through this without shifting after all. Instead of questioning who she was and why she was there, he jerked the knife from his belt and hurled it end over end toward the daemon with three arrows sticking out of his chest still trying to get to the blond. Then he arced out with the blade in his hand and struck the other advancing daemon, catching it across the chest. Blood spurted, the daemon howled. Again Orpheus yelled, "Run!"

The first hybrid, the one still in human form, lay writhing on the ground. Two daemons Orpheus could handle—they weren't trained warriors; they were scrappy fighters—so long as the females fled. He chanced one look over his shoulder as he fought against the monsters, couldn't see his target. She'd obviously taken off, but the blond was still there, lining up her arrows and pulling a throwing star from her waistband, then hurling it like a pro.

Throwing stars? Who the bloody hell was this chick?

Not his concern, he told himself as he sliced out with his blade, used his legs for leverage, knocked one beast to the ground and whirled on the other. If she wasn't going to listen and split, he couldn't be responsible for what happened to her. But he kept her at the edge of his vision just the same. Made sure the daemon close to her stayed on the ground. Blood spurted, howls echoed, and just when he thought the fight was almost over, the hybrid she'd originally hit with her arrows—the one who hadn't yet shifted—let out a bone-chilling scream and morphed from human form into the biggest damn daemon Orpheus had ever seen.

The blond cursed. Orpheus looked just in time to see the daemon closest to her scramble to his feet, then backhand her across the face and send her sailing twenty feet. Her body slammed into the ground. Her bow and arrow went flying. The throwing star in her hand became a whir of silver as it ricocheted against a tree trunk. From across the clearing, the big daemon—the leader—growled, "She's mine."

Orpheus had a split second to decide what to do.

He let go of his daemon. The glow consumed him. Clothing ripped, bones cracked, and another roar echoed through the forest, only this one, he knew, came from him. From that part hidden deep inside. The part he rarely let out. The part he'd been cursed with from birth. The part that, even now after three hundred years, he couldn't totally control.

Beast replaced man. Instinct overruled logic. Through hazy vision he watched the blond scramble backward on the moss-covered ground, her violet eyes wide and fear-filled. And though déjà vu filtered through his turbulent mind as he looked at her, his plans, his one true goal, what he was doing out here in these woods to begin with, began to slip out of his grasp. Only one thought spiraled in, swirled, and took hold, replacing everything else.

One thought that consumed him.

Feed.

I shouldn't have been so eager to prove them wrong.

The thought revolved in Skyla's head as her fingers closed around the rock. Athena, the head of the Siren Order—Zeus's personal band of highly trained assassins—had tried to talk the King of the Gods out of sending Skyla on this assignment, but Skyla had argued she was ready for action again. Never mind that she was only weeks out of a battle that had nearly left her dead. She wasn't about to let some shitty hybrid force her into retirement.

Of course, now, surrounded by three—no, make that four—hybrids, all bigger than the one who'd left her bloody and bruised in the first place and who were each eyeing her as if she were prime Grade A beef, she thought that maybe she shouldn't have been so bull-headed. Maybe just this once she should have at least *listened* to Athena's rationale.

Damn it, if she could just reach her dagger. It, like her bow and arrows, was charmed and could inflict more damage than a regular weapon. But daemon hybrid skin was tougher than most, and since her arrows weren't doing much to stop these monsters, even it was no guar-antee. Her mind raced with options. Feminine charms definitely weren't going to work in this situation. Her only hope at this point was to deflect and incite.

The closest daemon growled and stepped toward her. But a voice at his back stopped his feet. "I said she's mine."

Skyla looked past the first to see another—bigger—daemon stalking across the ground with murder in its glowing eyes. Her adrenaline surged. She gripped the rock and glared up at the closest daemon, the one who was backing off to make room for the big one.

"Can't do it yourself?" she taunted. "Oh yeah, you're a real badass, aren't you? Do you wipe his ass for him when he asks too?"

The smaller daemon's eyes flashed, but he stepped aside for the big one. If she could get them to turn on one another, she might have a chance. A slim chance.

"No one touches her but me," the big daemon growled.

She lifted the rock. Ground her teeth together. Felt the weight of her dagger in its sheath against her lower back. But before she could swing out and make contact with the rock, the daemon at the back of the pack—the one who'd only recently appeared—wrapped his meaty claws around the neck of the big monster and jerked him backward.

A roar poured from the mouth of the bigger daemon as his feet left the ground. The other two turned to look with shock and awe across their grotesque faces. The big daemon sailed across the small clearing, slammed into a tree trunk. Crumpled like a rag doll. A blur of claws slashed out until there was nothing left but bones and blood. The other two daemons, sensing fresh meat, turned and charged.

Skyla scrambled to her feet, grasped the dagger at her back and hurled it through the air. It hit one daemon square in the back of the head. He slammed into the ground face-first with a thud. As the other charged the remaining daemon, Skyla darted for her bow and arrow. She ran hard, slid across the damp ground, scooped up her weapon, then lined up her shot and hoped like hell she was aiming for the right one.

Her arrows sailed through the air in succession. Stuck into the back of the daemon still wearing a trench coat. Another slash of claws and all that was left was her, a bloody mess, and the man named Orpheus she'd followed into the trees.

Correction, the *daemon* named Orpheus she'd been sent to find.

Her chest rose and fell with her rapid breaths. Hands steady from years of training, Skyla kept her bow at the ready, her arrow aimed dead center at his chest in case he made any kind of threatening move. Though Athena claimed he was nonviolent and that after three hundred years he'd mastered control over his daemon side, the acrid scent of blood and the vile stench of daemon slime wafting on the breeze reminded her he was more beast than man, no matter what Athena said.

Her adrenaline surged as his glowing green eyes lifted to hers. She searched his face for any sign of the man she'd seen earlier. The man who'd tried to get her to leave before the battle began. She couldn't find him. All she saw was a monster. A monster born of the Underworld and intent on annihilation.

Skyla widened her stance, braced herself for one last fight. No, she wasn't going down this way. Screw Zeus and what he wanted from the daemon hybrid. Yeah, she'd been sent to gain his trust so she could complete her mission, but if it came down to her life or some stupid relic Zeus deemed important, she'd choose her life every time. No matter the consequences.

He stepped forward.

Skyla's pulse raced. She pulled the arrow back. "Stay where you are, daemon."

Chapter 2

ORPHEUS BREATHED DEEP, TRIED TO REGULATE HIS pulse. Energy and darkness radiated through his body—through his daemon body—urging him to strike again. To take. To feed.

The female pulled the arrow back, the tip catching what little moonlight filtered down from the forest's canopy. But there was no fear in her violet eyes. Only challenge.

Take her. Taste her. Feed.

He licked his lips. Took a step closer. Knew it would be so easy. To suck the blood from her veins. To tear into her pale flesh. In his daemon form, instincts ruled and the need was always there, even if he'd forcibly denied himself over the years. One taste wouldn't kill him. One bite wouldn't condemn him. He'd already been condemned to a fate worse than death.

He eased closer.

"Stay back," she said. "I'm warning you."

Something familiar in her tone stopped his feet. He tried to see through the wavering haze that always descended after he turned. But the golden glow of her hair and the violet of her eyes were all he could focus on. That and her voice. He inhaled. Exhaled. Tried to place her. Couldn't. All he knew was that he wanted her. Had always wanted her.

The bloodlust turned in on itself and twisted his insides until pain consumed him. The change came on as swift as the slice of a blade, even though he didn't consciously will it.

He stumbled forward a step, then another. The female's wide eyes came into focus just before something sharp sliced across his scalp near his ear.

"That was a warning. I said stay back."

He hollered, but no sound escaped his lips. He was already in the throes of the change. His body slumped to the ground and excruciating pain exploded everywhere—through his torso, his limbs, his fingers and toes, even behind his eyelids.

He gripped his stomach as a wave of nausea rolled through him, followed by two more that kicked the shit out of him. Bones cracked and reformed, blood raced like fire through his veins. A kaleidoscope of color burst behind his eyelids, melding with the torment that seemed to have no end. Just when he was sure that this time the change really would kill him, an ice-cold chill slid through every cell in his body, leaving him clammy and shivering in its wake.

He breathed deep to fill his aching lungs, teeth cracking together as he fought the cold. In the fuzzy aftermath that was his brain, he knew he'd be lucky to find enough strength to uncurl from his I-just-got-my-ass-handed-to-me fetal position.

But with the weakness came a rush of memory, and he groaned when he realized where he was and how the hell he'd gotten here.

Skata. He'd lost the female he was tracking. He couldn't even sense that weird light of hers anymore, which meant she was long gone. Which also meant he'd be starting from scratch all over again, and that this time she'd be watching for him.

Footsteps echoed off to his right. He opened his eyes. A pair of platform black boots decked out in silver buckles stopped directly in his line of sight.

For a heartbeat, he didn't move, barely breathed. If it was another hybrid, he was toast. No way could he defend himself right now.

Then the legs attached to those boots bent, and the being—no, woman—knelt in front of him. "You don't look so good."

She reached out to touch him. Obviously thought better of it and pulled her hand back. His gaze lifted. He focused on her golden hair. On smoky, made-up eyes with irises the color of a summer lilac. On porcelain skin that stretched across finely carved features. And for a split second, just a heartbeat, he knew he'd stared into that face dozens—no, hundreds—of times before.

She pushed to her feet and vanished, her boots crunching across sticks and rocks on the forest floor. Seconds later she reappeared and pressed a wad of fabric against the side of his head.

"Damn it," she muttered. "I thought you were attacking me, not…" She shook her head. "Never mind what I thought. You're lucky I fired a warning shot."

His memory was a maze of starts and stops. He had no idea what the hell she was talking about.

She pressed against his ear. Looked at the blood on the rag, pressed again. While she mumbled about daggers and poison and magic, which made zero sense, he stared at her face and tried to figure out what the hell was going on.

He knew her from somewhere. Was sure of it. Still couldn't place her to save his life.

"I think this is going to be okay. It's barely bleeding now. You know, if you'd told me you were shifting, this wouldn't have happened."

He still couldn't follow her, but lying on the ground when his head felt as if he'd shoved it in a washing machine during the spin cycle wasn't helping the situation. He knocked her hand away, then maneuvered to sitting, resting his back against the trunk of a tree for support.

"*Skata*." The forest spun. He pressed both hands to his pounding forehead and tried to quell the thump.

Shifting back always left him weak and out of it. If he'd fed in his daemon form, he'd be fine. Better than fine. He'd be as strong as the Argonauts. But that wasn't his goal, was it? No, he couldn't change who he was, but he could control it. Most of the time.

He glanced down, found his pants ripped through the calves and thighs, his shirt shredded. He was pretty sure he'd worn a jacket, but who the hell knew where that had gone? He was lucky he still had some kind of clothing left. Sometimes he was left bare-ass naked.

He moved to his knees, pushed to stand. The woman reached out to steady him.

"I'm fine," he managed in a raspy voice before she could touch him. "Though if you're hot to grab something…"

She shot him a *yeah, right* look. "I see one part of your brain is still working."

Yeah, his little brain, not his big one. Because he was way too aware of the human woman standing entirely too close to him on the bloody battlefield.

Sonofabitch. There were three dead-ass daemons lying on the ground that he now needed to get rid of. And he'd annihilated the fuckers in front of a witness.

A human witness.

The woman turned away, walked toward the hybrid he'd tossed near the shrubs. Her hair was windblown, there were streaks of dirt and blood smeared across her black clothes, and her right cheek was pink, as if she'd taken a hit there. But she didn't seem fazed. Or scared. And though nothing about the fact she'd just been through a daemon battle screamed "sexy," Orpheus couldn't tear his eyes away from her.

Who the hell was she?

The daemon's arms stuck out at an odd angle and twitched against the forest floor. She knelt by the crumpled remains, looked close. Orpheus opened his mouth to warn her away—daemons, especially hybrids, were hearty creatures—but before sound left his throat, she pulled a dagger from her lower back and decapitated the beast like a pro.

Two things occurred to Orpheus in the silence that followed. One, she'd definitely fought daemons before. And two, she was well trained on how to take them down.

His strength came back little by little as he watched her stand, wipe the bloody blade against her thigh, and sheathe it at her back. But when she turned and stalked in his direction, those kick-ass boots echoing in the still dark air and her hair trailing behind as if she were more supermodel than superwoman, Orpheus was struck again by the strange sensation that he'd met this particular female before. A long time ago. A lifetime ago.

"We'll need to dispose of the bodies." She stopped in front of him, gestured to the two mutilated hybrids to his left. "A fire this close to the concert will cause too much attention. We could weight them down and throw them in the river. Hopefully the remains will disintegrate before anyone discovers them."

Burning was the safest and quickest way to get rid of any evidence. Though Orpheus didn't give a rip what humans knew of the gods, even he realized the pandemonium that would result if they discovered that monsters like these, like him, roamed the earth. The female was right. Daemon remains decayed quickly—quicker than normal—but the question of how she knew that surged to the front of his gray matter.

She bent over, grasped the arm of the closest hybrid, but Orpheus blocked her with his hand on her forearm. Shards of heat penetrated his skin when he touched her, spread deeper, amping that arousal he shouldn't be feeling. "Before we do that, why don't you tell me just where you came from?"

She rose. "And ruin the mystery? Where's the fun in that?"

She was toying with him. He didn't know why, but the knowledge eased the tension inside him. "You're not Argolean." He tapped into his senses, this time focusing on her. On what he'd ignored before, because he'd been too distracted by his target to pay attention to her. "And you're not a god. I can't quite put my finger on it, but—"

"What in Hades…?"

She was staring at the ancient Greek text on his arms. The text marking him as a guardian of his race.

Damn it. When he'd lost his shirt in the shifting process, he'd forgotten all about the Argonaut markings. Markings he didn't want and couldn't wait to get rid of. Markings he'd inherited after his brother's death.

Her eyes darted back to his face, and confusion—
maybe even a little horror—slithered into their amethyst
depths. "You're an Argonaut? But I saw you shift. I saw
you turn into that…that thing." She shook her head.
"Daemons can't be Argonauts. They *can't* be chosen. It
goes against every law ever established. It goes against
the natural order."

She was definitely otherworldly, but he still didn't
know from where. And if she knew what he was, why
wasn't she slicing and dicing him like the others right
this minute? When she jerked her arm out of his grasp,
he didn't try to stop her. 'Cause, yeah, this whole
fucked-up situation went against his order too.

Damn you, Gryphon. And damn the gods for marking him in Gryphon's place. There was only one thing
he wanted now. One thing that would grant him vengeance against the sonofabitch god who'd cursed him
to begin with.

He stepped back, perched his hands on his hips,
breathed deep so he'd stay calm and not shift again. But
it wasn't easy. Because the fire in her eyes told him his
night was far from over.

"Screw whatever it is you want to know about me," she
said. "What I want to know is…who the hell are *you*?"

––––w––––

The agonizing cry of pain that echoed in his ears was his
own, even though his lips didn't move.

In his mind, Gryphon kicked out at the vulture attacking his right leg, but his body didn't answer the command. It never did, even though he wished and willed
and prayed for just an ounce of movement. Frozen in

place, he breathed deep through the pain and closed his eyes—the only part of his body he could move— blocking out the vultures and the view he'd looked out at for the last three months: jagged black rocks that made up the ground and mountains. Red-gray clouds above that swirled and boiled but never let loose the cleansing rain he sought. A canyon mere feet in front of him that dropped to a gurgling lava river, and a hot acrid wind that blew across the barren land, the heat so intense it seared what hair he had left on his skin, dried his eyes, and made him wish for annihilation.

But annihilation wouldn't come, just as moving even one limb was a pipe dream he should stop fantasizing about. This depraved land was his eternity. Tartarus. Hell in all its glory. And though today's torment would soon be over, he knew another would take its place tomorrow. When he awoke in the morning whole and healthy, just as he did every morning, only to be subjected to another round of torture more agonizing than the last.

Tears burned the backs of his eyes. Tears that would never fall. He turned his mind from the pain rippling through his body and imagined home.

Argolea.

The blessed realm of the heroes. Where his ancestors had dwelt. Where his Argonaut kin remained. Where his brother lived, whole and healthy and alive.

He felt himself flying, could see the entirety of his homeland as he looked down. The blue-green Olympian Ocean with its white sand beaches, the emerald green fields, the majestic snowcapped Aegis Mountains and the city of Tiyrns, gleaming white marble in the setting sun. He wondered if the Argonauts were in the castle or out on patrol. If Orpheus was with them as he should be. If his brother wondered where he was now. Did Orpheus care that Gryphon had been sentenced to Tartarus even though he'd never done anything to deserve it?

That's a bloody lie.

"No. It's the truth."

You've killed more than your fair share. The blood of innocents stains your soul.

"If I killed, it was done out of duty."

Ha! There is no duty in death. Only misery. Which you now well know.

The voice mocked him. He hated the voice. Fought against it. And yet it was the only constant in this ever-changing hell. "*I am an Argonaut. I did what was asked of me.*"

Not anymore. You're nothing. You're dinner. Look at you. You can't even move.

"I served. I saved—"

You're pathetic. Whom did you save? You can't even save yourself.

"I—"

Go ahead. I dare you. Save yourself, stupid. I'd like to see it.

His tears burned even hotter, but still no wetness slid down his cheeks. He focused every bit of strength he had left in an attempt to move one muscle. Just a fraction of an inch.

I knew it. See? You're worse than pathetic. You're navel lint. You're the crud on the bottom of the other Argonauts' shoes. You're—

"Stop it!"

—dead…

"So are you! If I'm dead, you are as well. Now who's the pathetic one?"

Silence descended. He waited. Listened. Hoped. Only the voice didn't even sigh. A bone-chilling emptiness slithered into its place until all he heard was the tearing of his flesh as the vultures continued to pick him apart.

"Wait. Come back. I didn't mean it. I didn't mean… Please? I'll be nice. I promise."

Nothing.

Dear gods, he was going crazy. He couldn't continue down this path, hoping and wishing for something that was never going to happen, arguing with himself only to spiral headlong into insanity when he awoke day after day after miserable day to be tortured all over again. There had to be a way out. Even if it was just up one level in this terror-filled infinity.

Blackness spiraled in. The end—at least for today—loomed close. Even though he couldn't move, his body felt heavy, his mind a brick falling fast. And as he separated from what was being done to him, tried to think of a way out of this never-ending hell, the irony wasn't lost on him. As a descendant of the famed hero Perseus, his power had been the ability to freeze his enemies for a few minor seconds, just enough time to get the upper hand. It didn't matter that he'd rarely used that gift. He was now paying for it.

Would always pay for it.

"Please."

There was no use begging. There was no one to hear him. Not even the voice. Blackness closed in until all he saw was one tiny pinprick of light.

He was alone.
Dead.
Forever.

———— ~~~ ————

How could Orpheus be both daemon *and* Argonaut?

Skyla's mind whirred with impossibilities as she stood in the trees, staring at Orpheus, and thought back to what she knew of the Argonauts. The seven strongest heroes had been chosen by Zeus himself to protect both the Argolean realm and the human world from Atalanta's daemons. Though Zeus and the other Olympian gods couldn't cross into the blessed realm, they sure as hell kept tabs on what happened there, and they were fully aware which descendents from each line served with the Argonauts. There was no way a daemon hybrid could have slipped in unbeknownst to them. And the fact that neither Zeus nor Athena had bothered to tell her cut deep.

Her spine stiffened. She was being played. There was more going on here than simply a daemon gone wrong who was pressing Zeus's buttons.

"Well?" she asked.

"Consider me gifted and talented." Orpheus grasped the dead daemon at their feet and dragged it across the damp earth toward the river.

His snarky comment wasn't lost on her. It was the same sort of response she would give when she didn't want to actually answer. How in hell was this all possible? The only thing clear at the moment was that he was moving more slowly than he had before. When he came back for the second dead daemon, sweat covered his forehead and blood began dripping from the wound near his ear all over again.

Daemons healed quickly. So did Argonauts. But apparently the shifting process took something out of him. Questions pinged around in her brain, questions she wanted—needed—answered. But she could see she wasn't going to get them now. Not with him in this condition.

She dragged what was left of the third daemon to the river herself. When she got close, she let go of the body, stepped over it, and grasped the legs of the daemon Orpheus was trying to hurl into the water. She could see he'd filled the beast's pockets with rocks and was having a hard time lifting him.

He stilled, stared at her for a long second. Moonlight accentuated the muscles in his jaw, the strength in his neck, the width of his shoulders. "Working with the evil daemon Argonaut now?"

"It's either that or watch you struggle. Consider it my good deed for the day. I've always had a soft spot for the underdog."

He harrumphed, hefted the daemon's upper body. "If under's the position you like, woman, all you have to say is when."

"Ha. The state you're in now, you'd never be able to keep up."

A glint lit his eyes, but he didn't respond. And that more than anything told her how much he was suffering. She helped him hurl the other bodies into the river and reminded herself to stay on her toes. He may look docile right now, but he wasn't. Not really. And even though he was sexy—tall, strong, with sandy brown hair that needed a trim and a day's worth of stubble on his chiseled jaw—he was still a threat. Though a threat that intrigued her.

When all the remains were disposed of, Orpheus wiped the sweat from his brow then stepped past her, heading back toward the clearing. She followed and slowed as he stopped to look down at her bow, lying on the forest floor.

Nonviolent. Athena's word echoed in Skyla's mind, but her fingers twitched at her side and the dagger felt heavy where it pressed against her lower back.

He reached down for her bow, turned, and handed it to her. Cautiously, she accepted it, still unsure of his intentions, then depressed the button on the end without a word, shrinking the weapon to a metal bar only six inches long.

"Definitely not human," he said. "Though that body…not bad. Since I know you're not Argolean either, that leaves only a couple of options."

She didn't answer. Wasn't about to tell him anything. But she recognized the heat in his eyes. Not a daemon heat or a battle heat, but a male heat. The kind that said he was interested. Her stomach tightened as she slipped the bar into her boot and waited.

"Not that I care." He shrugged. "Something tells me you're the sort of female who doesn't play well—or like to share—with others."

Maybe. But Skyla wasn't thrilled with the fact he could read her so easily either.

"I guess I'll be on my way." He turned toward the lights of the parking lot.

Panic closed in as she watched him stalk away. "Wait."

One eyebrow angled upward as he looked back over his shoulder, a sexy expression that warmed her blood. "For what?"

Yeah, for what? She searched her mind. *It's not because he intrigues you. It's because you have a job to do.* Zeroing in on his shredded pants and shirt, she said, "You can't walk around like that. You'll draw attention."

He glanced down at his nearly bare chest—his very impressive, very muscular bare chest. Then his *so what?* gaze jumped back to her face.

Skyla's cheeks heated. Even to her, the excuse sounded lame. But she still needed answers. And though she knew she could follow him again and see where he went next, she'd always been better at enticing information out of her mark rather than tailing him. After all, it was what she'd been designed to do.

So do what you've been assigned to do and get on with it.

"I have a room not far from here," she said. "There are clothes there. You're welcome to them. Plus, you need that wound covered before infection sets in."

He lifted his blade from the ground, found the scabbard a few feet away. "A room? You just conveniently have a room in this podunk town?"

Not exactly, but when she'd found out the female he'd been chasing had bought tickets to the metalhead concert, she'd had a feeling it might draw all kinds. And she'd *hoped* he'd show up looking for her.

Luckily, her intuition had been right.

Since she couldn't tell him that, she said instead, "I…like to be prepared."

He didn't immediately answer as he slung the

weapon over his back so the strap cut across his bare chest and crossed back to her. He stopped inches away. And though she fought it, the heat from his muscular body made her the slightest bit light-headed.

"Why would you care?" he asked. "You saw what I am. And you're the one who cut me."

She had. But that was before, when she thought he was going to eat her. Now…now things had changed and she wasn't sure why. She glanced down at his forearms again, covered with the Argonaut markings. Markings that should *not* be on his skin. "It's the least I can do."

"That must grate."

"What?"

"Thanking a daemon."

Her warrior shield came up even as she worked to keep her expression neutral. "If you hadn't been chasing that girl, she wouldn't have run into that pack of hybrids and I wouldn't need to thank you, now, would I?"

"No one asked you to intervene."

No, no one but Zeus. Though she wasn't about to say so.

She debated the best tactic. Knew—regardless of how attractive he was—that her feminine charms were her surest bet.

So get on with it.

Before she could change her mind, she eased a half step closer, then reached out to run her finger down the center of his sweaty chest. "It's up to you, daemon. I was just trying to be nice. If you're not interested—"

A jolt of déjà vu rippled through her when she touched him. As if she'd touched him like this before. Her words cut off midsentence. He sucked in a breath as if he felt it too.

Skyla moved back. Searched his face and tried to remember if she'd met him somewhere else. But she was sure she hadn't. He was a stranger...a daemon hybrid...her *mission*. Only, as she stared at him, her stomach clenched as if *he* had touched *her* and she'd enjoyed it. Immensely.

She stepped past him, more rattled than she wanted to admit. Weird. Residual energy from the fight? Memories of the last time she'd run into a hybrid and nearly died? It had to be. It couldn't be anything else.

"Where'd you get them?"

His voice stopped her feet, slowed her mind. She turned. "Get what?"

"The clothes." His boots crunched over sticks and dried leaves as he stalked toward her. His interest flared hot all over in his eyes.

Relaxing, because this was a role she knew how to play well, she rested her hand on her hip, shifted her weight in a way she knew accentuated her breasts. Males were all the same—human, hybrid, or immortal. If all went as planned, she'd have the information she needed from him before the night was over. "Worried they belong to an ex-lover?"

He chuckled. "No."

"No?"

He leaned in close, and even though he was covered in blood and moments ago had shifted into a monster, heat ignited in her abdomen. A heat that sent her back a step, right into the hood of a parked car. "Especially not since you haven't been able to stop staring at my ass since we left the river."

"That's not what I..."

He braced his hands on the hood of the car. Leaned in close. Until the warmth of his breath tickled her ear, sending tingles all along her skin. "Curiosity killed the cat. Or so humans like to say. Be sure this is a curiosity you're willing to gamble with, female."

He pushed away and threaded through the parking lot before she could think of a comeback. Before she could tell herself she'd just lost the upper hand. She was trained for seduction, but he seemed to be the one doing the seducing. If she let this go on without taking the reins, she'd be putting not only herself but her order in jeopardy.

And that...well, to put it in his words, that wasn't something she was willing to gamble with. She may not have a lot, but she had the order. It had saved her life. It had *given* her a life. No sexy, charming, or intriguing daemon would ever make her forget that.

Chapter 3

MAELEA CLOSED THE FRONT DOOR OF HER LAURELHURST home on the banks of Lake Washington and stood in the dark entryway, listening to the silence. So much silence. Years of silence. It was a wonder she hadn't gone insane from all that silence eons ago.

Like you aren't nuts already?

She ignored that thought because it would get her nowhere, breathed deep to slow her adrenaline. Not bothering to turn on the light, she crossed the marble floor and moved up the richly carpeted stairs until she reached her bedroom suite on the second floor. Lights shimmered across the water through her bedroom window, but tonight she didn't bother with the view.

She flipped on the bathroom light, stared at her reflection in the mirror. Her eyes looked haunted, her face sunken. In all her years, she hadn't felt like a ghost, but tonight she did. Tonight, after running into those daemons, she wondered what the hell she'd been thinking, going to that concert, searching for the dark one.

She'd known the big man chasing her. She could feel the darkness of the Underworld radiating from him.

Images of those daemons re-formed in her mind all over again, and to keep from freaking out, she crossed to the shower, flipped on the water. Careful not to look at her arms or legs as she peeled off her baggy black clothes, she stepped under the spray and scrubbed away any remnant of the night.

She towel-dried her hair, combed out the long black strands, then wrapped her body in a peach silk robe and headed downstairs to the kitchen. But as she started a pot of green tea to settle her nerves, then relaxed into her favorite plush chair in the parlor and stared out at the water of Lake Washington, the light inside her that was drawn to all that darkness leaped with excitement.

What if he was the one? What if she'd finally found her way to Olympus?

Fear and excitement, light and dark, they were each so much a part of her life, she didn't know where to start. Common sense told her she should have stayed at the concert, should have waited to see if he emerged from the trees after that daemon fight. If he'd tracked her there, he could find her home. But fear had sent her running. Fear and a need to formulate a plan. Though she might not age, she wasn't immortal like her parents. She had no godlike powers. She was simply female and fragile and alone. So very alone.

Just as they wanted.

Bastards.

What her parents didn't know was that she was determined. Now more than ever. And if the man who'd chased her tonight really was the one, she knew he'd come looking for her again. Next time, she'd be prepared. Next time, she'd do whatever it took to make her dream come true.

The kettle whistled and she bounced out of the chair with a renewed sense of purpose, then moved into the kitchen where she poured herself a steaming mug and tried not to get ahead of herself.

Only one thing was certain: She wouldn't wander this earth alone and silent like a wraith until the end of time. She wouldn't let the silence drag her to insanity. And no matter what, she wasn't about to become the dark thought Hades had cursed her to be.

—∿∿—

Orpheus followed Skyla up a flight of stairs and paused outside a blue metal door in the run-down rent-by-the-week motel on the edge of town.

As he stared at the back of her head, a waft of honey-suckle met his senses. The same fragrance he'd noticed in the concert crowd, in that clearing, and every second since. A scent that was oddly…familiar.

She reached up to the doorframe, felt around, flashed him a one-sided grin as her hand lowered with a key. "Stay here. I'll be right back out."

He didn't know what she was up to, but he waited in the hallway while she disappeared into the apartment then came out seconds later with folded jeans and a T-shirt slung over her forearm. She locked the door, replaced the key, then motioned for him to follow her again down the hall.

"What was that?" he asked.

"Neighbor. He's about your size. Works nights. Way too trusting."

He smirked as she stopped in front of another blue door and pulled a key from her pocket. A schemer, like him. Who'd have thought it? "I thought you said they were your clothes."

"I never said that," she answered, pushing the door open with her hip. "And no way you'd fit into my pants. If you did, I'd have to kill myself."

He eyed her pants. And her sexy backside. Told himself trying to find a way *into* her pants was a really dumb idea. He didn't have time to play with the blond, no matter what she was. He should be back out there already, searching for the dark-haired female again. But he didn't want to be. For just a few minutes, he wanted a break. Craved something just for him. Needed that connection with another person to remember he wasn't dead. Like Gryphon.

Thoughts of Gryphon brought back the tightness to his chest he'd been living with the last three months. He thought of the female he'd been chasing earlier. And the way the blond had talked to her in the crowd at that concert.

The two knew each other somehow. Why else would the blond have followed them into the trees?

She closed the door after him, flipped on the kitchen light. The place was a far cry from the Ritz. The kitchen spilled into a tiny living room with a wall of windows that looked out to an enclosed deck and the darkness beyond. The furniture was old, covered in brown and orange checked fabric that looked like something straight out of the seventies. The tables were wood veneer, and the draperies hanging on one side of the windows were made of some heavy off-white, smoke-stained material.

He turned a slow circle, took in the closet-sized kitchen with its avocado green Formica and matching fridge that barely reached Skyla's shoulder, the cracked vinyl brown chairs and matching table. And the short hallway off to his left, with its thick brown shag carpet, was bracketed by two doors, both dented and scarred from time and abuse.

He didn't doubt for a minute that this was nothing more than a stopping place for her, one that suited her as much as the Argonauts suited him.

"The bathroom's here." She moved down the hall, pushed the door to the left open, flipped on the light.

More avocado green countertop and a mirror over the sink that reflected hollow cheeks streaked with blood, pale skin, and hair standing out every which way.

He looked away from his reflection, moved into the doorway of the other room, where she'd disappeared. A full-sized bed with an ugly burnt-orange bedspread filled the space. A small dresser, nightstand, and lamp rounded out the room. "Gorgeous. You do the decorating yourself?"

She crouched in front of the dresser, pulled the bottom drawer open, and extracted a clean towel. "Oh yeah. Shit brown and puke green are my favorite colors. Aren't they yours?"

"Obviously. I'm a daemon, right?"

One corner of her lips curved. A sexy little grin that supercharged his blood. And again he was struck by the fact she didn't seem the least bit afraid of him.

She stood, held out the towel and clothes. "While you get cleaned up, I'll find bandages for your head."

He didn't bother telling her he didn't need bandages. Instead he took the clothes, pulled them against his chest so she could pass. Was just about to ask why she wasn't scared as a normal person would be, when her body grazed his in the doorway.

Her heat seared every inch of him, reigniting the arousal he'd felt back in the trees. Only this wasn't just sexual. No, this was something more. An awareness. A déjà vu feeling. A memory he couldn't quite bring into focus.

Her feet stilled. Her smile faded. And his stomach felt as if it flipped over when he realized she felt it too.

Who was she? What was she to him? And why the hell couldn't he figure out how he knew her?

She turned back toward the kitchen. "Take your time."

Why the hell was he so rattled around her?

Skata. Maybe that last shift had been one too many. Maybe he'd finally suffered some serious brain damage in the process.

Stepping into the bathroom, he shook off the thought, avoided the mirror. He didn't need to see his reflection to know he looked like shit. He felt like it too. And not just from the change. Months of searching, only to be met with disappointment, were taking their toll. He needed food. A couple hours of shut-eye. And to find that damn dark-haired female before he lost the Orb for good.

Steam filled the room as he let the water beat down on his battered body. He rubbed soap all over his skin, washed his hair with shampoo from a purple bottle that smelled way too girlie, then flipped off the water and dried with a towel from the rack. As he did, he caught sight of the ancient Greek text on his forearms that ran down to entwine his fingers.

Man, if the Argonauts could see him now. No, nix that. He already knew exactly what they'd say or do if they'd seen the switcheroo he pulled in that clearing. Daemons weren't just discriminated against in their world, they were the bitter enemy. If word got out he was half daemon, the Argonauts would be the first to crucify him, likely in Tiyrns Square, for all Argoleans to see. Forget the fact he was the last living descendant

of the famed hero Perseus. And never mind that he'd
helped their queen and all the Argonauts more times
than he could count. He tossed the towel away in disgust, jerked on the fresh jeans. To them he'd forever
be nothing more than a daemon. Useful one way: dead.

He tugged on the dark blue T-shirt that barely fit,
shoved his feet back into his boots, and finger-combed
his hair. Screw what he *thought* he wanted. There was
only one thing he needed right now. The Orb of Krónos.
Once he had that…well, then the tide would finally turn.

As for the blond…yeah, she was hot, but he didn't
have time for this. And the weird sensations pinging
around in his chest when he looked at her weren't just
delaying him, they were distracting him. So he'd go out
there, find out what she knew about his target, then be
on his way.

Decision made, he grabbed his weapon from the
counter where he'd left it and opened the bathroom door.
Steam preceded him into the hall, where the scent of
bacon filled the air. His stomach growled, and he turned
the corner to find the blond—shit, he should have asked
for her name—standing at the stove, flipping bacon and
scrambling eggs. She'd dressed in fresh clothes: another black shirt—this one, short-sleeved—a fresh pair
of slim black pants, and the same kick-ass goth boots
she'd worn earlier. But it wasn't her outfit that made the
room spin. It was the modern appliances fading into the
background that tipped the world out from under him.

Weathered stone, a baking hearth, and an old scarred
table filled the space. And at the counter, the same female, stirring something in a ceramic bowl. Only this
time she was barefoot, wearing a slip of a dress made of

gauzy white and tied at her narrow waist with a woven gold braid.

He reached out and gripped the hallway wall to steady himself.

She looked up. Her hand stopped moving. The bowl sat cradled in the nook of her other arm. A streak of flour ran across her right cheek.

A warm smile spread across her face. One filled with heat and mischief and knowledge. "Stop looking at me like that. Thou knowest that is playing with fire."

She went back to stirring. Looked back down at her work with a victorious grin. Turned to reach for something behind her.

But Orpheus felt like he'd just been sucker punched in the gut.

The air left his lungs on a gasp. The room spun again, flipped his stomach end over end. The scabbard fell from his hand as he reached for the wall with his other hand. He felt himself going down. Saw shadows barreling in from all sides. But was powerless to keep from fainting like a giant pussy.

"Daemon? Can you hear me?" The voice was muffled. Distant. Something hard pressed down on his chest. "Come on, already. Wake up!"

A crack echoed around him. His eyes flew open.

"That's it. Yeah, that's right, keep looking at me."

He couldn't do anything else. He stared up into amethyst eyes that sparkled like the Aegis Mountains in the early-morning sunshine. And felt that rush of familiarity all over again.

"There you go. See? Not so bad after all." Her voice wasn't so muffled anymore. "Let's get you up."

He didn't fight her when she pulled on his shoulders, maneuvering him around to lean against the wall, his legs kicked out in front of him. While his head continued to spin like a top, she went back into the kitchen, flipped off the stove, reached for bandages and other supplies, then came back and knelt next to him.

Honeysuckle wafted around him as she leaned close to look at the side of his head. But that vision of her in that old-time kitchen wouldn't leave his head. That and the knowing smile she'd sent him that spoke of familiarity on a personal level. An intimate level.

Shards of heat ricocheted everywhere she touched, sending a tingle down his spine that left him more off-kilter than before. "This looks like it's finally scabbed over," she said. "I know daemons heal quickly, but... well, you are not what I expected."

Neither was she. Whatever she was doing to him, though, he was about to put a stop to it.

He grasped her wrist, ignored the heat that flared beneath his fingers. "I want...answers."

Another jolt of déjà vu rippled through him. She looked down where he held her, and something akin to shock washed over her face. Then she pulled her hand free with a quick snap of her wrist, a motion that told him she was stronger than she appeared, and pushed to her feet. "You need food. We'll talk after you eat."

Screw that.

He'd never fainted in his life. Couldn't believe he'd done so now, especially in front of her. Whatever she was—witch, sorceress, immortal—she was playing some kind of mind fuck on him. Getting him to see and feel things that weren't real. His mother had been

Medean. He'd studied her craft, knew how to cast spells himself when the time was right, and was well aware of the power the dark arts could harness. He wasn't about to be manipulated by this female, in any way.

He pushed to his feet. Before she reached the end of the hall, he flashed in front of her, bringing her feet to a dead stop.

Surprise lit her eyes. Confusion followed quickly on its tail. Argonauts could only flash in Argolea. In the human realm they were limited to the same laws of nature as humans. But not him.

She dropped her supplies, eased back. "What...? How did you do that?"

"I'm full of surprises." He took a step toward her.

She moved back more. "What do you think you're doing?"

"I've had a shitty day and I'm tired of the head games." Her back hit the wall. He knew his eyes were glowing green, illuminating the dark hallway around them, but he didn't force his daemon back as he normally would. Right now he needed its strength. "I want answers, and I want them now."

He pressed a hand against the wall and leaned in close. Until the heat from her skin slid over his and the beat of her heart was all he could hear. "I want to know who the hell you really are. And I want to know what your being here has to do with me."

Chapter 4

SKYLA WASN'T ONE TO BACK DOWN FROM A FIGHT. BUT she'd seen the damage Orpheus could do in his daemon form. And this close, if he changed, there'd be no time for her to reach her weapons.

His hot breath washed over her ear, slithered down her neck, sent tingles racing along her spine. Tingles that warred with the danger she should be feeling. He smelled like the grapefruit shampoo she picked up a few days ago, and this close he was bigger than she'd realized, all muscle and sinew.

From the moment he'd followed her back to the run-down apartment she'd taken while she'd searched for him, she'd been overly aware of him. Of his size, of his movements, of the raw masculinity he radiated every moment. And she couldn't stop thinking about the power he'd wielded out there in the trees. Not just the way he'd decimated those daemons, but the way he'd put himself between her and danger. The way he'd tried to get her to leave. The way he'd told the other female to run.

What kind of daemon did that? Not one she'd ever met.

Her skin heated. That ache—the one she couldn't explain—slid from her stomach to settle between her legs. She'd used sex in the past to get close to a target, but this was different. This was *her* reacting to *him* instead of the other way around.

"I'm waiting," he said.

Good gods, what was wrong with her? He was man-handling her and she was getting turned on? This so wasn't the way she worked.

As she fought the strange reaction, she looked up into glowing green eyes. Eyes that slowly faded to gray as they stared down at her. Eyes not of a daemon, but of a man. Eyes that hypnotized her on a level she'd not experienced in over two thousand years.

She knew right then that no matter what he said or how he used his size or daemon to try to intimidate her, he wouldn't hurt her. If he'd wanted to, he'd have done it back in the woods. He wouldn't have saved her.

"Female, it's time you tell me—"

"Skyla."

"What?"

Her gaze slid to his mouth—a mouth she was suddenly tempted to taste. "My name is Skyla."

"Your name isn't what I want right now."

Heat thrummed in her veins. She stared at his lips. Firm and masculine. Licked her own. Kissing implied intimacy, and intimacy was something she'd learned long ago to avoid. But the need to touch him, to taste him, was right there, pulsing along her nerve endings, teasing her control. She followed the strong curve of his chin, and finally the delectable jawline. "What do you want, daemon?"

"Answers. Where did you come from? And how did you know the female I was follow—"

She rose on her toes, pressed her mouth to his jaw until the musky scent of him filled her senses and the salty taste of his skin exploded in her mouth. Then stilled because that was an action she hadn't planned and now wasn't sure how to finish.

He pulled away. Stared hard into her eyes. And in the silence that followed, she rationalized this was what she was supposed to do: seduce, gain his trust, use him to find what Zeus so desperately wanted. But suddenly this wasn't just about her job. That ache intensified until satiating it, with him, was all she could focus on.

"What are you doing?" he asked.

"The same thing you want me to do."

"I never said I wanted you to—"

She closed the gap he'd created before she could stop herself, pressed her body along his and her lips to the soft skin of his throat.

"*Skata*, female. I'm starting to think you're the one who has brain damage."

"Possibly. Is that a problem for you?" She kissed the pulse of his throat, found another, more delectable spot to taste and sample. Waited for him to drag her closer. Waited for a hint of that heat she'd seen earlier in his eyes.

When he didn't, she decided to pull out all the stops. "What's wrong, daemon? Am I too much for you to handle? Maybe the creature you were chasing is more to your taste? I bet you prefer your women docile, don't you?"

For a split second she thought he was going to pull away, but then a growl echoed low in his throat. His hands slid through her hair. He tipped her head to kiss her. But there were just enough synapses firing in her brain to remind her kissing was a no-go, and she jerked her head to the side, offering her neck instead.

He hesitated the briefest of seconds, as if caught off guard. "I like my women to scream." Then he pressed his body into hers along the wall. "Is this was you want, Skyla? Me to make you scream?"

Before she could answer, he nipped into her neck, sucked the skin, and worked his leg between both of hers until she felt the length of his erection pressing against her hip. And the way he said her name…

Yes. Gods, yes.

She moaned at the feel of him, at his lips on her throat sending shock waves of pleasure straight to her core. Her fingers tightened in the fabric of his shirt. She lifted her leg around his hip, ground herself against him. Pulled him even closer.

Danger excited her. Why else would she be reacting this way? Though the markings of the Eternal Guardians covered his arms, logic told her this daemon was no hero. He was prey. Someone cursed by the gods for reasons she didn't understand and wasn't supposed to know. And yet here she was. Rubbing against him in this crappy apartment hallway like a sex-crazed nymph. Desperate for more. Aching for something only he could give her.

On some level she knew she should stop…but that level was disappearing in the background, moving right out of her grasp. And as long as she didn't get emotionally involved, why couldn't she do this? She could complete her mission *and* enjoy it at the same time. And gods, it had been so long since she'd enjoyed anything. She deserved a few moments of release.

"More." She moved against him, dragged his head to the other side of her throat. Her hands slid down his muscular chest to grasp the hem of his shirt and pull it over his head. He broke contact long enough for her to toss the shirt to the floor. Across his face, the same need she felt reflected back at her.

His broad chest, covered with a sprinkling of dark hair, rose and fell with his labored breaths. He shoved his hands up under her shirt until it landed against the floor next to his, and his warm, strong fingers brushed her nipples. "What is this?"

"Breasts." She leaned closer, found his earlobe again. Gods, he tasted so damn good. Smelled even better. And that rod of steel rubbing between her legs was nice, but not nearly close enough. She wanted it closer. Wanted him deep.

"I know what these are," he mumbled, palming her breasts as she wrapped her arms around his shoulders, levered herself higher to rub against him right where she wanted him most. "I meant *this*. What's happening here? What the hell is it?"

"Let's not overanalyze." She just wanted to feel. To give herself over to the sensations rocking her world right out from under her. She'd worry about her mission later. "Take off my bra already."

The clasp popped with a snap, and the lace slid down her arms. She wriggled out of it and reached for him again. Pleasure arced through her pelvis as he hooked her leg over his hip once more and ran his fingers across her panties.

"Damn it." His mouth nipped at her chin, trailed hot, succulent kisses toward her ear that enraptured every part of her being. He couldn't seem to get enough of her either. She gasped in surprise when he undid the zipper on her boot, tugged it off, and threw it down the hall, then stripped her pants down her legs, underwear and all.

He hooked her bare leg over his hip again. Her pants looped around the boot still on her other foot. But when his fingers found her wetness, she barely cared.

Yes, yes, yes. This was what she wanted. The *only* thing she wanted. Why had she waited so long?

He stroked her, slid two fingers deep inside. A tremor ran through her body as his thumb brushed her clit. "What kind of enchantment are you casting, female?"

He seemed as bewildered as she at the instant attraction. This was more than a quick fuck and both of them knew it—even if they'd never in a million years admit it.

"No enchantment," she managed. "Need more."

A low rumble echoed through the hall, one she wasn't sure had come from him alone. She didn't have long to ponder because his mouth was back at her ear again, his tongue doing wicked things to her lobe. His touch consumed her, drew the air from her lungs, promised her something she couldn't see but needed. A zipper rasped. His fingers slipped free of her. She groaned at the emptiness but shuddered when he slid both hands under her ass and lifted. She wrapped her legs around his waist. Then nearly came out of her skin when the tip of his cock brushed her folds and he pressed her into the wall, filling her in one sharp thrust.

Pleasure rippled through every cell in her body, as if this was what she'd been seeking all her life. She tightened around him, cried out in protest when he drew away, then moaned all over again as he plunged deep. Those fireworks picked up in intensity until pinpricks of heat were all she felt. "Oh…"

"Like that?" He slid out, thrust back in again. Sweat slicked her skin as he plunged deep over and over until her eyes blurred.

"Yes, yes, more. Yes." She dug her fingernails into his shoulders. Tried to take him even deeper.

Her release barreled toward her. He grew even thicker inside. But it wasn't enough. Never enough. The climax she longed for was right there. Hovering out of her grasp. She shifted her hips, tried to find that one spot…

"*Skata*." He changed the angle of his thrust. "Here?"

"Yes. I—" Before she could brace herself, fire exploded through her core, so unexpected it stole the breath from her lungs.

She groaned, kicked her head back into the wall, and tightened around him as waves of pleasure washed over her. Waves that went on and on and triggered a feeling so sublime, it seared deep in her chest and grabbed hold of her heart like a vise.

But it didn't last. As the last wave dissipated, a sinkhole opened wide. She felt herself falling, tumbling into a black abyss of pain and suffering so intense she gasped. All around her, torment rang out like trumpets, and a grief she'd only experienced one other time settled in deep. Grabbed hold of her heart. Threatened to never let go.

A grief that had nearly killed her once. A grief she thought she'd left behind a lifetime ago.

Her eyes opened. His face was mere centimeters from hers, his jaw tight, his skin slicked with sweat, his eyes wide and unfocused. And reflected in those familiar gray pools she saw her past as clear as if it were the present. Felt the pain that had shaped her into the Siren she was today as sharply as if it had just happened.

"What…is…*this*?"

Words dried up in her mouth. She couldn't answer. Didn't know what to say. Couldn't believe the gods could be so cruel.

He couldn't seem to stop his body from moving, and she knew he was right at the edge where control has fled and biology takes over. He clenched his jaw, thrust harder, deeper, jostled her against the wallboard. Too shocked to do anything but hold on, her muscles contracted, and as she felt him grow impossibly hard inside her, knew his release was consuming him. But hers was long gone.

Tears she wasn't about to shed burned her eyes. He drove deep one last time and groaned, then held still, pinning her to the wall with his body. She tried to steady her racing heart. Couldn't. Tried to convince herself what she'd just experienced wasn't real.

But it was. Gods help her, it was. And a truth so horrendous she didn't want to acknowledge it as real…became crystal clear.

He wasn't just a rogue hybrid causing trouble for Zeus. He was more. And their meeting had not happened by chance.

He dropped his head against her shoulder, breathed deep. Braced one hand against the wall to steady them both. "My gods," he mumbled against her, his hot breath tickling her oversensitive skin. "Who the hell are you?"

She couldn't tell him. Not now. Not ever. But the déjà vu feeling she'd felt before now made a sick sort of sense.

She swallowed, braced her hands against his

shoulders, and pushed with what little strength she had left. "You're hurting me."

He immediately eased away, dropping her legs to the ground so she could stand. He wasn't hurting her—at least not physically—but he didn't need to know that. Hands shaking, she tugged her pants back on, reached for her shirt from the floor and shrugged it on, then found her boot, the whole time avoiding his eyes, trying not to notice the movements he made as he dressed, how similar they were to *his*.

How could she have been so stupid? Why hadn't she seen it from the very beginning? And why in Hades hadn't Athena warned her?

"Skyla—"

She turned for the kitchen. "I need to go."

"Wait a minute."

"There's food in the refrigerator if you're hungry."

He grasped her arm just as she reached the door. "Hold on. We need to talk."

Panic pushed in. A panic she knew would sweep her under if she didn't make tracks. So what if she looked like the weak female running from the scene after doing the deed? It wasn't embarrassment over what they'd done driving her. It was a need for answers. And for an explanation that made no logical sense in a world she'd come to rely on.

"Look," she said quickly. "You don't need to worry. I'm not fertile. Nothing will come of this."

"That's not what I…" His hand tightened around her arm. "*Skata*. What the hell just happened?"

She turned her face toward his. For a split second searched his eyes for some confirmation that what she suspected couldn't be true. But she didn't see it. For the first time since they'd met, she saw eyes she'd looked into hundreds of times before, thousands of years ago.

Cynurus. The man she'd loved with heart and mind and soul. The one she'd nearly sacrificed her order for. The one whose death still haunted her, even now, over two thousand years later.

The man *she* was responsible for killing.

Pain slashed sharp and deep. Dear gods, it really was him. Reincarnated into this…this monster.

"Skyla—"

"Forget you met me, daemon. Forget everything about this night. If you know what's best for you, you'll forget what it is you seek and you'll leave this realm. And you'll never return."

Chapter 5

THE FIELDS OF ASPHODEL WERE AS DEPRESSING AND desolate as Atalanta remembered. As she stood in the middle of the waving gray wheat and stared out at a dull gray sky, she remembered why it had been so easy to recruit souls from this forgotten land to build her army of daemons.

Those that dwelt here existed between life and death. Frozen in time. Almost as if they'd never existed in the first place. Though some were truly evil and would ultimately find their way to Tartarus to begin punishment, others, the ones who'd led unremarkable lives, were simply awaiting judgment. All wanted out, though. For one never quite knew how long a soul would wait in the Fields of Asphodel before receiving that judgment. It could be days. It could be millennia. The promise of a second chance—even in the body of a daemon—had been Atalanta's greatest enticement.

She walked through the field, the palm of her hand brushing the stalks of wheat, the entire meadow undulating in the breeze like an old-time black-and-white movie. Back then—when she'd recruited from this realm—she'd drawn power from the Underworld, where she'd resided. But now, after being expelled from Hades's realm and reestablishing her army in the human world, she found herself back in this gray and barren land. Only this time she wasn't just visiting.

She was an inhabitant. Trapped here by her disloyal son and the daemon spawn who shared her son's Medean powers.

Anger welled deep in her soul, burned her flesh until she tasted the embers on her tongue. She stopped, looked down at her once bloodred robes now as gray as the sky, at what was her milky skin now ashen and plain. She couldn't stay here. Every day that ticked by in the human realm was a day she would never get back. And there was so much vengeance to be had. So many Argonauts—her son included—to destroy.

"Mistress. I beg for yer attention."

Atalanta whipped around, stared down at the three-foot-tall troll-like creature whose pointy ears barely crested the wheat. "Galto, I've been waiting for word. I trust you've brought me something of use."

The creature she'd recruited to help her in this plight—the one who was supposed to be monitoring the inhabitants of this realm, his directive from Hades himself—rubbed his scaly hands together and glanced back and forth with large oval catlike eyes that dominated his triangular face. "I have, mistress. But…these fields have ears. If ye will come with—"

"I've waited long enough, Galto. Tell me your news. Now."

The creature swallowed hard. Though he knew, as she did, that she retained her godlike powers, she couldn't use them to free herself from this vile holding cell. She'd been trying for nearly three months and had come up empty. Her only hope was now this pint-sized…friend.

And if he couldn't help her, she'd use her powers to turn him to dust. She still had that much strength left.

He shifted on his feet. Leaned forward and whispered, "The gates to the human realm are watched. There's no passage through there."

"Bollocks." She twisted away, the wind blowing her black hair behind her as she stared at the barren sky above. *I will blast you for this, Demetrius. For every second I've been locked here. You and the daemon spawn who helped trap me here.*

"But…" Galto whispered at her back.

She glanced over her shoulder. "But what?"

He looked around again as if searching for eavesdroppers, stepped close, and motioned her down with his gnarled hand. She bent to hear his soft words. "But rumors circulate of an Argonaut in the Underworld. One sent here by magic, not death."

"An Argonaut, you say? Here in the Fields of Asphodel?"

"No, mistress." He glanced around again. "In Tartarus."

Atalanta stared down at the scaly creature as ideas, opportunities, plans solidified. Aside from death, there was only one magical force strong enough to cast people into Tartarus. And only one magical force strong enough to free them.

"Can you get me into Tartarus?" she asked.

"Of course, mistress. But the journey is fraught with danger."

She looked across the undulating gray field again, only this time she didn't see the drab wheat and colorless vegetation. She saw a way out. And a way to finally have her revenge.

"Danger, Galto, is only a matter of perspective. And where we're heading, it's worth it."

Skyla didn't stop at the gates of Olympus and announce herself as was customary after returning from the human realm. She bypassed the guards and headed straight for Athena's temple.

The facade was as gleaming and ornate as Zeus's palace, although the interior was a different story: plush furnishings, bold colors, rooms that bled from one richness to another and showcased the goddess's affinity for whimsy.

She passed through the main hall with its canary yellow walls and purple tile-framed mirrors, down three steps into Athena's living quarters where leather furnishings were paired with whitewashed tables and heavy eggplant-colored velvet curtains. She searched the whole of the palace before she realized the goddess wasn't there. Glancing toward the clock high on the wall, she realized Athena would be with the Sirens at this hour. Training for kills yet to be made.

She closed her eyes, pictured the Siren Compound—well within the walls of Olympus but outside the gods' domain—and flashed there, opening her eyes when the ground solidified beneath her feet.

Acacia and wild olive trees rimmed the compound. The five main buildings—Siren headquarters, the training facility, mess hall, and barracks—were made of wood, painted white to match the marble monstrosities of the gods but clearly meant for those less endowed. Bitterness brewing, Skyla skipped steps to reach the porch of the main building, pulled back the screen, and stepped into the lobby of the Siren Order.

Head shots of each Siren who'd ever served lined the white-painted walls, a veritable yearbook of those who'd served and died. But today Skyla had no desire to walk down memory lane. She wanted answers and she wanted them now.

The front desk was empty. She stepped out of the welcoming area, moved past Athena's empty office, and reached the end of the hall, where she glanced out the back window toward the training field beyond. Just as she'd thought, Athena was at work with a group of six Sirens—mostly new recruits—covering mortal-combat maneuvers.

Skyla crossed the emerald green grass. And as if the goddess sensed her presence, Athena looked up and frowned.

Athena straightened from a crouch, eyes still cast Skyla's way. "I'm afraid that's all I've got time for, ladies." She looked back at her newest recruits. "We'll take a short break. Get some water."

The newbies, three of whom Skyla had never met, sized Skyla up. When Skyla sent them a withering glare, they moved off toward the barracks across the field in a cocoon of whispers, leaving Skyla alone with her mentor.

The pain of betrayal burned hot in Skyla's veins, but she capped her anger, knowing there had to be a logical explanation. Something that made sense of a situation that couldn't possibly be real.

Athena braced her bow against the ground, brushed her chestnut curls over her shoulder. Though the goddess of war could have passed for a Victoria's Secret model, she was as tough as they came. Her blouse was white silk, her hip-hugging trousers jet-black, and her goth boots as kick-ass as the ones Skyla wore. Yeah, it made sense Athena was the head of the Siren Order. She could lure a man in with simply a look, then gut him even before he knew what had happened. "Well, that was quicker than I expected."

Skyla's stomach dropped. And in her mentor's eyes, she saw reality sharpen and clear.

"You know." Betrayal burned a hole straight through Skyla's gut. "You knew he was Cynurus and you didn't tell me?"

"Oh, Skyla. You make it sound like I set out to deceive you. I had no such intentions."

"What would you call it?"

Athena bent to pick up her throwing stars from the ground. "I call it an assignment, plain and simple. Who he is changes nothing. And had you not slept with him, you would never have known the truth. You did sleep with him, didn't you? That's the only reason you'd even know. My gods, Skyla. It's been years since you fucked a mark. It didn't even occur to me that you would screw a human, let alone a daemon hybrid."

It hadn't occurred to Skyla either. She hadn't understood the pull she had toward Orpheus. All she'd known was that between seeing him in that concert crowd and tending his wounds in that stopover apartment she'd taken while she waited for him to show up, he'd awoken some primitive womanly part of her she'd shut down eons ago. And in that moment of release, when they'd been joined and her guard had been stripped bare, she'd seen into his soul.

Athena's betrayal seared her heart. A heart she'd buried so long ago, she didn't realize it could still hurt.

"You should have told me. Keeping his identity secret was not your call to make. I had the right to—"

"To what?" Athena asked. "To decide his fate? That's not your job, Skyla. Your job is to do as you're told. If you remember, I tried to talk Zeus out of sending you on this mission, but you claimed you were ready, and I went along with you because I trust your judgment. Regardless, though, who your target *was* is of no importance. It's who he is *now* that matters. And what he's done."

Skyla stared at the goddess she'd once regarded as her friend. The only person who'd understood her. But now she realized Athena hadn't truly understood her at all. Not if she could so callously brush this aside as if it meant nothing.

"How is it even possible? He died. I saw his body. I…" She closed her mouth, swallowed. Couldn't say the words. Because even just thinking them cut with the fierceness of a jagged blade. He'd been her lover, her heart, the one person she'd been willing to leave the Sirens for. Until he wasn't.

Athena pressed the button on the end of the magical weapon. It shrank down to a six-inch metal bar, which she slipped into the leg of her platform kick-ass boots. "That was not my doing."

"But you know."

"What I know is irrelevant." She shrugged. "My guess, though? A meddling Fate."

"What would a Fate care about one man's actions?"

Athena turned to look past the Siren Compound toward the shimmering palaces of Olympus beyond. "More than you know."

Before Skyla could ask what that meant, Athena turned back to face her. "The man you were so ready to leave the Order for, Skyla, was so angry at Zeus for convincing his father Perseus to put another on the throne of Mycenae instead of him that he used you to gain access to Olympus and jump-start his revenge against the King of the Gods. He stole the air element right out from under Zeus's nose. An offense punishable by death. And when you couldn't kill Cynurus as you were *ordered* to do, Zeus sent others in your place to finish the job."

The stab of Cynurus's betrayal still stung, over two thousand years later. Skyla remembered all too clearly how humiliated she'd been when she realized she'd been duped, that he had in fact stolen the palm-sized gem that held the chthonic powers of the sky. And when Zeus had ordered her to kill him, she was so distraught over her misjudgment, she hadn't been able to think, let alone act.

She'd spent the long years of her life knowing that misjudgment had sealed his fate for all eternity. And she'd justified it by believing he was guilty. But now…

If he was truly guilty, as Zeus and Athena claimed, why would a Fate give him a second chance?

"Lachesis was pissed when Zeus stepped in and had Cynurus killed prematurely," Athena went on, oblivious to the painful memories washing over Skyla like a wave. "Why? I'll never know, nor do I care. My guess is she took her appeal to Hades and brokered a deal for a second shot at life for the bastard. And as he did back then, now, in the body of this daemon hybrid, he's pulling the same shit as before. Only this time he has his sights set on the Orb of Krónos. And ultimate control of everything. The soul is black, regardless of the body. Then as now, Skyla, that is the same."

The Orb of Krónos. Holy gods, that's what this was about? Athena had told her Orpheus was after a relic. One that held great sentimental value for Zeus. But that's not what this was. This was the source of ultimate power. The object that had the strength to release the Titans from Tartarus, to start the war to end all wars, and the power to control what was left behind.

Armageddon in all its glory.

"I covered for you, Skyla, for a very long time." Athena stepped close, and in her eyes Skyla could see she'd pushed the goddess past her patience limit. "And when Zeus wanted you cast out of the Sirens, I made sure you had a place to stay. I trained you. I molded you. I taught you everything I knew so that you'd never be misled again. Everything you have and everything you've done is because of me. Because I cared enough to see that you were never hurt by the lie that is love again. The Siren call to duty is one that is meant to be answered, served, then abandoned, and we never intended for you to serve this long. But to spare you, I alone allowed you to remain. You are not immortal, even though you choose to think you are. Before you start spewing accusations that will only have you cast out for good, I suggest you think long and hard about who used you and who was there for you when you needed it most."

Athena brushed past Skyla and headed down the hill toward the main building. As Skyla watched, a host of memories rippled through her mind, bombarded her heart, tore at her soul. But the clearest—the most excruciating—was the moment she'd realized the man she loved was gone forever. In those static seconds, it hadn't mattered what he'd done. All that had mattered was that she was alone.

Head spinning, Skyla moved toward the barracks. As she climbed the front steps, the sound of voices and laughter drifted to her from behind the structure. She ignored her sisters and headed into the lobby. The place was set up like a fancy hotel, with plush couches and chairs. Skyla bypassed the comfort and climbed the stairs to the right, heading to the third floor and her personal residence as her mind continued to flicker over events long since past.

"I knew that hybrid kicked your ass. I just didn't expect to still see you licking your wounds."

Skyla's feet slowed. Sappheire leaned against the wall, sharpening one of her many knives. The Siren's mane, a mixture of blond and brown and red, fell to her biceps. Her piercing blue eyes—for which she was named—were homed in on Skyla as if she could see past flesh and bone and deep into the soul.

For a second, Skyla thought her Siren sister was referring to Orpheus, and her skin prickled. Then she realized Sappheire's dig was related to the hybrid who'd injured Skyla weeks ago, not the hell she'd just been through.

"It surprises me you win any battles, if you think this is defeat." Skyla grasped the balustrade and turned for the next set of steps. She wasn't in the mood to get into a pissing match with Sappheire. It was no big secret Sappheire was itching to take Skyla's place as Athena's most trusted Siren. But today she didn't feel like dealing with Sappheire's shit. She had enough of her own to deal with.

Sappheire skipped steps and caught Skyla on the next landing. "Word is you're slipping, Siren."

Skyla's eyes narrowed. "The only slipping I'll be doing is on your blood if you don't back off."

Sappheire flicked a lock of hair from Skyla's shoulder. "Be careful whom you mark as your enemy, Skyla. You might just find yourself alone when you need me most."

Sappheire's threat lingered as she descended the steps. When she was gone, Skyla blew out a breath and continued to her rooms at the highest level of the building.

She'd been given this premier space when she'd become Athena's right-hand Siren, the one the goddess confided in the most and turned to when she had a problem. Skyla pushed open the door to her apartment and crossed the immaculate space. She'd taken pains to make this area her own. Comfy white furnishings, a mixture of glass and wood tables. And plenty of books.

She bypassed her kitchen, where she enjoyed baking—though no one but her knew that little secret because she never shared her goodies with anyone—and went straight for her bedroom.

This room was all her. Red velvet comforter, wrought-iron bed, plush pillows, and shelves along every wall lined with more books than a mortal could read in one lifetime. Some from Olympus, but most acquired over her many years spent in the human realm.

She stepped around a stack she'd yet to shelve and knelt on the hardwood floor near the window. After one deep breath that did little to settle her nerves, she pried up the slat closest to the window and reached inside the dusty hole for the box she'd stashed there thousands of years before.

It wasn't anything fancy. Just aged cedar that was now covered in a layer of dust. She blew the dust from the lid and rubbed her hand over the Siren symbol—the ancient Greek letter sigma, cut diagonally with an arrow and surrounded by an intricate bow with swirled ends and delicate edges. The same symbol branded into the skin over her right shoulder blade. The same symbol every Siren had been branded with when they'd joined the order.

Σειρήν.

Siren.

Her entire being was wrapped up in that one word. Her only reason for existing. When she'd buried Cynurus deep in her mind, she'd buried all her mementos of him in this box as well. But she'd never forgotten. She couldn't.

She opened the box, peered inside, extracted the drawing she'd done of Cynurus one night when they'd been relaxing in his home and he thought she was reading. And as she stared at the ancient picture, which was well preserved by the perfect Olympus air, she compared the man she once loved with the one she'd given herself to just today.

They looked nothing alike. Cynurus's features had been more refined, more aristocratic. Orpheus's were rugged, a little bit wild. But there was something similar in the slope of the nose, and the eyes…they were exactly as she remembered. Slate gray, deep set, and as intense as ever.

Why hadn't she noticed that right off?

Her heart leaped beneath her breast, beating so fast it was a painful whir in her chest. How could she have loved someone so much yet not really known him? How could she not have seen the darkness of his soul? Back when they were together, she'd never once anticipated he could betray her. She hadn't wanted to believe it. Had told Athena she was wrong. And then she'd seen the proof, from Zeus himself.

The gods had no reason to lie. And proof was proof. Yet…she still hadn't been able to kill him when Zeus ordered her to. But she hadn't stopped his death when her sisters had come to finish the job she'd started.

And now, nearly two thousand years later, a Fate had stepped in and given him another chance. What did that mean? Did it mean the gods were wrong? That he'd served his time? Surely a Fate wouldn't bring him back if he was truly as black as Athena and Zeus claimed.

She took a deep breath, let it out, repeated until the sharp stab was nothing but an ache just beneath her breast bone. Guilty or innocent, it wasn't her job to judge him, was it? Her job was to find out if he was really looking for the Orb.

So she'd use their connection to get close, pair up, and discover what he was really after. Learning that Athena had kept secrets from her for so many years changed every-thing as far as she was concerned. And the fact a Fate had stepped in to give him another chance…well, that told her there was something happening beneath the surface. Something even the gods didn't want her to know.

She wouldn't be a sheep led blindly into the night anymore. But if he was only after power and revenge, she'd do what she was trained to do, ex-lover or not.

She'd kill him herself. And she'd bury what he'd once meant to her forever.

Chapter 6

THIS HAD BEEN THE DAY FROM HELL. NOT ONLY HAD Athena nearly lost her patience with the most recent of her Siren recruits—gods, was the blessed well of recruits getting stupider by the hour or what?—she'd had to deal with her half brother, Ares, and she made it a point to avoid the conceited god if she could.

He was pissed at Poseidon for some slight he deemed reprehensible and he wanted Athena to send a few Sirens to fuck with the Lord of the Seas. Like she had time for that? Or wanted to take on Poseidon right now? She had her hands full with Zeus and Skyla and this whole damn Cynurus/Orpheus debacle.

Gods almighty.

She pushed Ares to the back of her mind, ran a hand over her hair, and climbed the marble steps to the archives. Inside the massive marble building, the scents of paper and ink met her nose. Columns lined the inside of the library, flanked by enormous wooden shelving units tricked out in decorative moldings. She wove through stacks of ancient leather tomes and stopped when she came across Skyla in a back corner, sitting at a mahogany table, books open all around her. "I thought I'd find you here."

Skyla glanced up, then refocused on her books, jotting notes on a piece of paper at her elbow. "Not a stretch, when you know this is where I come to do research."

The Siren was still pissed. Well, Athena couldn't blame her for that, now could she? "Does this mean you've decided to move ahead with your duties?"

Skyla flipped the book closed, pushed to stand. She was still dressed in the same clothes as before—black shirt, fitted slim pants, and kick-ass goth boots—but unlike before, her hair was pulled back in a slick ponytail and her makeup was fresh. And she was wearing her fighting gear—the leather breastplate with the Siren stamp and the leather arm guards that reached her elbows. "It does."

The Siren didn't sound excited. But at least she seemed resigned. That was as much as Athena could hope for.

"He's still looking for Maelea," Skyla said, folding her paper and slipping it into her right boot. "Now that I know this is about the Orb, I'm guessing he'll use her to locate the medallion. If you gave me all the information I needed up front to do my job, I'd be far more effective."

Maelea—technically known as Melinoe, but she'd dropped that name long ago—was the waiflike creature who'd wandered the earth for over three thousand years. Not a god, not a human, she was the daughter of Zeus and Persephone, conceived one dark night when Zeus descended into the Underworld and disguised himself as Hades, then seduced the Lord of the Underworld's wife near the banks of the River Styx. Zeus was always doing shit like that, causing trouble and making waves, but he got away with it because he was Zeus. King of fucking everything. It was no great surprise that Hades had been pissed at both his brother and his wife when he discovered their affair, or that he'd cast their bastard child out of the

Underworld, banishing the girl to the human realm, where she'd wandered ever since, caught between worlds.

Athena had given Skyla the hint before—that the daemon hybrid was tracking Maelea—but she hadn't told her why. "I'll expect an update when you find her."

Skyla nodded, stepped past Athena, and headed for the front of the library.

"Skyla."

Skyla hesitated but didn't look back. "What?"

There was still hurt there. Athena didn't feel bad for causing the Siren pain, but neither did she like the resulting resentment. "Duty has saved you. Remember that."

Skyla didn't move, and in the silence Athena sensed that the Siren wanted to say something but didn't. She simply nodded again and disappeared out the front of the archives.

Athena stared after her, trying to decipher what it must be like to be mortal. Though Skyla didn't age, she was still mortal in every sense of the word. She truly was the toughest Siren Athena had ever trained, but that didn't make her invincible. The iron shield she'd built around herself since Cynurus's death wouldn't last forever. And when it finally gave, Athena had a sinking suspicion the aftermath just might cause a host of problems for the whole of Olympus.

Unless, of course, Athena headed it off before that happened.

Footsteps echoed to her right. She didn't turn to look to see who'd joined her. She already knew who'd been lurking in the stacks because she'd told her to wait there until Skyla left. "Gather two other Sirens. I have a job for you."

Sappheire paused at Athena's side, her gaze straying to the front of the building. "Khloe and Rhebekkah are available."

"Good." Athena turned toward the blue-eyed Siren who would one day soon take Skyla's place. "Send them to Argolea. A new queen rules. I want them to enlist the help of the Argonauts."

"Toward what end?"

"To locate the warlock who holds the Orb of Krónos."

"And what if they won't? As far as they know, the hybrid is one of them."

"They will. Especially when you tell them what he really is."

"And what of her?" Sappheire nodded toward the door Skyla had just exited.

"Follow her. And report back to me what she and the hybrid are doing."

"You think she's compromised."

Athena chose her worlds carefully. "I think it's possible Skyla is letting emotions rule her actions."

"And if you're right?"

Loyalty was a sacred trait that couldn't be taught. But even to the gods, self-preservation trumped loyalty by a long shot. "Then you and I both know what has to be done."

~~~

Orpheus had been in a piss-poor mood ever since the blond with the hypnotizing violet eyes had ditched him three nights ago in her apartment. He'd replayed the events over in his mind and only two things were clear.

One, she was definitely otherworldly. Even if she

hadn't poofed right out of his arms, he'd have known it from the mind-blowing sex they'd had in her hall. Human females didn't blow his mind. Argolean females either. He'd even slept with a few goddesses in his many years and not even they'd rocked his world the way Skyla had. He tried to ignore the fact she was the only one who'd *ever* flipped him end over end like that, but couldn't.

He had to get the female out of his head. The only thing that really mattered—and the second point that was clear to him—was that the sex obviously hadn't been as earth-shattering for her as it had been for him. Evidenced by the way she'd run like the wind as soon as it was over.

Whatever. He didn't care. *Skata*, he shouldn't even be thinking of her anyway. He had more important things on his mind. Like locating that damn Maelea creature, the one he'd let get away the night he'd met Skyla. The witches in Argolea had told him she could sense energy shifts on earth. If that sonofabitch warlock Apophis was using the Orb's energy, Maelea would be able to feel it. And she'd be able to tell Orpheus right where the slimy piece of shit was hiding.

He stayed in the shadows of the ritzy Lake Washington neighborhood he'd tracked Maelea to. Two nights of waiting and she hadn't returned to the small town of Auburn, Washington, where the concert had taken place. But he'd lucked out when he overheard a conversation in a bar between two human males about the weird black-haired woman who routinely hung out at the death-metal concerts. What she'd been doing with the metalheads, Orpheus still didn't know. But he wasn't about to question a streak of luck, especially not when the waitress told him Maelea had mentioned living somewhere near Lake Washington in the Laurelhurst area.

He'd spent the last night running reconnaissance and he was pretty sure which house was hers. The daemon inside him could sense the light and dark warring within her. The new moon cast not a hint of light as he hid in the shadows and waited for the streetlights to go out. At this time of night—nearly two a.m.—not a soul was awake, but in this rich area, he knew neighbors looked out for one another. And a six-foot-six, two-hundred-seventy-pound stranger lurking in the shadows would draw attention he didn't need.

He shook off the feeling he was being watched, crept up the empty drive with its manicured hedge and towering trees blocking out the other houses. The property was a sprawling four acres right on the waterfront. Prime real estate he had no doubt Maelea had purchased back when land in the Seattle area was cheap. He briefly wondered how she kept her neighbors from asking questions about her ageless appearance, then brushed it aside. No doubt she kept to herself. He couldn't exactly see her at the neighborhood picnic, getting chummy with the local mom's club.

He moved around the back of the house, felt the daemon in him stir. Yeah, she was definitely in there. He could feel the blackness of her soul, along with that same odd light from Olympus.

Man, that would suck. Light and dark warring together within, never letting one get the upper hand, never giving the bearer any kind of relief. And he thought he had it bad.

The back patio curved outward, covered by a trellis of climbing ivy. He picked his way around patio furniture and up the three cement steps to peer in the back window of the house.

"Rethink that move, daemon."

He froze. Knew that voice. For some reason wasn't surprised to hear it here, now.

Slowly he turned and peered through the dark with his enhanced sight toward the woman who'd rocked his world just three nights before.

Correction—not a woman. Dressed in what looked like some ancient Spartan fighting gear with…shit, a very familiar symbol stamped on the breastplate…Skyla's affiliation suddenly made sense.

He turned back to peer into the house. No lights. Nothing moved. No sign anyone but a ghost lived here.

"I was wondering when you'd show up again."

"I thought I warned you to steer clear of this."

"Well, lucky for you I never do as I'm told." He glanced inside the window ledge at the LED that indicated an alarm system was turned on. "And at my age, I don't plan to start now." He took a step back, looked up at the second-floor window. Still no lights.

"I—"

"I've been trying to figure out what you are. We both know you're not human, though you put on a good act. You're definitely not a god. I'd have picked up on that right away. You aren't a Grace or a Muse—not enough class. For a minute I thought nymph." He shot her a look, from the swell of her breasts pressing up behind that leather breastplate to the knee-high black boots showcasing her shapely legs. "You screw like one."

A disgusted look crossed her features. Was that jealousy? No, not from her.

He turned back to the house. "Then I realized there was only one creature built like an X-rated Barbie doll able to kick a daemon's ass." He dropped the humor. "Tell your boss Zeus to go fuck himself."

"Cy—"

He didn't wait to hear what she had to say. He flashed inside the house, turned to look at her through the window. Her shocked expression said she hadn't expected he could flash through walls.

Get used to surprises, sweetheart. I sure have.

He shot her a salute and turned for the front of the house. In the entryway he stopped. Listened. His oversensitive hearing picked up one heartbeat. One even breathing pattern.

He grasped the old oak banister, climbed the curved stairs toward the second floor. The creak of wood behind him stopped his feet and brought his head around.

"Orpheus," Skyla whispered. "Rethink this move."

Skata. How the hell had she gotten past the security system?

"Look, lady," he said in an equally low whisper. "I know you've got a hard-on for me and all, but it wasn't that great. I'm not interested anymore."

She might be trained by the gods themselves, but she didn't hide the sting his words inflicted as quickly as she should have. For a tiny second he regretted saying them. Then the feeling fled.

"If you're determined to drag her into this, go ahead," she whispered in a hard tone. "But I'll not let you hurt her."

As if he cared. He reached the second floor and

looked right and left. The door at the end of the hall was open. He headed that way. Paused outside. Peered past the door into what looked like a bedroom suite that ran from one end of the house to the other.

The bed along the wall was empty. To his left, lights from windows that looked out at the street streamed into the room. From the right, dots of illumination peppered the darkened windows at the back of house. Ahead, a door that had to lead to a bathroom was cracked just an inch. And though he couldn't see her, he sensed Maelea close. Hiding like the ghoul she'd become.

He took a step into the room, conscious that Skyla wasn't far behind.

"She's not here," Skyla whispered.

Yeah, she was. He turned toward the female he still couldn't stop thinking about but who was quickly becoming a thorn in his side. "Why don't you see if she's downstairs."

"And leave you here alone? I don't think—"

The double doors to his right flew open. A high-pitched shriek echoed through the room just as a slight figure draped all in black charged, hands held high over her head, holding a blade as big as a machete poised to slice him in two.

He dropped back three steps. The female hurled herself at him, the whites of her fury-filled eyes blinding in the darkness. She slammed into his body. Another shriek filled the room as she sliced out with the weapon. "I will kill you!"

She couldn't have been more than five-five, a hundred and twenty pounds soaking wet. Didn't even knock him off his feet when she barreled into him. He easily overpowered her, grasped her forearms, and wrestled for the blade now only centimeters from his face. When he pulled it from her fingers, she screamed in denial. He tossed it to his left and flipped her around, her back pressed to his front, her arms pinned beneath both of his. "Stop. Now."

"I'll never stop," she screamed. "Never. Do you hear me?"

Bloody hell, she was stronger than she looked. With her arms still locked tight under his, he eased back a few steps until he felt the bed, dropped down, and pinned her on his lap, hooking one leg over both of hers to hold her still. "Stop fighting, do you hear me? We're not going to hurt you."

She continued to struggle, and when she realized she was trapped, finally stilled. But her chest rose and fell with her labored breaths, and Orpheus knew she was plotting a way out.

"Orpheus." Skyla stepped forward from the shadows, concern across her perfect features as the lights from outside reflected off her face. He hadn't lied when he said she was built like an X-rated Barbie. Not only was she the hottest thing he'd ever seen, that warrior-princess getup with the arm guards and breastplate and those ridiculous platform boots made him hard with just a look.

The female in his arms stopped breathing. And too late he realized *she* thought he was turned on because of *her*.

Not even close.

"Are you calm enough for me to let go?" he asked, careful to keep his tone even and his body still. "Or do I need to restrain you?"

Silence.

"Orpheus," Skyla warned again.

"I'm not here to hurt you," he said. "I just want to talk."

The female nodded once.

He didn't trust her, but she was no threat. And he didn't want to restrain her if he didn't have to. A willing hostage was way better than an enraged one. "Okay then. Nice and easy, you got it?"

Maelea nodded again.

He eased his leg off her lap, let go of her arms one by one. As soon as she was free, she bolted away and flipped around, pressing her back into the wall and searching the ground for her blade.

He rose, kicked it toward the bathroom door, spread his feet to use his size as intimidation.

"Now that we've got the awkwardness out of the way, let me introduce myself. I'm Orpheus. The chick in the Halloween getup over there is a Siren." Skyla flicked him an irritated look that only amused him. "You're familiar with Delia in the Argolean realm? She sent me to find you."

Confusion crossed Maelea's face. She shot a look toward the weapon behind him again. "The witch? Why?"

Delia was the leader of the Medean witch enclave that resided in the Aegis Mountains outside the Argolean city of Tiyrns. And she'd been a personal friend of Orpheus's mother and was now a friend of his. "I'm looking for a warlock named Apophis. He broke free of his prison in Argolea and crossed into this realm a few months ago. He has something that belongs to me. I want it back. It's as simple as that."

The female's wary eyes darted his way again. She

wore a long-sleeved black tunic that covered her hips, the sleeves so long they fell all the way to her fingertips, and a full, black, bohemian-style skirt that swallowed her slim frame. Straight black hair fell around her shoulders like a curtain. "What does that have to do with me?"

"I want you to tell me where he is."

"And what if I won't?"

"I'm hoping," he said carefully, putting a hint of malice in the words, "that won't be your choice."

Skyla's blond head darted his way, and in his peripheral vision he read the warning in her violet eyes, but he ignored it.

After a silence, Maelea said, "I don't know anything about any warlock."

She was lying. The daemon in him stirred as his patience waned. He took a step toward her. "Maelea—"

She pressed her hands against the wall at her back. Glanced past him to the weapon she'd never reach. "I'm warning you. Stay back."

He nearly laughed. But he was well past laughing. He needed to know where that shitty warlock was hiding. He took another step her way. "If you won't cooperate willingly, I'll have to come up with creative ways to make you talk."

"Orpheus—"

A howl cut off Skyla's protest. Both females turned to the windows at the front of the house. The daemon in Orpheus vibrated with excitement, sensing something otherworldly outside.

The howl echoed through the still night air again. Maelea's eyes went wide with fear. Skyla stepped past him and looked out the front window.

"Shit."

"What?" Orpheus reached her side and peered out into the dark.

"Hellhounds."

Three enormous doglike creatures with pointy ears, red eyes, and protruding fangs stood on the front lawn, looking up at the house.

"*Skata*." It wasn't daemons who'd been following him. It was Hades's miserable underlings.

"You really are on a roll tonight, aren't you, daemon? Is there a god you haven't pissed off yet this week?" Skyla shot him a *way to go, dumbass* look, then turned back to Maelea. "Shit, she's gone."

He whipped around. Sure enough, the room was empty. And Maelea's weapon of choice was missing as well. "Motherfucker."

Skyla pulled a metal bar from the inside of her boot. Seconds later her bow unraveled. She reached inside her collar and extracted what looked like a toothpick but which grew into a full-blown arrow right before his eyes.

"Now *that* is sweet," Orpheus murmured before he thought better of it.

"Check the first floor for her." Skyla readied her weapon. "Those things will tear her to pieces if she tries to run."

"Now you don't mind me being alone with Ghoul Girl?" He stepped toward the door. "How the tides have changed."

She twisted back to the window, slid the pane open a crack, and brought the bowstring to her shoulder. "If it's a choice between you and Hades's hounds, I'll take you any day."

"Gee, I feel so loved." He moved into the hall, intent on putting the Siren out of his mind and finding that damn Maelea before she screwed this up for him for good, but paused when a whisper met his ears.

You aren't now, but you were once, daemon.

He whipped around just as Skyla pulled the arrow back near her ear, let it go with deadly precision. He heard the whir as it spiraled toward its target, then the yelp and howl of the hound as its flesh tore open. And couldn't ignore the fact those words hadn't been in his head. She'd said them. Out loud.

The world spun. Blurred then cleared, until the bedroom walls disappeared and he was surrounded by trees. Standing in a field of green. The woman in front of him poised with her bow, exactly as she'd been in Maelea's bedroom. Only this time she was aiming for a target propped against the trunk of a tree.

She released the arrow like a pro. It sailed through the air, struck the target dead center with a resounding thwack. With a triumphant grin, she lowered the bow and turned to face him.

"*Your turn. Try to beat that, lover.*"

His lungs tightened on a gasp. And an ache, the same one he'd experienced in the hallway of her apartment two nights before, settled deep in his chest.

Holy Hades. Whatever head game the Siren was playing with him had to stop *now*.

A scream from the back of the house jolted him out of his trance. The trees and field disappeared like a wisp of fading fog.

"Maelea." Skyla passed him in a dead run.

Orpheus simply pictured the back patio and flashed

there. Feet from him, Maelea stood frozen, the blade she'd used on him earlier shaking in her hand as she stared out at the side yard and the hellhound growling an ominous warning.

The door crashed open behind him. Skyla leaped onto the patio, spotted the hellhound, and froze. "Orpheus! Behind you."

At Orpheus's back, another growl echoed. He looked that way to see another hound, its eyes glowing as red as death. Skyla and Maelea stepped backward toward him as two more hounds joined the fray, followed by the bleeding and pissed hound with Skyla's arrow sticking out of its shoulder.

"If you're thinking about shifting so we have a chance here," Skyla muttered, "I wouldn't object."

Orpheus couldn't agree more. Though the fact the Siren had flipped from trying to stop him to trying to help him wasn't lost on him. He tuned in to his inner daemon, felt his eyes morph to glowing green and the power of the daemon ripple through his limbs. In a rush he released the hold he kept on his dark side and unleashed control.

Nothing happened.

"Um…" Skyla raised her bow, pulled the arrow back as she cast him a frantic look. "Now would be a good time."

He focused deeper on the daemon's strength rumbling right beneath the surface. Pictured it consuming him as it had done so many times before.

Only again, nothing happened.

"Sonofabitch," he hissed.

Skyla's eyes darted from hellhound to hellhound. "Orpheus?"

Panic closed in. He could feel its strength, damn it. Why wasn't it working?

He reached for the knife he kept strapped to his hip. "I don't think that's gonna work this time."

"*What?*"

The hound directly in front of them chuckled.

It chuckled. Holy hell.

"Damn it," Skyla muttered. "This is not good."

"No shit," Orpheus tossed back. Damn it, what the fuck was going on?

Maelea's entire body shook as she backed into Orpheus. But this time she didn't seem to mind being close to him. "What—what do we do?"

Five bloodthirsty hellhounds against him, Skyla, and the quivering Ghoul Girl. He was a fierce fighter who knew a little magic. Even without his daemon, he and the Siren could probably survive these odds if they worked together, but not Ghoul Girl. They'd lose her in a heartbeat.

And he wasn't about to lose her. Not when she was the key to everything.

He thought of the lake behind them, a good hundred yards down the sloping grass. "You got a boat?"

Maelea swallowed hard. "Y-yes. A power boat. It's stored in the boathouse."

"You thinking about making a run for it?" Skyla asked in a low voice, her bow poised to shoot.

The injured hound growled low in its throat.

"Thinking about it," Orpheus muttered as the monsters slowly moved forward, forcing them back several steps and onto the grass.

He glanced behind him, toward the boathouse.

They'd never make it. Even injured, those hounds could run like the wind.

"You have something Hades wants," the hound to the left growled in a voice that was half man, half beast.

Oh, fucking fantastic. It could speak.

Orpheus reached into his pocket and pulled out the earth element. The one Queen Isadora had found and given to him months ago. Just before he'd left Argolea to find that warlock.

The monsters drew to a stop.

Skyla darted a look at the glittering quarter-sized diamond in his palm. The one stamped with the symbol of the Titans. "What the hell?"

All five beasts stared with rapt attention at the element he held. At the element that fit in one of the four chambers of the Orb of Krónos. Though the element held a special kind of power Orpheus had yet to tap, it wouldn't be fully useful until all the elements were joined with the Orb. Then the powers would combine and the bearer of the Orb would be stronger than Hades. Stronger, even, than Zeus.

And the monsters in front of him knew that.

Orpheus closed his fingers over the element and squeezed, harnessing the Medean powers bequeathed by his mother. He hadn't played with the element much since Isadora had given it to him, and he had no idea what to expect, but he wasn't against harnessing every shred of magic from it if he could.

But nothing happened, aside from the element growing warm in his fist.

The lead hound moved forward and growled. "We'll take that from you now, Argonaut."

The word *Argonaut* echoed in Orpheus's head. And he thought of his brother, Gryphon, confined to the Underworld because of that damn warlock. Of the moment Gryphon's Argonaut markings had appeared on *Orpheus's* skin. Of the real Argonauts, who didn't give a shit about him or what had happened to his brother.

His anger harnessed a flash of power. Medean magic shot down his arm and erupted through the earth element in his hand.

The ground shook in a violent blast of energy that knocked Orpheus back two feet. A hellhound shot forward with a snarl and a snap of its jaws. Maelea screamed. Skyla shouted something he couldn't make out. The other hounds howled in unison. And a roar that sounded like Hades himself rushing up from the center of the earth echoed everywhere.

Chapter 7

"ORPHEUS!"

Skyla lost her footing as a chasm split open between them and the hounds. She hit the ground with a grunt. One monster launched its massive body toward Maelea with a snap of its jaws. On her back in the wet grass, Skyla aimed her bow at the hellhound sailing through the air.

Its bloody teeth caught Maelea's arm. She screamed. Skyla fired, heard the hound cry out in agony, pulled another arrow, lined up another shot, and fired again. Before she could get to her feet, Orpheus was on top of the hound, driving his blade deep into the beast's flesh.

More snarls and growls echoed from across the chasm as the shaking died down. The other four hellhounds paced back and forth, waiting for their chance to strike. The bleeding hound lay dead at Orpheus's feet.

"You will pay, Argonaut," one hound growled across the distance.

Shocked, Skyla looked at Orpheus, who was shoving the earth element back into the front pocket of his jeans. Holy Hades. He already had one of the four sacred elements. No wonder Athena hadn't told her who he really was.

"Go fuck yourself!" Orpheus shouted.

Two hellhounds barked out their protest with a snap of their massive jaws.

Orpheus sheathed his blade in a scabbard at his back and bent next to Maelea. "How bad is it?"

Tears filled Maelea's eyes as she cradled her bloody arm against her stomach and shook her head.

Orpheus lifted her in his arms, then peered at Skyla across the damp grass before he hustled toward the boathouse. "If you're coming, you'd better haul ass, Siren. They're going to figure out how to cross that gap pretty quick."

Skyla shot their seething enemies a quick glance before realizing that escaping with Orpheus was her only choice at the moment. With her bow and arrow still in hand, she ran after him and caught up on the dock outside the boathouse. He kicked the door in with his boot. The little bit of light shining in from the watery opening at the end of the boathouse reflected the word *Olympian* painted across the side of the nineteen-foot motorboat.

"Fitting." She tossed her bow into the boat as Orpheus dropped Maelea in a seat and searched compartments.

"Where are the keys?" he asked Maelea.

"Hanging in the second compartment. There."

Skyla untied the boat and threw the rope in. She jumped in the back, picked up her bow and arrow. Outside she could hear the snarls and growls of the monsters as they raced across the grass. "Um…anytime would be good."

"Goddamn it." Orpheus opened panels and slammed them shut. The sound of claws racing along the dock outside echoed in the air.

"Orpheus?" Skyla readied her bow, aimed for the door.

"Found them!" Keys jingled as Orpheus jumped behind the wheel.

The outer door shattered into a thousand pieces.

"Now!" Skyla screamed.

The boat's engine roared to life. Orpheus punched the throttle. The hounds rushed into the boathouse. Skyla fired one arrow, readied the next shot just as the boat tore out of the boathouse and cut across the water.

She fell backward into the seat behind her. Water sprayed her face. When she found her footing and pushed up, the hounds were already pacing the end of the dock, their glowing red eyes tiny points of light far off against the shore.

They motored out of Union Bay and into Lake Washington. The dashboard lights highlighted Orpheus's sandy brown hair blowing in the breeze as he maneuvered the boat through the glassy water as if he'd done it a thousand times before.

To keep from staring at him, Skyla moved to check Maelea's arm. Looking at him made her wonder about that element. Where he'd gotten it and what he planned to do with it. And what else about him was the same as Cynurus.

Maelea jerked her arm back from Skyla's touch. After arguing with the girl for five minutes, Skyla finally gave up and sat on the other bench.

They slowed as the lake came to an end. "Through there." Maelea pointed toward a dock with her good arm. "There's a park."

Orpheus killed the engine and brushed past Skyla to tie the rope to the dock. A rush of heat swept over her skin where he grazed her, followed by a chill that left her with gooseflesh.

"How bad is the arm?" he asked, helping Maelea out of the boat.

"It's—it's fine." Maelea wrapped her good arm around her bad.

"Let me see it."

"No, it's fine."

When he grasped her hand and tugged it away from her body, moving the sleeve out of the way to have a look, she protested again. "I don't need—"

"What the…?"

Maelea broke the eye contact, tugged her hand away, and cradled her arm against her stomach again. "I told you it was fine."

Orpheus's jaw tightened, but instead of arguing he turned toward Skyla and said, "She's fine. Let's go."

Maelea took a step back. "I'm not going anywhere with either of you."

Orpheus rolled his eyes. Then whipped her into his arms.

"Put me down!"

"When you start listening to directions, we'll talk about it."

"You sonofa—"

"Where are you taking her?" Skyla asked, grabbing her weapons and hustling to follow as he strode down the dock toward shore.

"Where's the closest airport?" he asked Maelea.

"Airport?" Maelea repeated in surprise. "Why do you need an airport?"

Orpheus stepped off the dock and stopped on the grass, glaring down at the girl in the moonlight. "Let me explain this to you so you get it. I ask the questions, you provide the answers. If you give me answers I like, I'll consider answering a few of your questions. You got it?"

Maelea's mouth snapped shut. She glanced past Skyla to the dark lake beyond.

"Airport?" Orpheus asked again.

She pursed her lips. Looked as if she wasn't about to answer. In the silence Skyla could practically see the steam brewing in Orpheus as his patience waned, and she prepared herself for the worst. Now that she knew he was only after Maelea to get to the Orb, his reasons for protecting her the night of the concert made sense. But there were no daemons out here. No hellhounds either.

Finally, Maelea mumbled, "Snohomish County Airport. But it's at least ten miles from here. My house—"

"Is probably already toast," Orpheus told her, walking again. "And by now those hellhounds have reported back to Hades and told him you're with me. You're not safe on your own anymore."

Sickness slid across Maelea's face, and at his side, Skyla clenched her jaw at the way Orpheus was carrying the girl—the same way Rhett Butler had carried Scarlett up the stairs in *Gone With the Wind*. Orpheus picked up speed as he climbed a small knoll in the park. "We'll find a cab, head toward that airport. There's gotta be a charter plane we can catch there."

"Where to?" Maelea asked, cringing and clutching her injured arm as he jostled her.

"Was that a question?"

Her mouth snapped shut again, and this time her jaw clenched with barely contained anger.

Looking pleased, Orpheus said, "I've got a friend in Montana. He can take care of you there."

"Montana? But I live here!"

Orpheus's face went stony. Skyla drew to a stop,

her breath catching at what he would do to the injured female. She'd seen him in battle. Had seen the way he could shift into daemon form with just a thought. Why he'd screwed around and hadn't shifted back at Maelea's house she didn't know, but she'd soon find out. About that and the earth element. And just what he had planned.

Skyla waited for his eyes to change to signal he was calling up his daemon, but they didn't. "Do you want me to take you back to your house?" he asked.

Maelea stared at him. Swallowed. Seemed to debate her options. Slowly, she shook her head.

"Okay then." Orpheus resumed walking through the trees. "I think we're your only option at this point."

Maelea's gaze found Skyla, and it was clear she believed the hybrid. And didn't like it.

Be careful, female.

They reached Bothell Way, a major thoroughfare, in silence. Streetlights illuminated the four-lane highway. "There won't be any flights going out this late," Skyla pointed out. "Unless you're planning to hitch a broom to Montana, we need to hole up somewhere until morning."

"Then we'll take a train," Orpheus said. "But we're not sticking around here. I guarantee those hounds have our scent."

"Yeah, but we don't need to run all the way to Montana to lose them."

Orpheus ignored her—he was damn good at that—and looked to Maelea. "What about a train station?"

"Um…there's one close," Maelea said. "Edmonds. About twelve miles, maybe—"

"There won't be any trains leaving at this hour either," Skyla protested.

"Fucking fine, Miss Transportation Guru." Orpheus moved down the sidewalk. "We'll find a car and drive north to Bellingham, catch a train from there."

"Find a car?" Skyla liked that less than his idea to run for Montana.

Orpheus veered into a parking lot, where he dropped Maelea to her feet and peered into the window of a Ford Explorer.

"You're gonna steal that, aren't you?" Maelea asked.

"Sure as shit, I am." He used his elbow to knock out the back window. An alarm sounded. Seconds later he was in the front seat, bent down under the steering column, pulling wires free. The alarm clicked off, then the ignition roared to life. "Get in. Both of you."

Skyla stopped Maelea with a hand on the female's arm. "She's not in any condition to travel. And you're not the one calling the shots here."

She waited for the flash of green in his eyes, almost wanted it, because that would prove he was out of control and not thinking clearly, but it didn't come. Instead he turned very focused, very stubborn eyes her way. Eyes that were as gray as they'd been in Cynurus's head over two thousand years ago.

"Trust me, Siren, I am calling the shots. And I could just as easily have left you to deal with those hellhounds alone as rescued you."

"Rescue me?" she snorted. "On what alternate plane do you live?" But even as she said the words, unease slid through her. *Had* he rescued her?

Orpheus looked past her as if she hadn't spoken. "Who did the saving? You're the final judge here. Me or Rambo Girl there?"

Maelea's eyes widened, obviously not liking being caught in the middle. "I—I don't—"

"Stop tormenting the girl," Skyla snapped.

There it was again. That irritation that he seemed more interested in Maelea than her. What the hell was wrong with her? *Daemon hybrid*, she reminded herself. *Traitor to Olympus and just about every person on the planet*.

Orpheus eased out of the car and put his body between Skyla and Maelea, easily breaking Skyla's hold. "Ghoul Girl comes with me. Why don't you just head back to Olympus and tell your boss you failed?"

"Ghoul Girl?" Maelea's shocked expression would have been comical in a different situation, but Skyla barely cared.

She was suddenly too bowled over that Orpheus was suggesting she leave instead of making her go. From his reaction when she'd appeared at Maelea's house, it was clear she hadn't surprised him. He was tracking the Orb, and he knew she was there to stop him. Why the hell had he let her tag along this long?

His intense eyes stared into hers. And she had a flash of him glancing at her when they'd been running across Maelea's lawn, checking to make sure she was with them.

Why hadn't he left her there? And better yet, why wasn't he demanding the info he needed from Maelea right now and leaving her behind as well?

A thousand questions pinged around in her head. Melded with questions from the past, the ones regarding Cynurus's guilt or innocence—*his* guilt or innocence. And in the silence between them, she knew she had a choice. Walk away for good and let one of the other Sirens deal with him…or not.

Walking away would mean turning her back on the order.

Duty has saved you.

Athena's words trickled through her mind. Her mentor was right. The order *had* saved her. When nothing else could. But now she knew that order had also lied. The one question she couldn't get out of her head was why he'd been given a second chance.

She wasn't walking away from him. Not until she had the answers she needed. Not until she knew for sure he really was the black soul Athena and Zeus claimed him to be. Though she could now see the similarities between him and Cynurus, they didn't matter to her. She'd built up her barriers long ago. She'd look at this assignment objectively, keep her emotions out of it, and base her decision on the facts.

On what he did from here.

"If you think I'm letting this girl go anywhere alone with you, daemon, you're higher than a kite. Where she goes, I go."

She'd just made herself Maelea's protector. Her. A Siren. A lethal warrior trained not to protect, but to kill. Shit, she knew as much about protecting as she did about, well, Orpheus.

She ignored the irony in that thought and instead focused on Orpheus's gray eyes. His suddenly wicked gray eyes and his seductive mouth, curling up ever so slightly along one edge as his gaze slid from her face to her breasts, then lower. "I always liked to get high. I can think of one way that doesn't involve drugs. Just hormones."

There it was again. That transition from battle mode to sexual predator. How did he do that? And why the hell did it make her hot?

"Get in, Siren." His gaze lifted back to Skyla's mouth before she could think of something pithy to say in retaliation. Where it hovered until the heat of his stare pooled in her abdomen and sent shocks of electricity all through her body. "Before I come to my senses and change my mind."

―――

Spiders.

Today it was hundreds of spiders in all shapes and sizes and colors.

A scream echoed through Gryphon's mind as he lay on the flat obsidian rocks and stared into four giant, gaping eyes of a hairy arachnid the size of a grapefruit. He tried to move but couldn't. Tried to holler but was met with only the tapping of thousands of legs against rock, echoing in the humid air. Felt the sensation of those legs crawling over his skin and the sharp, angled fangs sinking deep into his flesh.

Death hovered just out of his reach. His vision swam as the creature on his chest lifted its front two legs and waved them wildly in the air in front of his face. Its fangs loomed dangerously close.

Another stab somewhere on his leg. A gasp of pain he couldn't inhale. Poison burning through his veins to mess with his mind.

"I have to get out of here."

You're not going anywhere.

"I don't deserve this. It's a mistake. It's—"

That's what they all say. But not all can be innocent. You sure aren't.

"I can't take it anymore."

You have thousands, millions of years yet to suffer. This is only the beginning. Just a taste of what you've yet to experience.

"Please…"

Don't beg. It's so…un-Argonaut. Man up and take it like the hero you used to be.

"I'll do anything. Anything…"

There is no such thing as anything. You should know that by now…

The voice faded to nothing. His mind fogged as un-shed tears and unanswered prayers washed over him. Inside he felt his body liquefy, pool, begin to slowly ooze out through every single puncture wound. He no longer felt the thousands of feet crawling across his body, no longer saw the spiders. A thick, white haze descended, and he felt himself drifting downstream, heading for a black abyss as vast as an endless chasm.

"Yes, finally…"

"I can ease your pain, Argonaut."

Gryphon's eyes flew open at the sound of the voice somewhere close. His vision cleared to reveal hundreds of multicolored spiders undulating across the length of his naked body. Sensation returned to his skin, along with the pain in his flesh. But even through his poison-laden mind, he recognized the voice.

This one didn't come from *inside*. It was female and deep. The sweet smell of candy wafted in the air nearby, mixing with the voice to tempt and tease and draw him back from the oblivion he needed.

"Yes, Argonaut. You know me well. Soon you will know me very well."

Atalanta.

His gaze darted from side to side as he looked for the female. He didn't care who she was. She was real. He wasn't alone in this forgotten hell after all.

"Help me!"

"I can take you away from all this pain, Argonaut. Would you like that?"

"Yes, yes, please, yes."

She chuckled.

A pale-skinned hand dropped down in his line of sight. Long tapered fingers lifted a giant spider from his chest and dangled the monster in front of his face. "Did you know there is a place within this realm where relief can be found? Where those who were sentenced long before you found refuge? Where the Elder Gods themselves rule a land more pleasurable than even Sodom and Gomorrah?"

Elder Gods. The Titans.

Gryphon's foggy mind spun as the words sank in deep. Zeus had cast the Titans into Tartarus at the end of the Titanomachy, the war between the Titans and the Olympians. And they'd been locked in the lowest level ever since, awaiting the day they would one day be freed by the Orb of Krónos.

"I can take you there, Argonaut. I know where it lies. I can save you from this never-ending agony. With me you can leave this torture behind for good and become powerful again. Whole. The warrior you once were. All you have to do is join me." Her voice dropped to a seductive whisper. "Be my *doulas.*"

Slave.

Some deep space inside screamed *No!* but it was drowned out by the thought of a world without pain. An end to this continuous torment.

The fact that Atalanta had been his bitter enemy in the living realm meant nothing. He wasn't an Argonaut any longer. His prior life was over. And he was willing to do anything to make this suffering end. Even if that meant sacrificing everything he'd once believed in.

"Yes, yes, yes. Anything you want. Just take this all away."

No!

A soft chuckle met his ears. "I knew I could count on you, Argonaut."

A whoosh of air streamed across his bare skin, sending the spiders scattering. A rumble sounded somewhere close and blackness spiraled in, then exploded into a thousand colors, fading like a clearing mist until a face appeared through the fog. A face with skin like alabaster, lips as red as blood, eyes of coal black, and a fall of long straight onyx hair that looked as if it were made of silk.

"Follow me, *doulas*."

His arms moved. Excitement leaped in his chest. But before his mind could tell his limbs what to do, he felt a tug, right in the center of his chest. A tug controlling him. Pulling him forward like a bull being led by a nose ring. Toward her. Until there was nothing. No sound. No pain. Nothing but endless emptiness fanning out in every direction.

~~~

Maelea didn't know what to make of her traveling companions. As she lay on the top berth of the stateroom they'd arranged in Bellingham and pretended to sleep, she listened to their quiet breathing and wondered if they were awake. Wondered also just how long until she could make a break for it.

She hadn't dared try on the drive to Bellingham. Hadn't tried when they'd stopped at that Walmart and Orpheus had dragged her in to buy a jacket and shoes so she'd blend in. Certainly hadn't tried at the train station when he'd booked tickets, not with the way Skyla kept watching her as if her head were about to spin around. She wasn't dumb. She knew Orpheus was right. Those hounds clearly had their scent, and if they stopped for any length of time, the monsters would be on them in a heartbeat. But that didn't keep her from planning for a way out when they finally reached their destination. Wherever that might be.

They'd switched trains in Everett around noon, had gotten lunch and hung out in the dining car as long as possible, then retired to their stateroom to get some rest and—Maelea knew—to avoid curious eyes. It didn't take a genius to see the three of them didn't go together. Skyla with her model-perfect body, Orpheus's sheer size and the dangerous air that seemed to hover around him, and Maelea, the quiet one who had a hard time looking either of the other two in the eye and wasn't even sure what she was doing here.

The need to bolt overwhelmed her, but she calmed herself by thinking about the alternative. Hellhounds? No, thanks. She was *not* about to tangle with Hades. For the time being, she'd wait and watch and make tracks only when she was sure it was safe. She wasn't wild about being with either of these two, but she sensed they didn't have plans to harm her.

At least not yet.

No one had said much since they'd returned to the stateroom. There was tension among all three of them, especially between Orpheus and Skyla. Tension Maelea was curious about but didn't dare question. Though she'd tried to doze as the train barrelled east toward the Rockies and dusk settled in, her mind was too full of images and sounds and the bitter reality that Orpheus was not the one she needed to kill after all.

The darkness she'd first sensed in him had diminished. How, she didn't know, but during the last hour she knew for certain his death would not grant her the access to Olympus she wanted. And that realization pissed her off more than anything, because thanks to him she now couldn't even go back to the sanctuary of her house in Seattle.

Stupid male. Stupid her for going to that concert in the first place. She was better off keeping to herself, but even knowing that, she couldn't seem to stop looking. It was the one major malfunction in her brain—the light pushing her to seek out the dark when what she should be content with was slinking into the shadows.

"You're staring at me, Siren," Orpheus said in a low voice.

Maelea went still and listened. They definitely weren't partners. He was marked with darkness from the Underworld; she was of Zeus's light. Another irony that wasn't lost on Maelea.

"I'm just trying to figure out which bones will be

easiest to break when you try to take Maelea out of here without me," Skyla said from the bottom bunk.

Now that was a fight Maelea would like to witness.

Orpheus chuckled. "So protective. One wouldn't expect it, coming from you."

"You don't know me."

"Not entirely. But I know way more than most. You're thinking about it now, aren't you? That's why you can't stop watching me."

Skyla grew quiet. The air thickened. And Maelea's unease at being in the same room with them jumped. Orpheus's suddenly husky tone spoke of intimate knowledge, but she couldn't imagine one of Zeus's warriors lowering herself to have sex with a daemon.

Not that Maelea had a whole lot of experience with sex as of late. She'd pretty much given up on that whole part of her life as she couldn't see the point in getting involved with a human when they'd eventually die. But she wasn't a virgin. Or a prude. She had cable, after all.

Or did. Before Orpheus ruined that for her too.

"You're full of yourself, daemon," Skyla said from below.

"No," he purred. "You were full of me. You're wondering what that would be like again. You're wishing you could have it right now. Admit it."

Maelea's skin warmed, and the realization that these two definitely had gotten busy hit her head-on.

Before she could stop it, her mind spun with images of their coupling. It would be fierce and rough. Both were warriors. No sweet lovemaking for these two. Judging by the power play between them before, it would be a fast, hard, animalistic struggle where one or both were eventually injured. And though she knew this was not a conversation she—or anyone—was meant to hear, for some reason she couldn't stop listening. Couldn't stop picturing them together. Couldn't stop herself from craving something…just as hedonistic.

"I thought you said it wasn't all that good," Skyla tossed back.

The seat below creaked, and through half-lidded eyes, Maelea watched as Orpheus leaned forward to brace his elbows on his knees and clasp his hands while he stared toward the bottom bunk. "But it was for you, wasn't it? I seem to remember you scoring my back with your nails and screaming for more. I felt it, when you came. Hard. All around me. I could make you come again, just as hard, right here, right now."

No way. These two weren't going to…Not with her in the room. Were they?

The chair creaked again as Orpheus moved forward until he disappeared from Maelea's view. The bottom bunk groaned.

"Careful, daemon," Skyla whispered.

"You don't like it careful, though," he whispered back. "You like it hard and rough. That's how we're the same."

"We're not the same."

"We're more similar than you know. Tell me you don't want just a little."

Skyla sucked in a breath that echoed through the car. Maelea's skin grew warm as she pictured the scene: him touching her, her responding. And for just a second, she wished it was her he was talking to. Not because she was attracted to him, but because part of her would like to know what it felt like to be wanted again, even half that much.

Orpheus's chuckle drifted up to Maelea's ears. "I thought so, Siren. All you have to do is beg."

"You'd like that, wouldn't you?" Skyla asked. "Me to beg. Well, I'm not going to. This isn't happening again, daemon."

"A challenge." Amusement echoed in Orpheus's husky voice. "Let's make a little wager. I get you to come without using my hands, and you tell me just what kind of enchantment you're casting on me."

"I'm not casting an enchantment."

"Then you'll tell me whatever the hell this weird connection is we seem to have."

Silence drew out through the car, mixed with the craving swirling in Maelea's blood. A craving she hadn't felt in years and didn't want. What was the point of looking for someone special? Just to get her heart broken all over again?

No, thank you.

Olympus. That would be her relief. That was what she needed to stay focused on. Not silly relationships that would never amount to anything important. Look what sex had done for these two—created tension and distrust, two things Maelea didn't need more of. The sooner she got away from Orpheus and Skyla and got serious about her goal, the better off she'd be. Because now more than ever, she was determined to make it to Olympus no matter what it took.

Once she was there…maybe then she'd think about sex and relationships and finding someone special again. When she was finally where she was supposed to be.

"I'm not having sex with you again," Skyla said. "I already made that clear."

"No sex," Orpheus answered. "My clothes will stay firmly in place. So will yours, I promise. What do you say? Afraid I'm that good?"

"I *know* you're not that good, daemon."

"Then take the bet."

"What if I win?" Skyla asked.

"Then I tell you whatever you want to know."

"You'd answer my questions?"

Silence. And then, "Three," he answered.

"Any three?"

"A bet's a bet."

For a heartbeat, no one spoke. And in the quiet, Maelea had a sinking suspicion they *were* going to go for it. Right here. Her stomach tightened with a mixture of anticipation and dread.

"Well?" Orpheus whispered.

Chapter 8

ORPHEUS KNEW HE WAS PLAYING WITH FIRE. JUST sitting across from the Siren in the confined sleeping car, he'd been juiced to the max. Now, seated next to her on the bottom bunk waiting for her answer, the heat from her body swirled in the air to mix with some sweet honeysuckle scent from her skin that left him lightheaded and on the edge of control.

Gods, he wanted her. Wanted to taste her again. All of her this time. Even knowing who and what she was.

The easy move—the *smart* move—would have been to ditch her ass in Seattle. But he hadn't. Partly because he needed to know what this weird connection was between them. Partly because she was no real threat until he actually had the Orb. And partly because seducing her in the meantime was a way to screw with Zeus. If there was one god Orpheus didn't mind screwing with, it was the King of the Gods.

"Well, Siren?"

Her eyes lifted to his, held. Brilliant violet eyes, the color so unusual he wondered if they were real. The color so familiar he was sure he'd looked into them before.

She pushed her hand against his chest. "You're radiating heat, daemon."

So was she. And her touch only amped the fire in his blood to lava-hot levels. Her hand flat against his sternum sent a shot of wicked heat through his chest. A hand that wasn't moving or forcing him back farther. "I'll take that as a yes."

A crash sounded outside in the hall. Skyla jumped to her feet. Before he could reach for her, she was out the door and into the narrow hallway.

"Sonofabitch." Frustrated, he pushed off the bench, looked out to see a steward picking up plates from the floor.

"Excuse me," the steward said when he caught sight of them. "Sorry for the disruption."

The steward quickly swooped up the dropped utensils, set them back on the tray, then disappeared down the corridor.

Orpheus looked at Skyla, a good foot away from him. The door between this car and the one behind clanged shut as the waiter left. With a one-sided grin, Orpheus stepped toward her. "Where were we?"

She held out her hand and eased away. "We weren't anywhere."

"Yes, we were."

He moved closer. She moved back again. Damn, he liked this nervous side of her. Way more than the seductive one. What would she do if he kissed her? Like he'd wanted to kiss her in the hallway of her apartment? Those lips were made for kissing. Plump, tender, so damn sweet, he was sure they'd taste like candy.

"We were right about…" He maneuvered her around until her back hit the wall, slapped a hand against the surface to trap her between it and him. "Here. Weren't we?"

She pushed against his chest. Didn't budge him. He leaned close, stared at her enchanting lips, and imagined them opening to take him in. Her mouth would be warm and wet and, he bet, just as slick as her sex. The need to taste her overwhelmed his senses. He moved in, saw her eyes widen in surprise.

He liked that he threw her off-kilter. Liked that she was remembering all too well how they'd fit together. He wanted that fit again, this time with her mouth locked tight to his as he drove inside her.

"Yeah," he said, staring at her lips, "we were right here."

Just as he moved to kiss her, she turned her head, offering her neck instead. "Maelea is just inside."

He focused on the pulse beneath her skin, remembered how sensitive she was there. "Ghoul Girl's asleep, trust me."

"That's like asking a mouse to trust a starving lion."

"With you, sweetheart, I am a lion. An insatiable lion."

She tensed when he nuzzled her ear. And he smiled at her nervousness. It meant that whatever this was, it wasn't the same thing she had with all her marks. He wasn't stupid enough to think she was tagging along with him and Maelea because of *him*—or even Maelea, as she wanted him to think. She was here because Zeus had sent her to get the Orb. And still that didn't stop him. Not yet. He was having way too much fun tempting her.

Her hand rested against his chest but she didn't push, and the way she tipped her head farther away told him she liked what he was doing.

He kissed the soft, soft skin beneath her ear. So it wasn't her mouth. He'd take her mouth later. When he slid inside her.

She drew a deep breath, let it out slowly. Her body relaxed against him. "I…uh…thought there was to be no touching."

"With my hands. You never said anything about other body parts."

Her throat worked as she swallowed. He followed the movement with his eyes and brushed the tip of his nose across her jaw again, barely scraped his lips over her neck.

"Someone could walk by."

His lips curled as he pressed them to a mole at the base of her throat. "That makes it more exciting. And I don't remember you objecting in that apartment."

"I obviously wasn't thinking clearly then. I seem to have that problem when you're around."

His chest expanded. He liked that. Liked it a lot.

He nudged her knees apart with his leg, pressed his thigh between hers as he kissed her neck again, as he pressed his lips to the electric skin just behind her earlobe. A tremor ran through her body, one that made his jeans even tighter.

"I know how to ease that problem." He skimmed his nose across her earlobe again, inhaling a deep whiff of her sweet scent that went right to his head like a drug, pressed his leg just high enough so his thigh rubbed against her mound.

Her chest rose and fell with her deep breaths. She was definitely aroused. Probably already wet.

Gods knew *he* was aroused. Ever since she'd shown up at Maelea's house, he hadn't been able to stop thinking of her. Shit, that was a lie. He hadn't stopped thinking of her since he'd seen her at that concert. It didn't matter that he'd already had her. He wanted her again. Here. Now. However he could get her.

He breathed hot against her neck, watched as the

pulse in her throat picked up speed. Her fingers drifted down his side to rest on his hip, dangerously close to the bulge in his jeans. And his blood heated to near boiling at the thought of her fingers so close to his cock.

Her gaze followed her hand to his hip, hesitated. She swallowed, as if she was imagining taking her own delicious sample.

He swelled harder against his zipper, imagined her mouth around his shaft. He didn't dare move his hand away from the wall for fear he'd forget all common sense and take her, losing their bet before it even got started. "You're teasing me, Siren."

Her dark, spiky lashes lifted to reveal amethyst eyes heavy with desire. "I was just wondering what happens if you come first. We didn't factor that into our bet."

He nearly came right then, just from the possibility in her words. It was his turn to swallow. "That won't happen."

"Why not?"

"Because I learned to master control long ago."

She raised her right thigh, slid it up over his hip so his erection sank in the vee of her body until he felt the heat of her sex through the denim and cloth separating their skin. Her hands roamed up his chest to rest against his pecs and squeeze ever so gently. Ripples of sensation flowed from that spot, through his abdomen and lower. "I saw your control in my apartment, daemon. Something tells me you don't have quite the control you think you do."

When she pressed her hips forward and his cock rubbed against the cleft between her legs, he knew she was right. If he wasn't careful, he'd explode long before she even warmed up.

He glanced down at her chest, at her luscious breasts lifting and falling beneath her thin black shirt. Thankfully, she'd taken off the breastplate and arm guards in their stateroom, but he liked the fact she was still wearing those stripper boots. He wouldn't mind if she wore those and nothing else as she wrapped her legs around his waist and screamed his name.

"So, what do you say, daemon?" She pressed forward, stroked his erection with the heat between her legs. "Why don't we make the bet a little more interesting?"

He was vaguely aware their power positions had reversed, that she was trained thoroughly in the art of seduction and knew how to strip a male of every thought so she could get what she wanted, but this wasn't about him. It was about her. And giving her a little of the lust-drenched mind she'd drugged him with the last few days.

He pressed his cock against her heat, rubbed until she sucked in a breath. Yeah, she was wet. He could feel it. "What do you have in mind?"

She pressed back. "Let's say if you come first, you walk away from Maelea and leave the poor girl alone."

His hips stilled. He focused on her determined yet very aroused eyes. Eyes that set off a tremor of déjà vu deep in his chest. "Why would a Siren care about someone like Maelea?"

"I don't."

For a second he thought she was lying, then he realized she wasn't. "So this little bet is a way to make sure I don't use her to get what I want." When she didn't answer that thought, another crept into his mind. "Which prompts the question, why would a Siren try to *stop* her mark? There's something you're not telling me."

She focused on his shoulder. And in her silence he knew she didn't have an answer. At least not one she could voice. But it was there, hiding behind her familiar and entrancing eyes. An answer that explained what their connection was and why she was all he'd been able to think about since the moment they'd met. Even to the detriment of his one clear goal.

The door at the end of the hall creaked open. Skyla's head darted that way and her hands pressed hard against his chest, pushing him away from her succulent body.

Another steward came down the corridor toward them, a tray in his hands. He stopped when he caught sight of them, looked from face to face. Understanding dawned in his eyes just before he coughed and a rush of pink spread up his cheeks. "Um. Sorry. I just need to get through."

Orpheus stepped back against the opposite wall to make room, but he knew his irritation reflected in his eyes. Only…they didn't flash green the way they normally did when he was irritated.

The man ducked his head and was out the opposite door in a flash.

Skyla stepped away and cleared her throat. "I need some air."

"Hold on." He reached for her but wasn't quick enough to grasp her.

"Thanks, but no. I think we both need a good shot of distance right now. I know I sure do."

She disappeared out the door before he could think of a reason to make her stay. For a brief moment he considered following, then remembered Maelea in the stateroom. He couldn't leave Ghoul Girl alone. She was waiting for the first opportunity to run, and contrary to what Skyla thought, he didn't intend to harm the waif. But he would use her to get what he wanted.

And what he wanted…It was time he remembered his goal and stopped screwing around with the Siren who'd obviously been sent here to get rid of him. She was a distraction he didn't need. And though he didn't know why, he had the strangest feeling that being close to her was messing with his daemon.

She was right. They did need distance. Distance so he could call back that part of him he both hated and needed at the same time. Once they got to the half-breed colony, he'd ditch her ass. Because without his daemon…he'd never get what he wanted most.

—⁓—

There were benefits to being the Lord of the Underworld. Chief among those benefits was that souls weren't just scared of you, they cowered. And though Hades ruled Hell in all its glory, everything that happened within his domain eventually found its way back to his ears, no matter how secret.

Which was how he'd learned Atalanta once again roamed his realm.

He stared at the relief in front of him, carved from the purest marble in the human world. The image of him and his two brothers, Zeus and Poseidon, immortalized as they stood on the top of Mount Othrys, the home of the Elder Gods, after they'd defeated Krónos and the Titans and locked them deep within the bowels of Tartarus.

Their victory in the Titanomachy had been long fought and hard-won. And in that moment when he'd stood there with his kin, the strength of everything they'd accomplished had flowed as rich as wine through Hades's veins. But it had been fleeting. For as soon as Zeus had locked their father, Krónos, in Tartarus, he'd taken command of the heavens, bestowed the oceans on Poseidon, and left the afterthought to Hades.

The same bitter resentment he'd held for thousands of years rushed through him, heated his blood, and burned his eyes. He'd wanted the human realm, had *deserved* it. But the Fates had fucked him there, hadn't they? According to them, the human realm was subject to free will. No god could rule it. No god, that is, except the one who possessed the Orb of Krónos, the magical medallion that held the four chthonic elements—earth, air, water, and fire—and granted the owner powers never seen before, not by any god.

He'd waited long years to find the Orb. Had come so close to controlling the human realm when he'd held it in his hands, thanks to his power-hungry wife. The irony that the daemon hybrid Orpheus had been the one to find the Orb in the realm of the blessed heroes wasn't lost on him. Orpheus was more than anyone knew. More than a daemon, more than a witch, more even than the Argonaut he'd recently been branded. Only one being truly knew what he was. One Fate he couldn't wait to destroy when he finally had that Orb in his hands for good.

The air stirred at his back and without looking he knew his wife stood behind him, waiting for his attention.

"I take it you've returned with news."

"Yes, my lord," she said in a sickeningly sweet tone. A tone he knew was meant to placate and deceive. "You were right. She went after the Argonaut in Tartarus."

He turned Persephone's way. She stood five feet from him, her fall of silky black hair framing her powerful shoulders to hit near her narrow waist. As a god herself, she was near his height at close to seven feet, and her flawless skin and ruby red lips drew his attention as they always did. The daughter of Demeter, the goddess of fertility, Persephone was every god's—and human's—wet dream. His included. Even after all these long thousands of years, she was still the only female he desired day after long, miserable day. Not that he didn't occasionally want—or take—others, but when it came down to it, she was his. In every sense of the word.

He narrowed his eyes on her smiling face, knew, as he always did, that she was scheming to get the Orb and rule the human realm herself.

Getting his hands on the Orb was turning into a clusterfuck of missed opportunities, but that's what made this whole thing fun. And he'd gotten so bored with the torturing-souls thing. He was enjoying the chase as much as he would enjoy the moment he had the Orb and all four elements and could say fuck you to the Fates and every other god—including his two brothers. Every other god except his beloved wife. The wife who was as devoted to him as he was to her, and who would never stop scheming for a way to take charge as *his* master.

A wicked smile curled one side of his mouth as his gaze roamed her luscious body from head to toe. He had to love a woman who could match him in wickedness. Clasping his hands against his spine, he took a step down the three marble stairs. "So she's found the Argonaut Gryphon within Tartarus. What does she plan to do with him?"

Persephone turned as he walked by her toward a window that looked out on his realm. Lava boiled and popped, jagged black mountains rose in the distance. And like a breath of air, the moaning of souls being tortured in the most horrendous ways floated like a song on the breeze. "She's taken him to Sin City."

With his enhanced eyesight, he could see a soul far across the valley, in the center of a circle of rabid dogs, about to be devoured whole. Hades's energy thrived on each soul he obtained, and his powers grew every time a soul was tortured within his realm. In this case, the man had enjoyed great wealth from the underground dog-fighting ring he'd run in the human realm. It didn't bother Hades in the least to know that reliving those fights, with the human as the victim, again and again and again was a just and fair punishment for the man. In all likelihood, it was probably better than he deserved.

"Sin City, you say?" His gaze scanned this level of the Underworld. A good distance from Tartarus, where Atalanta was now scheming with the fallen Argonaut. He had no doubt she'd make the Argonaut Gryphon her bitch in every sense of the word. He knew all too well how she fucked not only with a male's body, but his mind. While the sex had been hot enough, the aftermath with his wife, when she'd learned he'd lost the Orb, had been less than stellar. The question was, what did Atalanta plan to do with the Argonaut? She hadn't been sentenced to the Underworld herself. She'd simply been trapped in the Fields of Asphodel by her son and his witchcraft. But it was clear she planned to use the Argonaut to her advantage. Somehow.

"Yes," Persephone answered. "She was granted

access to Sin City, and word is she's meeting with Krónos soon."

Hades had no doubt his father would relish a go at Atalanta. The bitch was hot. But she was also unpredictable. And Hades didn't put it past her to use her feminine charms on Krónos to get what she wanted. Which was undoubtedly to find a way back to the human realm and to get her hands on that Orb.

Unfortunately, the area Krónos and his Titan goons had set up in Tartarus was the one and only part of the Underworld Hades couldn't see into. Which meant he didn't know what they did in their depraved corner of hell. Knowing his good ol' dad, though, it was as immoral and degenerate as it could get, not that Hades cared. So long as the bastard stayed locked down there, things were fine. It was the wild card Atalanta and what she might promise Krónos that left Hades with a bitter taste in his mouth. "We have someone on the inside?"

"Tantalus is there."

Tantalus. The human who'd cut up his son Pelops, boiled him into a soup, and served it to the Olympians when he'd been invited to join them for a meal. One corner of Hades's mouth curled at the image of that banquet. Tantalus had been condemned to Tartarus by Zeus himself, but Hades had granted the soul special privileges other inhabitants didn't have, simply because he loved the fact Tantalus had had the balls to pull that one over on Zeus and the other egomaniac Olympians.

"Tantalus is perfect. I want to know exactly what she has planned."

"Yes, my lord," Persephone said.

Hades turned back to his wife, moved close to her.

She didn't cower from him, and he liked that. Every other female cowered because they knew what to expect. Persephone loved his perversion.

She braced her hands on his forearms as he slid his arms around her waist and dragged her close, as he sank his teeth into her neck and drew the sweetest taste of her blood. Blood and pain and desire swelled in his mouth to heighten his need for her.

"There is one other thing," Persephone said, tipping her head to grant him more access.

"Mm?" He ran his tongue over the bite mark, healing it with his powers, then taking another bite from her flesh in a more delectable spot.

"This part you might not like."

He lifted his head, stared down into her emerald eyes. "Tell me."

She never once looked away, but he saw the quick flash of fear before she masked it with steel resolve. Something else he admired about her. Even when she knew she was going to piss him off, she didn't back down. She'd meet his fury head-on even when it left her battered and bruised.

"Orpheus has found Maelea."

The slow, red rage he always felt when the bastard child's name was mentioned slid through his veins and pummeled his chest. He'd banished her to the human realm, couldn't kill her because those fucking Fates had meddled where they shouldn't be meddling. But he wished only for that stain to die. While he didn't have a problem with his wife screwing around on the side, the reminder that his brother Zeus had succeeded in seducing his wife right here in his realm and had created a child with her was a humiliation not even Hades could forget.

He dropped his hands, moved back mere inches. Never took his eyes off his treacherous wife. She was to blame too. Still was to blame. "And?"

She drew a deep breath. "And I sent hellhounds to stop him, but they got away."

Hades looked past his wife to the marble relief again. Only this time all he saw was betrayal, not victory. A betrayal he would douse with vengeance. "And the bastard?"

Persephone frowned. "My daughter is not a bastard. But yes, she got away with him. I didn't send the hounds there to harm her."

No, of course not. Persephone loved that fucking stain. Even though that love made Hades hurt his wife time and again.

"What would he want with the bastard?"

"I don't know."

Hades looked back at her, only this time he didn't see his wife's beauty anymore. He saw deception of the most calculated kind.

"Find out," he said through gritted teeth.

"Of course, my lord," she said in that sickeningly sweet voice again. The one that this time energized his anger. "Anything for you, love."

She turned for the door, and for a second he thought of stopping her, of dragging her back by her hair and bending her over the altar behind him to punish her. But he didn't. Because right now he had more important things than her insolence to deal with.

When she was gone, he snapped his fingers. The

four-foot-tall troll-like creature emerged from a small door hidden in the wall and dragged a lame foot behind him as he scuffed across the floor. He stopped to look up at Hades with his green scaly hands and twisted, too-long nails pressed together in subservience. "Yes, my lord."

"Orcus, where is that stain Maelea?"

It was Orcus's one job in this realm to monitor Maelea for Hades at all times. If Zeus so much as made even the most minute contact with the girl, Hades had just cause to strike her down. It was an agreement he'd made with Lachesis, that meddling Fate, when he'd cast Maelea out of his realm and banished her to the human world eons ago. He'd waited and watched for that opportunity, but so far, over three thousand years later, Zeus hadn't shown even an ounce of interest in his bastard daughter. But perhaps now, monitoring her might come in useful after all.

"She's on a train, heading east."

A train heading east. Hades looked out the window again at the depravity he'd worked so hard to create, all within the Underworld. For the last two hundred years or so, Maelea had taken up refuge in the Seattle area. She ventured out, but she stayed close to home. Until now, that is. "With Orpheus."

"Yes, my lord. There's also a Siren with them."

Hades whipped around. "A Siren? Which one?"

"Skyla."

The eldest and most fierce of Zeus's assassins. Oh, this just got better and better. Zeus was after the Orb too, it seemed, and he was using his Sirens to track Orpheus, then no doubt take the Orb by force when they found it. But why would Orpheus need Maelea?

He rubbed a hand over the patch of hair covering his chin as he thought through the possibilities. Maelea had no powers. At least none he was aware of. But what if she was somehow linked to that Orb? He wouldn't put it past his brother Zeus to bestow on her some gift the King of the Gods could one day use to his full advantage.

He dropped his hand. "Send the hounds."

"They're on a train, my lord. Traveling at rapid speed."

"I'll deal with the train. Have the hounds kill Orpheus and the Siren. But leave Maelea to me."

"But the Fate, my lord—"

He slashed Orcus a look that struck fear to the center of the scaly creature's soul. "The Fate cannot interfere because I won't harm the bastard child. I have other plans for her. Now stop asking asinine questions and do as you're instructed."

When Orcus slithered away, Hades looked back out at his view, clasped his hands behind his back, and scanned the flaming red horizon. No doubt Lachesis would be pissed he'd sent the hounds to kill her precious Orpheus, but he could handle the loss of Orpheus's soul. Yes, the soul of a hero had been a prize worth fighting for over thousands of years, but for the chance to find the Orb and rule what was rightfully his, Hades would gladly go back on the deal he'd made to give the hero a second chance at life. He didn't care what role Lachesis claimed Orpheus played in the balance of the world. All he cared about was getting his just due.

And after all, some things required sacrifice. Even on his part.

Chapter 9

MAELEA LAY STILL AS STONE AS THE DOOR TO THE stateroom flew open and clanged shut again. She held her breath and listened, wondering if Skyla and Orpheus were about to pick up where they'd left off. Feet shuffled, the steady in-and-out breaths of one mouth floated in the air. Followed by a muttered "*Skata*."

When a thwack sounded from below, she peeled her eyelids apart and tried to see what was going on. From her vantage on the top bunk she could just see Orpheus standing in the center of the room with his hands on his hips, staring down at Skyla's leather armor, which was strewn across the floor near the wall.

Obviously, things had not gone so well out in the hall.

"I know you're awake up there, Ghoul Girl, so stop holding your breath."

Maelea still hadn't decided what she thought of Orpheus. Yeah, he'd saved her from Hades's underlings back at her house, but he hadn't done it for her. He'd done it because he wanted something from her. Kidnapping was kidnapping, no matter the reason.

She pushed up to sitting on the top bunk, drew her legs to her chest, and wrapped her arms around herself as she glared down at him. Outside, the moonlit snow-covered mountains sped by, an eerie sea of light and shadow.

Orpheus frowned up at her. "Stop looking at me like I'm going to eat you alive. Have I yet?"

"No, but that doesn't mean you're not planning to at some point."

"Nice comeback, Ghoul Girl. There's hope for you yet."

He flopped down into the chair he'd been sitting in before, tapped his long masculine fingers against the armrest. They sat in silence for several minutes, the rhythmic rocking of the train and wheels clanking along the tracks the only sounds. Finally, when she couldn't stand it anymore, she worked up the courage to ask the one thing she needed to know. "Where are you taking me?"

"Montana."

"You said that already. Where in Montana?"

"A friend's place."

"What friend?"

He scowled up at her. "Does it matter?"

"To me it does. You've made me a prisoner."

His gaze shifted back to the empty bottom bunk. "No, Ghoul Girl, Hades and your precious pop made you a prisoner. I've just changed your holding cell."

Anger welled in Maelea's chest but she pressed her chin to her knees to keep from antagonizing him. Though it burned, what he said was true. Hades and Zeus had both made her a prisoner in this realm. No one cared for her. No one looked out for her. She was alone in every sense of the word.

"Look," Orpheus said. "We're going to be there soon. Things will go a lot smoother if you just tell me right now where that sonofabitch warlock is. Then I can be on my way."

She knew exactly which warlock he was talking about. And why Orpheus wanted to find him. But she knew if she told him what he wanted to know, he'd be gone and she'd still be held captive. Wherever the hell he planned to leave her. Her anger swelled at the way she was being treated like a prisoner. She lifted her head to tell him to go to hell when she sensed a vibration radiating from deep inside the earth.

For a second, she didn't move. But when she felt it again, she jumped off the upper berth and rushed to the window. The vibration grew stronger until it shook her very core.

"Stop the train. We have to stop the train!"

"What?" Orpheus pushed to his feet as she rushed past him.

She pulled open the stateroom door, looked right and left. At the far end of the corridor, near the rear door, she spotted the emergency brake box mounted to the wall.

She took two steps. His hand wrapped around her bicep and jerked her to a stop. She whipped around, tugged at her arm. "Let me go!"

"What the hell are you doing?"

"An earthquake's coming. We have to stop the train."

Orpheus's brows drew together. "How do you—?"

"Because I felt it!" she yelled. "Who's the one person in the bowels of the earth who wants to stop you from reaching your destination?"

Understanding dawned in his eyes. He ducked his head back under the stateroom door, looked to the windows. And she knew he saw exactly what she did—they were coming up on a mountain pass. The valley they'd just traveled through would soon close down into a narrow gap where miles and miles of snow would be easily dislodged from those peaks under the force of a god-induced earthquake and bury not only this train but everything in its path.

"Shit." He let go of her and sprinted to the end of the car.

She followed, her breaths fast and labored as he searched the box.

"Turn away," he commanded.

Maelea covered her face and whipped around. Glass shattered at her back. She looked over her shoulder just as he reached inside the broken box and grasped the emergency stop cord.

"Hold on to me!" He gripped a curved metal railing near the door with one hand. With nothing else for her to grasp, she wrapped her arms around his waist and buried her head in his massive chest.

No alarm sounded, but the shriek of metal against metal as the brakes were applied was so loud, it rang with the shriek of a thousand Muses screaming. Orpheus wrapped his free arm around her shoulder, held her close. The train jerked violently and threw them around the corridor like jumping beans in a can.

Maelea slammed her eyes shut and screamed but didn't dare let go. Pain ricocheted through her limbs. When the shaking finally stopped and she opened her eyes, she realized they were on the floor in the corridor, Orpheus's big body cocooned around her like a protective blanket. The train had completely stopped. She looked up to see he was still holding on to the metal safety bar above.

"Holy shit," he muttered. "You'd better be right or we're gonna get our asses thrown off this train."

Maelea opened her mouth to tell him she was more

than right, but stopped short when she heard a rumble that was not the train. Low at first, and growing in intensity with every passing second.

"Fuck me," Orpheus muttered, climbing to his feet and hauling her with him. He dragged her back into the stateroom. "Grab your coat." He rushed to the window and pulled up on the red plastic emergency release lever at the bottom of the window.

The vibrations inside Maelea grew at an exponential rate. She located her jacket and tugged it on.

The strip of rubber along the bottom of the window peeled free. Orpheus threw it behind him, then grasped the metal handle attached to the bottom of the window and pulled up on that too. The window opened inward, separated from the hinge above. Using both hands, Orpheus grasped the entire thing and pulled it out of the way, tossing it on the floor against the wall.

"Attention passengers," a voice echoed over the speaker system. "The train has come to a complete stop. Please remain in your seats while we tend to the delay."

Orpheus froze. He turned for the door.

"There's no time!" Maelea screamed. "It's coming now!"

"Sonofabitch stupid Siren," Orpheus muttered as he pushed Maelea toward the window. "Go!"

Maelea grasped the window frame and climbed from the chair he'd been sitting in earlier to the window ledge. "Why aren't they telling those poor people to get off the train?"

"Because they don't know what we know. Now *move*!"

"Gods," she whispered, "they'll all die."

Orpheus pushed her out the window. "Haul ass!"

Maelea closed her eyes and jumped. She smacked into the frozen snow with a grunt, rolled to her side. Pain radiated from her shoulder outward, along with the jolt of ice-crystal-coated air streaking into her lungs. But the violent shaking grabbed her attention and forced her eyes open. That and the deafening roar from somewhere above.

Orpheus was on his feet at her side before she could find her balance. He yanked her up. She jerked around and looked up at the colossal mountain, one whole section of snow dislodging and rushing down the slope with plumes of white that engulfed and devoured every boulder and tree in its path, the entire mass heading right toward the front of the train.

"Run!" Orpheus jerked her by the arm away from the river of snow.

Maelea's legs kicked into gear and she tore after Orpheus as fast as she could. They raced past the end of the train, past humans opening their own windows and peering out at them, shouting questions. Past screams and horror-filled eyes, as understanding dawned.

The roar grew louder. She turned to look back just as the deluge of white slammed into the front four cars, devouring them in billowy clouds of powder that shot spirals and columns of snow up from the mammoth slide.

A gasp tore from her mouth. She hadn't realized she'd stopped on the tracks some hundred yards away and was staring back at the devastation until Orpheus turned her by the shoulders to face him.

"Focus, Maelea. Take this." He shoved the handle of a knife the size of her forearm into her hand, closed her fingers over the end. "Stay with the humans back here and keep your damn coat on." He jerked the zipper up to her chin. "Help will be coming. I'll be back for you."

Her wide eyes shot from the knife to him. "Wait." He was already jogging back toward what was left of the train. "Where are you going?"

"To find that damn Siren."

He wove through the twenty or so people who'd managed to escape from the end of the train and were standing on the tracks, staring at the devastation with horrified expressions. They obviously hadn't seen her yet.

Her gaze shot back to the knife, and then she turned to look down the empty track behind her. The track that shot off to the horizon and disappeared in the moonlit snow. She could run. This was her chance to escape. She took a step toward freedom, then stopped short.

Three hellhounds emerged from the trees and moved onto the tracks, their glowing red eyes blinding orbs of light far off in the distance.

Isadora's pulse raced as she waited for Callia to finish her examination. Beside her, she felt her mate's anxiety as if it were her own. The exam was routine, and she felt fine, but there was always the possibility something could go wrong, and Demetrius knew that better than anyone.

Three months into her pregnancy and he was already a bear to live with. But he was her bear, so she cut him some slack, at least this early on.

Callia lifted her hands from Isadora's bare stomach and opened her eyes. A smile spread across the healer's face. "Everything's good."

The air rushed out of Isadora's lungs on a long breath

and she smiled, looking up at Demetrius. "See? I told you, worrywart."

Her big strong Argonaut husband scowled down at her. "There's still six months to go, *kardia*."

She knew he was worried some genetic mutation from his mother was going to seep into their baby, but she didn't share his fear. This baby was a blessing, not a curse. And once it was born and he saw that for himself, he'd believe, just as she did.

Callia reached for a clipboard, jotted notes. "You can sit up now." As Isadora pulled her green sweater down and swung her legs over the side of the exam table in her half sister's clinic, Callia added, "Heartbeat's strong. You're measuring right on, and I don't sense anything out of the ordinary. How's your appetite?"

"Like a bird," Demetrius said.

Isadora shot him a *shape up* look, then glanced back at her sister. "Better. The nausea's mostly gone."

"Good," Callia said. "You're in the second trimester now. Your energy level should perk up too." She winked at Demetrius. "You might want to rest up, big guy. This is the honeymoon phase, when a pregnant *gynaíka* needs plenty of sex."

His cheeks turned red and he darted Isadora a *holy hell, tell her not to say stuff like that* look.

Isadora laughed, her pulse definitely back in the relaxed range. Gods, she loved this Argonaut.

A knock sounded at the door.

"Come in," Callia called.

Zander poked his head into the room. "Hope I'm not interrupting."

"No." Callia's face brightened as he stepped in and

closed the door. "We're done here. Miss me already, did you?"

With a cheesy grin, the oldest Argonaut of the bunch moved toward his mate and kissed her cheek. "Always, *thea*, but it's not you I'm here for right now."

Callia's brows lifted. "Oh, no?"

"No," he answered, looking toward Isadora. "It's you I need, actually."

Isadora's smile faded as her feet dropped to the floor and she stood. Beside her she felt Demetrius tense. "What's happened?"

"We have visitors who are requesting an audience with the queen. They're with Theron at the castle."

"Why does that sound ominous?" Isadora asked as she took the cardigan Demetrius handed her and they headed for the door.

"Because it is," Zander mumbled, stepping aside to let Isadora pass.

"Zander?" Callia asked.

"It's okay, *thea*, but you might want to tag along too. Just in case Isadora needs you."

Isadora didn't know quite what to expect when she reached the castle, but when she stepped into her father's old office, which was now Theron's headquarters for Argonaut business, she realized just how accurate Zander's comment had been.

The two females standing on the great alpha seal in the middle of the floor turned when she entered the room. Theron, the leader of the Argonauts, stepped past them and greeted Isadora. "Thanks for coming right over, Your Majesty."

Isadora let his formality pass without correcting him

as she normally did. They'd grown up together. Theron had been her father's most trusted confidant amongst the Argonauts. And at one time they'd been betrothed, though there'd never been a love match between them. Thankfully, Theron had found his soul mate Casey, Isadora's other half sister, before they'd been bound. Which had given Isadora the time she'd needed to realize that she was Demetrius's soul mate. But at their core they were friends, and she respected and admired Theron now as they worked together for the good of their world.

Tension hung like a thick cloud in the room as Isadora moved forward to greet their guests. Both women were close to six feet tall, one with curly red hair, the other with chestnut locks. And both were dressed like warriors, with leather breastplates that bore the stamp of the gods, arm guards, and knee-high black platform boots.

Sirens. In Argolea. This couldn't be good.

"Your Highness," the redhead said as they both inclined their heads in a brief bow. "Thank you for seeing us on such short notice."

"You're most welcome," Isadora answered, very aware the observers in the room were as curious about this meeting as she was.

"This is Rhebekkah," Theron said, gesturing to the redhead, "and Khloe. They've come with a request from Athena."

Isadora didn't need to catch Casey's skeptical look on the far side of the room to read her sister's mind. She and her two half sisters shared more than just their father the king's royal blood. They shared a link to the Horae, the ancient Greek goddesses of balance and order. She had no doubt that Casey and Callia's Hora markings were vibrating just as hers was, indicating a major imbalance.

"It's not often we get a request from Olympus." Isadora moved toward Theron's desk and leaned back against the aged mahogany. Theron stepped up on her left, Demetrius on her right, flanking her with their size and support, both staying far enough away to let her take the lead. "What can we do for Athena?"

"We bring Athena's condolences on your father's passing," Khloe said.

A small space in Isadora's chest pinched at the mention of her father, who'd finally passed from old age not more than a month ago. He'd been a great king but a lousy father. They'd never been close, but he'd instilled within her a love for their realm and an honor to serve, and for that she would always be grateful.

"Thank you. That means a great deal to me."

Both Sirens nodded.

"But," Isadora added, "something tells me my father's passing isn't the reason you're standing before me now."

The Sirens glanced at each other and then Khloe said, "It's no secret that in these tumultuous times it is as important as ever to maintain balance within the human realm."

No one knew that more than Isadora. "I agree."

"There are those who would choose to destroy the balance the gods have created," Khloe went on. "One in particular, who seeks the Orb of Krónos for personal gain. I'm sure you're aware of the Orb's significance."

Oh, was she ever. Not that they needed to know that little detail. "I was under the assumption the Orb had not been found," she lied.

"Unfortunately, it has. By a warlock who once inhabited your realm."

Apophis. Yep, Isadora knew him too. And she was fully aware he was lurking somewhere in the human realm, in Gryphon's body, waiting for the chance to use the Orb and build his coven of witches so he could one day overthrow Zeus.

"Interesting." Isadora crossed her feet at the ankles, braced her hands against the solid desk. "But I'm not sure what that has to do with us."

"Athena respectfully requests the help of your Argonauts in locating the warlock," Rhebekkah said, "and the Orb."

Isadora narrowed her eyes. "Correct me if I'm wrong, but the Orb isn't of much use without the four basic elements."

"You're correct. It's not."

"So you're telling me the Sirens are having trouble locating one insignificant warlock who is unable to harness the true powers of the Orb? And you want our help because he's of this realm?"

"Not entirely," Khloe said. "Normally, we wouldn't need to enlist the aid of your guardians, but our efforts have been diverted. You see, it's one of your own that seeks to take the Orb from the warlock and disrupt the balance of the human realm. We have Sirens working to head him off, but he already has one element. Perhaps more."

Orpheus.

Their visit suddenly made a whole lot more sense.

She pushed away from the desk, stepped toward the windows, and looked out at the emerald green fields beyond the castle. Far off in the distance, the Olympic Ocean glimmered in the sunlight. "One of our own, you say?"

"Yes," Khloe said, turning after her. "An Argolean. One with a history of causing imbalance within the human realm. He also happens to be a daemon hybrid. I'm sure you can understand why Zeus does not want to see the Orb fall into his possession."

Skata. Orpheus's lineage was one secret she'd kept for many years. And had hoped to forever keep from the Argonauts.

Isadora caught Casey's surprised look before she turned back toward the Sirens, careful to keep her face as neutral as possible. "So you want us to find the warlock before this Argolean hybrid does."

"Yes."

"And what of the hybrid?"

"We'll take care of him."

Isadora didn't like the sound of that at all. She glanced toward Theron and read his *no way in hell* look. He wasn't Orpheus's biggest fan—not by a long shot— but even he knew Orpheus had helped the Argonauts on several occasions.

She refocused on Khloe. "I'll speak with my Argonauts and see what we can do. Unfortunately we're stretched thin as it is. We recently lost a guardian, as I'm sure you're aware, and with the increase in daemon-hybrid activity, in addition to Atalanta's daemons still roaming the human realm, my guardians have their hands full."

"Of course," Khloe said, though her olive green eyes screamed her skepticism. "If they could keep a lookout and report back anything they hear to us, though, Athena would be most appreciative."

"I'm sure that won't be a problem," Isadora lied.

"And if you happen to come across this Argolean hybrid, I would appreciate the same."

"Of course," Khloe replied in what was very clearly the biggest lie of all.

Loud footfalls echoed from the hallway. Isadora looked toward the door just as Titus stepped into the room and froze, his hazel eyes shifting to Isadora, the Sirens, over to Theron, and back to Isadora again.

Isadora moved toward the Sirens and held out her hand. "Please send my best to Athena."

"Thank you, Your Highness."

They each grasped her hand in turn, bowed slightly, then turned for the door. Titus moved back to let them pass.

When they were finally alone, Theron said, "Titus, close those doors."

A lock of wavy hair fell free of the leather tie at the nape of Titus's neck as he shut the double doors and turned to face the room once more with *no way that was real* eyes. "Was that what I think it was?"

"Yeah," Theron muttered. "*Skata.*" He pinned Isadora with a hard look. "You don't seem surprised by the announcement good ol' O is a hybrid."

Isadora caught Demetrius's gaze at Theron's side and drew from his strength. He knew the truth about Orpheus too. He'd been in Atalanta's lair. He'd seen Orpheus's glowing eyes. Though Orpheus hadn't shifted then—at least when she'd been there—it had been more than clear what he really was.

She looked back at Theron. "I'm not."

"Holy Hades," Zander said. "Orpheus is a hybrid? All this time? How the hell is that even possible?"

Isadora raked a hand through her short hair as shock

rippled across the room. Even she had no explanation for that one. Orpheus was Argolean, Medean, *and* daemon. It made no sense, and yet there he was.

"He's an Argonaut now, too," Theron pointed out with a dark look that said this was not at all what he'd expected or wanted. "Don't forget that. As the last remaining descendant of Perseus's line, he's got Gryphon's guardian markings. Man, this is a clusterfuck. An Argonaut-daemon hybrid. Wait until the Council catches wind of this."

"Don't forget Orpheus is also Lucian's nephew," Isadora said. "And even before we lost Gryphon, he was next in line to take Lucian's place when the Council leader retires."

Titus snorted near the door. "Now that's something I'd like to see."

"No way a daemon hybrid will ever serve on the Council of Elders," Theron said. "*Skata.* When did you find out?"

Isadora dropped her arm and stepped into the middle of the room. "When I discovered his lineage is irrelevant. What remains is that this is Orpheus we're talking about. Before we even found Casey, I had a vision that Orpheus would somehow be important to our cause, and he's proven that time and again."

She knew her foresight wouldn't be enough to convince them, so she turned to Zander and Callia, both of whom looked as shell-shocked as Theron. "And let's not forget, without Orpheus's help you wouldn't have your son Max now either."

Zander put his arm on Callia's shoulder, pulled her back against his chest protectively.

Isadora turned from face to face, pleading a case

she'd known from the first day she'd assumed the crown she'd one day have to make. "Orpheus is of no more threat to us than Nick is."

She knew the reference to Nick Blades, the leader of the half-breed colony in the human realm—a colony made up of Argolean-humans—would resonate with the group. Aside from being their biggest ally in the human realm, Nick was also Demetrius's half brother, and he wanted to see Atalanta and her daemons destroyed as much as they did.

"We would be remiss if we aided Athena and her Sirens in their quest to persecute him," she added.

"Orpheus has always had a hard-on for power," Titus pointed out. "He kept that damn Orb after Max brought it to us. Shit, he practically gave it to that warlock and started this whole damn mess."

Before she said the words, she knew Titus read them in her mind, but she said them anyway, for the benefit of the others. "We know he did that in an attempt to save Gryphon's life. He had no idea that warlock's energy had destroyed Gryphon's soul or that the warlock would harness the Orb's power to take possession of Gryphon's body."

Titus crossed his arms over his massive chest. "Doesn't change the fact Gryph's in Tartarus right now because O fucked things up."

No, it didn't. Just as it didn't change the fact the Argonauts stuck together. They were all still mourning the loss of their brother in battle. And even though Orpheus now had Gryphon's guardian markings, he would forever be an outcast as far as they were concerned. The one responsible for Gryphon's death.

Theron pinched the bridge of his nose as if he had the mother of all headaches. "We're not saying Orpheus is the enemy, Your Highness. We're just pointing out his track record isn't so great. And now that we know he's a hybrid on top of it all…"

Theron let the words linger, and Isadora's protective wall where Orpheus was concerned sprang up. She owed him her life. More than her life. She owed him for saving Demetrius in Atalanta's lair and for helping her stop the Council from executing him. She also owed him for protecting the life of her unborn child, a child who she was every day more and more convinced would play an important role in this world. She wasn't about to let Zeus or Athena or any Siren "take him down."

"His intentions are not at all what you think."

"How does anyone know *what* he thinks?" Theron asked. "He's a hybrid, for shit's sake."

Footsteps echoed in the hall again, followed by the crack of the door opening. Before Isadora could answer, Cerek peeked in the room, his short brown hair mussed as if he'd just run through a wind tunnel. "Um, guys. Sorry to interrupt, but we just got a message from Nick at the colony. There's trouble."

"What kind of trouble?" Isadora asked.

"Hellhound trouble. Nick's sentries killed two earlier tonight while out on patrol."

"*Skata*," Theron mumbled. "Why the hell would Hades be sending hounds to Montana?"

"He wasn't," Casey said, stepping over and touching her mate's arm. "He was sending them for Orpheus." She glanced from Theron to Isadora. "Where would Orpheus go in the human realm if he was in trouble?"

"The colony," Isadora breathed. "He and Nick are friends."

"Yes," Casey said, looking to her sister, the *we have to warn him* more than clear in her eyes.

"That's not all," Cerek added. "There's something else you might need to know. Ever heard of Maelea?"

"Zeus and Persephone's daughter?" Callia asked, with a wrinkle in her brow. "What does she have to do with all of this?"

"Nick's got a friend in Seattle. One who keeps tabs on otherworldly events in the area. Maelea's been living there near Lake Washington, blending in, not causing any trouble. Apparently a portal opened and closed near her house earlier, not once but twice. A hellhound was killed. And the female's now missing."

"*Skata*," Theron muttered, shooting Isadora a *see?* look.

"Holy shit," Zander murmured. "Now Zeus's interest in O is starting to make a lot more sense. Hades's too."

Yeah, Isadora was thinking the same thing. And hating where her thoughts were heading. She looked toward Cerek with a whole new urgency. "Tell Nick we're on our way."

Demetrius, who'd been silent through the entire conversation, stepped forward. "*Kardia*."

"Don't worry," she said to him, sure she wasn't easing his fears. She knew he remembered what had happened the last time she'd crossed into the human realm, but this was different. This time they weren't going alone. "You're coming with me. Several of you are. This isn't something we can ignore any longer."

Chapter 10

SKYLA NEEDED A DRINK.

She eyed the bottle of Jameson behind the bar in the dining car. If she were home on Olympus, she'd down the whole damn thing. Here on earth, she needed to keep her wits about her. Especially around the hybrid.

Holy...*mother*. She lifted the glass of ice water she'd ordered to cool down after her run-in with Orpheus and downed the whole thing. Her barriers needed strengthening if he was able to get to her so easily. Daemon, she repeated to herself. *Daemon*. Why the hell was she flat out ignoring that part of him?

A loud shriek of metal against metal echoed through the car. The cup of ice flew out of her hand. Screams echoed. Skyla fell forward. She smacked into a booth, hit the floor with a thud. As she pushed up the train came to a stop. She looked out the window and saw a river of snow rushing down the mountain right toward her.

Oh...*fuck*.

Snow plowed into the train, sending it end over end like a matchbox car tossed into a clothes dryer. Skyla sailed backward, crashed into the wall. Her head cracked into glass. Pain nudged the conscious ends of her mind, but the screams echoing around her dragged at her attention. That and the smash of glass breaking, of snow pouring into the car and sucking out every last molecule of air.

When she tore her eyes open, silence met her ears and nothing but a vast empty darkness surrounded her. A frigid cold darkness.

Oh...*gods*.

Instinct had her clawing at the snow. She managed to get her hands up near her face, was somehow able to dig enough snow out of the way to create a pocket of air. Drew deep breaths to tamp down the terror.

Common sense nudged the panic to a manageable level as she lay cradled in the snow, her fingers numb, her arms and legs packed against icy-cold walls. She had no idea if she was facing up or down, how the dining car was lying in the snow, or if the car had been ripped to shreds by the avalanche. The fact the snow hadn't hardened yet told her she hadn't blacked out, but that didn't ease her anxiety.

Orpheus's image flashed in her mind. The way he'd looked when she walked away from him in the sleeping car. The disappointment on his face. The yearning in his eyes...

Stop.

She smacked her head against the snow behind her. Told herself to stop being a fool. He wouldn't be looking for her. He was a daemon. He knew why she was here, and even though he was playing her own seduction game—for whatever reason—that didn't mean she meant anything to him. That didn't mean he had any desire to see her live.

A shiver racked her body. Panic closed in again. Panic over the fact she was by herself here in the dark. That no one would find her. That no one would miss her when she was finally gone. The Sirens would move on. Sappheire would likely take her place as Athena's favorite. She had no family left, no close friends. She was over two thousand years old, with countless battles fought and won under her belt, and her life had been reduced to this moment. To dying in an avalanche in the middle of frickin' nowhere. Alone.

Don't panic. Stay calm. Using her brain had always worked for her before. Somehow, it had to work again.

She kept her breaths slow and shallow. Used her fingers to claw out more space around her face. Wiggled her body to make room before the snow hardened and she was truly stuck.

From somewhere to her right, a muffled sob reached her ears.

She froze, listened.

Another sob. Then a scream.

"Who's there?" she asked.

The crying cut off. Silence met her ears.

"Who's there?" Skyla asked again.

"Me," a muffled voice echoed. "I'm…here. I'm here."

Relief pulsed through Skyla's veins. She wasn't totally alone. "What's your name?"

"K-Katie," the small voice said. "I'm eight. I—I can't find my mom!"

Skyla tried to turn that way. She didn't have much room, but her flailing earlier had created enough space around her so she could move. Able to get her hands in the vicinity of the voice, she started digging. Snow fell into her tiny pocket of air and began packing near her feet but she didn't care. The fact she wasn't alone was all that mattered. "Keep talking to me, Katie. I'm trying to get to you. My name's Skyla."

"S-Skyla is a weird name."

"It is," she agreed as she dug. Her fingers were numb, her heart pounding hard in her chest. But she kept on digging, because anyone was someone.

"I—I'm cold," Katie said.

"Me too, Katie."

"I'm so scared."

Skyla's fingers broke through and closed around flesh and bone. Katie gasped. Skyla continued digging, using her arms and legs to move the snow around as much as possible until the small child was only inches from her. When she could manage, she wrapped her arm around the human girl and pulled her close, the heat of her upper body against Skyla's torso a stark improvement over the ice-cold snow packed tight now up to her waist.

"We're going to die," Katie sobbed against Skyla's chest.

"No, we're not," Skyla lied. But even she knew things weren't looking good. The utter darkness around them signaled they were buried deep. She ran through options in her head and decided trying to dig out was better than lying down and dying without a fight. On a deep breath, she let go of the girl and reached out to give it her best shot.

Her fingers dug into ice-cold snow. From somewhere deep below, a rumble echoed. Fear wound its way around her heart just as the earth shook with a force that knocked Katie into her and brought snow falling down around them.

"Skyla!"

Skyla grabbed onto the girl. "Take a deep breath, Katie! Fill your chest with as much air as you can!"

The shaking continued until Skyla wanted to scream.

She knew they were dropping deeper into the snow, farther from salvation. She held tighter to the girl. Katie sobbed against her chest.

The shaking stopped. Skyla went right to work, digging around their faces to create another pocket of air. Then stopped short when she heard a noise.

She stilled. Listened.

"Is that…?" Katie started.

The sound echoed again. Muffled, but distinct. A voice.

Hope leaped in her chest. No, not one voice, Skyla realized. Several. There were people out there.

"Here!" she screamed. "We're here!"

"We're here!" Katie yelled at her side.

The voices increased in intensity, and then a flicker of blue light cut through the darkness. Then another, and another, until the snow near her face began to break away piece by frozen piece.

Adrenaline coursed through Skyla's body as she struggled toward the light. Snow flicked into her eyes. Then a hand broke through, followed by another voice. This one not muffled, but clear and strong. "We've got another one!"

Relief was like the sweetest wine. Warm and brisk and encapsulating. Katie sobbed out her excitement.

"Grab my hand," the voice yelled.

Skyla grasped Katie's arm, pulled it up. "Take the girl first!"

Snow kicked back in Skyla's face as Katie was drawn up and out of the hole, then Skyla reached for the hand held out for her and used her boots to dig in for leverage so she could climb.

Bright light burned her eyes as she was hauled out

of the broken windows of the railcar. Voices echoed around her. She held up her hand to block the glare and saw dozens of people digging in the snow, some holding flashlights to aid the rescuers. A shiver racked her body, the night air decidedly colder than it had been in that frozen pit. From the corner of her eye, she saw someone whisk a blanket around a young girl with dark hair. Saw a man and a woman rushing toward the girl. They grasped her in a tight hug and rocked her back and forth.

And even though Skyla was free, that rush of emptiness washed through her again as she watched. She'd sacrificed that—love, companionship, a family—for the Sirens. To stay on Olympus doing what Zeus commanded because it was safer to remain numb inside than to feel anything again.

Through hazy vision, Skyla watched Katie's parents lift the girl into their arms and carry her away. And as she swiped at her frozen cheeks she told herself it was melting snow, not tears. Sirens didn't cry.

Her chest pinched with the weight of the emptiness around her until it was hard to draw a single breath. Then the image of Katie and her parents was blocked by a body rushing toward her. A body with wide shoulders, a broad chest, and a pair of intense gray eyes that drew her in like a lifeline.

"You stupid Siren." Orpheus's arms were around her before she realized it was him. In a whir of movement he jerked her tight against his warm body, slid his hands into her wet hair and lowered his mouth to hers.

Her mind was still a blur of sensations, but the heat of his lips, the roughness of his whisker-covered jaw, the way he kissed her like a man starved, overwhelmed every one. She was alive, she'd been found. And she wasn't alone.

She reached for him, dug her numb fingers into the fabric of his shirt, opened her mouth and drew him in. Then she kissed him back as she'd promised herself she would never kiss anyone ever again.

Someone moaned. She wasn't sure if it was her or him. All she knew was this kiss. This moment. This man, daemon, Argonaut, *whatever*, who tasted of promises and regrets and a thousand other emotions she couldn't define in the moment.

He kissed all thought out of her head, and when she was sure he'd demolished a few thousand brain cells in the process, he drew away and stared down at her with those achingly familiar eyes. The ones she couldn't get away from. The ones she'd never been able to forget.

Someone threw a blanket over her shoulders. He tugged it tight at her chest, pulled her close to his warmth again, and whispered in her ear, "If you're trying to impersonate a Popsicle, you're doing a damn good job."

Skyla had obviously hit her head harder than she'd thought, because she couldn't seem to process anything yet. And when he scooped her up in his arms like a damsel in distress, it took several seconds before she realized what he was doing. She pushed a hand against his chest, a hand that was shaking and did nothing to stop him. "I…I can walk."

Was that her voice? It didn't sound like her. It sounded as if it came from someone else. She was strong, confident, a warrior. Not someone who needed tending. She should tell him to stop and put her down. Wasn't a hundred percent sure she wanted him to.

He didn't look at her, just kept walking with her cradled in his arms like some fragile woman. "I'm sure you can. Humor me for the time being, would you? You go acting all Rambo Girl on me and the humans around here won't know what the hell to think. And I'm pretty sure they've had enough surprises for one night."

He stopped at a grouping of humans near the end of the train, which hadn't been swallowed by the avalanche. The cars were dislodged from the tracks but somehow appeared to still be in one piece. Gentler than she expected, he set her on a boulder near a fire someone had built, tugged the blanket around her shoulders again, and mumbled something to the woman next to her. Then he turned and headed back to the buried cars.

She was aware someone was checking her head, knew bandages were being applied, and that another voice was asking her questions to see if she had a concussion, but all she could focus on was Orpheus thirty yards away, searching for more survivors, digging with the humans, all while wearing nothing more substantial than jeans, boots, and a long-sleeved henley.

Her chest tightened. Her mind spun. She ran her fingers over her lips, lips that were still tingling from his kiss and alive with heat.

She was too rattled to do anything but sit by the fire and watch Orpheus work from a safe distance. Someone offered a jacket. Around her, people recounted the earthquake and the avalanche.

Earthquake. Yeah, earthquakes happened, but here?

In the Rockies? Stopping the train she and Maelea and Orpheus were traveling on? This was not a coincidence. Her mind drifted to the hellhounds back at Maelea's house. There was only one person who could be linked to both. Too late she remembered she'd left her armor in their stateroom on the train, which was now probably covered in snow.

The ground shook. Skyla gripped the rock she was sitting on, pushed down the panic. When the shaking stopped, shouts echoed in the distance, and men ran toward a buried railcar that had somehow rumbled to the surface.

Her mind flashed to another rumble, another moment when the earth had opened before her. That shaking hadn't been god-induced, just as this aftershock seemed too gentle to be generated by Hades.

She searched for Orpheus. Couldn't find him. Pushed to her feet and dropped the blanket on the rock.

"Skyla?"

She ignored her name being called from around the fire. Stepped past fallen trees and boulders that had been dislodged from the ground. Moved through the dark and into the woods, searching. And finally spotted him…a good twenty-five yards from the others, hidden from view behind an outcropping of rock, his hands extended in the direction of the still-buried cars, his eyes closed, the earth element shining in his palm like a falling star.

Her breath caught as she watched him harness the magic of the element with something seated deep inside him. Something she was sure not even Zeus knew he possessed. The ground shook again. A rumble echoed.

Shouts grew to her right, and she looked that way to see another group of men run to yet another railcar that had risen to the surface of the snow.

Suddenly, how she and Katie had been saved made sense.

Her gaze shot back to Orpheus. Only he was no longer focused on what he'd been doing. He was staring right at her. And his eyes were no longer the familiar gray she knew so well. They glowed a blinding green that lit up the night.

———— ∾∾∾ ————

Orpheus had gotten used to people being afraid of him. Most of the time he relished it. But the stark shot of fear in Skyla's eyes as she stared at him across the snow hit him dead center in the chest in a way that not only knocked him for a loop, it pissed him off. Especially after he'd just saved her life.

He pocketed the earth element, stalked toward her, and tried to ignore the fact some small part of him cared what she thought. As he worked to calm the daemon inside, he realized he should be glad he was having such trouble. It meant his daemon was back. And judging from what he'd spotted in the woods behind Skyla, he knew he'd need that daemon sooner rather than later.

Confident his eyes had returned to their normal color, he stopped in front of her, gave her a quick once-over. She'd found a coat at least, but he didn't miss the bandage near her right temple and the purple and black bruise bleeding out from beneath it. Yeah, she was alive, but if she hadn't run from him in the corridor of their railcar in the first place, she wouldn't have been trapped in that avalanche. Wouldn't have that wound now. Wouldn't be looking more shell-shocked than confident as she stared up at him.

Guilt was another thing he'd gotten used to over the years. But he pushed it down as he'd learned to do and looked past her to the humans beyond. "Where's Maelea?"

"I…I haven't seen her. I thought you knew where she was."

"She sensed the earthquake before it hit. I was able to get her off the train and away from danger. I left her on the tracks with a group of humans before going back." *To find you.*

When she didn't answer, only continued to stare at him as if he had three heads, he gripped her arm at the elbow, turned her toward the others, and started walking. "We have a problem."

"What kind of problem?"

"A hellhound problem."

Skyla scanned the forest. "Where?"

"About a hundred yards past the last railcar, down the tracks. I counted at least three."

"They travel in packs of five."

"I know."

The fifty or so humans who'd survived the avalanche were about to meet a death they couldn't even imagine. *Bloodbath* wasn't a term Orpheus used lightly, but that's exactly what would happen if he didn't do something to stop it.

They reached the last railcar. The wheels were dislodged from the tracks but the car still stood upright. Darkness loomed beyond the wreckage, towering trees and mountains, a mixture of inky darkness and shadows eerily lit by the moon high above. And far off in the distance, a red glow that flickered and disappeared.

"Are you up for a little hunting?" he asked, still looking out at the snow-covered trees.

"Get me to my armor and I'm with you. What about Maelea?"

At least the Siren sounded normal again. He headed around the end of the last car, then back up the other side, where they had a modicum of privacy. "Let's hope she wasn't stupid enough to run off by herself."

They reached their sleeping car, which was still upright too. The cars on both sides had separated, the door of the car behind butted up against their stateroom window—the one he'd pulled open so he and Maelea could escape. He planted a foot on the mangled car at his side for leverage as he climbed up and dropped into their wrecked stateroom.

A chair lay on its side, pillows from the top berth were scattered about, and Skyla's armor was strewn over the floor. As Skyla climbed through the window, he reached out to her, slid his hands around her waist, and helped her jump down from the sill. The long, lean line of her body pressed against his as she gripped his shoulders and eased to the floor.

For a moment he remembered their little bet. What he'd wanted to do to her out in the corridor. His blood warmed. His pulse picked up speed. When her gaze flicked to his and her cheeks turned the slightest shade of pink, he knew she felt it too.

She took a quick step back. Broke the contact. Moved to pick up her armor. "What's the plan?"

War strategy. She had an easier time talking about

that than the attraction still simmering between them. But could he blame her? It was a helluva lot easier for him to think about how to kick some hellhound ass rather than the kiss she'd laid on him out in the snow. The one that was still smoking through the toes in his boots.

He pushed his hands into his pockets, fingered the earth element as she took off her coat, tied the garment around her waist, then strapped on the breastplate and arm guards. Man, she was sexy. All long legs and willowy curves. Built, obviously, to seduce. But he liked that about her. Because it meant when this thing between them eventually burned out, he'd have no regrets about whatever came next.

"I was thinking we'd lure them out with my daemon," he said. "You wait in the trees until we've got them all. I take down what I can, you swoop in and get the rest."

She turned his way, her golden hair waving behind her as she moved. "Are you sure your daemon will come out and play this time?"

"Sweetheart, my daemon's ready to play anytime, anywhere. Just say the word and he'll be there."

"Hm." She stepped over the chair, crossed to the small bathroom door. "I'll feel better about that when I see it for myself."

"A pregame warm up? Siren, you surprise me." He reached for the button on his jeans. "I'm not sure we have time, but I'm ready to give it a try if you are."

She huffed an exasperated sound as she grasped the handle of the door, pulled it open. "Get real."

He smiled because he knew he'd gotten under her skin.

A scream echoed through the small space.

Skyla let go of the handle and jumped back, the dagger strapped to her lower back already in her hand.

Orpheus rushed over, peered around the corner into the bathroom, and spotted Maelea crouching on the floor with his blade in her hand.

"Holy Hades." He reached in and grasped the girl by the shoulders, hauling her up and out of the bathroom. "What the hell do you think you're doing?"

"What the hell do you think I was doing?" She wriggled out of his grip, dropped down on the lower berth, breathing heavy. "There are hounds out there."

Skyla moved to Orpheus's side, slid her blade back in its sheath. "We saw them. We were wondering what happened to you."

"I heard noises outside so I hid in the bathroom," Maelea said. "I'm not stupid, you know."

"No, you're not," Orpheus said. "You were smart to hide."

She glared at him. "What other choice did I have? Run? Then Hades would have exactly what he wants. He hasn't paid me any mind in all this time, but since you came after me, twice now I've had to run from his underlings. Thanks for that, by the way."

Orpheus's spine stiffened because what she said was true. That guilt he'd gotten good at ignoring came back tenfold.

"Maelea—" Skyla started.

Maelea tossed Orpheus's knife to the floor, pulled her legs up to her chest, and curled into herself. Conversation done.

Skyla looked at Orpheus and tapped her wrist with her index finger, indicating they didn't have time for this.

"We're going to take care of the hounds," Orpheus told her. She didn't answer. "You'd be wise to stay here until we come back and get you."

Still nothing from her.

When long seconds passed without an answer, he finally glanced to Skyla again, who nodded toward the open window and the hellhounds that waited for them.

"We'll be back for you, Maelea," he said as he climbed out the window and helped Skyla to the ground. "Sit tight."

"Where else would I go?" Maelea muttered with a wicked bite as they walked away. "All I have left is this holding cell you created for me."

Chapter 11

SNOW CRUNCHED UNDER SKYLA'S BOOTS AS SHE MADE her way around trees and downed logs, careful not to give away her location, her eyes ready for anything that might jump out at her. She knew Orpheus was somewhere to her left, circling the hellhounds' position from the other side, but she couldn't see him. He moved like a shadow—silent, deadly, utterly undetectable until the last second.

For that she was glad, because she was sure those hellhounds could hear her from a mile away. Her pulse pounded in her ears and every step she took seemed to echo across the empty forest. Moonlight filtered through the tall pines to cast eerie shadows on the snow.

A branch cracked to her right. She lifted her bow and arrow. Her heart beat hard against her ribs as she waited. For a long moment only silence met her ears, and then a rustle echoed above her. She shifted, aimed her arrow, then released her pent-up breath when she realized it was only an owl, his *whooooo* echoing through the darkness like an ominous warning.

Holy Hades. Relax already!

Hellhounds were a piece of cake. It was daemons—hybrids—she should be worried about. Like the one somewhere out here in the dark.

Something red darted between trees twelve feet in front of her. She shifted in that direction. When two red dots peeked out from behind the tree, she didn't hesitate.

Her arrow whirred through the air, struck something with a hard thwack. A yelp echoed in the trees. She grasped another arrow from her collar, lined up her next shot. A black shadow loomed ahead, followed by a low growl, then the snarl and snap of jaws and the pounding of paws against snow as the injured beast charged.

She didn't think. She acted. Just as she'd been trained. One, two, three arrows sailed from her bow, struck the hound dead in the chest. It hollered a sickening sound, then dropped to the ground. Its massive body sailed across the snow as if on a sled, stopping at her feet.

Steam rose off the corpse. Blood poured from the four arrows sticking out of its flesh. Its bloodred eyes were open and glassy. Howls to her left drew her attention.

Damn it. Where was Orpheus?

Her adrenaline shot up. As feet—lots of feet—pounded across the earth in her direction, she looked up and around, searching for safety. She hooked her bow over the branch of a pine and pulled herself up.

She got her legs up under her, managed to reposition so she was sitting on the tree limb, one boot braced against the trunk. She lined up another arrow and waited.

Within seconds, three hounds bounded into the clearing, their eyes beady points of red light, their mouths open, fangs dripping something vile. A fourth hound, bigger and blacker than the others, ambled to the edge of the trees, his gaze pinned right on her.

She aimed toward the big one, the leader.

His lips curled in a snarl—no, not a snarl, a smile—and a low growl echoed across the snow. "Come down, Siren."

Where the hell was Orpheus?

She fired. The big hound stepped aside, narrowly

dodging the arrow. He barked toward the other hounds. With gnashes and snarls they hurled their big bodies at the base of her tree, shaking it, snapping at the bark and biting enormous pieces from the trunk.

She grappled for the trunk and pushed up to her feet. The shot was hers but she couldn't steady herself long enough to take it. Where in the bloody hell was Orpheus?

A roar echoed from below just before a violent tremor shook the bow out of her hand. Her heart shot to her throat. She reached for her weapon, the ancient wood grazing her fingers. But she was too late. It sailed out of her reach, fell to the ground with a crack. With one hand wrapped around the tree trunk, she reached into her waistband and grasped a throwing star. She didn't aim, just hurled. A howl from below said she'd hit something.

Another violent shake knocked her off balance. A yelp slipped from her lips as she went flying. Frantic, she grappled for the branch, caught it, the bark digging into her bare, sweaty hands as she fought to hold on.

Damn it, Orpheus. Where are you?

He wouldn't have left her out here alone. He wouldn't have double-crossed her like this, would he?

Would he?

She sucked in a breath, tried to adjust her grip. The hounds below growled and barked. She knew this was it. As soon as she let go she'd be eaten alive. At least if she died here she'd die in battle. There was honor in that. Or so she hoped.

Her fingers slipped again. A rumble shook the ground and the tree and everything around her. The branch jerked out of her grasp. She screamed as she went down.

Was sure she was lunch. Her boots hit the snow-covered ground with a thwack, and her legs went out from under her, a jolt of pain shooting up her spine as she collapsed.

In an instant of confusion she realized the shaking had come from the ground, not the tree itself. The hounds all lay on their sides as if they'd been knocked off their feet. Head spinning, she scrambled for her footing, grasped the bow to her right, and lined up another arrow. The dazed hounds lifted their heads, shook out their manes, and growled. She released one shot after another, impaling them with as many poisonous arrows as she could.

Two went down. The third stumbled her way with murder in its bloodred eyes. She shifted that way, was just ready to let loose, when the hound's eyes bugged out and he froze, then dropped to the ground at her feet.

Her adrenaline pulsed in the out-of-this-world range. A rustle echoed from the edge of the trees. She drew her bow that way, then saw Orpheus stalking toward her. A quick glance down and she realized his blade stuck out of the back of the hound at her feet. She scanned the tree line again and spotted the lead hound—the big one—lying bloody and dead amid the brush.

Relief was swift and consuming. As consuming as it had been when he'd swooped her into his arms after she'd come out of that frozen pit and kissed all thought right out of her mind. "How did you—?"

"I thought we agreed you'd wait for my signal." Orpheus crossed the snow with a frown. He looked like a man, like the sexy devil-may-care man she'd come to recognize and even anticipate, not the daemon she'd expected.

He stopped when he reached the last hound, braced his boot against its back, and yanked his blade from its flesh.

After wiping the beast's blood on its fur, he sheathed the blade and set those sexy, smoky, smoldering eyes on her.

Eyes that were so familiar and definitely annoyed. "Well? And you can stop pointing that damn thing at me anytime, Siren."

She lowered her bow, couldn't seem to quell her racing heart. "I expected something cataclysmic like, I don't know, a daemon to charge out of the trees or something."

"Sorry to disappoint you. Next time I'll try to remember you like blood and gore more than flesh and bone."

She didn't. She liked him. More than she should. And she was way too relieved that he hadn't really betrayed her to think clearly yet. "Your daemon didn't want to come out and play after all?"

His jaw tightened. Emotion flashed in his eyes before he tamped it down, but she noticed, his eyes didn't shift to green as they normally did when he was angry. "Guess not. Must have shriveled in all this cold."

The sarcasm hit her as defensive, not playful. "You used the earth element, didn't you?"

"That and a little witchcraft. You can thank me later." He patted his pocket. "This thing comes in handy now and then."

Yeah, she could see that. Not that the knowledge that he held it eased her racing pulse.

Her hands shook as she depressed the end button on her bow, stuffed the rod it became into her boot. Why couldn't she stop thinking about that kiss? About the fact he was standing next to her now looking like a hero? She glanced away so she wouldn't be distracted by those eyes. "I meant to ask, how is it you're able to use witch—?"

A rumble echoed through the trees. On instinct she scrambled for her bow, swiveled. But Orpheus's hand against her arm brought her head around. That and the heat from his fingers searing her skin. "Easy, Rambo Girl. That's a chopper. My guess is the authorities have arrived."

The accident. Right. There would be humans looking for the missing passenger train.

"We should get back before Maelea decides to run," he said as he let go.

Maelea. With one sentence he'd just reminded her what they were all doing here. Whatever thought she'd had about telling him to touch her again disappeared like the moon setting behind the mountain.

They reached the forest edge and stepped onto the tracks in tandem. Choppers were parked beyond the wreckage. Rescue personnel moved survivors from danger to safety. But the activity didn't catch her eye. The woman standing still as stone at the end of the train did. The one with her arms folded across her middle, her eyes focused right on them. The one Skyla had pretended to protect so she could tag along on this little adventure. The one Orpheus seemed to have some protective instinct toward.

"Well, at least she didn't run," Orpheus said, heading in Maelea's direction.

"Yeah," Skyla muttered as she followed. "Aren't we lucky?"

Sin City lived up to its name in every way imaginable.

From the balcony of Atalanta's suite, Gryphon

looked over the stone balustrade out at the sea of depravity. Fountains gurgled bloodred water in the center of the square, and lust-filled moans echoed up to his ears. Naked bodies were draped across the benches surrounding the fountain like blood-starved daemons in need of a fix. Some were grouped in pairs, but most were engaged in hedonistic acts of three and four, in plain sight of anyone who wanted to watch. In invitation to anyone who wanted to join in.

Here in Sin City, anything went. Orgies, gambling, highs never experienced in the living world…if it could be imagined, it was here. The Titans had set up a racket sweeter than anything Vegas had to offer. Pleasure, self-indulgence, no strings—all drugged the inhabitants and kept them from contemplating leaving, as lotus flowers had done to Odysseus and his crew when they'd anchored near an island off the shores of North Africa eons ago. And the only thing the Titans required in exchange for this pleasure-filled escape from the tortures of Tartarus was utter and complete allegiance. Krónos believed he would one day be released from the prison his sons had locked him in. Every soul he stole from Hades down here was one more soldier who would be bound to serve in his army when he was finally free.

"See something you like, *doulas*?"

His stomach clenched as Atalanta moved up behind him. He hadn't heard her enter the room, but he should have expected it. She seemed to know where he was at all times.

Her hot breath washed over his nape, sending a shiver down his spine. She was slightly taller than he was, and a thousand times more powerful. As her *doulas* he was bound to do her will. So far, since being here with her in Sin City that will had consisted of waiting on her hand and foot, running her errands in the acrid streets, dodging danger in Krónos's city to bring her whatever she asked for. And sometimes—though he hated it—it included serving her guests and allowing them to berate and humiliate him. He wasn't proud of his station. It was demeaning to be ordered around. Degrading to know your life was held in someone else's hands. But it was better than the torture he'd endured in Tartarus.

A million times better.

Some deep-buried instinct told him to fight back, but he ignored it. Though when her hand brushed his bare back and she leaned even closer to his ear, his stomach tightened with unease.

"I do so like to look at you, *doulas*. You are quite a specimen."

That unease quadrupled. And a worse kind of torture— one she'd yet to unleash but which he worried hovered around the next bend—haunted his every thought.

This is not who you are.

He swallowed hard, worked not to recoil from her touch. Didn't want to do anything to piss her off. But as he stared out at the black mountains and hazy red sky far off in the distance, he couldn't quite remember who he was anymore.

Once, before that torture in Tartarus, he was sure he'd been someone. That he'd been part of something. He didn't know what that was, exactly. Didn't know who might be missing him right this second. But he was sure of it. Once, he'd made a difference.

"What is it?" Atalanta asked, coming to stand in front

of him. He hadn't noticed she'd stopped stroking his back, that her hands now cupped his face, tipping it up to hers.

She was beautiful. Even he couldn't deny that. Porcelain skin, large onyx eyes, jet-black hair as silky as the most delicate satin. And her body bested that of any Siren. But her soul was evil. Her eyes as empty as his. And even though he'd vowed to be her *doulas* for all eternity, he never forgot that. Not even for a moment.

"Nothing," he managed.

She brushed a finger across his cheek, wiped away a tear he hadn't known had slipped from his eye. A tear he didn't even know he could cry. "My *doulas* is unhappy?"

He thought of the alternative to her humiliation. He couldn't go back to the torture of Tartarus. An eternity with her, no matter what she made him do, was a billion times better than what he'd been through under Hades's control.

"No," he said. "I'm whatever you want me to be."

"Good boy." She brushed her hand down his cheek, then stepped past him. "I think I have something that will make you very happy. We've a meeting with Krónos in an hour."

She walked back into the gaudy bedroom with its gold-plated everything and moved behind a screen. Her bloodred robe landed on a side chair. She held her hand out. "Bring me my dress."

Gryphon crossed to the emerald green gown hanging from a hook on the far wall, removed the hanger, and offered it to her. The gauzy white curtains blew gently in the breeze from the open arched windows. "What do we want with Krónos?"

Fabric rustled as she wriggled into the gown. Stepping out from behind the screen, she turned her back, lifted her long black hair. "Zip me."

He grasped the zipper at the base of her spine and slowly zipped it up her back until the two halves of the dress came together just beneath her shoulder blades.

"A great many things," Atalanta said. The emerald green gown was so long, it draped across the floor even when the straps were over her shoulders.

She didn't elaborate, and he knew not to question. Turning to face him, she leaned close and brushed her index finger over his lips.

His unease at what she had planned, the fear of the next round of humiliation she decided to unleash, exploded in his belly.

"Now you'd best get ready." She sent him a wicked smile. "I want you dressed appropriately for this meeting. It's quite important to our future. Wear the leather I got you."

She slid her hand down his naked chest, around to his back, then lower to pat his ass through the loose cotton pants he wore. The only thing he wore. "Do not disappoint me, *doulas*."

She disappeared out the arched doorway without another word, her heels echoing on the marble stairs as she left.

In the silence, Gryphon turned back to the depraved view of Sin City as sickness rolled in his stomach.

Fight back. Run. Leave.

He wanted to, but where would he go? Like it or not, he was stuck here. With Atalanta. His only hope at this point was that she'd continue to be satisfied with the degrading and humiliating things she made him do. If she wasn't…

Bile pushed up into his chest. He didn't want to think about what would happen if she wasn't. Because for him, no matter what she plotted next, there was no escape.

Chapter 12

KALISPELL, MONTANA, WAS THE CLOSEST CITY TO THE accident. Rescue personnel loaded survivors into helicopters and airlifted them away from the wreckage. It took several hours, but by morning Orpheus eventually found himself in a town he didn't recognize, with two females who were both shooting daggers his way anytime he caught their gazes.

Maelea, he got. The female hated him with a passion. She wasn't happy about being with him—anywhere— and even though he and Skyla had succeeded in killing those hounds, Maelea didn't seem reassured he could keep her safe. And her constant distrust as to where he was taking her grated on his last nerve.

And then there was the Siren. He glanced out the window of the car-rental office to the lot beyond, where Skyla and Maelea waited. The Siren had been hot as fire when he'd kissed her after dragging her from the wreckage of that avalanche. Then cool as ice since they'd killed the hounds. He couldn't follow her mood swings. Didn't know what the hell he'd done to piss her off this time. All he knew was he still wanted her. Common sense told him to be rid of her, but something in his chest said he wasn't done with her yet.

"Focus, dumbass," he muttered, turning back to sign the paperwork for the car.

The sales clerk looked up with a perturbed expression. "Excuse me?"

Great. Caught talking to himself. Fucking fabulous.

Since he frequented the human realm whenever the hell he wanted, he kept cash reserves here. Was familiar with how things worked. Even had a number of false identities, so he could skate through society when he needed. Pulling them off usually wasn't a big deal. Unless he wasn't paying attention. Like now.

He tried for a smile that came out more as a sneer. "Nothing. Is that it?"

The clerk folded the papers, slipped them in an envelope. "Yes. They're bringing the car around now."

"Perfect."

Orpheus pushed the glass door open and crossed the frigid parking lot toward the females. The morning sun beat down on the piles of snow still littering the pavement, but as the temperature was near freezing, it did shit to warm anything up. Maelea still wore the coat they'd bought for her in Everett, had her arms folded across her stomach, her gaze directed to the pavement. Skyla, dressed in those stripper Siren boots, fitted black pants, and a jacket that all but swallowed her whole, stood at Maelea's side, gnawing on the inside of her lip and glaring in his direction.

Such love. From both of them. They were obviously more than thankful he'd saved their lives. Why the hell hadn't he just let them both die? There had to be an easier way to find that rat bastard Apophis. He didn't need this grief.

He was all but ready to announce that when Skyla glanced from him to Maelea and back again. The look in her eyes was not one of anger or hatred, but jealousy.

The ground tilted beneath his feet. He felt the parking

lot shift and twirl. And then he was standing in a room, large columns rising to a ceiling he couldn't see, gold and marble and richly colored drapes and rugs filling the space. A woman was next to him, sitting in a chair, looking at a book. Her long red hair was pulled up on the sides and clipped at her crown, while the rest of the heavy mass fell down her back. She laughed, looked up, and smiled.

Pretty. She was pretty with that red hair and those shimmering green eyes. But he didn't recognize her.

He leaned over her, pointed to something in the book. The woman placed her hand on his forearm and laughed again.

From his right, a sound echoed. Skyla stepped into the room wearing a long white gauzy dress tied at the waist with a gold sash. She looked from him to the woman, then back again. And before he could say anything, she disappeared the way she'd come in.

He wasn't sure what the hell he was seeing. He was there, but he wasn't. Watching it as if it were a movie, but seeing through the eyes of an actor. He felt himself floating through the corridor, following Skyla. She turned when she reached the wide front marble terrace. More columns lined the front of the building and down the twenty or so steps, a city lay beyond, tall mountains to the right and left, and water—an ocean of blue—as far as the eye could see.

"Skyla!"

She whipped around, shot him a scathing look. The same look she'd just sent him in the parking lot. The same look he'd gotten used to seeing this whole last day. *"I thought you weren't going to marry her."*

"I'm not."

"Then what is she doing here?"

"Visiting. Her father sent her."

"Visiting." She all but vibrated with rage. And hurt. And jealousy. A jealousy that for reasons he couldn't explain rocked him to his knees. *"Fine. Then go to her."*

She turned, rushed down three steps before he grasped her by the arm and whipped her back to face him. *"I don't want her. I want you."*

"Why? She's a princess. She's exactly what they want you to have. All I am is—"

"Mine." Her heat was intoxicating. Her body like a thirst he could never quench. He wanted to shake some sense into her. Hated that she'd think he'd want anyone but her. Didn't she have eyes? *"You're mine, Siren. Just mine. Understand?"*

"Orpheus?"

The steps, the view, the palace beneath his feet faded like a thinning mist. Orpheus blinked once, twice, shook his head to clear the fog. When focus came back he found himself in the parking lot, looking into the same gemlike eyes, only these weren't soft and desire-filled as they'd been on those steps when he'd taken her into his arms. These were wary and confused and more than a little intimidating.

"What's with you?" Skyla asked. "I'm the one that was nearly toasted. Twice. And you look like you have PTSD. See anything wrong with this picture?"

He had no idea what she was mumbling about. He heard her words but they didn't register. He turned to Maelea for help, only the look she sent him said he was on his own. And from the way they were both staring at him as if he'd grown a third eye, he knew he'd just had another of those weird-ass visions.

Fuuuuuuuuuuuuck. He rubbed both hands over his face. Tried like hell to settle the pounding of his heart. Didn't even come close. What was happening to him?

"Orpheus?" Skyla said again. "Are you tripping on drugs or what?"

He wished.

He pressed his fingers into his temples until pain shot through his skull. "Just tired. I'm fine."

Only he wasn't. Even he knew he wasn't fine. He was way the fuck freaked-out. Because that didn't seem like a vision to him. There were emotions in there. Emotions still pinging around in his chest like a billiard ball bouncing off bumpers.

That had felt…like a memory.

Which was *not fucking* possible.

An engine purred, then the attendant pulled the SUV up, stopping at Orpheus's left. Thankful for the distraction he reached for the keys, but Skyla was right there, taking them before he could.

"What do you think you're doing?" he asked.

"Driving. No way I'm getting in a moving vehicle with you when you're lapsing into la-la land every few minutes."

"I'm not—"

"Climb in," she said to Maelea.

Maelea eyed them both as if they were certifiable but opened the back door of the Tahoe and slid inside the car without a word. Skyla sent Orpheus a superior smirk.

"You don't even know where we're going."

"So you'll tell me. Now, are you coming along or

not? I can just as easily leave your ass here as I can rescue you."

It was what he'd said to her in the parking lot back in Seattle after they'd gotten Maelea away from those hounds. But the memory of that vision—the emotions— rolled through his chest again before he could be impressed that she remembered, tipped him off balance in a way he'd never been before.

Who was she to him? And why couldn't he figure it out?

"Look, daemon. I know it chaps your ass to be saddled by a female, but deal with it." She climbed into the SUV. Slammed the door. Shot him a *hurry up already* look through the windshield.

And in the cool morning breeze, he knew he could be an ass or try to lighten the mood. They still had several hours before they reached the colony. Regardless of what was happening in his fucked-up head, he really didn't want to spend those hours dodging her daggers.

He climbed into the passenger seat. Latched his seat belt. As she put the vehicle in drive and pulled out of the lot, he rested his elbow on the windowsill. "For the record, Siren, I like being saddled. Reverse cowgirl is my favorite. When you're ready to ride, you just let me know."

She snorted and flipped on the radio. Loud.

He chuckled all the way to Whitefish, Montana.

Skyla didn't know what to expect when they reached their destination. In her head she'd pictured little cabins. Maybe a small lodge. A dozen or so people. Tepees probably wouldn't even have surprised her, considering Orpheus had described the inhabitants here as refugees. But when Orpheus told her to pull off the pothole-riddled one-lane dirt road she doubted a car had driven over in years and park inside a cave, she started to wonder what the hell was up.

He was being cryptically quiet. Had been since they'd passed Whitefish and that irritating laughter had died down. After giving her directions, he'd lapsed into silence and they'd driven the remaining three hours deep into the wilderness without another word. Several times she'd glanced into the rearview mirror to make sure Maelea was still there. Thankfully—or unthankfully—the female was. Though Skyla wasn't thrilled with the way Orpheus treated her, the girl was growing more defiant by the minute, something Skyla sort of liked. At least she was showing some spunk now, whereas before she'd seemed more like a mouse. Skyla had very little use for females who passively let others tell them what to do.

Isn't that what you've let the gods do all these years?

She shook off the thought. She was *not* Maelea. Not by a long shot. And why was she even comparing herself to the girl when it was Orpheus she should be concerned with?

He'd had another one of those weird zoning-out spells in that parking lot in Kalispell. She'd seen him do that now three times. Was that somehow related to his daemon? Was that why he couldn't shift? Part of her was still irritated he hadn't shifted back there in the woods when they'd been hunting those daemons and she'd nearly been lunch. Another part—a part she was trying hard to ignore—was glad. There was something sexy about him in his Argolean form kicking ass. Really freakin' animalistic sexy.

She tamped down the desire stirring in her core as she climbed out of the vehicle, tugged on her jacket again. The car doors closing echoed around her in the dark space. She'd driven deep enough into the cave where the vehicle wasn't visible from the road anymore.

Orpheus pulled out the flashlight he'd bought in Whitefish and flipped it on. A steady beam of light lit up the darkness and the cave walls around them.

"Are you sure about this, daemon?"

"Just keep up," he answered.

Skyla didn't really have any other choice. She nudged Maelea in front of her and the two followed Orpheus and the light deep into the cave.

They walked nearly twenty minutes. Shivers racked Skyla's body. Every now and then her boot would slip and she'd twist her ankle on the uneven rocks. From up ahead she heard a noise.

She grasped Maelea by the arm to stop her. The light kept moving. Unease rippled through Skyla as the cave grew dark and a voice she couldn't make out echoed ahead.

"What is it?" Maelea whispered.

"I don't know." Skyla pulled the dagger from her back. "Stay behind me."

She stepped in front of Maelea. Stilled. No sound echoed from the direction Orpheus had gone. For a moment she thought of calling out to him. And then a light cut through the inky darkness, followed by the clomp of boots. Skyla lifted a hand to block the glare.

"This isn't a pit stop, ladies," Orpheus said in an irritated tone. "We're almost there."

Relief rushed through Skyla's veins. She sheathed her dagger, nudged Maelea forward.

Orpheus nodded toward the bend in the tunnel behind him, his flashlight pointed up to illuminate the darkness. "There's a sentry right around the corner. He'll take us the rest of the way in."

He stepped aside to let Maelea pass, but when Skyla reached him he moved back until he partially blocked the tunnel.

She had to turn sideways to get by. Her chest brushed his in the process and warmth spread from his body into hers at the contact, followed by a zing of déjà vu she remembered from the night he'd pinned her to the wall of that apartment in Washington. Her feet stumbled, her cheeks heated at the memory. And the desire she'd worked so hard to forget flared hot all over again.

"Scared you lost me, Siren?"

His voice was as soft as a husky whisper, and his gray eyes, dark in the low light of the cave, simmered with mischief. A mischief that tugged at her and drew her in.

"No," she lied. "Afraid you lost me, daemon?"

"I was. In that avalanche."

Her stomach tightened at the emotion she heard in his voice. A hot, needy, wanting sound she'd not heard in thousands of years.

He disappeared into the darkness again before she could think of something to say. And alone, her chest squeezed so tight it hurt to draw air.

Daemon. Traitor. Hero.

The words revolved in her head. She tried to ignore

the last one, reminded herself the first two were all that mattered. But those words were drifting out of her reach. Moving away from what she associated with him. And the last echoed loudly in the space left behind.

Her head felt heavy by the time she pulled it together and reached him, a good twenty feet ahead in the tunnel. As he'd said, a sentry waited for them, a man dressed all in black with dark hair and a menacing look, standing in the center of what appeared to be a rock-walled room with tunnels jutting off in different directions. Though he carried a lantern that illuminated their location, Skyla's Siren senses kicked into high gear. Guns were anchored to both his hips and a knife with a series of jagged teeth was strapped to his thigh. She'd stayed alive all these years by paying attention, and she easily recognized the threat in the man's eyes as he caught sight of her.

She reached back for her dagger, but Orpheus grabbed her fingers and tugged her close before she grasped it. "Thought you got lost back there. You ready or what?"

She shot him a *back off* look he didn't heed. Tried to pull her hand away. Couldn't wrench it from his grasp.

The sentry gave her another once-over, then motioned with his hand as he turned and headed down a tunnel to their right. "This way."

Orpheus leaned close to her ear. "Don't piss them off."

She didn't miss his deadly serious tone or the *I'm not kidding* look in his eyes when he eased back. And her unease at where he was taking them shot up another notch.

Their guide didn't speak much, and his pace was quicker than theirs. But after a series of turns through a maze of tunnels Skyla was sure she'd never remember, they eventually reached a door at least ten feet high made of solid steel.

The sentry flipped up a piece of what looked like rock on the wall but obviously wasn't. Underneath, a keypad was backlit by a green glow. He typed in a code, then the door slid open to reveal a room with stone walls, a concrete floor, lockers and cabinets along one whole side, and a man as big as Orpheus standing in the center of the vast space, his hands on his hips, his amber eyes less than thrilled that they'd arrived.

"I had a feeling I'd be seeing you," the man said.

Orpheus tugged Maelea into the room. Her eyes were wide with fear but she let Orpheus pull her along, didn't even flinch at the contact. And that irritation that he so obviously cared about Maelea's safety reared its ugly head all over again in Skyla's chest.

"It's nice to see a familiar face," Orpheus said.

"Uh-huh." The man turned skeptical amber eyes toward Maelea, then to Skyla. After a long beat of silence that amped Skyla's already tightly strung nerves, he pushed a button on the wall near an elevator. "From the looks of the three of you, I'm guessing you'll be needing food and clothes and somewhere to rest."

"That would be good," Orpheus said. "We appreciate it."

The elevator opened with a ping. The man held out his hand, waited while Maelea and Skyla stepped into the car, then followed Orpheus in. He punched a button on the panel, turned, and crossed his arms over his massive chest, locking his stare on Skyla.

He knew who she was. She could see it in those eyes. Only this guy wasn't just a man. He was something more. He was bigger than Orpheus and that was saying a lot. His blond hair was cropped short and he wore large gauges in his earlobes. And dressed all in black with those guns at his hips, the fingerless gloves, and that long scar down the left side of his face, he screamed threat in every way imaginable.

"Nick," Orpheus said into the low hum from the elevator, "this is Skyla and Maelea. Ladies, this is Nick Blades, leader of the Misos colony."

Nick didn't answer. Didn't even spare Maelea a glance. And as tension filled the car like a helium balloon inflating, Skyla realized this was one of the few half-breed colonies scattered across the globe. Argolean-human survivors of Atalanta's war who'd taken refuge together. It was well known on Olympus that Argoleans placed no value on the Misos mixed-breed bloodline and that their past king refused to grant them protection because of societal discrimination. Since Zeus refused to get involved in anything Argolean related, he left them alone as well. Obviously, from the look of bitter contempt in this guy's eyes, he knew that and thought less of Zeus than he did of the new Argolean queen.

Which meant he thought even less of her.

Her anxiety amped and the weight of the bow in her boot reminded her she needed to be careful.

The elevator door opened. A wall of arched windows looked out over a view that seemed to come straight off a postcard. Blue-green water in every direction, snow-capped mountains surrounding a lake. Even an eagle swooping through the air to catch a fish, then sailing high once more.

Maelea's eyes grew wide but still she didn't speak. Skyla turned a slow circle and took in the two-story stone room with its high peaked ceiling, intricate iron chandeliers, multicolored throw rugs, and fancy Russian furnishings.

She'd have bet her throwing stars they were in a castle. But a castle out here? In the middle of a lake? In the center of nowhere? It made no sense.

Footsteps echoed behind them and Skyla turned just as an attractive woman with a slight limp stepped down from the staircase that curved up and to the left.

"This is Helene," Nick said. "She'll take you someplace where you can freshen up and relax. Orpheus and I have things to discuss."

Skyla knew those "things" meant her. "I won't—"

Orpheus leaned toward her, his hot breath and low voice millimeters from her ear. "Go with Maelea. She's liable to jump out a window if we aren't there to stop her."

When he eased back, Skyla saw the spark of mischief in his eyes, but the tight line of his jaw belied the carefree attitude. And the fact he'd obviously picked up on Nick's animosity toward her nixed her jealousy and made her that much more determined to stay.

She opened her mouth to tell him just how little she cared about what Maelea did or didn't do when he mouthed the word *please*. And just that fast her resistance wavered. As if he had some magical control over her.

"I'll come find you both when I'm done down here," Orpheus said.

She felt she shouldn't go. But she couldn't seem to say no. She found herself nodding as she stepped away from him.

The female, Helene, smiled and held a hand out to the stairs. "You both look tired. Come. This way."

Skyla gripped the intricately carved mahogany banister and looked down at Orpheus as she followed Helene and Maelea. The heat of his stare burned into her soul, and as she climbed the stairs she remembered that day at Perseus's castle when she'd gone to tell Cynurus she'd thought it over and she was ready to leave the Sirens for him.

He'd been with that Arcadian princess, the one his parents had wanted him to marry. She'd walked in on them doing nothing more dastardly than looking over a book together, but Skyla had been devastated, as devastated as if he'd been kissing the woman right in front of her. Never before had she realized the difference in their social status until she saw him with the sort of woman he should be with. He was heir to an entire kingdom and she was nothing…nothing more than an assassin. No royal blood, nothing to offer him except embarrassment when his family found out who and what she was. She wasn't even a commoner. She was lower than that. She was someone who did Zeus's dirty work, who killed and schemed and who had only met him because Zeus had targeted him as a nuisance to be dealt with.

Her heart squeezed tight as memories, emotions she'd long buried, came back tenfold. He wasn't the same man he'd been then but there were similarities, and she was starting to see the things she'd loved about Cynurus in Orpheus. His worry over Maelea, his compassion for humans, though she was sure he'd never cop to it. And then there were the moments when he looked at her the way he was doing now. As if he wanted her the way he had then. As if she was the only female for miles and he was a man who'd been denied far too long.

She had to pull her gaze away, to break the connection before it sucked her under. Head spinning, she realized Helene and Maelea were gone. A quick shot of unease filtered through her before she heard their voices from the stairs above. She picked up her pace and reached them on the next level, where they were walking down a wide corridor lit every few yards or so with ornate sconces on the red-papered walls. Large arched doorways led into rooms she couldn't see. Beneath her feet, a lush blue rug with tiny white flowers ran down the middle of the hall.

"What is this place?" Skyla asked, interrupting something Helene was telling Maelea.

Helene's limp was more obvious as she glanced over her shoulder. "The castle was built by a Russian grand duke who sought exile in the United States in the late 1800s. He had it built for his wife, who was Romanian. Unfortunately, they were both killed before they could reach the States, as were their families. Since his wife was also a Misos, the castle fell into the hands of the Russian Misos colony. It sat empty for more than a hundred years. For whatever reason, no one from that colony wanted to relocate here. When our colony in Oregon was destroyed by Atalanta's daemons, Nick found out this was available, and here we are."

She stopped in front of a door, turned the knob, and pushed the heavy mahogany mass open so Maelea and Skyla could enter the room.

It was a suite, not a room, with high arching windows, again looking down to the water, and a four-poster bed so big there were steps to climb into it. A fireplace ran along the left wall, a formal couch and high-backed side chairs placed in front of it. And beyond, a doorway Skyla guessed led to a bathroom.

This one room was as big as Skyla's entire living space back on Olympus. A room clearly made for a princess, not a mere commoner. Definitely not an assassin.

Helene flipped on the lights, illuminating the jewel colors in the furnishings and the thick velvet comforter on the bed. "We were lucky they'd furnished most of the place. Though I have to admit sometimes it can be a little creepy."

Skyla turned a slow circle and noticed the dainty wallpaper, the heavy curtains, the intricate touches like fancy curved iron grates over the vents and rich cherry hardwood floors.

"The bathroom's through here." Helene pushed open a door on the far side of the room. "The suite across the hall is just like this one. You're welcome to it," she added for Skyla. "I'll have the cook send up some food for you both."

She moved past Skyla to the door. Skyla turned to look after her. "How is it no one's found this place?"

"Our sentries are good, that's how. Get some rest. I'm sure Orpheus will be up to see you when he and Nick are done speaking."

Orpheus.

As the door closed, that space in Skyla's chest tightened again and the word *hero* echoed even louder.

How did this female—Helene—know Orpheus? The way she said his name indicated a familiarity. A friendship. She'd sensed the same connection between Orpheus and Nick earlier.

Daemon hybrids didn't have friends. They were

loners. And they didn't care about others. They didn't protect them or rescue them from avalanches or worry about what they thought or felt. A lump formed in her throat, a big one that told her everything she knew about the world around her was being shot to hell the longer she spent with him.

"I'm going to take a shower."

Skyla had nearly forgotten she wasn't alone. She looked toward Maelea standing near the windows, an *I hate this place more than I hate you* look on her face.

"Go ahead," Skyla said, ignoring the look, too frazzled to deal with it right now. "I'll be here."

"Of course you will be," Maelea muttered as she disappeared into the bathroom and closed the door behind her.

A tiny part of Skyla felt for the girl. She'd lost her home, her anonymity, and Nick obviously wasn't happy Orpheus had brought her here to the colony, but at least she was alive. If she'd stayed at her house in Seattle, she'd be dead now.

Dead.

The word echoed in Skyla's mind as she moved to the windows, looked out at the blue-green lake around her quickly fading in the dusk of evening. For so long Cynurus had been dead to her, but he was alive. In Orpheus. Alive and so very close.

Water lapped at the rocky shore. A flock of birds soared far off in the distance. From this view, there was no way to get to the island unless you had a boat or helicopter. And that was good, because it meant surprise was thwarted by the water, the jagged mountains surrounding this lake, and the mass of caves they'd come through to get here. They were safe for the time being.

But not safe from the memories bombarding her from all sides. The ones of Cynurus that were mixing with what she'd learned of Orpheus the last few days and the emotions toward him that had nothing to do with the past and everything do with the present.

What if Athena was wrong? What if Orpheus wasn't the monster they all wanted her to believe he was? What if he was after something that had nothing to do with the Orb? Questions revolved in her mind, but the biggest one—the one that wouldn't leave her alone and made her heart beat faster—sounded loudest.

What if he really was a hero after all?

Chapter 13

"EITHER YOU'RE THE BIGGEST FUCKING IDIOT ON THE planet or you've got balls of steel. Currently I can't decide which. Both, I'm sure, are going to get me killed in the long run."

Here it came. Orpheus turned from the stairwell and the Siren who was continuously tipping his world off its axis and redirected his attention toward Nick. He chose his words carefully because though he and Nick were more friends than foes, the half-breed had a temper. And he was unpredictable, especially when that temper reared its ugly head. "How'd you know I was coming in?"

Nick crossed his arms over his massive chest. "Oh, let me see. It could have been my guy in Seattle informing me they'd found a dead hellhound near Lake Washington. Or it could have been news that Maelea was missing from that mansion she calls a house."

Shit. Orpheus should have expected Nick would have all ears to the ground. He kept close tabs on what happened around his colony. He had to, to ensure the safety of his people.

"Or," Nick went on, "it could have been the earthquake from hell—which, by the way, we don't get many of up here in Montana. But my money's on the two dead hellhounds my scouts killed not far from that train wreck. All of which combined has *dumbshit* tattooed all over it. And when I think of dumbshits, your name pops right to the top of the list."

"Two hellhounds?" Orpheus asked, ignoring Nick's rant.

"Two," Nick repeated.

Orpheus's brow lowered. "We killed five. Which means they aren't running in normal packs."

"Your powers of deduction are mind-numbing."

"Your guys find signs of any others?"

"No."

Something definitely wasn't right. "Well, thanks to your crew for rounding them up."

"Don't thank me," Nick said. "If it were up to me, you and your little entourage never would have been allowed entry into the colony. And what the hell are you thinking, dragging Maelea here? Pissing off one god wasn't enough for you? You had to go for two just to add a little spice to the mix?"

Yep, this was what Orpheus had expected when he'd seen the sentry's reaction in the caves. "I don't think she'd appreciate being referred to as part of my entourage."

"I don't fucking care what she appreciates," Nick snapped. "Doesn't change shit about who she is. Hellhounds, Orpheus. I'm gonna have Hades on my ass now. And thanks to you, Zeus too, if that Siren is any indication of things to come."

"If we had anywhere else to go, I'd have taken Maelea there and kept you out of this, but we didn't. I'll be gone by morning, so you have nothing to worry about. The Siren too. Zeus isn't after Maelea, trust me."

"Trusting you is like trusting a fucking Fury. What about Hades?"

"Hades doesn't want Maelea either. He wants me."

Or rather he wants what Maelea is going to get for me. If she ever cooperates.

"You'll understand if that doesn't leave me all tingly inside," Nick said. "And I didn't hear you say anything about taking Zeus's bastard with you when you leave tomorrow."

That's because he wasn't. Orpheus rubbed a hand over his mouth. If Hades had figured out Orpheus needed Maelea to find the Orb, he'd hunt Maelea himself. And that meant this was the safest place for her, where Nick's sentries could keep her hidden and safe. "I'm pretty sure she likes being called Zeus's bastard less than being part of my entourage."

"You're a fucking moron," Nick muttered.

Yeah, well, he might be, but if there was one thing Orpheus knew about Nick, it was that the half-breed would just as soon turn out someone in need as he would side with the gods. "What did you mean, if it were up to you we wouldn't have been allowed entry into the colony?"

Nick held his hand out to the door behind him. "See for yourself."

A strange feeling tingled low across Orpheus's back. He pushed the door open. Inside the long room with its conference-style table and windows that looked out at the now-black lake, he spotted Queen Isadora, her sister Casey, Theron—the leader of the Argonauts—and Isadora's new husband Demetrius.

Oh, this was just fucking terrific.

"Why don't you sell tickets," he mumbled to Nick. "There's bound to be fireworks now."

"Deal with it," Nick muttered. "I've had to for the last few hours."

The door closed behind them. Isadora's concerned brown eyes bored into his. For whatever reason, she seemed to think he had some hero streak inside him. He didn't have the heart to tell her that whatever heroic qualities were in his lineage had skipped right over him and shot straight to his younger brother Gryphon.

Or at least they had. Before Gryphon's soul had been lost to Tartarus.

He pushed that painful thought aside and focused on the here and now. She looked better than she had the last time Orpheus had seen her. She'd gained a few pounds and her face was no longer pale and sunken in. And the slacks and sweater were a major improvement over the gowns she used to wear. Behind her, Demetrius's jaw was set in a tight line as always. The Argonaut may have softened around the edges thanks to Isadora, but that didn't mean he'd softened toward anyone else, even if that anyone else had helped save his life. Then there was Theron, leaning against the table with his hand on his wife Casey's shoulder, watching Orpheus with an *I always knew you were gonna fuck things up* look on his face.

"Let me guess," Orpheus said. "You're all here on vacation. No, wait. Some kinky swingers' honeymoon." He caught the flash of annoyance in Theron's eyes but ignored it. "You know, if it were me, Isa, I'd have gone for a sunny beach, not a creepy castle in the middle of nowhere. But then what do I know? Maybe kinky twisted shit turns you all on."

Isadora shot Theron a warning look before he could respond, the shy little princess she used to be nowhere to be found in the confident queen she'd become. She stepped forward. "Tease all you want, Orpheus, but you know why we're here."

"No, I can honestly say I don't. Don't tell me you screwed the kingdom already, Isa."

"Tell him," Nick cut in. "Tell him what you told me."

Isadora sighed. "We had a few visitors at the castle. Two, to be exact. Sirens. Sent by Athena to enlist the help of the Argonauts."

"Help how?" Orpheus asked.

"In locating Apophis and the Orb of Krónos."

Interesting. "Why?"

"Because Zeus wants it for himself."

"That I get. But why come to you? And the Argonauts?"

"Zeus knows you're looking for it. And he obviously also knows your link to the Argonauts."

Of course he did. Zeus kept his ear to the ground too. Or rather his Sirens did.

His mind drifted to Skyla and their last few days together. But this news wasn't anything he didn't already know. He was well aware she'd been sent by Zeus to seduce him, snag the Orb when he finally found it, then kill him. They were both toying with each other in the meantime. What didn't make sense was why the hell Zeus would think his chosen Siren couldn't get the job done.

"Why are you telling me this?"

Isadora's eyes softened again. "Because I sensed those Sirens weren't telling me the whole truth. And because I'm worried about you."

"You need to give up this crazy hunt for the Orb, O," Theron cut in.

Orpheus ignored Theron. "What did you tell them? The Sirens?"

"That we would do what we can. Which," Isadora added with a lopsided grin, "means nothing."

Nothing. If it were up to Theron and the Argonauts, it'd be something.

"Why don't you tell them about your traveling companion," Nick said at Orpheus's back.

Shit.

"Maelea?" Isadora asked. "We already know."

"Not that one," Nick said. "The *other* Siren."

Isadora's surprised eyes skipped back to Orpheus. "You're traveling with a Siren?"

Man, he was so fucking ready to kill Nick. He didn't have time for this shit. He still had to convince Maelea to tell him where the Orb was tonight so he could make tracks and find that shitty warlock. "The Siren is none of your concern. Yours either," he said, shooting Nick a glare. "I can handle her."

Isadora looked at her husband standing across the room with his hands shoved into the front pockets of his jeans, then to her sister and Theron leaning against the table, all three sporting the same *what the hell did you expect?* expressions. When she refocused on Orpheus, though, her eyes weren't filled with the same indifference. They brimmed with worry. A worry that stoked his annoyance with this whole damn situation. "Orpheus—"

"Isa," he mocked. What he wouldn't give to call up his daemon and be done with all of them.

A frown turned her lips. "I know you can take care of yourself, but three Sirens in two days? That's not good. Even for you."

"You just worry about yourself, okay? I'll worry about me."

A knock sounded at the door. Nick answered with a yes, and seconds later a dark-haired half-breed popped his head into the room. "Um, Nick. We've got a situation."

"What now?" Nick asked.

He handed Nick what looked like a palm-sized computer and ran his finger over the screen, calling up an image. "Sentries just spotted them. Two beyond the outer perimeter. Doesn't look like they've figured out we're here yet, but their tracking skills are among the best. They'll figure it out soon enough."

"Fucking A," Nick muttered.

"What?" Theron said, letting go of Casey and stepping forward to look at the screen.

Nick pinned Orpheus with a hard look. "I just figured out what happened to the rest of the hellhound pack."

"What do you—?"

Nick turned the screen so he could see the two Sirens lurking in the woods outside the cave where they'd left their vehicle. "Man, you are major-league fuckup if I ever saw one." He glanced toward the male who'd brought him the news. "Get Kellon and Marc and take them down quietly."

"Hold up." Demetrius moved closer to Isadora. "You go killing a Siren or two and that's bound to get back to Olympus. Orpheus is right. Zeus has never paid any attention to Maelea before, which means odds are good he's not after the girl like we thought. He's after Orpheus, just like O said. And that means killing his warriors isn't going to do anything but piss him off more than he already is."

Unease rippled through Orpheus. Why the hell was he being tailed by two more Sirens? Something smelled rotten. Little by little it was becoming clear Zeus didn't trust Skyla as far as he could throw her. Which begged the question…why had he assigned her to Orpheus in the first place if he knew she was going to fail?

"Good point," Theron said. "What are you thinking?"

"I'm thinking disorienting them is a better bet," Demetrius answered.

"A spell?" Orpheus asked, surprised Demetrius was embracing his Medean heritage so easily. The last time he'd used his powers, it had been to help Orpheus banish Atalanta to the Fields of Asphodel. But that had been out of pure hatred rather than anything else. As far as Orpheus knew, Demetrius hadn't used his gift since.

"Or two," Demetrius said. "But I'll need your help. I'm still a little rusty."

Spells tumbled through Orpheus's mind. The idea had potential, but it wasn't a done deal. "We might be able to work something." He looked to Nick, then Theron. "But we'll need your help too."

Both nodded in agreement, and Orpheus found himself shocked that the Argonauts were willing to help him out on this. They could just as easily hand deliver him to Zeus.

Trying not to look as bowled over as he felt, Orpheus laid out the plan, and when he was done caught the nods and agreement of the others.

Who would have thought it?

They moved for the door.

At his back, Isadora said to Casey, "Why don't you and I go have a talk with that Siren upstairs."

Orpheus's unease reignited. *Yeah, Isa, you have a nice little chat with the Siren*. Butter her up. Because when he got back, he intended to put an end to their games and find out what was really going on.

—◦◦◦—

"Think this will work?" Demetrius whispered.

Crouched beyond an outcropping of rock on a gentle slope in the darkness, Orpheus peered down the twenty or so yards toward the small clearing below where the two Sirens—his tail—were scanning the trees, their superior Siren senses obviously picking up the fact there was more to this forest than met the eye.

"So long as Theron and Nick do as they're supposed to, yeah," Orpheus answered in a low voice. "I think it can work. You sure those aren't the two that visited Isa at the castle?"

"They're not."

Orpheus studied the two drop-dead-gorgeous Sirens below. "Yeah. Guess you'd know. Pretty hard to forget a body like that."

"I couldn't care less about their bodies." Then, under his breath, "C'mon, Nick."

Not for the first time, Orpheus found himself impressed Demetrius and Nick seemed to be getting along. They'd hated each other for years. Though they shared the same mother, the same link to the gods, Demetrius had grown up in Argolea and trained with the Argonauts, whereas Nick had been banished to the human realm because of his mixed-breed heritage. Orpheus now knew that was because the Council had seen him as a threat and had wanted to have him killed. All because he had something the rest of them didn't. He was a true demigod. Half human and half god. More pure than any in Argolea.

It explained a lot about the man. But Orpheus still wasn't sure what had been the catalyst for the brothers' truce. He suspected it had something to do with Isadora. Something more than the fact that she was now queen. He thought about mentioning it, then decided not to. It didn't much matter to him either way. He had more important things to worry about.

But as they waited for Nick and Theron to make their move, one question Orpheus had been wondering since Demetrius and Isadora had come back from that island popped out of his mouth before he thought better of it. "Aren't you afraid the honeymoon phase is going to wear off?"

"I don't know what you mean."

"With Isa. Let's get real, Argonaut. You are who you are. Just because we sent Atalanta to the Fields of Asphodel doesn't change the fact she's your mother. Doesn't change the fact what's evil in her is evil in you."

Demetrius's jaw clenched. "Isadora knows what I am."

"Yeah, but aren't you afraid at some point she's going to realize it—you—were a mistake? I mean, good sex only lasts so long. And gods know Isadora wasn't getting any before you, so it's not like she had a lot to compare to. But that infatuation will wear off soon enough. I mean, she's the queen of Argolea, and you're—"

"Why do you care so much?"

Why? Orpheus wasn't sure. Maybe because he still couldn't believe someone could love evil. And maybe it was because a small part of him was jealous. Not jealous that Isadora was taken, but jealous of how easily she'd brushed aside everything she'd known for years to be true about Demetrius and had found the one thing in him no one else could see.

He frowned because he knew the last wasn't it. "I don't. I'm just wondering when I can sit back and say 'I told you so.' The train wreck's coming. You know it is."

Demetrius's jaw clenched harder and he turned his attention back to the Sirens below. "You're the train wreck, Orpheus. Case in point, the mess you left back there in the mountains."

Yeah, he might be a fuckup, but he was smart enough to know he wasn't marriage material. Wasn't even relationship material. What he had going with the Siren was nothing more than straight-up sexual attraction. Which, as he'd told Demetrius, would burn out soon enough. Tonight, if he had anything to say about it.

His mind drifted to Skyla, and before he could stop himself he wondered what she was doing right this minute. A burst of desire rippled through him when he pictured her kiss-me lips and that made-for-sin body. Which both lit him up and pissed him off at the same time.

The brush to the left of the Sirens rustled, and Orpheus's adrenaline shot up when he saw Nick stumble into the clearing. The Sirens both pulled their bows, just as he'd seen Skyla do a dozen times. As they'd planned, Nick was covered in blood, crimson streaks all across his chest and thighs, and both Sirens caught the scent immediately, went on high alert as he dropped to the ground at their feet.

A shout echoed from the trees. One Siren shifted her bow in that direction. The other kept her arrow trained on Nick. Seconds later, Theron drew up short at the clearing's edge, his parazonium—the ancient Greek dagger all Argonauts carried—in hand. He lifted both

arms when he caught sight of Zeus's assassins. "Don't
shoot. I'm an Argonaut."

The first Siren stepped back near the second. Their
wary gazes darted between Nick, facedown in the grass,
and Theron. "What are you doing out here?"

"The same thing you are. Hunting. Two from your
order came to Argolea in request of our help."

"Who?" the one on the right asked.

"Khloe and…" He seemed to think for a minute.
"Reanna, Remea—"

"Rhebekkah?" the second Siren asked.

"That was it," Theron said. "Rhebekkah. Said you
two were hunting Orpheus." He nodded toward the
ground, slid his parazonium back into its sheath at his
back. "Here he is."

The Sirens exchanged glances, then looked toward
Nick. "How do you know it's him?"

Theron chuckled. "O's not hard to miss. Shitty attitude, fuck-off mentality. I could sense him a mile away.
The fact he shifted into one of those shit-for-brains daemons was also a dead giveaway."

So Isa had told Theron and the others that he was
a hybrid. Wonderful. One more thing for them to hold
against him.

"Where did you find him?" the multicolor-haired
Siren asked.

"In the mountains. Hiding. The other two got away.
Two females. But this is the one you want, right?"

The Sirens looked unsure. The second—the dark-
haired one—stepped closer to Nick, nudged his shoulder
with her kick-ass boot. The same boots Skyla wore. The
first lowered her weapon, moved closer to Nick too.

The second looked up at the first. "I think he might be dead."

They both refocused on Theron as they depressed the end of their bows, shrinking them down to nothing. "He was to be brought in alive, Argonaut," the first said.

"Whoa. Wait. No one told me that. You wanted him alive?' He scratched his head, perched one hand on his hip. "Well, damn. That creates a problem, doesn't it?"

"A big problem," the second said. She cut a look at her partner. "Athena will not be happy."

"Especially not when she finds out Skyla got away," the first replied.

So these two Sirens were hunting Skyla too. Orpheus's suspicions as to Skyla's real intentions bloomed all over again, stringing his chest tight as a drum.

"We'll take it from here, Argonaut," the first said. "You're free to go."

"Are you sure?" Theron asked. "I mean, I wouldn't want you…ladies…to get into any trouble over this."

The second sent a hard glare his way. "Leave now, Argonaut. Before we change our minds and decide you're better off dead too."

A shocked expression rushed across Theron's face. He held his hands up again and stepped back toward the dark forest. "Okay, okay. Hint taken. Good luck, ladies."

He disappeared from view. And beside Orpheus, Demetrius tensed. That was their cue.

"Wait," Orpheus whispered.

The multicolor-haired Siren leaned down toward Nick and muscled him over onto his back. When she caught sight of his face she swore loud and clear.

Nick's eyes popped open. "Now that didn't sound all sweet and seductive to me."

He kicked the legs out from under the brunette. She landed on her ass with a thud. The first reached for her bow, but Nick was already on his feet.

"Now," Orpheus said. He and Demetrius cast the illusion spell before she could pull her arrow, multiplying Nick by a hundred times all across the clearing.

"Fuck," the first Siren muttered as she shifted her bow right and left, not sure where now to aim.

"No thanks," Nick muttered, the mouths of all the illusions moving to disorient the Sirens, "we're really not in the mood."

The Sirens glanced from one image of Nick to another, then at each other. Finally, knowing they were likely screwed, they lowered their weapons. Though they might look cornered, Orpheus knew they weren't. He'd seen Skyla in that position more times than he could count.

"Now the rest," Orpheus whispered.

He and Demetrius focused their powers, called on their Medean heritage. The chant grew up around them, echoed in the still night air. From below, a Siren asked, "What was that?"

"Oh, just a little surprise," Nick said with a smile in his voice.

The Sirens' voices faded into nothing as the chant grew louder and Orpheus and Demetrius whipped the disorientation spell into a frenzy. When it was finally done, Orpheus opened his eyes to look down at the clearing, where both Sirens were lying on their backs in the grass, passed out.

"Did it work?" Demetrius called.

The images of Nick faded as their concentration broke, leaving only the real Nick standing in the meadow. He knelt near the multicolor-haired Siren and felt along her neck. "Yep. Pulse is strong. Though I'm pretty sure they're both going to have major-ass headaches when they come to."

Orpheus picked his way down the hill and stopped in the clearing next to Theron, who'd reemerged from the trees. "A major headache is an understatement. When they wake up they won't remember a thing, not about what happened here or anything about this forest. Though I did like seeing their faces when you multiplied. I'd love to pull that one on their boss."

"Don't wish for things you don't really want," Nick answered as the SUV Orpheus had rented in Kalispell pulled into the clearing next to them and the same half-breed who'd informed them of the Sirens' presence climbed from the vehicle. "He's gonna be pissed when he finds them."

"Where are you taking them?" Orpheus asked.

"Aidan's gonna drive them south," Nick said. "There's a Titan posing as a human down in Texas. Figured we'd leave them with him. He'll get a kick out of tormenting Zeus and Athena."

Nick looked to Orpheus. "We've got what, twenty hours?"

"Give or take," Orpheus answered.

"Piece of cake," Aidan said. "In twenty hours they'll be tucked in safe and sound and Zeus'll be pitching a conniption fit, wondering what the hell happened to them."

That wasn't the only fit Zeus would be pitching.

While their toying with his Sirens couldn't be linked directly back to the colony or even to him, Orpheus had a feeling somehow it would catch up with him. Shit always did.

Chapter 14

A KNOCK SOUNDED ON THE DOOR BEFORE SKYLA could decide if she was going to stay while Maelea finished her shower or go look for Orpheus.

She really wanted to go look for Orpheus.

"Come in," she said, her stomach grumbling when she remembered the food Helene had promised to send up.

A slim blond stepped into the room, smiled. She was petite, with short, messy hair and dark brown eyes. Behind her, a dark-haired woman entered, this one taller than the first. Neither held the tray of food Skyla was hoping for.

"I'm glad you're still here," the blond said. "I'm Isadora. This is my sister Casey. We came up to make sure you have everything you need."

Isadora…Casey…The names were vaguely familiar. But there was something about them that didn't jell with the other colonists Skyla had run into. "You're both Misos?"

"I am," Casey answered. "My *half* sister isn't. She's—"

The names finally clicked and Skyla's eyes widened. "The queen of Argolea."

Isadora clasped her hands in front of her, nodded. "Very good, Siren. The gods are obviously keeping tabs on what happens in our little part of the world."

Of course they were. They had to. There was that whole self-preservation thing going on.

The small of Skyla's back tightened. No weapons on

either of them, not that she could see, but that didn't mean they weren't a threat. What was the queen of Argolea doing at a half-breed colony?

Isadora moved farther into the room, stopping near the couch in the small sitting area. "Orpheus and Nick went with the others. They'll be back soon."

"Others?" Skyla asked, not moving from her spot near the window.

"My husband." Casey nodded toward the other woman. "And the queen's husband too. Both of whom are Argonauts."

Well, of course they were.

"We came up here," Isadora said, "to discuss your interest in Orpheus."

Ah. Now this was starting to make more sense. "Since he's one of your warriors, my interest in him obviously concerns you."

"Yes," the queen answered. "Greatly."

"Orpheus doesn't need you to be concerned for him. If you knew what he is, you wouldn't be."

"I know exactly what he is," Isadora answered. "And though you may see that as a negative, I see it as the opposite. I'm not about to let anyone—especially you— ruin him."

The queen's last words hung in the silence between them, a ridiculous warning from a petite creature any Siren would ignore. But Skyla wasn't ignoring it. Because only one thought revolved in her mind as she stared at the queen. "You care for him."

"I do. While he's not the easiest person to get along with—"

"You can say that again," Casey mumbled.

"—he is not defined by that part of himself he keeps carefully locked down."

His daemon side. The queen was talking about his daemon, which meant she did know what he was.

"It makes him unpredictable," Skyla managed.

"Unpredictability is often an asset, especially in a war the likes of which we are embroiled in. Regardless of that unpredictability, Orpheus has shown his link to the ancient heroes more times than I can count. If he was only what you or Zeus say he is, he wouldn't give a damn about me or my sisters or our world. And the truth is—whether he will admit it or not—he does."

Tingles spread through Skyla's chest. And that word, *hero*, the one growing louder and louder in her head whenever she thought of Orpheus, increased to the sound of a blaring trumpet. "How?"

"Excuse me?"

"How does he give a damn?" Her neck grew hot and sweaty. "Give me an example."

Isadora looked at her sister again, and when Casey nodded, she said, "I can give you several. He saved my life. He saved my husband's life. He saved our other sister's son Max's life. Together with my mate's help he was able to send Atalanta to the Fields of Asphodel, thereby giving us the chance to hunt her daemons and get a leg up on this war. But none of those are as important as the reason I'm about to give you."

Skyla's chest tightened. And in the queen's words, every suspicion she'd had about Orpheus was confirmed.

Hero.

She moved toward the bed, sat down on the edge before her legs gave out.

"Three months ago," the queen went on, "an Argonaut was injured in our realm by a powerful warlock who'd banded forces with Atalanta. Gryphon, Orpheus's brother, suffered a tremendous blast of energy during that fight that left him weak and nearly dead. Our healers did all they could for him, but it wasn't enough. When it became clear that Gryphon's body had regained its strength, but that his soul was slowly dying, Orpheus gave up whatever personal plans he had for the Orb of Krónos and brought it to Gryphon. Even without the four elements, the Orb has powers beyond explanation. But the warlock's energy had destroyed enough of Gryphon's soul that he was able to take possession of Gryphon's body, thereby sending Gryphon's soul to the Underworld."

The Underworld. *Oh gods*.

Skyla's breaths grew quick as Orpheus's intentions—why he was seeking the Orb of Krónos—suddenly became clear. She reached out and gripped the post at the corner of the bed, knowing what was coming even before the queen said it.

"I'm sure Zeus told you Orpheus is after the Orb for power and glory." Isadora's eyes grew hard. "But he's not. He's after the Orb so he can harness its powers and travel into the Underworld to save his brother's life. A life he feels responsible for losing. He won't admit that to you if you ask. He won't even admit it to me. And sometimes I'm not even sure he can admit it to himself, but that doesn't change the truth. The *ándres* who has been there every time we've needed him for whatever reason is more a hero than most in our realm. And he's more a hero than you or I could ever hope to be."

Hero. The word was there again, roaring through her mind like a freight train.

"And when you say he is an Argonaut," Isadora continued, "you may be right—now—but he was not one by birth. He was passed over by the gods to serve. Those marks on his arms? They only appeared after his younger brother's soul was sent to the Underworld."

"Siren?" Casey asked. "Are you okay?"

Skyla swallowed hard. Tried to nod. Wasn't sure she succeeded.

Dear gods, she'd been right. Zeus and Athena were lying to her. Lying because they wanted the Orb for themselves. Not to rescue a soul, like Orpheus, but to ensure no one became more powerful than them.

Hero. The word sucked up all the empty space in her head, shoving aside every last doubt she'd had about Orpheus because of his daemon. Whether he purposely hadn't shifted or couldn't anymore didn't matter. He was still heroic, even with the daemon.

"You said he was with the Argonauts." Skyla's mind was a thick hazy soup of lies long told and so easily believed. "Why? Where?"

"They went to deal with your tail," Isadora answered.

"My what?

"You've had two Sirens following you for quite some time." Casey brushed her hair over her shoulder. "And they weren't the same two that came to Argolea to request the Argonaut's help locating the warlock who has the Orb."

Skyla's head darted up. "Sirens from my order came to you?"

"Yes," Isadora said. "I take it from your reaction this is news to you?"

Big news. Enormous news. Yeah, Skyla had yet to check in with Athena as she was supposed to, but if the head of her order had already sent Sirens to tail them and also to Argolea to request help, it meant she'd never trusted Skyla in the first place. It also meant if Skyla didn't follow through on her orders and kill Orpheus, as Zeus wanted, her future with the Sirens would come to a dramatic end.

Of course, maybe that was the plan all along. A sneaking suspicion took root in the bottom of her stomach as she gripped the mattress. Maybe Athena had set Skyla up to fail right from the start.

The Siren call to duty is one that is meant to be answered, served, then abandoned, and we never intended for you to serve this long.

Reality was a sharp, swift slap to the face. Athena had said the words clear as day, and Skyla had heard them but hadn't realized their meaning.

"Siren?" Casey asked again. "Are you sure you're okay? You look a little green."

No, Skyla wasn't okay. Not by a long shot. Because this suddenly was not another of the thousands of missions Zeus had sent her on over her long life.

This time, she was the prey.

Chapter 15

HADES WAS IN A PISS-POOR MOOD. HIS HELLHOUNDS had failed. Scouts had found them in the mountains of Montana with Siren arrows through their hearts.

Orpheus, the Siren, and that stain, Maelea, were nowhere to be found. Not even a trace of them remained.

He tapped his long fingers against the intricate armrest of his blackened throne and waited for Orcus to bring him news. Yeah, he'd lost track of Maelea, but that didn't mean he was out of options. He was the Lord of the Underworld because he anticipated his enemy's next move. And he was rarely wrong.

If Atalanta was plotting something in Sin City with his father, Krónos, and the soul of the Argonaut Gryphon, it meant her escape plan was imminent. And if she promised Krónos enough, his lying shit-for-a-father would tell her exactly where the Orb could be found. Even though Krónos was locked in Tartarus, he was connected to that damn thing. He knew its every movement in the human realm.

Hades ran a hand over his chin. Once Atalanta got out, what would she need? Her army of daemons had disbanded when she was sent to the Fields of Asphodel. They now roamed the earth in secret, causing havoc, but they were no longer organized thanks to the Argonauts. She couldn't rely on them. She'd need her slave's help locating the Orb. And a soul needed a body, to be of any use in the human realm. He stroked the patch of hair on his chin. The Argonaut Gryphon's body was still alive, wasn't it? Possessed by that warlock, Apophis.

Apophis…

Hades's mind skipped back to his last confrontation with the warlock. In Demeter's temple on the island of Pandora. The warlock had been trying to take the earth element from Isadora. Hades had intervened, wanting the element for himself. Thinking back, he realized there had been something different about Apophis that day. Not just the warlock's newly acquired—and improved—body, but a strength the aging warlock shouldn't have possessed in the human realm, even in the young Argonaut's skin.

"*Motherfucker.*" Hades pushed out of his chair. The warlock had the Orb. He'd had it the whole time. And Hades had been so intent on getting the stupid element from the little queen, he hadn't even noticed.

He turned a slow circle. Pictured his precious wife. Persephone would have known, of course. During the month she'd had access to Isadora's power of foresight, thanks to the deal she'd made with the then-princess to save her sister's life, Persephone had been able to see where each of the elements and the Orb were hiding. That's how he'd known Isadora was going to find the earth element in the first place. But his wife had neglected to mention the Orb. The Orb she undoubtedly knew was with Apophis right now.

"That traitorous little wench…"

"I'm sure you couldn't possibly mean me."

Hades whipped around to find a Fate sitting on his altar, her legs crossed, her diaphanous robe hanging off her lithe and wrinkled body to float to the blackened floor. Annoyance at the interruption and bitter hatred for the creature who screwed with his life vied for his attention. "You are a wench of another kind."

Lachesis smiled, the bitch, but it faded quickly when she said, "And you violated our agreement."

He rested his hands on his hips. She was talking about her precious hero. Like he fucking cared about Orpheus right now. "I did no such thing. The weasel's still alive, isn't he?"

"Yes, no thanks to you." She tipped her head. "Hades, I shouldn't have to remind you, you cannot send hell-hounds to kill him. We made a deal."

"My hellhounds are the ones who are dead."

"And rightly so. But that doesn't change the fact you tried to destroy him. And while I'm at it, I'll remind you that you cannot kill Maelea either."

No shit, which pissed him off even more. He dropped back onto his throne and looked past her to the window beyond, irritated to the nth degree that he had to deal with her shit now. All the gods hated the Fates, but none more than him. Especially her, because she came here with conditions no immortal should be able to demand, especially in his damn realm. "I wasn't after the fucking stain."

She slid off the altar, floated across the ground. A petite creature he'd like to backhand into eternity. Only he didn't dare. Because like it or not, the Fates were stronger than any god. Not fallen angels like him and the other gods, but the real deal. The Creator's right hand...wenches.

"You're afraid he's going to succeed."

He scoffed. He wasn't afraid Orpheus was going to succeed. He just didn't want the moron to muck up his plans for the Orb before the so-called hero crashed and burned.

He cut his glare from the window to her. "Your precious hero won't succeed at anything. No matter what I do to him, his true colors will reveal themselves soon enough. A soul cannot be changed. And a black one is black for all eternity, Lachesis. I know that better than anyone."

"Not even the daemon you cursed him with has turned him completely, Hades. There is good in him still."

"Very little. Let's not forget he stole the air element from Zeus in the first place. That in his second chance at life—a chance you insisted he deserved—he's fucked with the Orb more times than I can count. It might look like he's doing good, but he's only out for himself. And as soon as he finds the Orb again, you'll see how little good there is left in him."

She held his gaze a long beat, a beady-eyed stare that boiled the blood in his veins and made him dream of vengeance. Of getting his hands on the Orb once and for all and showing her the true meaning of power and just what she could do with her meddling.

"Do not send your hounds after Orpheus again," she warned. "I will strike them down if you do. And instead of worrying about my hero, perhaps you should turn your attention to your wife. She plots against you."

A wicked smile curled his mouth. "I know. Ain't it grand?"

Lachesis didn't answer. Only faded to nothing until he was once more alone in his temple.

His humor died. As much as he admired Persephone's ruthlessness, his own wife would not beat him at this game.

"Orcus!" He pushed out of his chair again as plans and options whipped like a tornado through his mind. "Where is that little bastard?"

By the time Orcus dragged his lame leg into the room, Hades was pacing the blackened stones, thinking through every step. "Yes, my lord."

"Find my wife."

"But Maelea—"

"Forget the stain for now. I'm more concerned with what Persephone's up to. Find her and follow her and report back her every move."

"You think she knows something, my lord?"

"I think she knows everything. And while you're at it, find out what Tantalus discovered in Sin City. I want to know what my father is plotting with Atalanta."

"Yes, my lord."

The creature ducked his head, slithered out of the room. And alone, Hades clenched his jaw. It shouldn't be this hard to keep everyone in line. They were all plotting against him, wrestling for control of something none of them deserved. His father, his brothers, the Fates...even his precious little wife.

Of course, that plotting and deal making behind the scenes would make it all the more enjoyable when he finally had the Orb, wouldn't it? And when everyone—the meddling Fates included—finally bowed to him for good.

—◆◆◆—

It was after midnight by the time Orpheus made it back to the colony. He fully expected Maelea and Skyla to be sacked out somewhere, but he didn't care if he had to yank the Siren from a deep sleep. She was *going* to tell him what the hell was going on.

Isadora and Casey were sitting in the grand hall on the fifth floor of the castle sipping tea when he and the others stepped off the elevator. Enormous stone pillars rose around the outskirts of the room, separating the living space from the hallway. Isadora's face brightened when she saw Demetrius at Orpheus's back. "How did it go?"

"Good," Nick answered.

"Piece of cake," Theron grinned, walking around the couch to sit on the armrest near Casey and pull her close. She smiled up at him and leaned in as he kissed her temple. "Those Sirens don't have a clue what hit them."

"And we're sure Zeus can't link them back to us?" Isadora asked.

"Nothing's a hundred percent certain, *kardia*," Demetrius said, sitting in the chair next to her, "but those Sirens aren't going to remember anything. When they wake up though…" His voice trailed off as he looked to Nick.

"When they wake up, what?" Isadora asked.

Nick scratched the back of his head and shot his brother a *keep your trap shut* look. "Nothing. They'll just be wondering what the hell happened, that's all."

"Why do I get the feeling there's something you're not telling me?" Isadora asked.

Because there was. Nick hadn't informed Isadora his guys were leaving the Sirens with a Titan. Even though a few hadn't been condemned to Tartarus with the others at the end of the Titanomachy and still roamed the earth,

Zeus hated them with a passion. If Isadora knew they'd left the Sirens with one just to screw with the King of the Gods, she'd be less than thrilled. In fact, she'd be irate. Orpheus wasn't getting in the middle of this one.

"Where's Maelea?" he asked.

"Upstairs." Isadora set her tea on the coffee table. "Asleep."

"And the Siren?"

"She said something about needing air," Casey answered.

Disbelief rippled through Orpheus. "You let her leave?"

"No." Isadora pushed to her feet. "She's still here. The guards know to keep a lookout for her."

"Take the elevator to the top floor," Nick said to Orpheus. "There are a number of turrets and towers on the south end that no one uses because of the wind. If she wanted privacy, that's where you'll find her. I'll double-check with the guards and make sure she didn't pull anything funny."

That thought didn't put Orpheus at ease. There were measures taken when outsiders visited the colony, steps to make sure they couldn't find their way back. Skyla couldn't leave on her own now unless she was escorted out. But knowing her, if she'd suddenly decided to split, she could have seduced any one of those dumb guards to get free. And they would have fallen for her seduction skills a hell of a lot faster than he had.

Orpheus clenched his jaw, turned back for the elevator. Nick's voice stopped him. "What are you gonna do with her?"

Orpheus pushed the call button. "Get rid of her, once and for all."

Nick crossed his arms over his chest. "If you decide to let her live, make sure she can't find her way back here. And if you don't...clean up the mess."

Orpheus didn't answer as the elevator door opened. From inside the car, he heard Nick say, "So this means you're all taking off, right?"

"No," Isadora answered. "At least for tonight, we're staying."

Fucking fantastic. Just what Orpheus needed. The sooner he got the info he needed from Maelea, the sooner he could get the hell out of here and away from all of them. But first he had the Siren to deal with.

He took the elevator up another ten floors to the top as Nick had directed and stepped out into an empty space. Unlike the other levels, this one was nothing but stone floors and towering columns, void of furniture and rugs. A wall of windows looked out into the blackness.

He crossed the long room, pushed the arched doors open, and stepped out into the cold. A gust of wind lifted the hair from his forehead, and a shiver ran down his spine. Shrugging deeper into his thin jacket, he searched the flat, barren terrace covered in a thin layer of snow that ran the length of the south wing. No movement caught his attention. Nothing seemed out of the ordinary. He tuned in to his enhanced daemon sense—which, thankfully, still worked—and picked up nothing. To the right he spied a curved set of stairs that disappeared up into the darkness.

The Siren had to go. Didn't matter that she was hotter than sin. Or that he felt connected to her on some weird-ass plane. She was a distraction he couldn't deal with anymore.

The stone steps curved up and around. His boots crunched on snow as he skipped steps to get to the top. He paused when he spotted Skyla standing across the small terrace, looking out into the darkness, a trancelike expression on her perfect face.

Gods, she was beautiful. Even pissed off and ready to be done with her, he couldn't deny that fact.

For a second he thought she was asleep. But then he realized she couldn't be. Not standing straight with her eyes open. He took one more step onto the terrace and another gust of wind slapped him in the face, sending shivers over his skin. Skyla's hair blew away from her cheeks, but she didn't so much as quiver in the cold.

His aggravation regarding her and her Siren sisters came back tenfold. Along with his stupidity for not kicking her to the curb when he should have. "Getting new orders from the mother ship?"

She jerked in his direction. "Orpheus."

Why the hell did he like it when she said his name with that sexy Siren voice? He was so freakin' gullible it wasn't even funny. He set his jaw. "Well? Did Zeus give you the go-ahead to use me as a pin cushion with those fancy arrows of yours or are you supposed to wait until I have the Orb?"

A guilty expression rushed across her face. It was the first time he'd mentioned the Orb to her. They both knew why she was here, but neither, it seemed, wanted to admit it.

Well, screw it. This ended here. Tonight. No more games.

"I…" Her platform boots crunched on the thin layer of snow as she took a step toward him. She'd ditched the breastplate and arm guards, leaving behind only a thin cotton shirt and light black jacket that hit at her hips and led to slim black fitted pants grazing her legs. "I wasn't talking to Zeus. Or Athena. She wouldn't answer me, actually. I was…thinking."

Yeah, right.

She took another step toward him, her expression wary. She obviously sensed his animosity. That, or his eyes were glowing, signaling his daemon hovered close. Only it didn't feel like his eyes were glowing. And though his daemon *was* there, it wasn't as prominent as usual.

"Queen Isadora told me you and the others went to throw the Sirens off our trail."

Isa had talked to her? Fabulous. Just what he needed. "Worried about them?"

"No, they can handle themselves. They're well trained."

"Backup?" he asked. "For when I decide to kill you?"

Another shot of guilt rushed across her face before she glanced away. For the first time he noticed the scattering of patio furniture on this terrace. A couple of chaise lounges stacked together near what looked like a room made of glass. Inside he could see shapes, like other furniture stored for safekeeping.

"Perhaps," she said, "but I don't think that's why they were sent."

Orpheus brought his attention back to her, crossed his arms over his chest. Reminded himself he wasn't up here to take in the scenery. He was here for answers. And to get rid of her. "Then why were they sent? I think it's time you stopped fucking with me and laid it on the line. We both know you want the Orb. We both know

Zeus sent you. What I want to know is why he sent other Sirens to tail you."

She bit her lip, the first blatantly nervous move he'd seen her make since they'd met. And a trickle of unease settled in his belly. "He sent them because he doesn't trust me."

"And why doesn't he trust you?"

"Because he's not stupid," she muttered.

He was just about to ask what the hell that meant when she took another step toward him, this time with determined eyes. Eyes that said she'd just gone on the offensive. "You weren't chosen by the gods to become an Argonaut. You only got those markings when your brother died."

His spine stiffened. And the memory of what had happened to Gryphon whipped through him like a hurricane, pulling tight whatever was left inside his chest until it was hard to breathe.

That damn Isadora.

"I'd already started to suspect you were after the Orb for something other than what I'd been told, but now I know for sure. You're going after the Orb to save him, aren't you?"

Why was she moving toward him? He took a step back. "I don't know what you're talking about."

"Yes, you do. You're just so used to working alone, you'd rather everyone go on thinking you're a sonofa-bitch out for his own gain than have them know you're trying to do some kind of good."

He wasn't trying to do good. He was simply trying to right a wrong that shouldn't have happened. His brother was the hero, not him. He'd done more bad shit in his

life than most. He was the one who deserved to be in
Tartarus, not Gryphon. All Gryphon had done was try
to make the world a better place.

"I'm not having this conversation with you. You can
believe whatever stupid fairy tale you want. I only came
up here to tell you it's time for you to leave. Maelea's
staying here and your Siren buddies are gone. I'll take you
back to the forest, but from there you're on your own."

"You're letting me go? Just like that? Your friends
aren't afraid I'll tell Zeus and the others where their
colony is located?"

"I'll make sure you don't remember." He turned for
the steps. "Let's go."

"No, I'm not going back." When he looked over
his shoulder, he caught the challenge in her eyes. "I'm
going with you to the Underworld."

"You are higher than a kite." He stepped down,
waved his hand in a *come on* motion. "Move your ass,
Siren. I don't have all day."

No sound echoed behind him. He looked back across
the patio. She stood in the middle of the space with her
arms crossed over her chest and her boots shoulder-
width apart in a very clear *make me* pose. "Afraid you
might actually need my help, daemon?"

"I don't need anyone. And I sure as hell wouldn't
trust you if I did."

"No, you wouldn't, would you? That's why I moved
Maelea. You either take me with you or you can spend
the next two weeks searching for her in this mausoleum."

He moved back up to the terrace. "No, you didn't."

"Think again, daemon. Maelea knows the people
here don't really want her. She'd happily stay in a hole

in the ground if it meant she didn't have to face them. Trust me when I say she's locked up safe and sound in a portion of this castle with enough food and water to last her for several weeks at least."

There was just enough gloating in her eyes to make him wonder if she'd done exactly what she claimed. "Why, you little—"

A victorious grin cut across her perfect face. "Ah, now that's more like it. Have you noticed your eyes don't turn green anymore when you're mad?"

He'd have had more luck following her train of thought if she were speaking in a foreign language. All he knew was that she was fucking with his plans. Fucking with his head again too, standing there looking gorgeous and defiant and totally turned on by his temper.

He crossed the patio, stopped in front of her. Used his size and strength as intimidation factors. "Tell me where she is."

She pursed her lips. "Mm, I don't think so. Tell me you're going after your brother."

Maelea would be quaking in her shoes. But not Skyla. No, she liked confrontation. "Siren, I'm not in the mood for games."

"Oh, but you like games. That's why you've kept me around this long. That and the fact you couldn't hurt me if you tried. There's too much honor in you for that."

"There's no honor in me."

"Oh yes, daemon. There is. Way more than you think."

The last of his patience slipped away. The need to prove he was nothing but the monster that lived inside bubbled through his restraint.

He grasped her by the bicep, whipped her around so

her back was plastered to his chest, and held her immobile. She sucked in a surprised breath but didn't fight back. "We're done playing games," he breathed in her ear. "And your usefulness has run its course. If you don't want to get hurt, you'll tell me where Maelea is. And then you'll do as I said and leave this place for good."

Her body trembled against his, but he sensed it wasn't fear that sent that shiver down her spine. It was arousal. A twisted, wicked, steaming arousal that triggered his own depraved need. A need that locked on tight whenever she was near.

"Go on," she whispered, pressing that cute little ass of hers back into his groin. "Hurt me. I dare you."

Chapter 16

SKYLA SHOULD HAVE BEEN COLD. SHE'D BEEN UP ON this windy terrace for the last twenty minutes. But everything she'd learned tonight, coupled with what she'd already known, mixed together with the heat from the warrior at her back to fuel the fire in her veins.

She'd wanted him from the first. Before she'd known who he was. Before she'd realized their connection. Before she'd discovered his soul wasn't black, as she'd been led to believe.

She'd wanted him the moment she'd seen him in that crowd. Had been attracted to the danger. To the unpredictability. To the way he said *fuck you* to the world as if he lived life with no boundaries. Yes, there were moments when she glimpsed Cynurus in him, but the man he'd been before wasn't what called to her now. What called to her was the man he'd become, daemon and all. At some point over her long, carefully ordered years, she'd forgotten what it felt like to live. She'd forgotten what it felt like to want. He'd brought that back for her.

Orpheus.

Her heart skipped double time as she pressed her hips back against his groin again, teasing him with what she knew he'd been watching since they met. "Don't have it in you daemon? Don't tell me when it comes right down to it, you're all talk."

"You're trying to seduce me again, Siren. Comes

easy to you, especially when you're in a bind." His fingers grazed her breast. She drew in a breath as heat penetrated her skin. "But I've been teased enough. We both know you have no intention of following through."

This time she did, though. This time it wasn't about getting what Zeus wanted. It was about getting what she wanted. "Daemon—"

He grasped her shoulder and whipped her to face him. Before she caught her footing, he picked her up off the ground and tossed her over his shoulder.

She pressed her hands to the small of his back, tried to angle herself up. "Okay, put me down."

His boots clanked as he crossed the veranda. "You want down?"

He tossed her from his shoulder. Chilled air swept up her spine. A gasp caught in her throat as she felt herself falling. Darkness surrounded her, and for a second she wasn't sure he hadn't thrown her over the side of the railing.

Then her back hit something crunchy soft and icy cold, and she realized he'd dropped her on one of the chaise lounges left up here in the weather. The thin layer of frigid snow matted her hair, sent shivers down her spine. She tried to push herself up, but he straddled her body before she found her feet and grasped both of her hands, yanking them high above her head against the back of the chair, pinning her in place.

He leaned close, his hot breath washing over her ear to heat her chilled skin, his thighs brushing the outside of her hips to send quivers of delight straight to her center. "I think maybe it's time you took a turn on the other side. See what it's like to be the prey instead of the hunter."

Her blood heated at the image he painted, and any thought of fighting back quickly fled from her mind. "Planning on seducing me, daemon?"

His teeth closed over her earlobe. "And then leaving you hot and bothered."

Oh, *yesssss*.

His kissed the sensitive skin behind her ear, worked his way down her throat. Anticipation curled in her stomach. There was just enough mean in the way he nipped at her flesh to tell her he was good and truly pissed, but it didn't hurt. And if his plan was to get back at her, he was failing miserably. Because this was exactly what she wanted.

He captured both of her hands with one of his, slid the other down her torso to cup her breast. While his lips and teeth continued their assault on her throat, she arched her back, offering him whatever he wanted. His mouth stilled against her skin, his hand hesitated over her breast. Knowing she'd just surprised him, her lips curled in a self-satisfied smirk. Until, that is, he grasped her shirt at the neckline and yanked, ripping it in two all the way to her waist.

She gasped. Struggled beneath his hold. Icy air washed over her torso. In a move too quick to follow, he flicked the front clasp of her bra, freeing her breasts. Her nipples pebbled in the cool air and shivers raced over her flesh. "Orpheus…"

He let go of her bra, reached over the side of the chaise. When his hand came back she spotted the handful of snow and her eyes grew wide. "Orpheus—"

"Cold or turned on. Let's see which it is."

He balled the snow together. Her stomach caved in as he brought it toward her skin. Holding her breath, she flicked a look at his gray eyes and saw the flash of arousal hidden behind his wicked stare. No green. No daemon. Just an arousal that superheated her blood all over again.

She bit her lip and watched as he grazed the ball of snow against the underside of her breast, then slowly circled her nipple. Icy-cold sensations sent gooseflesh all over her body. The snow was so cold, pinpricks of pain stabbed her flesh but quickly melted against her warmth, creating a river of liquid that dripped off her naked breast to splash cool and wet against her belly.

"I think you like that, Siren."

She did. More than she would ever have expected. The circle grew smaller until the icy-cold wetness brushed across her nipple, sending shards of pleasure right to her core. She bit down harder on her lip to keep from moaning, dropped her head back against the chaise, and closed her eyes. Arched her back again. Offered even more.

He chuckled, moved the snowball to her other breast, repeated the circle, the tease, the wetness and heat. Caught between torment and ecstasy, Skyla lifted her hips and moaned when she felt his erection hovering just above her.

"Oh, no, no, no. You're not in charge of this, Siren."

He moved away. Let go of her hands. Fabric brushed her hip. Cool air washed over her thighs. She peered up to the twinkling sky above as he tugged her pants down her legs, exposing every last inch of her.

Yes.

She pushed up on her elbows, thankful her pants were stretchy so she could spread her thighs to make room for him. Moonlight washed over his thick hair and broad

shoulders. He was still wearing the thin jacket from before, was probably warm and snug in his clothes, while
she was out in the elements shivering, but she didn't
care. Because the desire rolling through his gaze was
enough to heat whatever chill the night brought with it.

"I never used ice on you," she pointed out.

"Are you cold? I figured for an ice princess like you,
this'd be nothing new."

A pinprick of hurt cut through her chest, but she
pushed it aside, because again he was right. She had been
an ice princess. For way too long. But that changed now.

He trailed the melting snow down her belly to the
top of her mound. She sucked in a breath when the ice
grazed the sensitive flesh between her legs. Frigid cold
water dripped down her overheated skin to pool beneath
her ass against the frozen cushion. And though she told
herself his twisted torture shouldn't be turning her on,
she knew it was. Cold and hot warred with pleasure and
torment as he ran the ice over her clit again and again
and jolts of electricity lit up her groin with a heat she
hadn't realized she'd been missing.

She dropped her head back and closed her eyes, this
time giving in to the sensations and moaning as she lifted
her hips. He kept up the assault on her clit with the ice,
but his warm fingers slid lower, against her quivering
flesh, then finally inside her where she wanted him most.

"Oh, *yesssss*." Her elbows went out from under her.
Her back landed against the now-damp cushion. She
groaned, turned herself over to him, all but begged for
more. He stroked her clit with the ice, searched deeper
with his fingers until all she wanted was more.

"Definitely enjoying." He withdrew, pressed back in

with a second finger. She gasped at the tight feel and pressed her hips against his strokes. At some point the ice must have melted because she felt his warm fingers against her clit, in stark contrast to the cold, but she was too gone to care how or with what he was touching her. The fiery edges of an orgasm she'd gone too long without hovered just beyond her reach.

Just before it crashed into her, he withdrew. Cool air washed over her skin again, and the cushion at her sides dipped. She opened her eyes, anticipating him climbing over her to take and taste, only when she looked up he was standing at her feet, staring down at her with a self-satisfied expression. One that reeked of victory and shone with distrust.

"You're good, Siren, but you're not that good." He tugged the jacket from his arms, tossed it to her. "Get your stuff together and meet me back in the great hall. And you'd better hope Ghoul Girl's exactly where she's supposed to be."

He made it two steps away before her iced-over brain clicked into gear and instinct took over where logic should reign.

She was on her feet in a flash, tugging her pants back up, her boots clicking on the cold stones beneath her heels as she threw his jacket on the ground. Her ripped shirt slapped open against her sides as she grabbed his arm, spun him back to face her. Surprise erupted in his gray eyes, followed by a shot of anger that tightened his face, but he didn't intimidate her. She'd seen enough from him over the last few days to know that even with his daemon, he had too much honor to hurt a female. Even one who'd been sent to kill him.

She stepped close before he could block her, twisted around so her back was to his front, held tight to his forearm, and shifted her center of gravity back, lifting him off the ground and tossing him over her shoulder to land on the chaise he'd just had her pinned to.

He landed with a grunt. The legs of the chaise snapped beneath his weight and a splintering sound echoed across the veranda.

She tugged off her ruined shirt, leaned over, and dropped it on his chest. "I am that good, daemon." She moved to the door and paused with her fingers on the handle, glanced back over her shoulder with her best *I dare you* look. "And you're wrong. This time I do intend to follow through. The question is whether or not you're man enough to deal with it."

The room was hexagonal. Four walls were solid— two on each end. The two long walls between were made only of glass, separated by thick, intricately carved wooden beams. A wide archway over each window rose to dramatic wooden trusses that lifted two stories to the roof's peak.

There was more patio furniture in here, stacked against the far-end walls and what looked like a door. Mismatched cabinets and wooden tables were piled against one glass wall. A blackened fireplace and empty bookshelves took up space on the other side of the room, and a series of boxes that weren't marked had been pushed up against the fireplace as if left there and forgotten.

"Follow-through, huh?" Orpheus's voice echoed from the doorway. Tingles of anticipation raced down her spine as she turned. He stood in the shadows, a menacing mixture of heat and the need she'd known would follow. "You wouldn't be playing me again, now would you, Siren?"

She rested her hands on her hips, stepped wider to form what she knew was a very attractive V with her lower body. The cool air tightened her nipples, the moonlight accentuated her curves. She cocked her head and pulled up her sexiest Cheshire Cat grin. "Me? I'm done playing. How about you, cowboy? You said when I was ready to ride to tell you. Well, I'm ready."

For a heartbeat neither of them moved, and then before she could gasp he was across the floor, tugging her tight against his rock-hard chest, drawing her mouth up to his, and claiming her lips as if they were his own.

Heat replaced chill. Need circumvented want. Electricity jolted through her entire body, forcing out common sense. She grasped his thin henley in both hands, slid her tongue into his mouth to tangle with his, used her grip to lever herself up when his hands rushed down to her ass and he lifted her.

"Orpheus—"

"Wrap your legs around me."

She did, hooked one arm around his shoulders, used the other to tug his face to hers and kiss him all over again. Her butt hit something cold. She didn't realize he'd carried her across the room until he dropped her on a desk pushed up against the glass wall.

Why hadn't she wanted to kiss him before? He tasted of mint and madness. Of desire and longing, all the things she knew she tasted of as well.

"Skin," she mouthed against him as she clawed at his shirt. He broke the kiss long enough to let her drag it over his head, then took her mouth again in another hot, wet, mind-numbing kiss that drove her closer to the edge.

Gods, this was heaven. This was home. This was everything she'd been missing.

She fumbled with the button on his jeans, finally gave up, grasped the two halves of his waistband, and pulled hard. The button popped and flew across the floor. He tore his mouth from hers and looked down, his bare chest rising and falling with his labored breaths, that scruff on his cheeks from days without shaving so damn sexy, it was all she could do not to take a bite out of him. "Impatient?"

"Yes." She pushed both hands inside his pants, slid them past his hips. "You. Naked. Now."

Desire darkened his eyes. He growled, then his mouth was back on hers, this time with frantic kisses stealing her breath while she shoved his pants and boxers down to his thighs. His cock sprang up, hard and hot and pulsing. She wrapped her hand around the thickness, smiled against his lips when he groaned and pressed himself into her hand.

She hadn't gotten to explore last time. She wanted that now. To find out for herself just what made him gasp. Which brush made him groan. How long it would take to make him come.

He fumbled with her pants again as she stroked him, pushing them down her hips. She lifted, wriggled so he could slide them down her ass. Grew frustrated when the fabric bunched against her boots.

He pulled his mouth from hers. "These have to go."

He grasped her pants at the waistband and ripped them right down the middle as if they were nothing but paper.

A surprised laugh fell from her lips. "Now who's impatient?"

"Me." He wrapped his hand over hers, still covering his cock, guided it close to rub the head against her clit. She shivered, gasped in pleasure. "Is this what you want?"

"Yes." She closed her eyes, let go with her hand to give him control. The head of his cock pressed against her opening, sending the first tendrils of pleasure pulsing through her core.

"Too bad, Siren." He pulled away. Her eyes flew open in surprise. He stepped back, grasped her body, and flipped her over onto her stomach. "Not what I want."

Her breasts smashed into the solid wood. Her boots grappled to find their footing on the floor. He kicked her legs wider and leaned over her, pressing his hips up against her ass. And then she felt his cock brushing her folds all over again.

"Now this…this is what I want." He thrust deep. She groaned at the hard length of him sliding into her. He dragged her back an inch as he withdrew. She dug her fingers into the edge of the table and groaned when he thrust again. Pleasure radiated outward from her center. He withdrew, drove deep again and again, jostling her against the table.

He brushed her hair over her shoulder as he continued to pound into her, leaned close to her ear. "This, Siren, is follow-through." His fingers grazed the Siren marking on her shoulder blade. "I like this tattoo."

She couldn't answer. Was too focused on his wild plunge and release and plunge again. Her orgasm barreled closer. She closed her eyes, pressed back against him. Groaned for more. And then she felt his fingers slide beneath her hips and brush her clit.

That was it. All she could take. The orgasm he'd teased and taunted exploded, radiated through every cell in her body. She cried out as it swept through her. But unlike the last time they'd been together, this time it was all pleasure. No heartache, no pain, no bitter memories of the past spiraling in to ruin the moment.

His thrusts increased in speed. As the edges of her orgasm faded, she heard him grunt, realized he was close. She looked back over her shoulder, tightened around his length, trembled when he grew twice as hard inside her. She wanted to feel him come. Wanted to watch as he lost control the way he had before. Only this time she planned to enjoy it. Every last second. "Mm, yes, Orpheus. Hard. Just like that."

"Tight. So tight." His fingers shifted to her hips, dug into her skin. She pushed back against him as he drove again and again. "Ah, fuck, Siren."

"Yes. That's exactly what you're doing. Mm…keep doing it. Don't be gentle with me. Make me come again."

Her words did exactly what she wanted. Made him harder, forced him deeper. On a long groan he shoved deep one last time and held still. His cock jerked and pulsed deep within her. His release triggered another in her, this one not quite as big as the last, but just as pleasurable. And so incredibly hot she knew she had to have it again.

He fell against her back and sucked in air. "Holy gods…"

A smile turned her lips. Not exactly. But she doubted a god could do it any better.

She pressed up on her hands, looked over her shoulder at his flushed face and tousled hair. Loved that she'd reduced him to a quivering mass of muscle and bone. "Follow-through?"

His heartbeat raced against her spine and his chest continued to rise and fall as if he was having trouble regulating his breathing. "Yeah, I guess that's what you call it."

"Not quite, daemon." She shifted her weight back against him, pushing him off her. He slid from her body, stumbled back a step. Looked down with surprise. She flipped over, wriggled off the table. Stood in front of him.

"Siren—"

His pants were still around his thighs, which was perfect. She ran her hands down his chiseled abs, taking a good hard look at his body in the moonlight shining through the windows.

Just as she'd imagined, he was all corded muscle and gathered strength, covered in smooth, tight, enticing skin shades darker than her own. Keeping her eyes locked on his, she slid to her knees.

His cock, which seconds before had been at half-mast, sprang up thick and engorged and big. Bigger than she'd expected. "Not fair, daemon. Are you trying to make my job easier?"

"One of the few benefits of being an Argonaut."

"Mm." She closed her fingers around his shaft, loving the pulse and life she felt in her palm, the soft flesh sliding over the rock-hard center as she stroked him from base to tip, the musky smell of both of their releases radiating from his skin. "I can think of a few more. Tell me what you want me to do."

"Skyla—"

Gods, she loved it when he said her name. "No more games, Orpheus. Not tonight. Tonight I just want you." She licked her lips. Watched as his eyes grew wide in anticipation. Her sex throbbed all over again as she leaned in and licked the very tip of his erection. "Should I stop or keep going?"

The doubt she'd seen in his eyes melted away. He grasped the back of her head and his fingers slid into her hair, tightened around the long locks. "No, don't stop. Don't you dare stop now."

She smiled. Trailed her tongue around the crown. "So what should I do instead?"

He tugged her head forward and a wicked grin turned his lips. "Why don't you start by sucking my cock?"

Oh, he was a naughty, naughty daemon. And she loved that about him.

She opened her mouth, closed her lips around his length. Drew him all the way to the back of her throat. Grew hot and achy and wet all over again when he hardened against her tongue.

Follow-through had its benefits too. And before this night was over, she planned to prove to him just what those were. Every single one.

Even if doing so left her wondering…where the hell she now fit in the world.

—◆◆◆—

Gryphon wasn't sure what Atalanta could want with Krónos, but just being in the Elder God's lair left a sick and horrific feeling in the pit of his stomach.

"Don't fidget, *doulas*." Atalanta sent him a hard look as they waited outside Krónos's private quarters.

Gryphon turned away from the fifteen-foot-high black iron doors to look at the wallpaper in the sitting area, patterned in swirls that looked like droplets of blood, and the naked pictures of bodies entwined hanging on every wall. He tried to ignore the horrifying moans coming from the other side of that door, but he couldn't ignore them completely. Dread coursed through his veins.

To distract himself, he stared at the drawings. Found one he could focus on without being sick. The image of two bodies locked in a heated kiss. As he studied the lines and swirls, he scratched at his thigh, tried to ease the tightness of the leathers Atalanta made him wear. This image—unlike all the others—wasn't pornographic in nature. It could be any two lovers anywhere in the world. It might have even been him once.

Had he had a lover like that? Did he know what it was to be connected to someone on such a primal level? Not sex for sex's sake but the joining of hearts? He searched his feelings, tried to find any ghost of a memory that told him he'd once been loved, that he'd experienced what he was seeing in the picture, but came up empty.

Maybe he hadn't deserved it. Maybe he'd been so awful in the living realm this was as much as he could hope for. Maybe this new hell was more than he deserved.

He waited for a voice—any voice—to tell him he was wrong, but there was none. Only the echoing moans from the other side of that door.

"Doulas? It's time."

The double doors opened, and he followed Atalanta into an ornate room. Leather couches, arching windows that looked out over Sin City, Grecian pillars, and richly colored rugs. A wall of books covered one whole side of the two-story room, but what captured his attention was the man—no, god—standing to the right. Unhooking a female from a metal contraption mounted into the cement wall with hooks and chains and restraints.

The female's nakedness was quickly covered with a blanket, but Gryphon didn't miss the lines of blood running down her skin or the whip that lay on the floor at Krónos's feet. As two servants escorted the weeping female through a door to the right, Krónos dried his hands on a towel and turned to greet Atalanta.

"Well, well, well. I heard a rumor the wicked witch of the west was back in the Underworld. I just never expected to see her with my own eyes."

The Elder God wasn't what Gryphon had pictured. Sure, he was tall—over seven feet at least—but he didn't look a day over forty. His hair was short and dark, with only a smattering of gray at the temples. His body was strong and lean, covered in jeans and a short-sleeved button-down. He was muscular as most gods were, but it didn't seem he could smite one with a look. There was no indication he could overthrow the world if he escaped from this prison. If anything, he looked like a normal, albeit tall, human.

Atalanta, dressed in her curve-hugging, cleavage-baring emerald gown, smiled and pursed her plump, fiery red lips. "When I heard what you'd done with the place, I just had to see it for myself."

"You lie so well, Atalanta. It's obvious you've honed those god qualities you wrangled from my son. Do you like what you've seen so far?"

She slanted a look toward the door the girl had been taken through, excitement lighting her dark eyes. "So far, I do."

Krónos leaned a hip against a long mahogany desk set near the windows. "No wonder Hades was tempted by you. Now why have you disturbed me during my...playtime?"

She slinked toward him, ran her fingertip down his shoulder to stop at his bicep. "I've come to make you an offer."

"There's not much you can offer me that I don't already have. Look around you."

"How about freedom?"

When he didn't answer, she turned back to Gryphon, where he still stood near the doors. "Do you see my *doulas* over there? He's not just man candy. He's an Argonaut."

Argonaut. The word revolved in Gryphon's mind but meant nothing to him.

Krónos slanted him a look. "I'd not heard an Argonaut had been killed and banished to Tartarus."

"He wasn't killed. He was sent here by magic. His body remains in the human realm, where a warlock possesses it. But the soul and body could be easily reunited if one wished it."

"A warlock, you say?"

"Mm-hmm." She moved closer to the Elder God, rubbing her breast against his arm in a move Gryphon knew was as calculated as this meeting. "They'll come for him, Krónos. I guarantee they're hatching a plan as we speak. You know how loyal and heroic those Argonauts can be."

Krónos studied Gryphon a long beat, then looked back to Atalanta. "What does this have to do with me?"

"I want you to gift him the darkness of the Underworld."

Gryphon tensed near the door. He didn't know what that meant, but it couldn't be good. And he didn't want anyone to rescue him. He remembered the torture he'd endured in Tartarus. Sin City, as gruesome as it could be, was a thousand times better than what lay beyond its gates.

"You want me to make him a god?"

"No." Atalanta laughed, running her fingers up Krónos's chest. "I want you to give him just enough darkness so he belongs to me."

Krónos tipped his chin down. "Why?"

Her voice hardened. "Because the Argonauts stole from me what was rightfully mine. And because with him, I'll have a better chance of finding the Orb. Your Orb. And then I'll be able to release you from this prison your sons locked you into." She leaned into him and whispered, "Imagine being free of this city. Of this realm. Imagine the two of us, ruling the world."

He stopped her from kissing him with two hands on her arms. "Why do I need you?"

"Because I can leave the Underworld anytime I want. You can't."

He studied her so long Gryphon wasn't sure if the Elder God was going to kiss her or tear her limb from limb. And the word *Argonaut* kept spinning in his head. Something about it struck him as familiar, but he couldn't remember why.

"How do I know you won't fuck me when you're free?" Krónos asked.

A licentious grin curled her mouth. "I never said I wouldn't fuck you."

"Answer the question, Atalanta."

"You don't," she said, sobering. "You'll just have to trust me."

"I learned not to trust a long time ago." He let go of her, leaned back. "However, I am willing to make you a deal."

"What kind of deal?"

He nodded toward Gryphon. "I'll gift your *doulas* there with what you ask and give you six months to find the Orb and all the elements so you can free me from Tartarus. If you don't, I'll drag that sonofabitch back here and I'll program that darkness inside him to drag your ass back as well. And that girl you saw in here earlier?" He leaned close. "If you don't get me the fuck out of here, you'll be her."

Atalanta's face blanched. "Six months isn't long enough to—"

"Tantalus, come in here," Krónos called.

A male dressed all in white with scars running down both cheeks emerged from the door to the right. "Yes, my king?"

"Bring me my glass."

The male disappeared, then reemerged with a flat object covered with a velvet cloth. He handed the object to Krónos, bowed, and retreated through the door.

Atalanta watched with wide eyes as Krónos removed the cloth and tossed it on the desk behind him. "You have a looking glass?"

"All the better to see you with, my dear." He waved his hand over the glass. "Show me my heart's desire."

Atalanta looked down at the glass and gasped. Her gaze shot toward Gryphon, then back to the glass again. "How…? I thought—"

"I had a feeling our warlock was one and the same." He set the glass on the table behind him. "Six months. You can either take the deal, or we can strap you to the wall now."

She shot a look at the shackles and chains mounted behind him. And for a minute, Gryphon's chest warmed at the idea of Atalanta bound to that wall. Then the warmth dimmed, because he knew if she was strapped up there, he would be too.

Take the deal, take the deal, take the deal…

He didn't know what the deal really was, but something inside told him it was infinitely better than letting Krónos have his way with them.

Atalanta held her hand out to the Elder God. "I accept."

Krónos's lips curled in a malicious grin. He closed his hand around Atalanta's and dragged her close, trapping her between his legs. As she sucked in a surprised breath, he looked over her shoulder to where Gryphon stood, hoping—praying—to be sent from the room.

"Tell your slave to get his ass over here," Krónos said in a low voice, his soulless eyes fixed on Gryphon. "We're going to have a little fun, just the three of us, to seal the deal before I tether you together."

Chapter 17

ORPHEUS DIDN'T DARE MOVE.

His heart beat like wildfire against his ribs as Skyla lay draped over him, her face pressed into his shoulder, her warm breath fanning his neck while she worked to slow her pulse.

Somehow they'd made it to the floor. One of them—he wasn't sure who—had had the good sense to throw cushions down so they weren't sprawled on the hardwood. But another round of mind-blowing sex and his third—fourth?—screaming orgasm weren't what kept him still. No, what kept him from moving a single muscle were the images flickering through his mind like some old-time movie set on fast-forward, with Skyla's face as the constant. The ones that had started just as he'd climaxed the last time and were still flashing for his eyes only in both black-and-white and color like a collage set to silence.

Her, smiling. Dressed in a white gown, her hair piled in braids on the top of her head. Standing on a balcony with a blue-green sea behind her. Wearing her Siren fighting gear. In a courtyard, talking with people he didn't recognize dressed in what looked like sheets. With the other Sirens in a field of green. Lying naked on a bed of blue silk. Looking sated and sexy and completely worn-out.

Holy *skata*. He was seriously losing it. Like

certifiable, strap-me-in-a-padded-cell, fast-track-to-the-loony-bin losing it. He shut his eyes, gave his head a swift shake, opened them again. The images were still there, though if anything playing faster now.

Skyla drew in a deep breath, let it out slowly, relaxed everywhere against him. "I hope that was enough follow-through for you, because I'm officially beat. I think you broke me."

He'd have laughed if he wasn't already freaking the hell out. And shit, she was making herself comfortable, which meant she wanted to snuggle. When all he wanted to do was beat feet for the door and get away from her. Panic clawed its way up his chest, but he worked to keep from hyperventilating so she wouldn't know he was wigging out. "Good to know."

She chuckled, burrowed in deeper. Gods, she had to feel his racing pulse. She probably thought he was still jacked up from the sex, which he was, but shit…what the hell was with the images? Now she was naked, swimming in the ocean? Okay, this twisted fantasy shit had to end here.

He squeezed his eyes together tight, willed his brain to stop dicking around. "Why wouldn't Athena answer you?"

"What?" The surprise in her voice wasn't the least bit sexy, and that's what he needed. To get the topic away from earth-shattering orgasms so he could get his mind off naked skin browning in the sun.

"Athena. You said the goddess wouldn't answer you. Why not?"

"Oh." She shifted off him, just enough so her hip was against the cushion but her arms and legs were still draped across him. He'd never been claustrophobic before, but right now he felt like he couldn't breathe. There was so much pressure in his chest. Fresh air would be good. A lot of it.

"I suppose it's because she doesn't expect me to complete this mission."

"And why not?"

She pushed up on her elbow. "Are you okay? You seem, I don't know, tense. I thought sex was supposed to relax a man."

"I'm not a man, Siren." But because he caught the slightest bit of hurt in her eyes at his terse voice, he worked to keep the bite from his words when he added, "I don't ever really relax. Curse of the daemon inside me and all that. Answer the question. Why wouldn't she think you'd complete this mission?"

She blew out a long breath, played with the thin patch of hair on his chest. "A few weeks ago I was injured in a fight. With a daemon hybrid. He got the jump on me. I was careless. If it hadn't been for my sisters, I probably wouldn't have survived."

The images came to a stop, the last one fading in a poof of smoke. "Where?"

"Where what?"

"Where were you injured?"

"Italy."

"Not *where*, idiot. Where?"

"Oh, here." She smiled as she turned so he could see the long scar that ran from just under her right breast, diagonally across her ribs, and around her hip to the small of her back.

"Holy shit." He'd felt the puckered skin when he'd been exploring her body, but in the shadows, with her twisting all different ways, it had been hard to see. Carefully, he ran his fingers over the scar and examined it in the moonlight. "This was only a few weeks ago?"

"Yeah. Luckily, we Sirens heal fast too. It'll be just a thin white line soon." She eased back down next to him, grazed her fingers over his chest hair again. Sent shards of heat through his torso. "Anyway, I convinced Athena to let me come on this mission. She wanted me to stay behind. Didn't think I was ready."

He thought back to that first night. In the trees behind the amphitheater. The quick flash of fear in her eyes when she'd seen those hybrids change. The one she'd masked quickly and probably wouldn't ever cop to. "And that's why she won't answer you? Because she thinks you're weak?"

"Not just that." He could sense from her words and what she wasn't saying that there was more. He waited, though he wanted to shake the answers out of her more than he liked. "I've been with the Sirens a long time. And when I took my vows, I thought I was doing something good, you know? Helping Zeus keep balance and order in the universe. Over the years, though…well, let's just say that recently I've seen the world from a different perspective. And I'm realizing that what Zeus and Athena have led me and the other Sirens to believe all these years isn't the entire truth."

Orpheus could have told her that. His first reaction was to ask why she hadn't figured it out sooner, but then he thought about what her life as a Siren must be like. Living on Olympus, surrounded by gods, separated from the living realm, and only going there to do Zeus's bidding. If you're taught one thing and are never shown anything different, it would make sense you'd see that as truth, wouldn't it?

"How long have you been with the Sirens?"

She didn't answer.

"Skyla?"

"A long time," she finally answered. "A lot longer than the rest. I, uh, met your forefather."

"Perseus?" He stared at her for confirmation, barely believed what she'd just said could be true. She continued to play with the hair on his chest and wouldn't meet his eyes. "Are you telling me you're over two thousand years old?"

She cringed. "Two thousand six hundred and four, actually."

No way.

Her eyes slowly shifted to his. "Surprised?"

Floored. And he'd thought he was old. Shit, he was a baby compared to her. "Are all the Sirens—?"

"No. Most serve only a few hundred years. That's the goal, anyway. My mother was a Siren. Zeus tends to recruit from past Sirens he deems worthy. Good genes, you know." She smiled, but he was still too shocked to smile back. "I was two when I started my home training. At the age of twenty I took my vows, was inducted into the order. I moved to Olympus, spent the next few decades mastering my skills, but didn't begin formally serving with the Sirens until I was about forty. It's common for a Siren to give three, four hundred years to the order, then leave to marry and raise a family. From that point they're usually granted a blessed life, much like the Argoleans, if they so choose."

"But you never left. Why?" He couldn't imagine dedicating his life to anyone. Hell, he'd spent his three hundred years being pissed the gods had overlooked him to serve with the Argonauts even though he was the eldest from Perseus's line, but now that he had the markings, he didn't want to be tied to them. Certainly couldn't see giving twenty-five hundred years to them, even if he could.

She shrugged. Slid her fingers down to his sternum. "Just never had a reason to."

Again, he sensed there was more she wasn't saying. And the hurt he saw flash over her features before she masked the emotion told him loud and clear something dark in her past was the reason she'd stayed hidden behind the order and hadn't ventured out to truly live.

Who was he to judge her, though? Wasn't he doing the same thing? Using his daemon as a reason to remain closed off from others, to keep from finding some sort of happiness in this life? He knew it existed. Hell, if someone could love Demetrius, then anything was possible.

His pulse picked up speed and his skin grew hot again. Only this time it wasn't panic or even desire warming him from the inside out. It was something else. Something that filled the empty place in his chest he'd lived with since the day Gryphon was lost. Something he wasn't sure he was ready to face.

"I wasn't going to tell Athena where we are or where we're heading next," she said, her sexy voice cutting through his thoughts. "I was just trying to check in so she doesn't send more Sirens after us."

"Why?"

This time, she met his stare head-on. No fear, no worry, only determination shone in her amethyst eyes. "Because she sent me to do a job, and I'm doing it."

He knew that answer could be taken in a variety of ways. She hadn't said she was going to turn him in, but she hadn't said she wouldn't either. Or that she wouldn't eventually kill him if she decided that's what needed to be done.

She yawned, snuggled back into him. "Give Maelea an hour or two to sleep, then we'll go ask her where it is. She looked exhausted when I left her. She's growing on me, daemon. In a petulant, irritating, teenager sort of way. The more I'm around her, the more I sort of like her."

Her eyes slid closed, her face relaxed. Maelea wasn't the only one who was exhausted, he realized. His Siren looked as though she could sleep for a week.

His. It was the first time he'd thought of her as his. She wasn't, though. Never would be. They were on opposite sides of a war that was only just beginning. And this moment of truce didn't do anything but reinforce that fact.

His chest ached at that realization, and as she drifted off to sleep in his arms that place inside that had seemed so full only moments before deflated, leaking out all the warmth right along with it. He lay still, tried to regulate his pulse so it would drop out of the stratosphere and he could think straight. Tried to figure out what the hell he needed to do next.

And knew only one thing for sure.

Skyla was not his goal. The Orb was. Everything hinged on that. And it was time he remembered that fact.

Orpheus's boots echoed through the dark corridor as he moved down the hallway toward the room Maelea had been given. He hoped like hell Ghoul Girl was in there and that the Siren had been lying when she'd said she'd hidden her away. He didn't have time to play hide-and-seek, and he definitely wasn't in the mood.

Thoughts of Skyla lying naked in the moonlight, hair fanned out around her, eyes closed in sleep, filtered through his mind, but he pushed them to the side. Walking away from her tonight was the first smart thing he'd done since he'd met her. He was done being a schmuck. No matter how great sex was with her, no matter how much he wanted to go back to her and do it all again, it wasn't worth compromising his goals. Those images of her that had been rolling through his head when he'd climaxed? Those thoughts of her being *his*? Those were prime examples of how twisted his brain was becoming with every minute they spent together.

He sensed Maelea from the hallway outside her room even before he came to her door. The same light and dark warred inside her that he'd noticed the first night, but the light didn't repel his daemon now as it had then. He felt the daemon move inside him, but the beast didn't come screaming to the forefront like usual. Didn't make any attempt to do anything but lie down and sleep, which was just plain weird.

He didn't have a clue what was happening to him, but he knew Skyla was right. His eyes hadn't once shifted green since they'd taken down those hellhounds after the train wreck. And though he knew his daemon was still in there somewhere, calling on its strength was becoming harder and harder to do.

He glanced at his watch. Two thirty-two a.m. Ghoul Girl was probably asleep, but he needed what was in her brain. And if he didn't get it now, he'd have to deal with the Siren.

And he was done dealing with the Siren. Way done.

He lifted his fist, knocked. Seconds passed in silence, then a small voice said, "Come in."

The room was dark, but through the moonlight shining in from the tall windows he could see Maelea sitting cross-legged on the bed, a white billowy nightgown fanning out around her, her long black hair falling past her shoulders like ribbons of silk. No surprise registered on her ashen face when he stepped into the room, and he figured that made sense. She was the daughter of Zeus and Persephone. If he could sense her, she could probably sense him as well.

He closed the door at his back. "Not tired?"

"I don't sleep much."

That made two of them.

He scrubbed a hand over his head. Tried to forget Skyla's fingers skimming through the hair at his nape when he'd kissed her after the train derailment and the electrical charge that had sent through his body. "I came to talk to you about—"

"Is it true?"

"What?"

"About your brother? Is it true he was sent to the Underworld and that you seek the Orb to save him?"

Isadora, damn it. He loathed the way the queen kept sticking her nose where it didn't belong.

"It is, isn't it?" Maelea persisted when he didn't respond. "You need the Orb to rescue him."

He hated the fact that everyone seemed to know his plans before he'd even solidified them. Why did they think he was anything but the seething daemon inside him? Isadora, Skyla, now Maelea. They all thought he was some kind of heroic Argonaut when the truth was, inside he was the same as he'd always been.

He perched his hands on his hips, shot her his most wicked glare. But he could tell from the expectant look on her face that she wasn't the least bit intimidated by him anymore. Which only pissed him off more.

"Where is it?" He locked his jaw. His fists itched to hit something. But for Ghoul Girl, because he needed her help, he killed the urge so as not to scare her.

She looked down at her dainty hands, resting in her lap. "The darkness is leaving you. At first I thought you were the one I was supposed to…" Her voice trailed off and she swallowed. "But I realized pretty quickly that you weren't him. It'll be gone soon. Does it leave you feeling empty?"

He had no idea what she was talking about, but the lack of animosity in her voice was new. And unsettling. "How do you—?"

"I sense darkness. I'm attracted to it. Something I can thank my mother and her wretched husband for, I guess." She twisted her hands in her lap. "I wish mine would go away. I'd relish the emptiness."

The anger left him as swiftly as it had hit. And in the silence he realized, yeah, they were more alike than she knew.

That emptiness in his chest that had consumed him the instant Gryphon's soul was lost opened up like a chasm between worlds, the pain as stark and fresh as the minute it had hit. Before he thought better of it, he crossed to the bed. She looked up in surprise when he reached for her hand, pushed the sleeve of her gown up, and turned her wrist over, revealing the thin white scars all over her inner forearms. "Something tells me you can't handle any more emptiness."

She jerked her arm back, cradled it against her body, and glared at him. "What do you know?"

A lot, female. More than I should.

He sank onto the side of the bed, leaned forward to brace his arms on his knees. Three hundred years wandering this world and the next alone, and the one person he understood more than any other was the forgotten ghoul-like soul who'd been trapped between worlds. Trapped just like him, only in a different way.

Gods, life was one big fucking ironic twist of fate, wasn't it?

"I know pain reminds you that you're alive," he said, surprised his voice didn't catch in his throat. "Trust me, I'm not judging you. I've caused enough pain—mostly to others—for the very same reason. But scars aren't always on the outside."

She was silent beside him. He turned to look at her. Saw the way she was watching him with wary eyes. Recognized it was the same way he regarded others. Yeah, they were the same. And because of that, she of all people would be the one to understand. If he was going to find the Orb, he had to take a chance.

"Being alone isn't the worst thing that can happen to a person, Maelea. Yeah, loneliness sucks, but it won't kill you. But being forgotten…" He looked down at his forearms and the Argonaut markings that should be on his brother's arms, not his. "That's the death sentence, isn't it? My brother's soul was sent to Tartarus because of me. I'm not going to let him be forgotten. Not when I can do something to save him."

They stared at each other long seconds, and that emptiness in his chest grew because he sensed even though he'd gone out on a limb here, she wasn't going to help him. If she didn't tell him where to find the Orb, he didn't know where he'd go next.

"I didn't intend to bring you here," he said, hoping to make her understand. "I just needed to know where the Orb is. When those hellhounds showed up at your house, I knew you wouldn't be safe there anymore. That's why I brought you here. Not because I wanted to hurt you. No one can find you unless you let them. Not Hades, not Zeus, not any of the gods."

"Do you think his soul can really be saved?" she asked in a quiet voice. "You and I both know what the darkness can do. What if you find him, only he's not the brother you remember?"

That emptiness opened so wide that for a second Orpheus feared it would swallow him whole. He'd already thought of that but dismissed it. His brother was the real hero, not him. It had only been three months. Gryphon was strong enough to survive in the Underworld for three months. He had to be.

"True heroism can't be turned. Not by any darkness."

"I hope you remember that."

His brow lowered. She looked back down at her hands and took a deep breath before he could ask what that meant. "The warlock is in Greece. Gathering witches to bring into his fold. He channeled the power of the Orb in an induction ceremony. I felt it as late as yesterday. I'm not sure what he has planned, but from what I know about warlocks, they draw strength from—"

"From the witches they suck into their coven." Orpheus pushed off the bed. Of course, it made sense. Apophis needed new witches to regain his strength. Which meant right now he would be at his weakest, before he'd had time to train and mold and draw from their growing powers. "Where in Greece?"

"In the hills outside the city of Corinth." She rattled off coordinates.

Excitement and the first inkling of hope filtered through his chest. "Corinth was where Medea fled after she killed Jason's children. It makes sense the warlock would go there in the hopes of harnessing that evil energy. Thank you."

"Orpheus. Wait."

With one hand on the doorknob, he paused. She climbed off the massive bed, a slight, frail creature who seemed nothing like her mother or father. But he sensed there was strength in her yet untapped. And he wondered when she'd see it for herself.

She crossed to the bureau, pulled open the top drawer. She extracted the skirt she'd worn earlier and reached into the pocket. Then she crossed to stand in front of him and held out her open palm. "You might need these."

Two golden coins lay cradled in her palm. "Oboloi. How do you—?"

"My mother. Just in case Hades ever tried to pull me down to Tartarus. Take them. You'll need them to get past Charon."

The ferryman who carried souls across the River Styx to the Fields of Asphodel, where they would await

judgment. Yeah, he would need them if he had any chance
of getting past the first obstacle in the Underworld.
Surprise mixed with gratitude. He took the coins, slid
them into his pocket. "I can't thank you enough."

"Prove me wrong. Knowing a soul can survive the
darkness of the Underworld will be thanks enough."

"I won't forget you," he said as he left the room.

"Then you'd be the first," she whispered.

Chapter 18

ISADORA COVERED HER MOUTH AND YAWNED AS SHE approached the bedroom Nick had directed her toward. She and the others had stayed up late into the night discussing not only Orpheus and this situation with the Sirens, but war strategy with Nick and what the Argonauts could do for the colony now that it had been relocated here to Montana. Atalanta's daemons had recently struck a village high in the Rockies—both human and Misos residents decimated—and there were increasing reports all over the Pacific Northwest about strange killings and even stranger creature sightings. The Argonauts, along with Nick and his men, were trying to track down what daemons they could and destroy them before more lives were lost. And they all agreed they needed to get a handle on the violence before a new otherworldly power decided to take advantage of Atalanta's absence and make the daemons their own. Or before Atalanta returned herself.

That last thought was foremost in Isadora's mind. She didn't for a second doubt that Atalanta was plotting her way out of the Underworld right this minute.

"You shouldn't be up this late."

Demetrius's concerned voice cut through Isadora's thoughts and she smiled at her mate as he pushed the bedroom door open and let her pass, careful, she noticed, not to touch her. He was always careful not to touch her. At least when others could see. "I'm fine. Besides, you know as well as I do that Nick won't come to Argolea. That means I have to catch him when I can. And at least tonight he seemed agreeable."

Most days he wasn't. Though she and Nick had formed an alliance and were sharing their knowledge and manpower in this fight, she knew how hard it was for Nick to be around her. Especially when Demetrius was in the room.

"He can't stand to see us together," Demetrius said at her back, closing the door behind them. "I know how he feels and I can't blame him. Sometimes I wonder if you'd be better off with—"

"Don't say it." She turned to face him, knowing this fear came from the very bottom of his soul. The soul he still didn't think would ever be good enough for her, even after she'd bound her life to his. "Don't even think it. He is not the one I want, Demetrius. He's not the *ándras* I'm in love with. He's not the one—"

His hand captured hers. He yanked her close, cutting off her words. She bumped into his solid chest, then groaned when he lowered his mouth and kissed her in that way that made her toes curl against the carpet.

Touching him was always like this. Electric. Exhilarating. Explosive. Like the very first time they'd kissed on the island where Atalanta had trapped them. If the goddess had planned to use Hera's soul-mate curse to her advantage, she'd failed. Because their connection wasn't a curse at all. It was the best part of her life.

His big, strong hands framed her face. He coaxed her lips apart with his tongue, slid into her mouth when she opened for him. He tasted like the coffee they'd had earlier and the sin she wanted to experience now. He changed the angle of the kiss, took her deeper, drew her so close he was all she could feel and see and know.

She was breathless and aching with need when he eased back. His eyes, those dark pools of obsidian, tugged at her soul. "Gods, *kardia*. I hate what Nick's going through, but I can't let you go. Not even for him. And I've wanted to kiss you like this all day."

Her fingers tangled tight in the fabric of his shirt. He was so big—everywhere. All solid muscle and brawny sinew. She loved that about him. Loved that his size— which had once scared her to death—was such a huge turn-on now. "You'd better never let me go. And for the record, Argonaut, I've wished you'd kiss me like this all day."

He pressed his lips to her temple, trailed hot kisses across to her ear that curled her stomach. "You know why I can't. Because as soon as I touch you I just can't stop."

He captured her mouth again. Kissed her long and slow and so completely, she melted. She felt his arms encircle her, felt her feet lift from the floor. Knew he was carrying her to that big bed but couldn't think of anything except getting him naked and taking him deep into her body, right where she wanted him most.

He laid her out on the bed, nudged her knees apart, and climbed over her. "Ah, *kardia*. You drive me absolutely insane, you know that?"

She smiled, traced the line of his thick dark eyebrows. "Nice to know I still hold sway over you, Guardian."

"You always will." He turned his lips into her palm, kissed her softly. "I—"

A knock sounded at the door.

She captured his jaw and drew him back to her. "Ignore it."

His lips found hers again and he flicked the button on her slacks, had both hands inside her pants and was pushing them down her hips when the knock sounded again.

"I know you're both in there," a voice called. A familiar voice. "I can hear you getting all hot and bothered. Keep your panties on for a few more minutes, Isadora. I need to talk to you."

Demetrius broke the kiss again and growled, "Orpheus. He's got the worst damn timing."

Isadora sighed, not about to argue with her mate. But she did need to talk to Orpheus and knowing the *ándras*, if he was awake now, at three a.m., there was no telling if he'd still be here in the morning.

She kissed Demetrius one last time and pushed against his shoulder. He rolled off her. "Time-out. Let's give him a few minutes. We can pick up where we left off once he's gone."

Demetrius didn't look so sure as she stood and buttoned her pants. But she smiled because she very definitely planned to continue to prove to him he was the one she wanted—the only one she wanted—as soon as Orpheus was gone.

She smoothed out her blouse and hair and crossed to the door. When she opened it, Orpheus had one hand braced high on the doorframe and looked anything but pleased that he'd had to wait. "You missed a button."

Isadora glanced down, realized her breasts were nearly hanging out. She didn't even remember Demetrius undoing her blouse. Cheeks heating, she quickly covered herself as Orpheus stalked past her into the room as if he owned it.

Demetrius pushed up on his elbows. "Your timing sucks, O."

"It always has," Orpheus answered. He turned to Isadora. "I need to ask a favor. And don't go falling over from shock, but I figure since you've asked me for a hell of enough favors over the last year, you can give me one without question."

Isadora had, but that didn't mean she was going blindly into any "favor" with Orpheus. "What do you need?"

"Your mate."

Demetrius's brow lifted. "What for?"

As Isadora came around to stand at Demetrius's side, Orpheus said, "I've located the warlock. Since I can't be in two places at once, I need your help keeping him immobilized until I get back."

"Back from where?" Demetrius asked.

"The Underworld."

"You're going after Gryphon," Isadora breathed, relief flooding her veins as she pressed a hand against her throat. "We can get the other Argonauts to help you. It—"

"No," Orpheus said in a hard tone. "No one else. I don't want them there."

"But—"

"No one else," he said in a louder voice, cutting her off. Then to Demetrius, "Just you. You owe me too."

Regardless of the fact Demetrius did owe Orpheus for saving her life—they both did—Isadora knew her mate would agree because he wanted Gryphon back as much as Orpheus did. All the Argonauts did, but Demetrius especially. He partly blamed himself for what had happened to Gryphon in that warlock's chamber at Thrace Castle.

Demetrius pushed off the mattress. "When?"

"Now," Orpheus answered. "He's in Corinth." He gave Demetrius the coordinates. "You can meet me there?"

Orpheus could flash on earth. It was one of his gifts. But Demetrius couldn't. Which meant he'd have to open a portal back to Argolea, then another to Corinth.

Demetrius reached for his coat from the chair where he'd thrown it when he and Isadora had stepped into the room. "Are you sure he'll still be there by the time we arrive?"

Orpheus's eyes darkened. "He'll still be there. He's gathered a new horde of witches and is knee-deep in training."

"Wonderful," Demetrius answered. "You sure you don't want the other guys to tag along on this? Remember the last time we tangled with Apophis's witches?"

"These ones won't be anywhere near as strong. And Apophis will be weak right now. You're the only one I need."

"Think again, daemon."

Skyla stood in the doorway wearing a white long-sleeved button-down cinched at the waist, with a dark belt and a pair of pants that looked three sizes too big. Her hair was tousled, eyes shadowed from lack of sleep, and the intensity in her gaze told everyone in the room she wouldn't be forgotten.

Or left behind.

Isadora watched Orpheus's scruffy jaw tighten and a scowl creep over his features. Her first impression in the great hall had been right. There was definitely something going on between him and the Siren. Something that went well beyond predator-prey and hinted of involvement.

She'd asked herself several times why Orpheus hadn't eliminated this Siren right from the start. Sure, she was every male's wet dream, built and beautiful, but Orpheus wasn't one to be easily swayed from his goal. Isadora knew that better than anyone. And she'd had her first inkling of an answer when she'd seen the Siren's reaction to the news that Orpheus's brother was trapped in the Underworld. Now she knew for certain there was some kind of connection between these two. His look didn't say *You can't tag along because I want to kill you* but looked more like *I don't want you around because you could get hurt.*

And Isadora couldn't help it. She grinned. Oh, these stupid males and their twisted sense of heroics. Demetrius had tried that protective bologna on her and look how well that had kept her away. Judging from the headstrong Siren blocking the doorway, there was no way Orpheus was getting out of here without her.

And knowing that, Isadora's estimation of the Siren went way, way up.

"Go back to bed, Siren," he growled.

"I would," she tossed back, "but it was suddenly too cold for my liking. Lucky for me I found these clothes in a box up there. What do you think?"

Demetrius and Isadora exchanged glances, and from her soul mate's *what the hell?* expression she knew he was noticing their connection too.

"I couldn't care less about what you wear," Orpheus ground out, "and I don't need or want you or your help."

Skyla didn't answer. Only smiled sweetly, which,

Isadora guessed from Orpheus's locked-jaw reaction, was way out of character for her.

Orpheus looked at Demetrius. "Are you ready or what?"

"Ask him if Maelea told him where the entrance to Underworld is located," Skyla said to Isadora.

"Fuck," Orpheus muttered.

Skyla grinned wider. "No thanks, daemon. Not right now. Maybe later, though."

To Isadora, Orpheus said, "Go get Maelea for me, would you?"

"I wouldn't bother," Skyla said. "She doesn't know where the entrance is. And this time I'm not lying. Persephone purposely hasn't told her for safety reasons. It's common knowledge if she crosses into the Underworld to see her mother, Hades has the right to strike her down. On earth she's safe."

Orpheus's shoulders tightened but he didn't look away from Isadora. "Who else do we know who might know how to get to the Underworld?"

"No one," Isadora answered, not sure she wanted to be stuck in the middle of this. "I mean, I've heard rumors of the Bermuda Triangle, but—"

"Good luck finding that," Skyla muttered. "How long are you willing to search, daemon? It could take days, weeks, months even. Think he's got months left in him?"

She was talking about Gryphon, and from the fury in Orpheus's eyes it was clear he didn't like her bullying her way in. Skyla didn't look the least intimidated by him, though. The tension in the room kicked the temperature up a good three degrees.

"You're not going," Orpheus said. "You'll slow me down. I don't have time to hop a plane."

"You don't have to. Unlike Maelea or your Argonauts, Sirens can flash on earth, just like you. Though I'm definitely jealous of the flashing-through-walls thing." She grinned. "Get used to the fact I'm going with you, daemon. It's called follow-through. You taught me all about follow-through."

"Motherfucking sonofabitch," Orpheus muttered as he headed for the door.

Skyla shot Isadora another grin and then followed.

As boots echoed across the gleaming hardwood, Demetrius reached for Isadora's hand. "*Kardia*—"

"Don't worry." She squeezed his fingers, loving that he reached for her even though the others were technically still in the room. Maybe there was hope he would slowly come around after all. Maybe it was a sign he was giving up this fool's idea she'd be better off with his brother. "I'll have Casey and Theron take me home with them. Go. Just whatever you do, be careful."

"I will." He lowered his head, pressed a swift, warm, gone-way-too-fast kiss to her lips. His hand grazed her belly and warmth shot up from the spot, spread through her ribs and chest and encircled her heart. "Take care of my daughter."

"Son," she countered, grinning like a fool because it was the first time he'd called their baby anything but "it."

"Let's hope not." He kissed her again, then pulled back. And in his dark, mesmerizing eyes, heat pooled. A heat that would have to sustain her at least a little while longer. "We'll finish this when I get back."

"You bet that cute ass of yours we will, Argonaut."

He cast her a devilishly handsome smile as he followed the others out of the room.

Alone, Isadora wrapped her arms around her waist and sighed. She hated lying to him, but if he knew she had no plans to go back to Argolea right now he'd never leave. And for his own mental well-being, he needed to be with Orpheus and help save Gryphon.

When their footfalls turned to silence, she blew out another breath, closed her eyes and focused, drawing on the internal power of the Horae, the ancient goddesses of balance and wisdom. The winged omega marking on her inner thigh heated and vibrated, and she knew the markings each of her sisters shared were vibrating as well. As the ancient power flowed through her, she triggered that internal communication system she and her two sisters had been perfecting over the last few months.

Demetrius might want her to go home, and Orpheus might not want her help, but neither was getting what he wanted right now. This was bigger than both of them. This was bigger than them all.

———⁓———

The mountain air was thick and muggy, the result of a warm front that had moved through the area. As Skyla stood in the shadow of a large palm tree, she glanced toward Orpheus, deep in conversation with Demetrius ten feet away.

He'd barely said two words to her since they'd flashed to Corinth. And though a part of her was a little peeved over that fact—especially considering what they'd done to each other only hours ago—Skyla couldn't help but be impressed. Orpheus knew how to blend in with human society. He barely seemed fazed by cities or technology or unknown terrains. And that, she supposed, was how he'd survived so long, hiding in the shadows, crossing back and forth between worlds, tormenting the gods whenever the opportunity arose.

A small part of her liked that about him. Liked that he didn't give a shit what people—or gods—thought of him. And this new infatuation had nothing to do with the fact he was sexy as all get-out in those jeans that hugged his ass and that tight black button-down that accentuated his muscles. Or that he had a hard look about him, one that screamed badass to the core. What intrigued her were the inconsistencies in this image he worked so hard to portray. The moments of gentleness he'd never cop to. The concern he hid from those around him. The worry she knew he felt for his brother but wouldn't discuss.

That was the real Orpheus. Not the daemon he wanted her to think defined him. Not the troublemaker he wanted the world to see. More and more, the word *hero* kept revolving in her mind whenever she looked at him. What she didn't quite understand was why he couldn't see it.

The word *hero* made her think of the lies Athena had told her, and before she could stop it her mind drifted to Olympus. Tension pulled at her chest. Zeus would not be happy when he found out she'd failed at her mission. If he sent other Sirens to finish the job as he had last time…

Orpheus stepped toward her. His jaw was scruffy, his gray eyes like polished granite in the sunlight. And though she could tell from his scowl he was trying to put distance between them after what had happened last night, the memory of his mouth, of his hands and tongue and what he could do to her with only a look heated her insides and drew all other thought from her mind. Zeus and Olympus and her future included.

She wanted him again. More than she had last night. And that was new for her. The last time she'd wanted someone had been thousands of years ago. When she'd been infatuated with Cynurus. Though they were technically the same…this was different. It was stronger. It was hotter. It consumed her on a level that wasn't even close to the same.

His eyes narrowed as he drew close. "I don't like that look."

She smiled, loving that she put him on guard. It meant he was feeling the same damn thing as she. "What look?"

"The one that says you're plotting something."

Need pulsed through her. She *was* plotting something. What she was going to do about her order. How she was going to keep Zeus from going after him. When she was going to get the man in front of her back in bed, hopefully sooner rather than later.

He nodded to the west. "Apophis's compound is just on the other side of those hills. Probably guarded by a dozen witches."

"He'll be expecting an attack," Demetrius pointed out, moving up on his side.

Orpheus scrolled through screens on his fancy phone. "Which is why he'll never see us coming."

Skyla glanced from male to male. "What are you two planning?"

Orpheus grinned, tucked his phone in his back pocket. A sinister twist of his lips did wicked hot things to her blood and told her he was planning his own *something*. "To lure him out. With a new recruit."

Oh, no. She took a step back. "You two are Medean, not me."

"Yes, sweetheart, but you've got the goods. Apophis only likes females. Special females. I'm thinking maybe you can be of use after all."

A shimmer of foreboding rushed down her spine. Yes, she wanted him, but something told her what he had planned wasn't anywhere near what she had in mind.

"Relax, Siren," he said. "You may like this. Would I ever lead you astray?"

Yes, yes he would. And he'd enjoy every minute of it. The problem was, so would she.

Chapter 19

SKYLA WASN'T SCARED. SHE'D BEEN TRAINED NEVER to show real fear. But then, a warlock hiding out in the human realm with godlike powers didn't exactly put her at ease. And pretending to be a virginal witch, when she was anything but, also didn't leave her overly reassured this crazy plan would work.

The hem of the thin white gown they'd bought for her grazed her thighs, made her itch to scratch her legs. The sandals were way too open for her taste and she felt naked without her armor. Since there'd been nowhere to hide her bow in this getup, she'd relinquished it in favor of the blade strapped high on her thigh, and the little spell Orpheus had cast on her—the one he'd *said* was necessary for this ruse—didn't sit well with her either. In fact, it made her thighs ache.

She tried not to fidget as she waited inside the circle Orpheus and Demetrius had cast. The earth element was heavy in her palm. In the clearing, surrounded by dark hills filled with cypress and oak and pine that towered above like decrepit old men, moonlight filtered over the stones and branches and wild orchids littering the ground, making the entire area look gray and barren rather than colorful and alive.

She could feel the energy invoked by Demetrius and Orpheus somewhere out in the trees. Knew the earth element in her fist was amping that energy. And she was sure Apophis could feel it too. Magic recognized magic, and she had no doubt the power from the circle would eventually draw the warlock from his hiding place. But a small part of her stiffened just the same. Orpheus was still frustrated with her for pushing her way into this quest. She just hoped that hero streak she knew was inside him showed itself when Apophis finally appeared. Because earth element or not, without her weapons there was no way her warrior skills were a match for a warlock.

Branches crackled to her right. She held her breath. Nothing moved around her, nothing but the air stirred by Orpheus's and Demetrius's incantations. Another crackle sounded to her left, and she tried to see through the darkness. Couldn't. The blade felt heavy against her thigh, the earth element hot against her palm. Neither slowed her pulse.

A figure stepped out of the trees. Her breath caught.

She'd known he'd taken the body of an Argonaut, but what approached was not what she'd expected. Dark blond hair, a youthful and handsome face with a square jaw covered in just a dusting of dark stubble. Unlike Orpheus, who had that dark, dangerous look, and Demetrius, whose scowl was downright frightening, this Argonaut was movie-star handsome, tanned from days in the sun here in Greece, body muscular and at the same time artistic, as if his shoulders and chest and thighs had been chiseled from solid stone.

But that blue glare coming from his eyes...that wasn't right. Whatever was *inside* him was definitely not Argonaut. And it was most certainly *not* heroic.

Apophis stopped just beyond the stones forming the

circle, tipped his head. Those eyes glowed brighter. "I feel power radiating from you, little one."

It was all she could do not to tell him what he could do with his power. But she bit her lip, reminded herself she was luring him in. It was no different from what she did as a Siren. Even if the virgin thing was a real stretch for her.

"I heard tales of a great warlock in the Peloponnese," she said in a sickeningly sweet voice, lowering her head in a subservient way. "I hoped we would meet."

His blinding gaze illuminated her body. "You are most delectable. There is promise in you."

Sickness floated up from her stomach. "I've been studying the dark arts for quite some time. I had a vision my master would soon come for me."

Oh, man, she was so going to hurl if this didn't end soon. "A vision?"

She nodded. And as they'd planned, opened her fist so he could see the earth element in her palm. "A vision that told me my master would unite a disk of great importance with this."

His eyes grew wide, their glow illuminating the clearing. "Where did you get that?"

"I stole it. From a man. I told you I've been practicing my art."

His eyes narrowed in deep distrust. "You are a virgin?"

Not even.

But Orpheus had been right. The warlock was attracted to that, the sick bastard. She knew why. He got some kind of enhanced power from the induction of a virgin into his order, but it pissed her off just the same.

"Yes, I am," she lied, hoping Orpheus's little spell was

working to block his ability to sense this particular aspect of her being.

"Open the circle."

This was the moment of truth. He couldn't enter without invitation. And she was safe until he did. "I can only open it for my master. How do I know you are he?"

For a heartbeat he did nothing. Then slowly he fingered the buttons at his chest, popped one, then another. And pulled his shirt open to reveal the Orb of Krónos lying against his toned skin.

Its power reached her across the distance. The earth element grew even hotter against her palm, so close to its home. No wonder Zeus was willing to kill for this thing. Even from here she could feel the all-consuming draw and command.

The energy of the circle fractured and opened. The warlock stepped inside. Skyla's pulse skyrocketed. She hadn't opened the circle, Orpheus had. And though she knew it was all part of the plan, that didn't ease her anxiety.

He approached slowly but with intent, and stopped only when he was a foot from her. He drew in a deep breath, held it. Smiled slowly. "This will be a very good union, virgin. You will be most important to the coven."

"Think again, warlock." Orpheus moved out of the trees with Skyla's bow in his hands, arrow trained on the warlock's heart.

As the warlock turned to look in his direction with fire in his eerie blue eyes, Skyla darted around behind him and sprinted for the opening in the circle.

"You," the warlock growled.

"Yes, me," Orpheus said, coming closer to the edge

of the circle, arrow still ready to strike. "You took some-thing that didn't belong to you and we want it back."

"We?" the warlock asked.

"We," Demetrius answered, coming out of the trees to the warlock's left, drawing his attention that way.

"You!" Fury erupted over the warlock's face. He lifted his hand toward Demetrius and hurled a bolt of blue energy that hit the edge of the circle and dropped to the ground, leaving behind smoke rising from the dirt.

Okay, that was cool.

"What's wrong, motherfucker?" Orpheus asked. "Too weak to break through one measly circle?"

Fury erupted over the warlock's face. He held both hands out, closed his eyes, and began chanting in a foreign language.

"Now?" Demetrius yelled over the warlock's words.

"Now," Orpheus answered, handing the bow and arrow to Skyla as she came up beside him. He took the earth element she offered, closed his eyes, created his own chant that mixed with Demetrius's.

The warlock's face grew bright red. Magic gathered in his hands. Energy shot forward from his palms and pierced the circle.

"Orpheus!" Skyla threw her weight into him, knock-ing him to the ground so the blast wouldn't hit him.

He rolled to his stomach, pushed to his knees, his chant never once missing a beat. Demetrius's voice grew louder. The warlock shifted Demetrius's way, tried to hurl the same energy, but this time the force hit the edge of the circle and dropped to the ground like a ball slamming into a wall.

He was weakening. Orpheus had been right: without

his witches, he lost his dominance. Magic was something Skyla was familiar with. After all, she lived on Olympus. She watched the gods conjure it without a second thought. But what she witnessed in that field between those two Argonauts, both of whom could trace some part of their ancestry back to Medea, was like an art form. Awe rippled through her at what they were able to do by focusing their gifts and working together.

When the warlock's energy was spent, his words cut off midstream, his eyes popped open. Every time Orpheus and Demetrius finished a verse, the warlock would yelp, as if he'd been shocked by some unseen electrical current coming from the ground. He lifted his feet, tried to jump away from the soil. After five minutes of yelping and screaming and dancing around like a chicken with its head cut off, he shrank to his knees in the middle of the circle, curled into himself, and whimpered like a child.

Orpheus opened his eyes. Grinned Demetrius's way. "Nice work."

Pulse still pounding hard, Skyla kept her arrow at the ready as Orpheus stepped into the circle and knelt over the warlock. Apophis didn't seem to notice. Orpheus reached for the Orb, but a pop sounded, and he jerked his hand back as if he'd been burned.

"What's wrong?" Demetrius called.

"He must have put some kind of damn spell on the thing."

Demetrius moved into the circle. "What are you thinking?"

Orpheus frowned. "I'm thinking we might not be able to get it off him until he relinquishes control of Gryphon's body."

"What does that mean, as far as holding him goes?"

Orpheus pushed up from the ground. "It means we'll have to make sure he's wrapped up nice and tight until I get back."

Back. From the Underworld. Skyla's stomach tightened. She'd known this was where things were headed, but her stomach tightened just the same.

"Let's just hope three days is enough time," Demetrius muttered, helping Orpheus tug the warlock from the ground and out of the circle. "He'll be pissed when he wakes up, and if his witches have honed their craft enough before you're back, I'll be in deep shit."

"I'll be back," Orpheus said.

Demetrius didn't look so sure as he led the warlock toward their vehicle hidden in the trees.

Alone, Orpheus perched his hands on his hips, tipped his head as Skyla shrank her bow. "You did good, Siren. That takedown was NFL-worthy. You been watching *Monday Night Football*? "

Skyla knew enough human culture to catch the meaning. And the compliment warmed her. More than she expected. "Physical contact, as you know, isn't a problem for me. I expected something a little more cataclysmic, though."

"Cataclysmic's overrated. Sometimes uneventful's good enough."

Not for her. But then she was a Siren. She always expected the worst.

She flicked a look at the earth element now hanging from a chain around his neck, just barely visible at his open collar. The thing unnerved her. Not only because it held so much power, but because he wore it as if it belonged to him. And though she didn't like where her mind was going, she couldn't help but wonder what would happen when he had the Orb to go with it.

She focused on his eyes. "You can go ahead and take the virgin spell off anytime."

"I don't know. It's got a certain…charm on you." His wicked gaze raked her breasts, slid down her waist, shifted to her thighs beneath the hem of the white gown.

And under that heated exploration, fire exploded in her veins. Whereas before his lusty looks had ignited a low simmer in her belly, now it stoked a full-blown blaze. He'd added a shot of something else to that masking spell, she realized. Some enhanced arousal he'd intended to use to punish her for not listening to him when he'd told her not to tag along. "This is funny to you, isn't it?"

"There's so little humor in my life, Siren. I have to take it where I can get it."

She leaned in close. Close enough to smell the sweet scent of a body hard at work mixed with an arousal he was trying not to show. "Then be careful, daemon. Because casting an arousal spell over me isn't going to change my mind about joining you in the Underworld. And you forget I'm a Siren. I'm used to getting all hot and bothered and avoiding release. You, on the other hand, might want to think twice about this. Because when we're walking through the Fields of Asphodel, I have a feeling you're going to have a helluva time forgetting just how horny you've made me, and what you know I can do about it."

She left him standing in the trees alone as she headed for the car, where Demetrius waited with the warlock.

And though it shouldn't give her satisfaction, the *holy hell* look on his face was enough to make her smile.

For now, that would be enough.

Orpheus had taken the arousal spell off Skyla right away. What he'd intended to use to torment the Siren had backfired. Big-time.

He swiped a hand across his sweaty brow as he followed her through the hills outside the city of Heraklion. It was midmorning. The sun was already baking his skin. They'd taken a boat from Corinth to Crete, landing in the northern city, then rented a car and driven to Psychro, where they'd left Demetrius with the warlock in an abandoned shack they found on the outskirts of town. Skyla had then dragged Orpheus to tourist shops in the village. All morning, as she'd been browsing shelves in one store then another, searching for gods only knew what, he hadn't been able to look away from those long shapely legs in the tight black leggings she'd bought, the flex of muscle in her shoulders against the sleeveless top she'd paired with them. And every time she smiled his way or he caught the mischievous twinkle in her eye, he was reminded of what she'd said in the woods outside Corinth.

I have a feeling you're going to have a helluva time forgetting just how horny you've made me.

Skata. Even without the arousal spell in place, she was teasing him to within a degree of boiling. He couldn't stop thinking about how she'd felt that night at the colony, how she'd looked in the moonlight of the tower, how she'd knocked him on his ass with just one taste. He was stupid to think he could torment her with a measly spell. Dumb to have agreed to let her tag along to the Underworld, when she had this screwy effect on him. Idiotic if he thought she was anything but the seductive Siren she'd been trained to be.

And yet...

Since they'd captured the warlock, she hadn't once tried to take the Orb. She didn't even act as if she cared that they had it. She seemed only concerned with getting to the Underworld and finding Gryphon.

Though he tried, he couldn't seem to tear his eyes from her. She stood in the sunlight at the top of the path, looking right and left, more gorgeous than she'd been the moment he met her. Every time he thought he had the female pegged, she went and did something completely unexpected. Like joining him on this trip to the Underworld, even though she didn't have to, or knocking him to the ground so the warlock's energy blast didn't hurt him.

Warmth spread through his chest. A warmth that was only going to distract him if he wasn't careful.

He tore his eyes from her, turned, and looked around the hillside. Told himself to pull it together before he forgot what he was doing here.

"Okay, Siren," he said, wishing he'd tossed a drum of water into his pack rather than a few measly water bottles. He needed to douse his frickin' head. Preferably a few times. "I'll bite. Are you trying to get me killed by sunstroke or exhaustion? Why the hell didn't we just flash here?"

She moved back toward him, her boots kicking up dust in her wake. When she reached his side, she handed him the water bottle. "Flashing would cause an energy

shift that would signal we're on our way. You don't
want that, do you? Besides, we're almost there. It's just
on the other side of this ridge."

"The entrance to the Underworld," he said, lifting the
bottle to his lips.

"Yes."

"Here on Crete. On Mount Ida."

"Yes."

"Where Zeus was born."

Mischief lit her eyes. "You didn't think Hades
wouldn't have a sense of humor about this, did you?"
She took the water bottle from him, replaced it in the side
pocket of her pack. Heat and life zinged across his skin
when her fingers brushed his, then was gone too fast.

As she headed back up the path, he eyed the sexy
sway of her ass. "Focus," he muttered, kicking his feet
into gear to follow. "I'd think Zeus'd put a stop to that.
It's gotta piss off the super king, doesn't it?"

"More than you know." They moved down the other
side of the ridge. A variety of cacti littered the landscape, along with indigenous herbs and cypress and
olive trees. "But he can't stop it, because Hades controls
the Underworld *and* its entrance."

"This seems like an obvious place for the opening."

"Obvious only if you understand the depth of Hades's
jealous mind."

"Right. How is it no one's found the entrance
before? Zeus's birthplace has been excavated by
human archaeologists."

"You've done your research." She flicked a look over
her shoulder. One that was way too damn sexy for his taste.

"When it comes to the gods, I do all my research."

"Location is only one part of the puzzle, daemon. You can't get to the Underworld without this." She patted her pack.

"That book you bought? The fifteen-euro piece of crap souvenir?"

"Trust me. It was fifteen euros well spent."

The path leveled out. Tall oak to their right indicated water was somewhere close. They picked their way around shrubs and trees in need of trimming and approached what looked to be the opening of a great cave.

A handful of tourists milled about, complete with cameras at the ready and sunburns on their pasty white skin. To their left a guide stood on a rock, reciting facts about the King of the Gods. Skyla nodded toward the entrance. "The Cave of Psychro."

"You mean the cave of psycho," Orpheus muttered. "Okay, smart-ass, what now?"

"Come on." She grasped the front of his shirt just beneath the element resting against his skin and tugged. Little tendrils of heat spread out from the spot where her fingers grazed, then cooled the second she let go.

She led them past the tourists and into the mouth of the cave, which opened to form a massive room. "The first hall," she told him, continuing past tourists who were snapping pictures and chatting about the cave's history. They passed through a narrow archway and headed for a series of switchback steps that descended into an even larger room.

Lanterns illuminated the darkness. The air grew cooler. Stalactites hung from the ceiling like ominous teeth ready to bite down, and voices echoed off the walls—whispers, laughter, even a scream now and then.

They headed down with the other tourists, careful not to do anything to draw attention, not that Skyla didn't draw her own attention. She was so hot, every guy in the area was checking her out, which sent a frisson of jealousy through Orpheus. Near the bottom, Skyla pointed to the right. "The Mantle of Zeus is through there. A huge stalactite that looks totally out of place. I won't even bother to tell you what it represents."

"If you tell me you know from experience, I may be sick."

She chuckled. "No, that's one thing this Siren has no experience with. You're spared." She nodded toward another opening. "There's also a pool in that room where offerings are often made."

"I take it we're not going that way?"

"Nope." She veered to the left, away from the crowds, and picked her way around rocks and stalagmites until they entered a smaller chamber, this one only big enough to hold a handful of people.

She pulled off her pack, dropped it to the ground, gestured to the doorway. "Make sure no one comes through."

Orpheus did as she asked. He blocked the doorway with his body so no one could come in or see what she was doing, and watched Skyla pull the book she'd bought this morning from her pack.

"There it is," she said, running her finger along the text. "Gates of Hades, Realm of the Dead, open thy doors so that we may pass from life to death." Her voice lowered, and she read words in ancient Greek Orpheus couldn't decipher. When she was finished, she stood still, waiting.

Nothing changed in the small room. Voices echoed

from elsewhere in the cave. He was just about to tell Skyla this plan was bogus when rock scraped rock and a vibration echoed through the floor.

No way.

A large stone shifted sideways, opening up a tunnel that disappeared into the dark.

Skyla reached for her bag and stuffed the book inside. Before she swung the pack onto her back again, she pulled out a flashlight and turned his way. "You ready?"

He eyed the darkness. An ominous wind whipped past his face, laced with a howling cry that could only come from torment and pain. Shivers ran down his spine, but the earth element burned hot against his chest. Hotter than before, urging him on. "Yeah, but I think you should stay here. I appreciate you getting me this far and all, but I don't need—"

"Daemon…"

He frowned back at her. "Siren."

But instead of the bullheaded response he expected, her face softened. "I'm going with you. End of story. And you're going to need me, regardless of what you think. I can charm a lot more than just silly men. Now stop arguing and hurry up. This thing won't stay open for long and we've only got one shot at it."

He wasn't sure what she meant by charming more than just men, but he knew from the determined look in her amethyst eyes she wasn't about to back down. They'd already been through this argument a dozen times and she hadn't once budged, even though there was a strong chance she—both of them—might never make it out of this alive.

She stepped past him into the tunnel. Chest tight,

the connection he'd felt to her from the first flaring hot beneath his skin, he followed. He paused and looked back when the rocks scraped again behind them, then slammed shut with a clank, sealing them inside.

Skyla's surprised gaze shot to his face. "Guess there's no turning back now."

No, there wasn't, was there?

Dread pooled in his stomach as he flipped on his light to shine down the corridor. Nothing but ragged stone walls, a dirt floor, and darkness beckoned.

That and doom. A hell of a lot of doom.

Chapter 20

SKYLA'S BOOTS CRUNCHED OVER ROCKS AS THEY MADE their way down the passageway. The flashlights illuminated the stone walls around them, the boulders and stalactites hanging from the low ceiling. Twice they had to maneuver around small pools of murky water as the tunnel continued its downward trek. The skeletal remains Orpheus flashed his light over were the third they'd passed since entering the corridor.

"Human?" he asked.

Skyla pushed up from her knees, where she'd been crouched. A leather satchel, work boots, a miner's cap with a burned-out light. "That'd be my guess. Archaeologist probably."

"Dumb shit," Orpheus muttered. "Had no idea what he'd found."

"Like the others."

He took the lead again. They walked a good fifteen minutes, the sounds of their boots tapping rocks and their steady breaths the only noises in the eerie tunnel. Just when she was sure they were going to continue into darkness forever, the tunnel opened up and the sound of water running echoed from ahead.

Neither spoke as they approached the water. Skyla shined her light up and around. The tunnel spilled out into a massive cavern, the ceiling so high it couldn't be seen. Black rocks edged a river of red, which twisted and turned and disappeared into darkness. Far off in the distance a dim light shone.

Orpheus slid the pack from his shoulder, opened the zippered pouch, and pulled out two coins. He handed one to Skyla. She looked down at the ancient obolos. Again surprised by the daemon at her side. "I hope you have a few more of these so we can get back across when we're done."

He hefted the pack over his shoulder. "No, but I've got a plan for that."

As the light grew closer and the ferry boat approached, Skyla's pulse picked up speed.

She was a Siren. When a Siren died, they were supposed to go to the Isles of the Blessed, not Tartarus. But what guarantee did she have that actually happened?

You've been doing Zeus's dirty work all these years. Why wouldn't you end up here too?

She nixed the thought as the ferry drew close and bumped into the blackened rocks that made up the shore. Charon, the mysterious ferryman, stood at the back of the small boat with his hands on a long wooden pole. Behind him, a lantern hung from a hook. He wasn't aged, as Skyla had expected. Dark hair with just a touch of gray, a lean body, long face and bright, knowing blue-gray eyes. Without a word he held out his left hand. Orpheus dropped his coin into Charon's palm. Skyla followed suit. Charon motioned for them to step on board.

Skyla drew in a breath. As Orpheus gripped her arm and helped her on board, a shot of warmth rushed over her skin. Charon said nothing as he dropped the coins into a pile on the boat's floorboards behind him, then used the long wooden pole to push them away from the shore. They began floating downstream in silence.

Darkness seemed to ebb and flow, and on the horizon a strange gray light grew. Skyla's spine tingled as she looked over her shoulder to find Charon staring at them with his intense eyes. She faced forward again, leaned close to Orpheus. "Friendly, isn't he?"

He eased down toward her so they couldn't be heard, and the musky scent of his skin filled her senses. "Something tells me it's better for us if he doesn't get chatty."

Skyla nodded, refocused ahead. The gray sky grew lighter until their surroundings were awash in the eerie, colorless light pushing out the darkness. Black rocks fanned out on both sides of the river, a desolate barren wasteland as far as the eye could see. Ahead, a dock fifty yards away beckoned.

The ferry bumped the end of the dock and came to a stop. Orpheus helped Skyla out of the boat again, and without another word Charon pushed off, turned the boat against the current, and headed back the way they'd come.

"So what was the plan about the extra coins?" Skyla asked as she watched the boat grow smaller and smaller in the distance.

"Hold this." Orpheus handed her his pack. And before she could ask why, he disappeared.

Startled, Skyla looked around, wondered where he'd gone. Then she saw him reappear on the ferry just behind Charon. He scooped up a handful of coins then disappeared again as if he'd never been there. Seconds later, he was standing next to Skyla.

He reached for her hand. "Put a couple in your pocket, just in case."

In case of what? she wanted to ask, but didn't. He stuffed a few coins in his pocket then dumped the rest in his pack.

"You don't think he'll miss them?"

"Let's hope not. Come on." He turned toward land, tugged on her sleeve. She followed him off the dock and up the slight rise of blackened rocks. At the top of the ridge, they both paused and took in the view.

"Holy gods," Skyla muttered.

Miles and miles of gray, billowing fields. Souls wandering as if they were lost. A feeling of desolation floating on the wind. And far off in the distance, black jagged mountains that rose out of nothing and melded with an orange-red sky.

"The Fields of Asphodel," Orpheus said. "Better than I expected, really."

"What were you expecting?"

"A lot more trouble before we reached this point."

So had she.

They headed down. A snarl to their left stopped Skyla's feet. She turned to look just as an enormous doglike beast with three heads emerged from behind a cluster of blackened rocks.

"Now this is more like what I was expecting," Orpheus muttered, reaching for the blade he'd strapped to his back.

Skyla placed a hand on his forearm before he could draw the weapon. "Just wait."

"Wait? Are you mad? That thing looks hungry. And not docile like Charon."

"If you kill Cerberus, you're going to draw all kinds of trouble we don't need." Skyla handed him her pack. "Trust me. This is why you brought me along."

She took a step toward the beast. Knew Orpheus was watching her with a *what the hell do you think you're doing?* look on his face. All three of Cerberus's heads growled an ominous warning.

"Skyla," Orpheus warned. "Wait."

She stopped three feet from the beast. His rancid breath washed over her. His fangs dripped something vile she didn't want to think about. When he growled again and bared those rows of sharp teeth, she opened her mouth and began to sing.

A couple of bars of the Brahms lullaby and the monster closed its massive mouths, curled up on the ground, and went to sleep. In the silence that followed, Skyla turned to Orpheus and grinned.

"What the hell was that?"

"Shh," she whispered, taking the pack from him and slinging it over her shoulders. "We don't want to wake him." She led Orpheus down the hill away from the sleeping beast. When they were far enough away she said, "That, daemon, was music."

"I know what music is," he snapped. "Where did it come from?"

"Come on, Orpheus. You know the stories. I'm a Siren." She drew the word out for effect. "Before we worked for Zeus we came from somewhere, right? Hot body, pretty voice, used to lure sailors in to meet their doom. Ring any bells?"

"Hits a little close to home," he muttered with a frown as he followed her down the incline. "All you Sirens can sing?"

She gripped both straps of her backpack as she stepped from stone to waist-high gray wheat. "Yep."

"So why didn't you use that little charm on those hellhounds back in Montana?"

"Works better one-on-one. If things had gotten dire, I would have tried it though."

His scowl deepened. And for reasons she didn't understand, the expression made her laugh. "You're mad because I charmed our way out of trouble?"

"I'm not mad. I just don't like surprises. Next time tell me what you have up your sleeve before you go walking up to some monster who looks like he hasn't eaten in three months."

And that's when it hit her. He wasn't upset she'd gotten them past Cerberus. He'd been worried she'd get hurt.

Her feet came to a stop. He moved past her. She watched the way the muscles in his shoulders and legs flexed as he moved. And warmth spread through her belly and up into her chest to encircle her heart.

He glanced over his shoulder. "What?"

Her heart picked up speed. A soft thump that quickly grew until it was pounding against her ribs. Pounding with the knowledge that she'd fallen for this daemon. Fallen hard, regardless of her job and his goal and the thousands of years of history separating his two lives.

"Skyla? Are you okay?"

His voice snapped her back to reality. The reality that they were in the Fields of Asphodel. In the Underworld. Marching for Tartarus.

"I'm fine," she said, picking up her pace and reaching his side. "Let's keep going."

But she wasn't fine. Not really. She was in love. She knew that now without a doubt. And judging by who and

what she was, something told her this love would be the
end of her.

―――

They'd walked through drab wheat fields for hours,
nothing but gray in every direction. Souls had floated
beside them as they crossed the plains, sad, depressed
souls with long faces and haunted eyes. At first, being
surrounded by the souls of the dead had unnerved
Orpheus, but he'd quickly gotten used to it. These souls
weren't malevolent. They were simply curious. And
something about the entire place left Orpheus with a bad
case of déjà vu.

It'd be a whole lot easier if he could just flash to
Tartarus and look for Gryphon, but he didn't know
where he was going, so that wouldn't help. Skyla could
flash in the human realm, but she couldn't here, and
though he hated to admit it, part of him was glad to have
her company.

They crossed from wheat to black rock when they
reached the mountains on the far side. The souls stopped,
stared after them. Some kind of unseen boundary kept
them trapped. Happy to be away from them, Orpheus
followed Skyla through the maze of razor-sharp rocks as
they began their climb over the jagged mountains toward
Tartarus. The gray sky gave way to swirling black clouds
and a fire red sky. And the farther they walked, the hotter the air grew until sweat broke out all over his body.
Unable to stand it anymore, Orpheus stripped off his shirt
and stuffed it into his pack.

Skyla tied her hair on the top of her head. Sweat
slicked every part of her skin, casting a sheen that

sparkled in the light. Tendrils of damp hair stuck to her neck and the soft skin behind her ear. He tried to keep his eyes on the path so he didn't fall and slice open his knee on the razor-sharp rocks, but his gaze kept straying back to her. To her compact body in that form-fitting tank and slim pants that molded her ass. To the way she walked. To her soft, soft lips that even now were moving in his mind, singing the tune she'd sung to Cerberus earlier in the day.

Okay, forget the fact that was a stupid move and she could have been eaten. What kept sticking in his mind was that he'd heard her sing before. He didn't know how or when, but he was sure of it. And that knowledge, coupled with the strange sense that he'd been here as well, left him edgy. Left him wishing they were in Tartarus already so he could stop thinking of her. Stop worrying about her. Stop wanting her.

They passed through a series of rocks that formed a ceilingless tunnel. On the far side, Skyla stopped and pointed down the hillside below. "Look."

From their vantage point, they could see the five rivers of the Underworld where they converged in a great swamp in the center of the massive valley. Volcanoes rose out of the ground, spewing molten lava, ash, and debris. More jagged mountains rose around the periphery, and everywhere souls screaming for mercy could be heard echoing on the wind.

Skyla dropped her pack at her feet, extracted her water bottle, and tipped her head back. Orpheus watched her lips against the plastic bottle, the muscles working in her throat. Remembered how it had felt when she'd all but swallowed him whole.

Heat coursed through every cell in his body.

She lowered the water. "We should rest here."

She was right. He knew she was right. But suddenly being alone with her in a confined space didn't sound like a good idea. Or it sounded way too good—that was the problem. He couldn't be distracted by her now. Not when he was so close to finding Gryphon.

They found an overhang to sit under. Skyla pulled the blanket from her pack and a bag of freeze-dried food they'd picked up in Crete before entering the Underworld. She plopped down and munched on a handful of trail mix. "Are you okay?" she asked between bites. "You look restless."

He dropped his pack, braced his hands on his hips, and paced the small ledge. "I'm fine," he lied. Then to keep her from figuring out what was really on his mind, he brought up the other thought nagging at his gray matter. "Don't you think it's weird Hades hasn't sent anything after us?"

Skyla crossed her legs. "Maybe he doesn't know we're here."

He pinned her with a look. "I have a feeling he sees everything in his realm. Besides that, Charon knew we weren't souls."

"What are you thinking?"

He raked a hand through his hair. "I'm thinking, every step along the way Hades has sent his hellhounds to kill us, but now when we're in his realm? Nothing? Something's up."

"Maybe he's waiting to see what we'll do."

"Or he's springing a trap."

She didn't answer, and in the silence he knew she was

contemplating that possibility. Fights he could handle.
An ambush he could deal with. It was the waiting and
wondering that drove him mad.

He kicked a pebble over the ledge. It smacked against
rock and dirt and dead tree limbs on its way down to the
swirling rivers below. The plastic bag crinkled as Skyla
slid it back into her pack. "Stressing over the unknown
isn't going to do you any good right now." She patted
the blanket beside her. "Come over here and sit down."

His pulse kicked up speed.

"Come on, daemon," she teased. "I don't bite." When he
glared over his shoulder, she grinned and added, "Much."

"No, thanks. I don't feel like being toyed with right
now." Besides, he didn't like the way she'd been looking at the element against his chest all day.

"I could sing to you."

He cut her another glare. "I don't think so."

She laughed. "Okay, if I promise not to touch you or
sing to you, will you come over here? You need rest.
There's no telling what we'll find down there tomorrow,
and if you're right, if Hades has something in store for
us, I'll need you at your best." She held up her hands. "I
promise I'll be good."

Her eyes glittered with mischief, but the concern in
her voice drew him over. He eased down on the blanket
next to her, rested his back against the rocks behind
him. Even though they weren't close enough to touch,
he could feel the heat radiating from her body. Could
smell the honeysuckle scent of her skin.

"Better?" she asked.

No, not better. Just being close to her made him hard.
And when he got hard, he thought of what sex with her

had been like. Hot and consuming in that apartment in Washington. Mind-blowingly erotic in that tower at the colony.

They sat in silence for several minutes. In the hot, humid air, he was aware of every breath she took, of the way her breasts rose and fell under her shirt, of the droplet of perspiration running down her neck to disappear beneath her collar.

Man, this wasn't going to work. He should be plotting strategy for tomorrow. Mapping their route. Not sitting here lusting after the Siren who'd been sent to kill him.

Gods, he was a fool for bringing her here. Why the hell couldn't he think straight when she was around?

"There's something I've been meaning to ask you," she said, her tempting voice cutting through the quiet.

Will you have sex with me again?

Why yes, yes I will. Where do you want me?

His skin grew hot, the air around him stifling.

"What?" he snapped.

"How is it you're Argonaut, Medean, *and* daemon? Those three don't seem to go together."

Relief rippled over him. As long as the topic steered clear of sex, he was good. "My father was an Argonaut. My mother a Medean witch. They met because he'd heard she and her coven knew where the Orb was hidden in the Aegis Mountains."

Her gaze strayed to the earth element at his chest. "She's the one who found it?"

"No. But her coven had found evidence of it. There were stories. He went to investigate."

"Did they fall in love?"

Orpheus wasn't sure he knew what love meant. Let

alone what it felt like. "I don't know. They hooked up. I was the result. But he didn't bind himself to her, if that's what you're asking."

"Because she was a witch?"

"Most likely. Witches aren't popular in the human realm, but they're even less popular in Argolea."

"So what happened?"

"She raised me in the coven until I was five. Then she died. The other witches didn't like the idea of an Argonaut's offspring left to their care, so they sent me to him. But since I didn't have the Argonaut markings…"

A lump formed in his throat. The same damn lump that always formed when he thought of his relationship with his father.

Except…*relationship* was too strong a word. They'd been strangers. Two people living in the same big house because of some warped sense of duty, barely speaking. Until the day his father had died.

"That must have been hard."

Yeah, hard. He nearly scoffed. He was the son his father had never wanted. Gryphon was the son he'd been meant to sire. Orpheus had sure learned about rejection early on. Something that had saved him.

"And the daemon part of you?" she asked.

He shrugged again. "I was born with it. I figure my mother must have been part daemon. I don't know, as I barely remember her."

Except for her face. Smooth skin, chocolate eyes, silky brown hair he'd loved to play with. Even now he could conjure up her image if he tried. He couldn't remember her voice or even the times he knew he'd spent with her, but he remembered her face.

Skyla tucked her legs under her, turned to face him, and eased her head against the rocks. "Daemon hybrids are rare, but they do exist and have for some time. But most we've come across have been the result of a human female and a male archdaemon mating. Regular daemons are impotent."

Yeah, he'd heard that too. Still didn't explain how or why he'd ended up part daemon. Unless you went with the "cursed" theory, which was the only one that made sense to him.

"Did your father know?" she asked. "About your daemon?"

He stared off into the distance. "No. After the backlash I got for my Medean gifts, I learned to keep that one secret. Gryphon doesn't even know."

"And how does Gryphon fit into all this? Is he Medean as well?"

Orpheus stretched his legs out, crossed his arms over his chest. "No. His mother was Argolean. Our father bound himself to her long after I'd moved out of the house. Gryphon's quite a bit younger than me."

"The chosen son," she said softly. "And yet you still love him."

He frowned at her. "You conjure things that aren't there. Are you sure *you're* not a witch?"

She smiled. "I hear the truth you work hard to keep hidden. No man ventures into the Underworld for a brother he doesn't love. Why didn't you ever tell him about your daemon?"

Orpheus's chest tightened. The Siren was mistaken. It wasn't love that had brought him here. It was guilt. A hell of a lot of guilt. Guilt for thinking he could play hero. Guilt for getting Gryphon hurt in that warlock's castle. Guilt for never telling his only sibling he was sorry for being such a shitty brother.

Guilt shifted to emptiness, opened that hole inside him all over again. Then was replaced with an anger he'd learned was the only emotion that could fill the void. "Because he's an Argonaut, and for a daemon, a *witch*-daemon, that means enemy. And in case you haven't figured it out yet, Siren, that damn hero gene in Gryphon is a major conflict to my interests. Look around you. We wouldn't be here now if Gryphon hadn't tried to save my fucking soul. Something I don't even have."

His frustration with the entire situation welled inside him, threatened to bubble over. His dumbass brother would never listen, not to the truth, even when it all but smacked him in the face. Because Gryphon was the real deal. A hero to the core. One who instinctively overlooked the bad and zeroed in on the good.

Except in Orpheus's case, Gryphon had been wrong. There was no good in him, no matter how much Gryphon wanted to believe there was.

"What makes you think you don't have a soul?" Skyla asked quietly.

Reality. That emptiness widened in the center of Orpheus's chest, dousing the anger with pain. A black hole of nothingness waiting to suck him in. "The energy that sent Gryphon's soul here should have done the same to me. We were both hit by the same power source that day. Except I survived and he didn't."

Because I don't have a soul to destroy.

"Maybe your daemon strength stopped it."

"Maybe you're naïve."

She smiled. "You have a soul, Orpheus."

He tipped his head her way. "I have a daemon, Siren, as you oh so eloquently like to remind me."

"Your daemon hasn't been very reliable lately."

No, it hadn't. Which pissed Orpheus off more than this entire conversation. Down here, the beast could be a real asset, but Orpheus knew it wasn't about to come out and play. Even now he could feel his daemon simmering beneath his skin, but it made no effort to unleash itself. Aside from a tremor now and then, it was as if the daemon barely existed.

"Whatever." He didn't have time to worry about what was happening to him. He had to figure out how to find Gryphon. "Doesn't change the facts. And facts don't lie. As a Siren you know that better than most."

She didn't answer, and silence settled between them. A silence that left him more edgy than before. To distract himself, he focused on the red-orange glow in the distance that was dimming but didn't completely go away, as if not even night could blanket the pain and suffering with comfort.

Skyla yawned, eased down to her side, tucked her hands under her face. Even though he fought it, Orpheus's gaze drifted her way and he watched the tendrils of damp hair blow gently against her skin.

"We'll find him, you know," she whispered.

His chest filled all over again as he watched her eyes drift close. She had a way of taming that emptiness inside him as no one had done before. Not even his brother. He wanted to chalk up her concern to the Orb, but the longer they were together, the harder that was to do. Logic told him she should have taken the Orb as soon as they'd immobilized that warlock. Or she could have let him venture into the Underworld alone and then stolen it when he wasn't looking.

But she hadn't done either of those things. She was here with him now, where she didn't need to be. Risking her life for someone she didn't even know.

Risking her life for him.

He leaned down until he was close to her ear, until her scent filled his senses and tempted him to take one simple taste. "Why do you care, Siren?"

She yawned. But instead of opening her eyes and looking up as he expected, she reached out and wrapped her fingers his. Fingers that were warm and soft and oh,so comforting in a way nothing else had ever comforted him before.

"The question isn't why I care, daemon," she murmured as she drifted to sleep. "The question is how long have I cared?"

Chapter 21

MORNING IN TARTARUS WASN'T MUCH DIFFERENT FROM night. The air was oppressive and suffocating. The heat sent sweat to every part of Skyla's skin. And the closer they ventured to Tartarus, the worse the moans and screams and cries for mercy grew in the distance.

She watched Orpheus carefully as they made their way down the jagged rocks. The scowl he'd taken on when they'd crossed the threshold into Hades's realm had deepened with every passing hour. Athena had told Skyla he didn't remember his past life, but she couldn't be sure he didn't remember the Underworld. More than once over the last day she'd seen the look of déjà vu on his face as he'd turned a slow circle and taken it all in.

For the first time, she thought of telling him about his past. About who he was, how they'd met, why she was with him now. But then she dismissed it. It would do no good. He wouldn't remember, and what was the point of bringing it all up now, when they were close to finding his brother?

Maybe if—*when*—they got out of this, she'd find a way to tell him. But even as the thought hit, something in her chest pinched. A warning that no good could come from a truth that was nothing but ancient history. He was not the same man he'd been then, even if the soul was similar.

They stopped at the base of the mountain, where

rolling hills of death and decay lay before them like grass on a knoll. She took a deep drink of her water, passed it to Orpheus. He sipped, then handed the bottle back to her. Their fingers brushed and heat raced over her skin. But when she looked at his face, he showed no response.

She capped the water and replaced it in her pack. "Where to now?"

He rested his hands on his hips where his jeans hung low, looked out in the distance. A layer of sweat glistened on his bare chest, ran down to his strong six-pack abs. The earth element lay against his heart, the mark of the Titans stamped deeply into the diamond, but it wasn't the element that captured her attention. With the hot air rushing past his face to ruffle his hair and the determined look in his gray eyes, all she could think was that he looked like a god. Like a sexy, muscular, all-powerful god. The only thing he lacked was cruelty.

"A hero's soul is valuable, right?" he asked, eyes fixed on the far off marshes. "I'm guessing Hades will have sent him for the cruelest sort of punishment. Close to the heart of the Underworld, where he can draw the most energy from Gryphon's suffering. I say we head there and see what we find."

Her heart expanded. When she didn't answer, he turned to look at her, his brow wrinkled in confusion. "What?"

The thump, thump, thump against her ribs echoed in her ears. And his revelation from last night—that he didn't have a soul—revolved in her mind.

Second chances.

Athena had told her he'd been given a second chance. That a Fate had made a deal with Hades for him to come back. What if his daemon was part of that deal? A way to ensure he wouldn't redeem himself? Except…except his daemon was fading. She was certain now he could no longer shift, and his eyes didn't even change anymore when he was irritated. Every time he did something good, like protect Maelea or help those people on that train or come to Skyla's rescue, his daemon seemed to grow weaker. And he did have a soul. She was sure of that. A soulless being would never do the things he'd done. A soulless being wouldn't care. Which meant…if the daemon inside him was nearly gone, that soul he was so sure he didn't have might be taking its place.

She stepped to him, brushed her hand against his granite jaw, let her gaze skip over his features. His tanned and weathered skin, the long slope of his nose she knew now really was linked to royalty, the deep gray depths of his eyes, and his dark eyebrows, cinched low as he stared at her as if she'd sprouted a second head. Then to his lips. Masculine. Hard. Yet so soft when they pressed against hers, when they opened to take her in.

She eased up on her toes.

He sucked in a breath. "What are you doing?"

"Kissing you."

His eyes grew wide. "Why?"

"Because, silly daemon, you are irresistible."

She grazed her mouth against his, just the slightest breath of skin against skin, heat against heat. He didn't move. Didn't reach for her. And as she slid her hands over his muscular shoulders and ran her fingers into the hair at the nape of his neck, then tipped her head to kiss him again, she smiled. Smiled because the circumstances of who they were and why and how they'd come to be here together in the middle of hell didn't matter anymore. The only thing that mattered was him.

Orpheus…

Ironic that Orpheus the legendary musician had been the one to tame the Sirens with his lyre when he'd sailed with the Argonauts on Jason's quest for the Golden Fleece. Though this Orpheus was no musician, he'd tamed her just the same. Awakened her. Shown her there was life beyond the order. Cynurus had stirred the need for a home, a family, a future inside her, but Orpheus was the one who'd stoked those cold embers and brought them back to life.

She slid her tongue along the seam of his lips, coaxing him to let her in. Used her strength to draw her body close until they were chest to chest, hip to hip, soul to soul. His hands settled at her hips. His fingers fisted in the damp fabric of her shirt. And just when she was sure he was going to let her in, he pushed back from her mouth and frowned down at her.

"I did take that arousal spell off you, didn't I?"

She laughed, eased in closer. Felt the warmth of the earth element between them. "You did. But haven't you figured out I don't need an arousal spell to want you?"

His eyes narrowed. "You're seducing me."

"No, daemon. I'm enjoying you. The two are very different. When I seduce, trust me, I don't enjoy."

For a heartbeat, he didn't speak. Just stared at her. Then he muttered "*Skata*" and brought his hands up to frame her face, drawing her lips back to his and kissing her with all the passion she'd been missing this last day.

She opened for him, drew his tongue into her mouth and savored that smoky, wet, dangerous taste on her tongue. The one that ignited fire in her blood and called to her on the most basic level.

His hands slid down her shoulders, over her sides, back to her hips again, dragging her closer to his erection. He took a step back, leaned against an outcrop of rock, and pushed one thigh between her legs, grasping her hips and dragging her close until she was rubbing up against him, growing breathless and sweaty all over again.

"Skyla, Skyla, Skyla," he murmured against her lips, then dipped in for another taste that drove her a little more mad. "You're going to be the death of me, Siren."

This time, she eased away from his mouth. "No, I'm not. I believe in you, Orpheus."

"You shouldn't."

"I can't help it. You keep doing things that prove to me you are not at all what you think you are."

"Don't put too much faith in me. I never live up to it."

She trailed her hand down his chest and laid it over the element resting against his heart, warm from a power that didn't come from his skin or hers. It came from within. Just like the strength that was hidden in him but which he couldn't see.

"Even a Fate can't see the heart of a person, and free will reigns in all men, you included. But something tells me your part in all of this doesn't end here."

His piercing gaze held hers, and though her need for him right here and now was great, it wasn't as great as her need for him to believe in himself. The only way she knew for him to do that was to find his brother and set right a wrong he felt responsible for.

She eased out of his arms but captured his hand in hers and smiled as she tugged him with her. His fingers closed around hers—strong, steady, alive. "Come on. We still have at least half a day's journey. And that's assuming we don't run into any problems. I want to get this done and get back to the human realm, where we can pick up where we left off."

He frowned but followed, his boots kicking up dust, his hand never leaving hers. "Where we left off was me being mad at you for pushing your way along on this trip."

She laughed. "Okay, then we'll skip ahead to the part where you're not mad and are thankful I came along."

"Am I?"

"You will be. Trust me."

———

"They've entered Tartarus, my lord." Orcus bowed his head in that subservient way that made Hades want to praise the disgusting creature by backhanding him across the room.

"And my wife?"

"Waiting."

Of course. Waiting for Orpheus to reach the Cursed Marshes. His wife would attack then. When the hero and Siren would be disoriented and unable to run. It was a good plan. A plan Hades himself would have come up with…if, that is, he only wanted the Orb.

But now, knowing the Siren was with the no-good hero, and knowing what Atalanta and Krónos had planned, the Orb wasn't enough. He wanted them all. The souls of two Argonauts, a Siren, *and* Atalanta. His power would surge with the blessed souls of the first three, and the last…well, he just wanted to see that bitch Atalanta suffer.

His father he'd deal with later.

"Bring me my wife."

"She will be most displeased, my lord."

A wicked smile turned up Hades's lips and he clasped his hands behind his back as he rocked on his heels and stared out at the swirling red sky. "I'm counting on it.

"Oh, and Orcus," he called over his shoulder.

The creature's scuffling stopped. "Yes, my lord?"

"Send Tantalus to the Cursed Marshes to tell them where they can find the Argonaut's soul. I'm ready to hurry this along."

The air grew stagnant and thick, the moans and cries for help so loud they were a never-ending buzz in Orpheus's ears.

As he followed Skyla across Tartarus, they stayed to the shadows as much as possible but found it impossible in places. They passed rivers of lava where souls were being thrown into the boiling streams, racks where souls were stretched and tortured with instruments that ranged from knives to scythes to chains. Everywhere, pain and torment rang out around them but none paid them any mind. They were allowed to pass as if they were invisible. Which just seemed…wrong.

As they walked by a particularly gruesome scene—a soul staked to the ground, being devoured by dogs— Skyla covered her mouth and looked away. "How does he decide who suffers what atrocity?"

"It's different for each soul."

Skyla turned his way. His feet stopped. Again that sense of déjà vu washed through him, the one that had grown stronger the deeper they'd delved into the Underworld. "I don't know how I know that. I just do. At judgment, Hades determines what punishments fit the perpetrator and he sets them up on a cyclical pattern. A day of each until the soul is killed, only to suffer through a new scenario the next day."

"That's awful," Skyla whispered.

It was. Horrendous. To know that day after day you'd be tortured until you died in different yet equally heinous ways, only to awaken and do it all again. An endless repetition of life, torture, and death.

Skyla slid her hand into his and tugged. "Come on."

He focused on her familiar amethyst eyes. Eyes that also brought a sense of déjà vu. Eyes he knew he'd looked into long before that day at the concert. "Skyla…"

"Yes?"

His chest filled again with that warmth only she could bring. "I…" *Why do I feel like I know you? What is this weird connection we have?* But he knew she wouldn't answer his questions. He'd tried that before. Maybe he should just stop questioning and be thankful she was here with him. To be in this place alone…

A shiver ran down his spine even in the blistering heat.

He shook off the thought and stepped toward her. "Yeah, let's go."

They walked another few hours until the barren ground shifted to wet, seeping marshes where all five rivers of the Underworld converged in a murky, bubbling, swampy mire. Souls could be seen floating amidst the muck, struggling to break free, but the surface was as impenetrable as glass, and the muffled screams echoed in the air.

Please don't let Gryphon be down there.

Orpheus had no idea how they'd get him out if he was.

A shout echoed to their left. On instinct, Orpheus pushed Skyla behind him and turned that way. She grunted and stepped free of his protection, then reached for her bow.

The voice grew stronger, and then a body came into view. A real body, not a soul like every other person they'd encountered. How Orpheus knew that he couldn't be sure. The souls looked real down here, but there was something about them that struck him as not complete.

The man, being, *whatever*, stepped out of the scraggly trees and stopped a few feet from them. He was dressed all in white, with dark hair, and two scars that ran down his cheeks. But he was definitely real. And very, *very* familiar. "You seek the Argonaut's soul."

Orpheus slanted Skyla a look. She had her bow up and ready to strike. "How do you know what we're here for?"

"Souls have ears," the male answered. "And secrets waft on the wind." His voice lowered. "Do not be so naïve as to think you were anything but allowed to venture this far amongst the dead. The Argonaut you seek is not among the Cursed Marshes. He's on the plains, over the ridge to the west."

Orpheus's gaze followed the sweep of the male's hand. "Why are you telling us this?"

The male stepped closer. "Because I've been told to." He slid a small teardrop-shaped vial of liquid into Orpheus's hand and whispered, "Even here, in the land of the forgotten, hope remains. Watch for the unexpected. They'll strike when you think you are free."

He turned and headed back the way he'd come.

"Hey!"

The man stopped. Glanced over his shoulder.

"Do I know you?" Orpheus asked.

"You did. Once."

Why that left Orpheus more uneasy than the fact this guy had approached them, he didn't know. He raised the vial. "What's in here?"

"Ambrosia. It has the opposite effect in the Underworld." The man turned and headed back into the mist.

"What do you think that was about?" Skyla asked.

Orpheus didn't know, but as he watched the male disappear, another shot of déjà vu whipped through him. "I think it means we need to watch our backs."

"Do we search the marshes or trust him?"

If Gryphon were here, it would take days, weeks, to find him. There were so many lying trapped in the shadows of the tall reeds. "What do you think?"

"It's your call."

Yeah. His call. His mistake to make, too. Only one of many he'd made during his lifetime.

He didn't know why, but that déjà vu said to trust the man. He slid the vial into his pocket. "We head for the plains to the west."

―――⟞⟝―――

Skyla's feet ached from walking and her back was sore from sleeping on the rocks. But she was a warrior, one who'd been through worse and had endured tougher conditions. The heat was a pain in the ass, but she was thankful for the tank that left her arms bare, and she was thankful too for the moody male at her side. Even if he'd grown quieter and darker with every step they'd taken in Tartarus.

They made it to the top of the plateau, damp with sweat and breathless from the climb. As Skyla passed Orpheus the water bottle, she scanned the horizon.

More souls being tortured in various ways. Some tied to poles, some locked in cages, some out in the open, being set on fire. Even though revulsion roiled through her, she knew she was growing numb to the atrocities. No single one struck her as any more vile than another. Until, that is, she caught sight of the male in the trees a good fifty yards away. The one hanging from chains, suspended from a limb high above. He was naked, while hundreds of thousands of snakes struck at his toes and ankles and legs.

"Holy gods." She hated snakes. Always had. She couldn't imagine a worse torture.

Orpheus turned and froze. "Gryphon."

He pulled the blade from his back and tore off across the field before she could stop him. Before Skyla could remind him about ambushes and traps and what that male they'd encountered had told them back at the Cursed Marshes.

Watch for the unexpected.

Skyla's heart shot into her throat. Pulling her bow free, she took off after him. And prayed this wasn't that moment.

Chapter 22

ORPHEUS SKIDDED TO A STOP AT THE EDGE OF THE trees. The horror of the scene sucked the air from his lungs. Gryphon dropped his head back between his shoulder blades and howled in pain.

Lift your legs, damn it! Why wouldn't he lift his legs away from the snakes striking out at him again and again?

"Gryphon!" He called out several times, but Gryphon didn't respond. The snakes formed a carpet of writhing bodies on the ground beneath him, blocking Orpheus's path.

"Holy gods." Skyla drew up beside him, her bow at the ready, her chest rising and falling with her labored breaths. "There could be anyone hiding in these trees."

"I don't care what's in the fucking trees. I care about getting Gryphon down." He waved the sword over his head. Jumped up and down and hollered to distract the snakes.

Skyla lined up her arrow and fired at the snake coiled to strike at Gryphon's bare, bloody toes. The arrow sliced right through the snake's neck, dropping it to the ground. As if they'd just taken notice that something else hunted their prey, the snakes on the edge of the mass turned and hissed in their direction.

Skyla took a step back. Orpheus followed. Three snakes with beady eyes, yellow markings, and heads like cobras wriggled across the ground right for them.

"Um, Orpheus?"

He swung out with his blade, decapitating one, and angled to the second. The third snake shot after Skyla.

"Orpheus!" She lifted her bow, fired. The arrow sailed through the air and sliced into the neck of the charging snake but didn't slow its pursuit.

There wasn't time for Orpheus to conjure a spell, wasn't even time to reach her with his blade and try to help. Some internal voice said, *Use the vial.*

He dug the vial from his pocket. Inside, the liquid glowed an eerie blue-green. The stranger had told them it was ambrosia. In the human world, ambrosia gifted immortality. If it worked differently down here…

"Here!" He threw the vial to Skyla, then struck out with his blade toward the snake still trying to snack on his flesh.

She caught the glass vial with one hand, twisted the lid. Then she tossed the contents toward the snake, reached for her arrow again, and lined up her shot.

Orpheus decapitated the snake in front of him, turned to help her, but realized he didn't need to. The glowing liquid hit the snake and immediately stopped its forward momentum. As if it had struck a wall, it jerked back, then a hissing sound echoed and smoke rose up around it. Seconds later nothing but ash littered the ground where the snake had been.

Skyla darted a look his way. "Whoa."

Whoa was right. But not enough. Orpheus looked back at Gryphon and the thousands of snakes below him. "Give it to me."

Skyla handed it over. Inside the glass, the blue-green liquid glowed bright, refilled to the top as if she'd never used it.

He ran toward the mass of writhing bodies and in the same motion Skyla had made, flicked the liquid out across the snakes.

Hisses roses up to meld with Gryphon's cries of pain, followed by the acrid scent of flesh burning and smoke rising up to fill the woods. The snakes, the whole lot of them, were reduced to nothing but smoldering ash.

He crossed the smoking remains, scaled the tree, and eased out on the branch to unhook the chains. "Hold on, Gryphon."

Gryphon's body dropped to the ground with a thud. Heart in his throat, Orpheus picked his way down the tree trunk to find Skyla already kneeling next to his brother, her backpack on the ground at her side, the blanket from inside it wrapped around Gryphon's shaking shoulders.

"Wh-who are you?" Gryphon asked, clutching the blanket to his bloody body, shivering as if he were in the Arctic.

"I came with Orpheus," Skyla said. "We're here to help you."

Gryphon's head shifted in Orpheus's direction but confusion creased his forehead. And in his light blue eyes there wasn't a single shred of recognition.

Orpheus knelt next to his brother. "We're gonna get you out of here."

"No!" Gryphon's eyes flew wide and he lurched to his feet, knocking Skyla back to the ground. "I have to get back to the city." His wild eyes searched right and left. Beneath the blanket he clutched tightly to his chest, shivers racked his body again.

Orpheus eased slowly to his feet. Held up his hands in surrender. "Easy, Gryph. No one's here to hurt you." From his peripheral vision he saw Skyla push herself up and circle around to Gryphon's other side.

"No," Gryphon said, backing up a step, his bloody bare feet scuffing over ash and razor-sharp rocks. "This is a trap. This is more torture. I won't stay. You can't make me stay! I'll find my way back to the city."

Orpheus didn't know what city his brother was talking about, but the pain in Gryphon's voice told him he'd seen and been through horrors no one should have to endure. He took a cautious step closer to his brother. "There's no trap. And no more torture. I promise. We're here to rescue you."

Gryphon's spine hit a blackened tree trunk. The whites of his eyes could be seen all around his blue irises. "And who's going to save you?"

Orpheus darted a look at Skyla. The one she sent back said *Good question.*

Orpheus took another step closer. "Gryphon—"

"Daemon," Skyla whispered. "These forests have eyes. I feel it. We need to get out of here *quick*."

Orpheus felt it too. The hair on his nape stood straight up. "Look, Gryph, we have to go. I promise nothing bad will happen."

Gryphon held up both blanketed forearms and slammed into Orpheus, knocking him hard to the ground. "No!" He darted past Orpheus and took off into the field.

He was real. Down here, at least, his soul took on a solid form. Orpheus's head spun from the hit and he rolled to his stomach, then pushed himself up. Skyla dashed after Gryphon and caught him just as he hit the knee-high grasses they'd crossed earlier. She hurled herself forward and grasped him by the waist. The two hit the ground with a smack, then disappeared from view.

Orpheus scrambled to his feet and tore after them. When he reached the grasses, Skyla had one knee pressed into Gryphon's bare chest to hold him down, her hands pinning his to the ground.

Orpheus's feet slowed, and in shock and disbelief he approached the pair, his heart in a fog, his head unable to grasp what he was seeing.

His strong, proud, invincible Argonaut brother was weeping.

Skyla glared up at Orpheus. "Help me here! He's freakin' strong."

Orpheus knelt at her side, grasped Gryphon's wrists with shaking hands. Gods...those damn gods. "We're gonna help you, Gryphon," he said, his own voice quaking. "I promise, *adelfos*. I promise nothing else will happen to you. We're here to get you out. I swear it."

Gryphon's eyes shot wide and he stopped his struggle. His terror-filled gaze darted right and left. "She's coming. She's coming. They're both coming..."

His words echoed in the air around them. Orpheus shot Skyla a look. In her *holy shit* look he saw the same thing he was thinking reflected back at him. Whatever *she* was or *they* were, they needed to be long gone before anyone showed up.

Together they hauled Gryphon to his feet. He whispered frantic, crazed words that made no sense as they wrapped the blanket around his body, darted nervous looks in every direction. Since there was nothing to be done about his bleeding feet, Orpheus slid an arm around Gryphon's waist, propped Gryphon's arm over his shoulder, and held him up. Skyla took the lead, her bow and arrow at the ready as they crossed the plains and headed back the way they'd come.

After only twenty minutes, Gryphon's shuffling and incoherent mutterings turned to thrashing and fighting. He tried to push away from Orpheus and screamed, "No! I won't let you take me!"

The blanket fell to the ground. Gryphon wrenched free of Orpheus's hold and turned to run back to the trees, but his legs gave out beneath him and he slammed face-first into the dirt.

"Skyla!"

Orpheus was at Gryphon's side in a flash, rolling him onto his back, trying to grasp his flailing arms. Gryphon was a big guy but he was weak, and the crazed, almost hysterical look in his eyes said he wasn't thinking clearly.

Gods, who could think straight in this hellhole?

"Gryphon, stop. Stop!" Orpheus grasped both wrists and pinned them over Gryphon's head. "I said stop!"

Gryphon lifted his head off the ground, struggled against Orpheus's grip, and through clenched teeth growled, "I won't let you take me!"

Skyla skidded to a stop at Orpheus's side, dropped her bow. "He doesn't know who you are."

"Holy fuck, how the hell are we supposed to get him out of here when he's fighting us? He'll have every daemon in the realm on us in minutes."

Skyla fell to her knees and began humming. A soft lullaby, like the one she'd tamed Cerberus with earlier.

Gryphon stopped his frantic thrashing. He looked all around to see where the music was coming from.

The lullaby morphed into a gentle ballad, one about hope and promises and finding where you belonged. And as she sang, as her clear, entrancing voice rang out across the plain, Gryphon slowly relaxed his muscles. One by one. Until he sank against the ground and his eyes drifted closed.

Orpheus was too stunned to say anything. He could only watch as she picked up her bow and pushed to her feet. "Let's go before something we definitely don't want to meet comes after us."

Chest warm, and not from the Orb, Orpheus hefted Gryphon into his arms. His brother was deadweight now, but that was okay. So long as he wasn't fighting them and drawing attention, Orpheus could handle it. And carrying the two-hundred-fifty-pound Argonaut kept his mind off other things. Like what a surprise the Siren had turned out to be and what he was going to do about her when they got out of this mess.

Neither he nor Skyla spoke as they made their way down the steep ridge and past the Cursed Marshes. Anytime Gryphon so much as stirred, Skyla would start humming again and he'd relax back against Orpheus's shoulder. Once, when they passed a soul being tortured—one tied to a stake being shot at by arrow after arrow—she stopped, stared in horror. But when Orpheus called out for her, she quickly picked up her pace and followed. It wasn't until hours later, when they reached the base of the jagged mountains that separated Tartarus from the Fields of Asphodel, that they paused to rest.

Orpheus eased Gryphon down to lean against a rock. His head fell against Orpheus's shoulder. The blanket was wrapped around his lean waist, his bare unmarked chest as muscular as it had always been, but the Argonaut Orpheus had known was nowhere to be found.

Orpheus's pulse pounded hard. He kept seeing Gryphon in that field, wild-eyed and crazed, scared out of his mind, afraid even of his brother. He swiped a hand down his sweaty face, dropped it against his chest. His fingers fell against the earth element.

"Don't even think about it." Skyla's bow was at her feet, a water bottle resting in her hand.

"Don't think about what?"

"The element. You can't give it to him."

"He needs it. He's weaker than—"

She stepped in front of him, blocking his view. "He's a soul, Orpheus. One who's been tortured by Hades and gods know what else down here. Giving it to him might be just what they want." Her gaze jumped from rock to rock in the jagged terrain. "Something watches us. And waits. I can feel it."

He turned to look around. He could feel it too. He just didn't know what that something was.

Her fingers closing around his brought his attention back to her. Fingers that were warm and alive and re-assuring. "Keep it on. Let it give you strength. Can you continue carrying him or do you need to rest?"

"No rest," he said, his throat thick. "We keep moving. I want out of this hellhole."

She nodded in agreement, let go of his hand, and handed him the water bottle. The loss of her touch was as stark as the barren wind blowing hot across the land.

"I figure six, maybe seven more hours until we reach the River Styx. If we can keep up this pace, that is."

Again he turned and scanned the hills, the feeling that eyes were watching sending tingles all along his spine.

That and a sense of déjà vu that he'd been here before. That he'd done this before. That failure was imminent.

―――᠁―――

Skyla's heart had been in her throat since she'd seen Orpheus's brother hanging from that gnarled and decrepit tree. And it had picked up speed when she'd seen the female tied to that post, being shot at with those arrows. The female she was sure she recognized as a former Siren. But it was the sensation they were being followed that put the urgency in her step and pushed her on even when her muscles ached from exhaustion.

Orpheus had barely spoken since they'd found Gryphon. Thankfully, her singing was keeping the guardian relaxed, but that didn't ease Skyla's anxiety. She wanted out of this shop of horrors as much as Orpheus did. And she never wanted to come back.

They climbed the mountain in silence, descended the other side as day shifted to night. But night here wasn't anything more than a darker version of a swirling red sky of gloom, so there was still plenty of light to push them on. At the base of the mighty mountains they passed into the Fields of Asphodel, the black, barren, and dead landscape of Tartarus replaced with shades of gray as if from a black-and-white movie.

Souls immediately rushed in their direction, floated around them as they crossed the fields of waist-high wheat, curious as they looked from face to face. Unlike the souls in Tartarus, these craved interaction. The ghostlike apparitions could almost be considered human if, that is, one ignored the depression and longing radiating from them like heat from a baking stone.

Skyla kept a keen eye out for any surprises. Twice she pulled her bow and arrow only to realize what she'd thought was a threat turned out to be nothing more than another curious soul.

The wheat fields ended as they reached the barren knoll and started their ascent to the top of the ridge where they'd run into Cerberus. She was ready with her arrow. Ready to sing again if she had to. But the three-headed dog was nowhere to be seen.

Orpheus leaned down to her ear. "His absence doesn't make me feel any more reassured."

Her either.

They crossed to the dock. Beneath their feet the River Styx swirled in shades of red and black.

"Will Charon come back or should we start swimming?" Skyla asked, eyeing the water, not sure she wanted to touch it. She was pretty sure she saw an arm floating by.

"He'll come back," Orpheus answered, hefting Gryphon's motionless body higher on his shoulder.

"How do you know?"

For a moment Orpheus said nothing, then his brow lowered. "I just…know."

Skyla's stomach tightened as she searched the distance for Charon and his ferry. Closing her eyes, she fought back the nausea. And for the first time she thought about what could have been, and probably was, done to Orpheus when he'd been trapped down here.

Nearly two thousand years. Gryphon was a muttering,

blubbering mess and he'd only been here three months. What must Orpheus have endured?

"Look. There." Orpheus pointed upriver. A light shone far off in the distance, growing brighter with every second.

Skyla swallowed around the lump in her throat and told herself not to think about what might have been done to him. He was alive, with her now. If he remembered anything she would have noticed. She glanced at his chest where the earth element lay hidden beneath the shirt he'd put back on, then up to his strong jaw and chiseled cheekbones, and finally to those eyes like melted silver. She'd do whatever she had to do to make sure it never happened again.

"Get out your coins," Orpheus said.

Skyla rifled through her pockets for the coins he'd given her earlier. The ferry approached, bumped against the dock. Charon didn't speak, but this time, unlike before, there was a pitying, almost sad look in his eyes.

Her hands shook as she handed him three coins, stepped onto the boat. Orpheus moved on after her, spread his legs to balance Gryphon's weight as the ferry pushed off and turned in the swirling red water. No one spoke as they traveled upriver. And though she tried not to notice, that feeling they were being watched lingered. As did the feeling everything was about to come crashing down.

They'll strike when you think you're free.

Her pulse picked up as they reached the dock, as the ferry bumped its way to a stop. Heart thumping beneath her breast, she climbed off the boat and reached for her bow and arrow again. The tunnel they'd ventured into at the start loomed ahead. Empty. Dark. The perfect hiding place for something or some*one* waiting to attack.

"Get my light," Orpheus said as the ferry pulled away and Charon disappeared into darkness.

Skyla reached into his pack, grasped the flashlight and flicked it on. Orpheus held out his hand. "I'll light the way. You just stay ready."

He was thinking the same thing as she. For some reason, that put her at ease. She nodded, brought her bow up, readied her arrow. They headed into the tunnel without a word.

A chill spread down her spine, the heat of Tartarus long gone. As they picked their way around stalagmites and eased through narrow corners, then passed pools of murky white liquid, she imagined the worst: Cerberus jumping out at them, Hades appearing in a poof of smoke, a fire daemon swirling in a vortex. But none of those scenarios came true. No apparitions, no interference, not even a sound, other than their boots scraping rock and their rapid breaths as they moved.

The tunnel came to an abrupt halt. Skyla stared at the wall of rock, the uneven edges and mottled stone, as Orpheus ran the light from floor to ceiling to look for an opening.

"There has to be a way through," she said.

"Don't suppose that book has any key phrases that'll open it?"

She shrugged out of the pack, reached in, and grasped the book. After flipping pages she frowned. "No, nothing."

One corner of Orpheus's lips curled, just a touch. "You could charm it with that Siren voice."

"My voice calms things. It doesn't destroy them like..." Her eyes widened. "Where's the vial?"

He reached into his pocket and handed her the glass vial the mystery guy in the marshes had given them. Skyla twisted the lid and flicked the glowing water at the rocks.

For a heartbeat, nothing happened, and then stone began to crumble.

"Get back," Orpheus called.

Skyla grabbed her pack and scrambled backward. The wall gave way with a crash of rock and debris until light shone in from the other side.

Light from lanterns inside the Cave of Psychro.

Relief rippled through her chest as she picked her way over the rocks and through the narrow opening. And when she reached the other side, when she set foot on the solid, dirt-strewn earth, she felt like dropping to her knees and kissing the soil.

They'd made it. They'd ventured to the Underworld, rescued a soul, and survived. How many people could say they'd done that?

Not many.

Rocks slipped and scraped one another as Orpheus stumbled through the opening, his brother still dead-weight in his arms. "Thank the Fates," he breathed.

Skyla's gaze shifted to Gryphon. "Look, Orpheus."

Gryphon no longer appeared solid, but ethereal, the only thing concrete about him the blanket still wrapped around his naked hips.

"Let's get him back to Demetrius. Quick."

She nodded. Headed for the arched doorway that had led into the next room. Too late she realized there were no tourists around. No people milling through the birth-place of Zeus.

In a poof of smoke, Hades appeared on the stairs that led to the bridge that would take them to freedom, all towering menace and malevolent doom. At his side stood Persephone, dressed in a gown as black as her soulless eyes, looking less than thrilled.

Skyla's feet drew to a stop. At her back, she heard Orpheus's steps still as well.

"What do you think, wife of mine," Hades said to Persephone without taking his eyes off Skyla. "That looks like stealing, don't you think?"

Persephone wrapped her long, clawlike fingers around the handrail at her side. "I would say that's most definitely stealing." Heat flared in her eyes. "Hello, Orpheus. It's good to see you again." Then to her husband, "Whatever shall we do with them?"

A wicked, sinister grin curled the right side of Hades's mouth, and dread dropped like a rock into the pit of Skyla's stomach. "I can think of several things."

Chapter 23

GRYPHON CAME AWAKE WITH A START. THE FOUL energy he felt in the air pulled him from the brink of unconsciousness where he'd been hovering for…he didn't know how long.

The snakes came back to squirm through his mind. He tried to push up, to get away, but couldn't. They were eating him, biting his skin, injecting their venom deep into his veins. Gods, the pain. There was so much pain. There was…

His mind stopped its frantic spin cycle. And he realized in a daze there were no snakes. Just the lingering memory of their striking, biting, slithering away only to strike again. Of spiders crawling over his flesh. Of vultures tearing at his muscles. Of monsters he couldn't name ripping his limbs from his body as if he were a rag doll. And burning. There'd been burning. He could smell the charred flesh as if it were happening now. But over it all, floating in every single memory, there was Atalanta. What she'd made him do. What she and Krónos had done when…

Agony churned inside him. Melded with shame and a sickness he couldn't ignore. He needed to run. He had to get away. He—

"*Skata.*"

The voice, a voice he recognized, brought him back around. He turned his head and saw the profile of his brother's face. Orpheus's strong nose, the solid cheekbones, the square jaw covered in what had to be three or four days' worth of stubble.

"O?" he whispered. Panic rushed in. No, no, no. His brother couldn't be here. Not in the Underworld. No one could be here. No one—

"The vial?" a voice just past Orpheus whispered. A female voice.

Gryphon realized he was sitting on the ground. He looked up past Orpheus but couldn't see more than watery shapes, one haloed in gold.

"They're immortal, remember?" Orpheus muttered.

"What about your spells?" the female whispered.

"They'd be as useful as your singing against these two," Orpheus said. "*Skata*, we get all the way back to the human realm and *this* is where it ends?"

Growls echoed somewhere close. Growls Gryphon recognized as hellhounds waiting to feast.

"Don't do anything foolish," Orpheus warned.

"Define *foolish*," the female snapped. "Because right now all options are on the table."

"You've caused me quite a bit of trouble, hero." Hades's voice rang out in a humorous tone somewhere close. "You find the Orb, you lose the Orb to my treacherous wife, you find the Orb again, then lose it to a scheming warlock." Hades chuckled. "You are all sorts of heroic, now aren't you?"

The Orb.

Gryphon's mind locked on those two words, and all of it, every detail of how he'd ended up in the Underworld, flooded his memory.

Orpheus didn't answer, just clenched his jaw and glared at the god.

"The soul of a hero is valuable," Hades said, obviously realizing he wasn't getting a reaction out of O. "But some things are worth more than a simple soul. For the Orb, you and your band of marauders can be on your way."

Don't believe him. Panic lanced its way up Gryphon's chest. No matter what he'd been through, it would be a million times worse for so many more if Hades got his hands on that Orb.

"Ignore him," the female next to Orpheus whispered.

Yes, listen to her! Gryphon shouted, scrambling to his feet. Only when he reached for Orpheus's arm, his hand passed right through skin and bone and muscle.

Gryphon's eyes grew wide. Lifting his hand, he realized he could look through it to the rock walls of whatever cave they were in. At his back, Hades laughed.

"Oh, to go from corporeal to ethereal. Must be a bitch." His voice hardened. "Now the Orb. The wife and I grow tired of this drama."

Persephone sighed.

Orpheus shot Gryphon a pitied expression, then his hand slid to his chest. To the outline of something beneath his shirt

"Orpheus, don't," the female warned again.

"I'm not letting him send you both back to the Underworld," Orpheus muttered.

"If you give him that, the whole world will become the Underworld," she countered. "Don't do it."

"Skyla…"

There was agony in the word. And emotion. An emotion Gryphon had never heard from his brother. Promise and pain and a future that would never be.

Gryphon looked down at his hands. His shaking, ghostly hands. His soul was in the human realm. He was free. He didn't have a body, but his soul…that's where the power had always come from. The power he'd gotten from his forefather and rarely used because it was unpredictable.

But unpredictable was better than nonexistent.

Before he could change his mind, he closed his eyes and focused in on that power. It would render him immobile, but what did it matter? He was a ghost here. Power flickered through his limbs, condensed in his chest, and shot up his spine. His eyes flew open and he zeroed in on Hades and Persephone, whom he could now see standing on cement steps ahead, smug expressions on their chiseled, perfect, immortal faces.

Someone gasped. A voice cursed—Hades's voice. And then as Gryphon continued to channel his power, all sound ceased.

His legs gave out. He crumpled to the ground. Or maybe he floated. Gryphon wasn't sure. The only thing he knew was that he felt like a deflated beach ball. He couldn't move, couldn't think, but he could hear.

"What the hell just happened?" the female beside Orpheus gasped.

"Gryphon, you super-fucking-smart sonofabitch," Orpheus exclaimed in an excited voice. "Help me get him up, Skyla."

Air whooshed over his back.

"He's a ghost!" she cried. "How the hell are we going to…?"

Weight pressed down on him. Fuzzy weight. A blanket. They were draping the blanket over him.

"Ah, good thinking, daemon," the female exclaimed. "Gives him solid mass."

Gryphon felt himself being hoisted into Orpheus's arms.

"We don't have much time," Orpheus said, jostling Gryphon as he raced up the stairs. "They won't be immobile for long."

"How did he do that?" Skyla asked, her voice breathless.

"His one gift," Orpheus answered, his own words breathless as he moved. "He gets it from Perseus. I can flash in any realm, even through solid walls, but his power is better. He can't turn things to stone like the legendary Medusa, but when he taps into the energy Perseus got from the monster, he can freeze things."

"For how long?" Skyla asked.

"Long enough for us to get outside."

"And then what?" she asked.

"Then we run like hell."

A crashing sound echoed. Voices hollered. Growls erupted far below.

Hurry. Hurry. Hurry…

"Orpheus!"

The last voice Gryphon recognized. Not because it had come from the female, or from the gods he'd just pissed off, but because it had come from his kin.

Theron. The leader of the Argonauts.

Sunlight burst over Gryphon's face. Warmth penetrated his soul. Orpheus was running, shaking him inside the blanket.

They drew to an abrupt stop, then Orpheus laid him against something cool.

Grass. He'd laid him in grass. "Stay here, Gryph. I'll be right back."

Gryphon's vision came and went. He focused long enough to look across the rolling field of brown toward a cave surrounded by olive and cypress trees. A cave they must have just run out of. The Argonauts were all there, blades drawn for battle: Theron, Zander, Titus, Cerek, and Phin. The only one missing was Demetrius.

Demetrius...The last time Gryphon had seen the guardian had been in that field outside the colony. After they'd rescued Isadora. When they'd been overrun by daemons. Just after he'd been hit with the warlock's energy that had sent his soul to the Underworld.

A female also stood with them. Dressed in knee-high boots, slim black pants and a tight-fitting top, her bow-string drawn back, arrow ready to release.

"Orpheus?" Theron called.

"I'm on it!" Orpheus called. He held out his hands and began chanting in that witch language of his. The ground rumbled. Hellhounds broke through the cave opening and charged. A blur of black slithered off to the right. While the Argonauts fought the beasts back, Orpheus continued chanting. Through the darkness Hades appeared, walking toward them in a swirl of smoke, with murder shining in his soulless eyes.

Orpheus's chanting grew stronger and something glowed red against the skin under his shirt. The ground rumbled again as if a great earthquake was building. Then the entire mountain came down, rocks and boulders and tree limbs crashing in to destroy the cave.

Teeth gnashed, a bloodcurdling howl echoed through the air. Gryphon watched as the Argonauts decimated the five or so hellhounds that had come through before the mountain had collapsed. The Argonauts and the female with the bow.

The battle was over in seconds. In the aftermath, shaking began, but this wasn't from the ground. It came from within. Gryphon could only curl into himself and the blanket. Voices drew close as he ducked his head. Voices of his warrior kin. Kin he couldn't face.

"Take him and go," Theron said. "Get him to D and that warlock, then get him the hell home."

"Hades will figure out a way through," Orpheus said, his arms sliding under the blanket to lift Gryphon off the ground. "He'll be pissed and he'll be coming."

"We'll distract until you're gone. Then we'll get gone ourselves."

"How did you know where and when we'd come out?" the female asked.

"The queen," Titus answered. "She and her sisters used their Horae powers to see what Hades had planned."

The ground shook again. And Theron added louder, "Get gone, already!

"On foot?" the female—Skyla?—asked somewhere close.

"No," Orpheus answered. "This time you're both otherworldly. At least for now. Hold on to me. We're flashing out of this one."

Before Gryphon could wonder what sort of "otherworldly" she was, he felt himself flying. Flying across time and space and away from the Underworld and all its horrors. But not away from the darkness that now lived inside him. And not away from the voice he heard cackling faintly on the wind.

Atalanta's voice.

Now we are both free. But don't forget you are mine, doulas. *Forever, you are now linked to me…*

—◆◆◆—

Orpheus hollered as they flashed to the abandoned homestead they'd found in the hills outside Psychro. Rock walls gave way to a thatched roof. Weeds and cacti overtook what used to be a yard.

The door jerked open just as they reached it and Demetrius's towering body filled the frame, his dark eyes darting to the blanket Orpheus had draped over Gryphon so he could carry him. "You got him?"

"Yeah. Where's the warlock?"

"In here." Demetrius led them to the back of the shack into what looked like a bedroom. An iron bed frame void of mattress sat against the wall, but the warlock—in Gryphon's body—was bound and gagged on the opposite side of the room, leaning against the wall, his eyes growing wide as Orpheus and Skyla stepped in after Demetrius.

The warlock struggled in his bonds, yelled beneath the gag. Fear shone in his too-blue eyes. Eyes that didn't belong to Gryphon.

"How do we do this?" Demetrius asked.

"I don't know," Orpheus answered. "Skyla?"

"This is outside the realm of my expertise, boys, but I think if you put his soul anywhere near his body, it'll know what to do."

That sounded like as good a plan as any. Orpheus tugged the blanket from Gryphon's back then laid him on the dirt-strewn stone floor, opening the blanket so his ethereal body came into view.

None of them spoke as they waited for something to happen. The only sound in the room was the warlock screaming beneath his gag and struggling with whatever strength he had left to break free of the chain holding his arms secured to the wall above his head.

At first, nothing happened. And then slowly Gryphon's soul began to slink across the floor, floating really, toward his body.

The warlock's eyes grew even wider. And he screamed so loud Orpheus was sure all Crete could hear him.

Very few moments stuck with Orpheus on a gut level, but that one did. Watching his brother's soul slide inside his body. Hearing the strangled scream of protest from the warlock. Seeing the warlock's ethereal spirit as it was forced out. The image of the warlock appeared in the air, his true form—old, wrinkled, with gnarled hands and fingers and the same glowing blue eyes. The fear-filled eyes surveyed the room, then exploded in the warlock's head. Then his ghostly body was swamped by a dark mist that dragged him down through howls of agony into the cracks in the stone floor until he was gone for good.

In the silence that followed, Skyla's shot a look at Orpheus. "Okay, that was wicked."

"Fucking wicked," Demetrius muttered. "Remind me not to piss off Hades."

"Too late," Orpheus told him. "We already pissed him off."

He knelt by his brother, ran his hand over Gryphon's cheek. Needed some kind of confirmation his brother's soul was in there. Gryphon lay slumped against the wall at an odd angle, his eyes still tightly shut. "Gryph, man, can you hear me?"

Gryphon stirred. With his hands still bound above,

his body twisted from side to side as if struggling to wake up. Then in a flutter of movement his eyes opened. Those same light blue eyes Orpheus had seen on his brother's face for over a hundred and fifty years stared up at him. "Or-Orpheus?"

Relief and something else, something he couldn't define, seeped into Orpheus's chest. "Thank you, *Dimiourgos*," he whispered. He reached for Gryphon's hands. "Hold on and we'll unhook you."

Gryphon looked up at his hands, bound above, then to Skyla and Demetrius, and finally back to Orpheus.

Heart still in his throat, Orpheus helped Demetrius unhook the metal cuff from his wrists. He rubbed at the red marks on Gryphon's skin. "It's over now. We're gonna get you home to Argolea where you can forget this ever happened."

In a flurry of movement Gryphon's arms came up, knocking Orpheus's hands away. He grasped the front of Orpheus's shirt with a death grip and tugged his brother's face close. Terror filled his wild eyes. "No. Not Argolea. Don't take me Argolea. Anywhere but there. I can't..." His body began to shake. His voice cracked. "Can't...can't go there. Not after...Don't make me go there..."

Heartache tore at Orpheus's chest. He grabbed Gryphon's forearms, the ones covered in the Argonaut markings, as they were supposed to be. "No one will make you do anything. You're safe now. I promise."

"No, no, no, you don't understand." Sobs overtook him. "She's out there. She's always out there." He let go of Orpheus's shirt, dropped back to the filthy floor, and rolled to his side, curling into himself.

Frantic to do something, Orpheus rubbed his hands against his thighs and whispered, "Who?"

Gryphon's body shook, a soul-deep tremble. And one word escaped his lips. "Atalanta."

Disbelief shot to Orpheus's chest, followed by a moment of clarity that whispered *Yes*.

He and Demetrius had trapped her in the Fields of Asphodel after they'd rescued Isadora from her lair. It was more than possible she would have recognized Gryphon for who and what he was down there.

Utter and complete helplessness consumed him as Gryphon's gut-wrenching sobs tore through the quiet.

Unsure what to say, what to do to help, he looked to Skyla. The pity and horror awash on her face said she was as lost as he was. Turning to Demetrius on his other side, Orpheus saw the guardian's clenched jaw and the mixture of fury and disgust etched into his features.

"The colony," Demetrius said in a hoarse voice. Then stronger, "We take him to the colony. There are healers there who can help him."

"Not Argolean healers," Orpheus countered.

"So we get Callia and bring her to the colony too."

Yeah, Callia. That was a good idea. Callia was the queen's personal healer and Isadora's sister as well. With her Horae powers, she'd be the one to help Gryphon through this.

Orpheus looked back down at his brother. Watched as Skyla draped the blanket over Gryphon's shoulders and ran her fingers through his hair, humming again, trying to soothe him. But when she looked up and her heartsick eyes met Orpheus's, he knew she was thinking the same thing he was.

Shame. Nothing could reduce a warrior to a quaking puddle of tears except shame.

Dear gods, what happened to him down there?

Sickness brewed in Orpheus's stomach as he swiped a hand across his forehead, tried to refocus. He'd worry about all of that later. Right now they had to get Gryphon away from this place. "He can't flash. Not in his physical state, not on earth. And I can't put him on a commercial flight when he's…like this."

"We'll charter a plane then," Demetrius said in a determined voice. "Isadora has human cash reserves set aside for emergencies. This qualifies."

Orpheus nodded even as a lump the size of a boulder settled in his throat. Yeah, this qualified all right. He'd thought getting Gryphon out of the Underworld would be the hardest obstacle they'd have to overcome. He hadn't considered what would happen after.

Hand shaking, he reached out to brush Gryphon's leg. A reassuring pat, for both of them. "It's gonna be okay, Gryph. Everything's going to be okay."

But Gryphon didn't answer. Only flinched out of Orpheus's touch as if he'd been burned. Then buried his head in his arms and wept harder.

Chapter 24

THE HOURS FLYING BACK TO MONTANA PASSED IN silence. The jet they'd chartered in Crete was roomy, with a couch along one wall of the cabin, captain's chairs on the other side, a galley, and a fancy bathroom. But none of them seemed to notice their posh surroundings. The horrors of the last few hours—the last few days—were too fresh.

Skyla kept Gryphon relaxed on the couch, running her fingers through his hair when he stirred, humming when he seemed to grow agitated, singing when they stopped to refuel and he looked like he was ready to bolt. He curled into himself as he'd done back in that shack, his back to the group, his face hidden. When he was still, several times Orpheus had peered over his shoulder, just to make sure he was still breathing. Sometimes Gryphon was asleep. Other times he lay frozen, staring wide-eyed at the back of the couch as if lost in a daze.

Demetrius spent most of his time in the cockpit with the pilot, and Skyla alternated between soothing Gryphon and tinkering in the galley, looking for food. She didn't speak much, but her singing helped smooth Orpheus's frayed edges too. And when she brought him a sandwich and sat next to him, then squeezed his hand before eating her own, that warmth returned to his chest. The same warmth he felt anytime she was close. Anytime she touched him. Anytime he thought about the way she'd protected Gryphon on their trek out of the Underworld, sung to keep him calm, and comforted him in that shack when Orpheus hadn't known what to do.

She was a rock. One who picked up the slack Orpheus left dangling, even though she had to be exhausted herself. While Orpheus's head spun with images from the Underworld and he couldn't seem to do much more than sit and stare at his brother, she made sure everything on the trip back to the colony ran smoothly.

And she hadn't even looked at the Orb under Gryphon's shirt, let alone tried to take it.

That last thought revolved in Orpheus's mind as they landed in the dark in Missoula. What was she waiting for?

Nick had a car ready to meet them at the airport. As they bounced along the road toward the colony, Skyla sat next to Gryphon and kept up her humming to keep him calm. Every time they switched surroundings, that wild-eyed look would return to Gryphon's face and he'd dart crazed looks around as if searching for…someone.

As they neared the colony, Gryphon tipped his head Orpheus's way. "I don't want to see them. The guys. If they're here…" His voice grew hoarse, but his eyes were clear. Clearer than they'd been since they'd found him. "If they're here, make them leave."

"Whatever you want, Gryph." Orpheus's throat closed around the words. As he squeezed his brother's shoulder, he caught Demetrius's gaze in the front seat. The guardian nodded once in silent commune, then looked out the dark windshield again.

The trip through the tunnels seemed shorter than when Orpheus had brought Skyla and Maelea through.

Had that been only days ago? Gods, it felt like years. So much had happened since then.

Nick met them in the vast cavern where various tunnels took off in a variety of directions and led them to the elevator. Gryphon seemed to have mellowed now that he was on his feet and walking on his own. Skyla left with Demetrius to fill the others in on what had happened while Nick took Orpheus and Gryphon up to find a room on the fifth floor of the castle.

Orpheus had the impression of pale blue walls and furnishings, but his focus was on his brother. He helped Gryphon into the room, settled him into a chair. After speaking quietly with Nick at the door, he learned all the Argonauts were here, eager to see Gryphon. He made sure Nick understood that might not be a good idea just yet.

Nick eyed Gryphon warily over Orpheus's shoulder. "You sure he's okay?"

"Would you be okay after three months in the Underworld?"

"No. That's why I'm worried."

"I'll stay with him."

Nick nodded but didn't look reassured. "Pick up the phone if you need anything. It runs to a central line."

As Nick's boots clicked down the hall, Orpheus closed the door and turned back to the room. Gryphon sat unmoving in the chair, staring off into space.

His body looked the same as always. Muscular, strong, healthy, albeit a little on the thin side. But the dead look in his eyes and the exhaustion lines on his face spoke of the strain on his soul.

Orpheus crossed the floor, helped Gryphon out of the

chair by grasping his arm and pulling him up. "Let's get you into a shower. The water will feel good."

Gryphon didn't fight him as he maneuvered them into the bathroom, with its wide glass shower and mirror that ran the length of the double vanity. But when Orpheus reached for his shirt, Gryphon swatted his hands. "I can do it myself."

"Are you sure?"

"I was dead, not stupid," Gryphon murmured, turning away. He pulled the shirt over his head, dropped it on the floor. Tugged the chain from around his neck and dropped that too. The chain that held the Orb of Krónos.

He hesitated before unbuttoning his pants. "Do you mind? I'd like some privacy."

"Sure. Yeah. I'll just be in the other room if you need me."

Orpheus eyed the Orb, lying on the floor at his brother's feet. His fingers itched to pick it up, but he fought back the urge. It wasn't going anywhere. As he stepped out and closed the door, he listened to make sure Gryphon didn't melt again. Long seconds passed with no sound, then the toilet flushed, followed by the shower turning on.

Orpheus moved away from the bathroom door and was just about to call down to see what Skyla was up to when a knock sounded to his right.

Before he could answer, the female he'd just been thinking of poked her head into the room. "Is it okay if I come in?"

Warmth spread through his chest. Warmth followed by worry. Would she try to take the Orb now? "Yeah. He's in the shower."

She stepped in, looking all long-legged and gorgeous with her hair tumbling down around her shoulders, just like always. "How is he?"

"Better." Orpheus glanced at the bathroom door, then back again. "I think maybe the worst is behind us."

"I hope so." She crossed her arms, looked around the room. "Not bad. Better than pink. That's the color they gave Maelea."

Orpheus had nearly forgotten about Ghoul Girl. He pressed two fingers against his right temple. "How is she?"

"Fine. The same. And the last thing you need to worry about right now."

Why did she care about him so much? Where was the kick-ass Siren who'd been sent by Zeus to kill him? Orpheus scrubbed both hands over his face. Confusion mixed with the exhaustion finally hitting him now that his adrenaline was waning. He dropped into the chair Gryphon had been sitting in earlier. "The Argonauts are here?"

"Yes. And the queen and her sisters."

"Fantastic." Another party. "Gryphon doesn't want—"

"Demetrius already told them. They're hanging out downstairs for now."

"That's gotta please Nick."

Skyla eased onto the armrest of his chair, her thigh inches from his hand. "Thrills him," she said sarcastically. "What's the story there? Between him and them?"

"He's Demetrius's brother."

She frowned, a pouty little look that made him itch to kiss it from her face. "I figured that out already, daemon."

"His *half* brother, smart-ass. Nick was persecuted by the monarchy because of his lineage."

"Which is?"

"He's an original hero. Sired from a human and a god."

Skyla sat silent for several seconds, then said, "Cool."

Orpheus chuckled. What was it about this female that tugged at him? Even now, when he knew he couldn't be anywhere but right here with Gryphon, when logic told him she was seconds away from snatching the Orb, he wanted to wrap her in his arms and drag her across the hall into an abandoned bedroom suite. Then find out all over again what it felt like to slide inside her body and get lost in her scent.

Him. A daemon who didn't form attachments. A witch who'd learned long ago to keep to himself. A male who never spent more than one night with any female.

And her. A Siren. Sent to seduce, steal, then take him down.

He eyed her leg. Ached to reach for her. To touch her. To let her remind him he was alive. To prove that he hadn't been forgotten.

He blew out a long breath and glanced toward the bathroom door. The shower was still running. "Maybe I should check on him."

Moment of truth. What would she do?

"Okay," she said as he pushed to his feet. "Are you hungry? I could call down and have something brought up."

He frowned. "Are you always this motherly, Siren?"

"Always," she mocked, crossing her shapely legs and leaning forward to bat her long dark lashes his way. "After beheading ogres all day long, I serve on the PTA board at night."

"You on a PTA board. Now that I'd like to see." He

knocked on the bathroom door. Drew up his defenses, just in case. "Gryph? You okay in there?"

Nothing but the sound of running water met his ears.

Orpheus knocked again. Got no response. He tried the handle and found it locked. A shot of panic rushed through him.

Skyla's boots clicked as she pushed off the chair. "What's wrong?"

"I don't know." Orpheus jiggled the knob again. "Gryphon? Answer me."

Nothing.

"*Skata*." Orpheus stepped back from the door, centered himself, and called up a simple spell to free the lock. A click resounded. He turned the knob.

Steam enveloped the room, fogged the mirror. Through the frosted glass he could see Gryphon standing naked under the spray, scrubbing at the skin on his arms. "Gryph? Are you okay? I knocked and knocked and you didn't answer."

"Can't get clean," Gryphon murmured. "Have to get it off. Just a little more." He stopped scrubbing, slammed both hands over his ears. "Stop!"

Gryphon shook his head violently, then went back to scrubbing at his skin again, murmuring faster, "Can't get clean. Can't get clean…"

Shit. He wasn't better. He was getting worse. That panic morphed to all-out dread as it pushed its way back up Orpheus's chest. "Come on, Gryphon. That's enough. Let's get you out."

Orpheus was aware Skyla was standing in the doorway as he reached for a towel and grasped the shower door, that the Orb was in plain view on the floor. But he didn't care. The only thing that mattered right now was his brother.

Orpheus pulled the door open. Then froze. "Holy gods…"

Blood ran like rivers from Gryphon's arms, his legs, his face and torso. His fingers were bloody stumps where he'd dug into his skin over and over, scrubbing harder with each pass.

"Gryphon, stop!" Orpheus threw the towel around Gryphon's shoulders and hauled him out of the shower. Gryphon hollered and hurled his weight into Orpheus, knocking them both to the ground with a crack. They grappled across the bathroom tiles until Orpheus got behind Gryphon, closed one arm across his brother's head, used the other to immobilize his arms, then hooked Gryphon's legs so he couldn't break free.

Gryphon struggled once, twice more, then collapsed against Orpheus and broke down, his entire body shaking with soul-rattling sobs. Water and blood ran from Gryphon's skin into Orpheus's clothes, dripped onto the floor around him. "I can't get it off," he cried. "It's all over me. Inside me. I just want it to go away. I just…oh, gods, make it go away."

His body convulsed in Orpheus's arms, and the sobs turned to full-body trembles Orpheus felt all the way to his very core.

Orpheus caught Skyla's horror-filled gaze in the doorway, where she stood still as stone. And his heart—the heart he thought he didn't have—contracted beneath the earth element still resting against his chest. "Get help," he whispered. "Find someone who can help my brother."

━━✠━━

It was hours later when Skyla peeked her head back into Gryphon's room. Though it was quiet, there were several people taking up space. Callia, Queen Isadora's personal healer, held Gryphon's wrist on the far side of the bed and glanced at the clock high on the wall. Theron conversed quietly with Isadora near the window. Skyla knew from her conversations downstairs that several other Argonauts had come and gone through the night, but Orpheus remained, sitting in a chair next to Gryphon, his elbows leaning on his knees, his hands clasped in front of him while he watched his brother sleep.

The image of the big Argonaut clawing at his flesh wouldn't leave her head. Neither would the blood that had covered him and the floor and Orpheus when Orpheus had tackled Gryphon in the bathroom. Every time she thought of what he'd been through in the Underworld, her mind skipped to Orpheus and the years and years he'd been trapped there himself. The gruesome things he must have endured. The fact that—thankfully—he couldn't remember them.

She'd considered telling Orpheus the truth about their relationship so many times. Had pondered what it would do to him to learn who and what he really was. But after seeing Gryphon, she knew she couldn't. It wasn't about her or what she'd be losing. She didn't want to hurt Orpheus. And bringing up the past would do only that. It would dredge up something that was better off dead and buried.

Heads turned. Orpheus looked over his shoulder,

eyes shadowed and bloodshot. But they brightened just a touch when they caught sight of her, and warmth flooded her belly in response.

He rose from the chair, all corded muscle and restrained strength. Though someone had given him a new shirt, his jeans were still stained with Gryphon's blood. As he crossed the floor toward her, the guardian markings on his forearms stood out in stark relief to the rest of his skin. Markings that technically shouldn't be there anymore, now that his brother was back.

He scrubbed a hand over the back of his head, his tired eyes and the stubble on his square jaw making him look sexier than she'd ever seen him. He stopped a foot from her, stuffed his hands in his pockets, was careful to keep his voice low. "Hey."

"Is he doing better?"

The agony Skyla saw in Orpheus's eyes tugged at her chest. "He's out. Callia gave him a sedative. Said he needed rest to let the"—he swallowed, faced her again—"wounds heal."

The wounds. Those crazed eyes. And Gryphon's voice. *I can't get it off. It's all over me. Inside me. I just…oh, gods, make it go away.*

She reached for Orpheus's hand, pulled it from his pocket, and squeezed her fingers around his, hoping to take the haunted look from his eyes. The one that said he remembered every detail as clearly as she did. "Come with me for a few minutes."

"I can't leave him."

"You'll be no good to him if he wakes and you're falling over from exhaustion."

"No. He needs me here." He pulled back from her hand.

"She's right, O," Theron said. "You need some rest. Callia and I will come find you if anything changes."

"He'll be out for at least another twenty-four hours," Callia added from the other side of the bed.

Isadora crossed the room, her ballet-style flats barely making a sound on the floor as she came to stand next to him. Beside the queen, Orpheus looked huge. She laid a hand on his forearm, right over the Argonaut markings, and not for the first time Skyla had the impression these two had some special bond. Not sexual, but…a friendship. "Go with Skyla, Orpheus. I promise when Gryphon wakes, we'll come find you. Everything will seem better after you've both gotten some sleep."

The frown on Orpheus's face said he didn't agree, but he finally nodded. Skyla stepped toward the door. A little of her worry eased when Orpheus followed.

In the long hallway his boots echoed like drumbeats as they moved toward the elevator. When they were inside the small car, Orpheus shot her a frown. "Since when do Theron and Isadora side with a Siren?"

She punched a button. "Since Demetrius explained what happened after we left the Argonauts on Crete. Apparently, you help one Argonaut, the rest are friends for life. Even if you are a Siren."

Orpheus didn't answer, but his scowl deepened and he crossed his arms over his muscular chest.

"Speaking of," she said, "I notice you still have the markings."

"I know."

He didn't say more, and she sensed he wasn't happy about that fact. Not wanting to push things, she let the topic drop as the elevator came to a stop and the door opened.

"Where are we going?" he asked.

"It's a surprise."

"Skyla," he sighed, "I'm really tired. One of the rooms across from Gryphon's would probably be bet—"

She took his hand and tugged him down the long empty two-story hall with its wall of black windows before he could dig his heels in. "Just humor me for a few minutes, would you? If you want to go back down and find a room closer to Gryphon after you see the surprise, I'll take you."

He scowled again, but let her pull him along. When they reached the double doors at the end of the hall, she pushed them open. Chilled air cut to her spine. She continued to pull him after her, heading for the curved stairs off to the right.

"I don't think it's snowed since the last time we were up here," he said at her back as they started up the steps.

She shot him a smile. Though she knew the events of the last few days weighed heavily on that soul he didn't think he had, she was happy that at least a little sarcasm was back in his voice. "Contrary to what you think, I'm not wild about snow."

"Could have fooled me," he muttered.

And oh yeah, the hero she'd come to care for was still in there. Hidden beneath a layer of pain she hoped to alleviate.

"Fooling you isn't as fun as it used to be, daemon." She tugged him to the upper balcony. "Okay, close your eyes."

He frowned but did as she asked. "If I get a snowball in the face, you're going to be in big trouble."

She grinned. "Will you spank me?"

"I'll do more than that."

Heat flooded her veins. *That* was the guardian she wanted to find again.

Her free hand closed around the door handle. She pulled him into the glass room behind her, shut the door. Warmth from the fireplace to the right dampened the chill, and the orange glow from the embers lit the room just enough.

"Okay, open your eyes."

Orpheus's lashes lifted. And his eyebrows immediately dropped low as he turned a slow circle. "Where's all the stuff?"

For the first time since she'd hatched this crazy plan, a sliver of unease slid through Skyla. "In storage somewhere else."

She watched as he took it all in. The couch and chairs positioned near the fireplace, the bookshelves on the far side of the room that were empty but for a few leather tomes, then past the dark windows to the other side of the room and the king-size bed with its blue comforter and mountain of pillows.

"What is this?" he asked.

Skyla's stomach tightened with doubt. "Your room. Well, if you want it, I mean."

When he slanted her a confused look, that unease pushed its way up her chest. She hated that she felt anything but confident. As a Siren, confidence was part of who and what she was. But ever since she'd met Orpheus, that confidence had been wavering. Because his was the first opinion that mattered. "Isadora suggested it, actually. A room of your own. She didn't think you'd be leaving Gryphon and going back to Argolea anytime soon."

Her voice trailed off because the whole idea suddenly sounded…lame.

"You did all this?" he asked, looking around again.

"Yes. Well, no, not all of it," she corrected. "Nick had a couple of his guys help me move boxes and chairs and haul furniture up here."

"You got Nick to agree to let me stay here?"

"Isadora did."

He turned to face her, but she couldn't read his expression. Was he impressed? Angry no one had asked him what he wanted?

He didn't answer her unasked questions. Instead he crossed the floor, stepped past the bed, and pushed the door on the far wall open. After flipping on the light and glancing around the fancy bathroom she'd been surprised to find behind the door, he switched off the light, then came back and stared at the bed. "Why?"

"Why what?"

"Why did you do this?"

"Because you need a place to unwind."

"No, why *this*?" He motioned to the whole room, accentuated by warm burgundy throw rugs and leather furnishings instead of the cold cardboard boxes that had dominated it before. "Why this room?"

Because it meant something to her. And she hoped it meant something to him as well.

A lump formed in her throat. She wasn't sure how to answer. Not without putting her heart on the line. A heart she'd only just rediscovered in the last few days. All because of him.

He crossed back to stand in front of her. "Well?"

She hated that she wanted his approval. More than she'd wanted anyone's approval before, even Cynurus's. Though they were technically the same. Gods, none of this made sense, and she especially hated how that made her vulnerable. Vulnerability wasn't something she had much experience with. "You don't like it? I told you if you didn't, you could find a different room downstairs. I was just trying to—"

"Why haven't you taken it?"

Her mouth closed. She stared up into his intense gray eyes. Eyes that seemed to be looking deep into her soul. It took several seconds before she realized he wasn't talking about the room but about the Orb.

Her gaze slid to his chest and the Orb she knew lay against his skin, hidden under the white button-down he wore. She'd seen the outline of it under his shirt after she brought help for Gryphon. Knew he'd put it on and that he'd probably already placed the earth element in its slot. And she knew right then that this was her defining moment. She could tease and seduce and imply all she wanted, but the only way she was ever going to prove her loyalty to him was to be honest.

"Because I don't want it."

"Zeus does."

"Zeus is going to have to learn to live with disappointment." When his eyes narrowed, she knew it was now or never. "I'm leaving the Sirens."

Skepticism crossed his handsome face. "Why?"

"Two reasons. The first is because now that I've seen that thing and felt its power, I know no god can have it. If balance is to remain, it needs to be destroyed. I know that can't happen before all the elements are found, but giving it to Zeus won't do anything but cause trouble. I'm sure of it."

"And the second?"

Right. The second. Skyla bit her lip. There was a jumping-off point, then there was a diving-off point. And right now she was either going to hit the water face-first and come up breathing, or she'd crash and burn in the bottom of an empty pit.

She pulled up her courage. "The second is that I can't in good faith stay with an order that wants me to kill the man I love."

There was no reaction from him, not even a muscle twitch in his jaw. And in the silence that followed, Skyla's anxiety amped a good three notches.

"You love me," he finally said. When she nodded, he added, "No one loves a daemon."

Her heart pinched. "No one but me."

For several long seconds he didn't say anything. And she still couldn't read his expression, had no idea what he was thinking or feeling. And then he frowned. "You are seriously fucked in the head, you know that?"

Her defenses came up. The same ones she'd used to protect her heart for far too long. A heart that was now battered and bruised and aching because she'd taken a chance and it had all been for nothing. "I—"

He closed the distance between them, grasped both sides of her face with his large, warm hands, then lowered his mouth to hers.

The air left her lungs on a whoosh. The fight slid right out of her body. As his tongue dipped into her mouth and she tasted the sweetness of him, she wrapped her hands around the guardian markings on his forearms and told herself not to let go.

There was urgency in the kiss. Mixed with relief and need. So much need it curled her stomach and made her whole body ache.

"Skyla, Skyla, Skyla..." She loved the way he mouthed her name against her lips, drew her closer with his arms until the long lean line of his well-defined body pressed up against hers. "They'll never let you leave because of me."

"It's not their decision to make." When he eased back and looked down at her with those soft gray eyes, her confidence shot up again. A confidence she now couldn't believe she'd been lacking. "It's mine. And I choose you. Daemon or no daemon. Argonaut or not. Zeus and Athena are wrong about you, Orpheus. You're not evil."

"How can you be so sure?" he whispered.

"Because I watched you with Maelea. I saw the way you protected her when you didn't have to. The way you protected me even though you knew what I was. And I saw the lengths you went to, to save your brother. An evil soul can't love like that."

"I don't have a soul—"

"Yes, you do." She tightened her fingers around his forearms. "One that deserves so much more than you've been given."

Emotion turned his eyes to shimmering silver. "Skyla—"

She rose up on her toes and kissed him, sliding her arms around his neck and drawing him even closer. "Let me love you, Orpheus."

She kissed him long and deep, groaned into his mouth when his arms circled her waist and his warmth surrounded her. She stepped back toward the bed, pulling him with her, loving the way he couldn't seem to stop kissing her, couldn't seem to stop touching her just as she was touching him. When her legs bumped the mattress, she eased back, tugged him down with her until they fell on the mattress and his weight pressed into her, the heat from his erection pressing into her lower belly, warming her from the outside in.

She yanked at his shirt, broke the kiss long enough to pull it over his head. His mouth was back on hers, kissing, licking, sucking as he found the buttons on her shirt and undid them, then tugged her torso up enough so he could wrench the shirt from her arms and toss it on the floor behind him.

The Orb fell against her chest. Warm and enticing. She ignored it and focused on him, sliding her hand over his rough jaw.

His gaze ran over the red bra she wore, down to her waistband. "Gods, you are so beautiful."

His hand followed, skimming over her cleavage, then down the line of her abdomen to trail heat to her belly button. She sucked in a breath even as a shiver raced down her spine. "It's not real. Once I leave the Sirens, I won't look like this anymore."

His warm, desire-filled eyes slid back to hers. "What do you mean?"

"I mean this Barbie-doll body is part of the gig. Once a Siren leaves, her body transforms back to the way it was before she joined the order."

His eyes narrowed with mischief. "Is this your way of telling me you were three hundred pounds with a hook nose before joining the Sirens?"

She ran her hands up his impressive arms. "Maybe not quite three hundred." When his eyebrows lifted in question, she smiled. "It'll be the same me. This is just the enhanced version."

"Explain 'enhanced.'"

"Well, for one, I'm not really this tall. Take about three inches off my legs. My hair isn't normally this blond, and if memory serves—and remember, it's been quite a while—my waist isn't quite this small."

"What about these?" His large palm slid up to cup her right breast.

Warmth puckered her nipple beneath the red lace. "Now those will likely stay the same."

That mischievous grin widened as he flicked the clasp, freeing her breasts to spill out into his hand. "I had a feeling they were real. I can always tell."

Her stomach tightened, and the humor faded as he lowered his mouth to her right breast, laved his tongue over her nipple, then drew her deep into his mouth to suckle.

Her fingers found their way into his thick brown hair and she arched her back, offering whatever he wanted. As much as he wanted.

He worked her over with his tongue, with his lips, with the wicked hot breath he blew across her nipples until they ached for more. She opened her legs so he could sink down into her body. So that long hard cock pressing against the fly of his jeans could rub right where she wanted it most.

"Orpheus…" She drew his mouth back to hers, kissed him deeply. Then eased back so she could see his face. "Will it bother you? If I don't look exactly the way I do now?"

His gaze started at the top of her head, traveled down the length of her body, hovered where their hips were locked together, separated by only his jeans and her pants. "I like this body, I won't lie. But it's not what I love about you."

Her heart tripped, and her voice cracked when she asked, "What you love about me?"

"Yeah, what I love." His fingers crazed her throat, traced the line of her sternum between her breasts, and hovered over her heart. "Every time I think about the way you cared for my brother…" He swallowed, and tears dampened his eyes. "You don't even know him."

"I know you."

One corner of his mouth curled. "Yeah, and you still cared for him, regardless."

"Orpheus—"

"No one's ever cared about me before. No one's put their life on the line for me. No one even considered it. You did it not only for me, but for my brother. I—I didn't think anyone could love me."

Her heart pinched all over again, and she ran her fingers over his stubbly jaw, the cap she'd kept on her emotions for so long finally blowing free. *I loved you before, daemon. It just doesn't even come close to how much I love you now.* "Then you thought wrong. And if you'll let me, I'll spend the next five hundred or so years proving just how wrong you were."

His gaze searched her face. "You will?"

"Well…" Her cheeks heated. "If, that is, you want me to. I might have some free time on my hands soon."

A slow, easy, devilish smile inched its way across his lips, and he pressed that heavenly erection against her mound all over again. "Oh, I want you, Siren. I've wanted you since you first set out to seduce me."

She lost herself in his kiss. Was so light-headed from his lips and teeth and tongue, she barely registered him kicking off his boots, sliding out of his pants, and dragging hers from her legs. But she definitely knew when his fingers brushed her wetness and his thumb circled her clit, sending a current of electricity racing through her body.

"Orpheus…"

"Like that?"

"Mm, yes. More."

He chuckled as he stroked her, seemed to enjoy it when her whole body quivered. As he slid two fingers deep inside, he continued to tease her clit with his thumb and lowered his head to her breast, flicking her nipple with his tongue until she moaned. She dropped her head back and lifted one leg so she could dig her heel into the mattress, granting him more access. Pleasure gathered beneath his hands, around his talented fingers sliding in and out of her sheath, along her nipples, where his tongue was doing insane things to her breasts. But it wasn't enough, wasn't ever enough when what she wanted most was so very close.

She hooked a leg over his hip and rolled him to his back, thrilled when she felt the naked, blunt head of his cock brush her aching folds. She wanted to taste it again, take it deep in her mouth like last time, feel his pleasure pulse along her tongue. But the throb between her legs was too great. The heat too intense to stop and readjust.

"Orpheus…" Her mouth was on his again.

"Hold on." He pushed her back. And she watched in awe as he tore the chain from around his neck and dropped the Orb on the floor along with his clothes.

Hero. The word revolved in her mind again. If she hadn't known it before, she knew it now.

"Now," he said, his hands sliding to her hips, guiding her, taking charge even though she was the one directing things. "Where were we?"

The head of his cock slid along her folds, pressed against her opening just enough to draw a groan from her chest, then retreated. She tightened her muscles, tried to lower herself down, met the resistance of his strong hands holding her still.

"Um…yeah," she managed. "I think…right there."

"There, Siren?"

"Yes." She kissed him. "Stop tormenting me."

"Tell me again." He lifted his head and kissed her long and deep and slow. "Tell me again what you did before."

She knew what he wanted. The same thing she wanted. "I love you, Orpheus."

He sat up so fast, a gasp tore from her mouth. But it turned to a groan when he pulled her hips down to his and thrust inside her. Flesh settled against flesh. His erection twitched inside her. He rolled her to her back and whispered, "Wrap your legs around me."

She did. Groaned again as he pushed in even deeper. He retreated, thrust into her again and again, stoked her already-roaring fire to within degrees of exploding. When it wasn't enough, he hooked his arms behind her knees, opening her wider, and drove himself one more reaching inch inside.

"Gods, Skyla," he said against her lips, "I love being

inside of you. I don't even care that you had to seduce me at the start to get us to this point."

She gripped his face with both hands. "I didn't seduce you, Orpheus. I didn't have to. That connection you kept asking me about is real. All I did was fight it. Way longer than I should have. Believe me. I've never wanted anyone the way I want you."

"Ah, gods, Siren." His eyes darkened and he lowered his mouth and kissed her again, this time as if he couldn't get enough. His thrusts picked up speed. She lifted her hips to meet him, wrapped her arms around his muscular shoulders, slick with sweat and flexing with his movements.

She knew his release was coming. She could feel it growing with every press and slide and groan and thrust and retreat. She lost herself in the feel of him—hard and hot and so very thick. And when he arched his back and his entire body quivered over hers—*inside* hers—she let herself go.

For the first time ever, she let everything she'd worked for, every disappointment and heartache along the way, every long lonely moment in a life that never should have been, finally go. And as he collapsed against her, as his head slid into the crook between her neck and shoulder and his hot breath washed over her flesh to tighten her nipples all over again, she ran her fingers over the damp skin of his shoulders and told herself there was no going back. Not for the order. Not for Athena. Never again for Zeus.

Not even when the King of the Gods sent her sisters to kill her, which she knew he would undoubtedly do soon.

Chapter 25

THAT CONNECTION YOU KEPT ASKING ME ABOUT IS REAL.

Images swam behind Orpheus's closed eyelids as he hovered on the edge of sleep. Images that blended with Skyla's words and refused to let him rest. Her standing in the chaos of that concert the night he'd been looking for Maelea. Protecting Ghoul Girl with that magical bow and arrow when she thought he was there to harm the girl. The way she'd kissed him after she was pulled from that avalanche. Covered in sweat in the Underworld, comforting his brother. The last few hours alone in this bed, as she'd used her body and voice to enrapture as she had from the start.

His daemon was gone. He didn't know how, but he couldn't feel it anymore. Not even a rumble of awareness. Something in the back of his mind said its absence was somehow linked to Skyla, but he didn't know how that was possible. All he knew was that for so long he'd lived by the push and pull of that daemon. To be free of it…it was like no other feeling in the world.

Save being inside Skyla.

That connection you kept asking me about is real.

Her image flickered again behind his eyelids. And though he knew he shouldn't be this content when his brother lay floors below, haunted by horrors Orpheus didn't want to imagine, he couldn't stop feeling alive any more than he could stop the steady thump of his heart.

And yet…

Something niggled at the back of his mind. The images shifted like billowing smoke, taking shape in different forms. Skyla again, only dressed differently. Speaking…more formally. Telling him…Telling him what?

Just as the first time they were together in this room, a kaleidoscope of images, all centered on her, cycled through his mind. Only these were clearer. The sounds growing louder. Playing like scenes from a movie. Until the great climax. And the moment the curtain was parted and the wizard finally revealed.

He jerked out of bed, a reflex of muscle and mind and complete and utter shock, and hit the floor with a thud that echoed through his bones. But the physical pain was fleeting. The emotional pain, the lingering torment, the years of torture, consumed him from the inside out. And betrayal, like a hot, sharp knife, sliced through what he thought had been a heart.

Skyla peered over the side of the bed, her hair rumpled, her eyes sleepy, her lips still swollen from his mouth. "Are you okay? What happened?"

Orpheus breathed through his nostrils to remain calm. But inside a firestorm had erupted and the blaze was consuming him in a flurry of flames for which there was no relief.

"Orpheus?"

"You knew they were coming. You left me there to die."

"What?"

The past, a past he hadn't remembered until just now, zipped across his mind. And the why and how and that connection he'd been feeling finally made sense. "We argued and you left. And they came in minutes later. The Sirens. *Your* Sirens. The ones you sent."

She eased up to sitting, tugged the sheet around her. A wary look passed over her features. Features that were still as beautiful as he remembered. Even now, over two thousand years later.

Two thousand years. Holy *fuck*.

"You've obviously had some kind of dream. Why don't you come back to bed and—"

"*That* wasn't a dream." He pushed to his feet, images now on fast-forward in his head, and scrubbed the heel of his hand across his forehead, only it did nothing to erase the pain. And the torment. And the horror. "I knew there was some connection between us. I knew you were lying to me from the start."

"Orpheus? Okay, just wait—"

The bitter bite of betrayal shoved out all the shock and awe from before. "Why don't you call me by my other name? The name my father gave me? The name my grandfather and your boss condemned."

She tightened the sheet around her breasts. In the dim light from the fading fire he saw understanding. And fear. For the first time since he'd met the Siren he saw true fear on her flawless face.

"Say my name, Skyla."

She swallowed. "I don't know what you're talking about."

"Say it."

She glanced across the room toward the fire so she didn't have to meet his gaze.

And in that moment, his restraint snapped.

The red rage of betrayal colored everything in his path.

He was on the bed before she saw him move, his hand wrapped around her neck, his knee wedged against her side as he pushed her down to the mattress. "Say my name!"

She gasped, let go of the sheet, and grappled for his fingers. But though she was strong and could easily give him a good knock-down, drag-out fight, she didn't try to tear his hand away, didn't retaliate in any way. Tears flooded her eyes. Tears that only inflamed his anger because he knew they were nothing more than another form of seduction. Seduction she'd been trained to use to get what she wanted.

"Say my name or I will crush your windpipe," he growled. "I swear it."

Tears spilled over her sooty dark lashes. "You weren't supposed to remem—"

His grip tightened. "Say it!"

"Cynurus," she choked out beneath his hand. "Your name was Cynurus. Your father named you after the mystical valley Cynuria between Argolis and Laconia, where it's said the Muses liked to play."

He let go and stepped back. And as he did he saw the past as clearly as if it had happened yesterday.

He was Perseus's son. Grandson to the King of the Gods. The son who was nothing but a major disappointment to his father. The grandson who'd been pegged as disloyal right from the start. And she was the Siren who'd been sent to kill him, not just once, but twice.

He'd fallen for her both times. Like a love-struck fool. All because somewhere deep inside he'd wanted to believe he deserved something more. That he was meant for things greater than himself. Just like the original heroes.

Stupidity slammed into him. Treachery followed

quickly on its heels. And sickness tore through his stomach to weaken his knees.

The "more," he'd gotten. It just hadn't been the "more" he'd wanted. Death at the hands of Zeus's assassins had gifted him two thousand years of "more" trapped in the Underworld. In a never-ending cycle of pain and agony and torture. Where he'd been forgotten. All because of her.

He turned away, because the rage inside was so strong it was either that or kill her. He swiped his pants from the floor where he'd dropped them hours ago. The Orb clanged against the hardwood and lay at his feet, the marking of the Titans staring up at him, the earth element gleaming where he'd slid it into its compartment only hours ago.

"Orpheus…"

Heat radiated from the Orb. Drifted up from his feet, infused him with the strength he lacked now that his daemon was gone. Reminded him what was constant in this world.

Not trust. There was none.

Not honesty. Honesty was a farce.

And definitely not love. Love was the greatest ruse of all. Designed to trap and enslave and ultimately destroy.

He lifted the Orb from the floor, slid the chain around his neck, and felt the power of the Orb surround him.

"Orpheus," she said in a frantic voice. "Wait. Let me explain."

He tugged on his dirty jeans, found his boots, shoved his feet inside. Picked up his shirt from the floor and pulled it over his head as he moved for the door.

She grasped his arm before he could turn the handle. "Wait. Please."

Her touch stirred what her voice couldn't. He whipped toward her, knocking her arm away. "Don't touch me. Don't ever think of touching me again."

"Orpheus." Tears streamed down her cheeks. Tears she was obviously working hard to conjure. She took a step back, gripped the sheet around her breasts with both hands, playing the part of the heartsick female remarkably well. But then she'd had years to perfect that role, hadn't she? Thousands of years.

"Just…just listen, okay? I didn't know at first. And by the time I did, I couldn't tell you. They said you wouldn't remember and I didn't want to…Everything…everything from then and now is so muddled. I was trying to figure out the truth about what happened back then and whether you deserved—"

His vision blurred and the red rage of retribution forced his feet forward. She closed her mouth with a snap, took a step back, her eyes wide, white halos all around her amethyst irises. Eyes he now knew he *had* looked into hundreds of times before. A lifetime ago, just as he'd thought.

He slammed his palm against the wall right by her head, a deafening crack that echoed through the entire room.

"Two thousand years, Siren," he said from between clenched teeth. "In hell. All because of you. Do not speak to me about what is *deserved*. Because right now I'm a hair's breadth from deciding you deserve to be ripped apart limb by limb and thrown to the fishes in the lake below us."

He took a step away from her, hating that even now, when he knew it had all been an act on her part, he still wanted her. Still craved her. Was still entranced by her just as he'd always been.

"And take a message to your fucking king while you're at it," he added, drawing on the Orb's strength so he wouldn't reach for her, wouldn't touch her, wouldn't ever give in again. "Tell him his grandson's back from the dead. And this time, *his* fucking days are numbered."

—◆◆◆—

Maelea couldn't sleep.

A dark energy had infiltrated the colony sometime during the night and she'd been awake since, checking abandoned corridors and balconies, looking for anything out of the ordinary. Drawn to it in a way that made her skin itch and her heart thump with excitement.

Footsteps echoed from the stairs. She slid into the shadows behind a large stone column in the great hall. Orpheus's boots grew silent as he hesitated at the bottom of the steps, glanced right and left. His hair was mussed, his shirt wrinkled, the jeans he wore stained with…blood? But it was his face that kept drawing her attention. The locked jaw like a slice of steel beneath his skin, the burning eyes, the unnatural energy that radiated from every inch of his rigid body.

She drew a sharp breath. This was not the same man who'd slinked into her room a few nights ago and spoken of loneliness and being forgotten. This was the man who'd kidnapped her from her home, killed those hellhounds as if they were nothing, and put her life in jeopardy.

His eyes narrowed on her hiding place. She held her breath, sure he could see her. Seconds later he turned and headed for the door at the far end of the hall.

Alone, she pressed a hand against her stomach and breathed deeply.

The clock over the fireplace told her it was close to five a.m. She needed to get back to her room before the colony awoke. She took a step for the stairs, then stopped when she heard voices. Female voices. She darted back into the shadows and waited for them to pass.

"Have you checked on Max?" Isadora asked.

The tall auburn-haired female strolling down the corridor with the queen of Argolea rubbed her forehead. "He was studying. Didn't want to talk to me. He's always studying."

"That's not a bad thing, Callia. He missed out on school during his time with Atalanta."

"I know, I know, it's just…"

"What?"

Callia stopped. "I knew the transition wouldn't be easy. I knew the honeymoon phase would wear off, but lately…I'm having a hard time getting through to him. It's like he doesn't want to talk to us anymore. Like he's turning into himself and his schoolwork."

"He has a lot of emotions to work though. He spent ten years with her."

"I know," Callia said, walking again. "I know he's angry and confused and trying to adjust to life in Argolea. It's just—" Her voice caught. "I love him so much. I don't want to lose him now that he's finally home."

Isadora squeezed her hand. "You won't. You and Zander will help him through this. He's lucky to have you."

Callia nodded, but she didn't look convinced. She stopped in front of the massive fire in the living area, where embers from last night's fireplace still glowed red.

"How about coffee?" Isadora asked. "That always helps."

"I think five minutes off my feet might do me better. I need to get back to Gryphon soon." Callia eased onto the couch. "And only one cup for you. Too much caffeine's not good for you and that baby."

The queen sat on the arm of a chair, said something Maelea couldn't hear, but Maelea barely cared. If the two females didn't leave soon, there'd be no way for her to reach the stairs without one or both of them seeing her. And while she wasn't afraid of them, she had no desire to "chat" or get to know anyone better in this place.

The two conversed quietly by the fire for a few minutes, then footsteps echoed from the stairs again and both turned that direction.

Maelea's gaze shifted to the stairs. Skyla's boots clanked against the hardwood as she skipped stairs to reach the bottom. She wore the same outfit Maelea had seen her in since the first, but this time the perfectly coiffed Siren was nowhere to be found. Her hair was a wild tangle around her face, her shirt inside out, one boot not zipped all the way to the top. And the panic in her eyes was a dead giveaway something had happened.

Isadora rose from the couch. "Skyla? What's wrong?"

"Maelea," the Siren said in a breathy voice as if she'd been running. "I have to find Maelea."

"I haven't seen her," Isadora said. "We've been with Gryphon. What's happened?"

"He took the Orb." Skyla pressed both hands against her eyes. "He remembered and he took the Orb and now he's gone. And I have to find him before he does something…"

Callia pushed up from the couch, followed Isadora across the floor to the base of the stairs where Skyla stood. She placed both hands on Skyla's shoulders, turned her into the light. "Calm down and tell us what happened. You're talking about Orpheus, right? What did he remember?"

"Everything," Skyla said in that same broken voice. "All of it. He…" She drew in a shaky breath, dropped her hands. "He's Perseus's son. Zeus's grandson."

"What do you mean, Perseus's son?" the queen asked. "Orpheus is only three hundred years old. How—?"

"He was given a second chance at life." When both looked at her as if she was nuts, Skyla waved her hands. "Two thousand plus years ago he stole the air element from Zeus. I was sent to get it back and then kill him. Only I didn't. I…we…we had…a relationship. And then I found out he really had stolen the element. I couldn't kill him at that point, but I didn't stop it either. I didn't think…" She closed her eyes, took a deep breath, opened them again to focus on the queen. "When Zeus sent me after Orpheus because he was hunting the Orb, I knew something wasn't right. But I didn't find out until later that Orpheus was Cynurus reincarnated. They told me he wouldn't remember his past life, but they were wrong. They were wrong about so many things. And I believed them. Just like always."

Isadora and Callia stared at the Siren in disbelief, and Maelea found herself thinking back to what she knew of Perseus and his son Cynurus, about whom she'd heard whispers but had never met. He'd done something to anger Zeus. Something more treacherous than simply being born, like her.

"I have to find him before he does something he'll regret later. He has the Orb and the earth element. And he thinks I betrayed him. He's angry and hurting. If he tries to challenge Zeus with the Orb…"

Callia shot a look at Isadora. "Theron needs to hear this."

"Go get him," Isadora said.

As Callia rushed off, Isadora added, "Now tell me what this has to do with Maelea."

"Maelea can sense energy shifts. She'll know if he tries to use the power of the Orb. She can locate him before he—"

Maelea stepped out of the shadows. Skyla's head came around and her mouth closed. Stopping in the middle of the room, Maelea rubbed her arms to ease the chill that had settled over her skin with this news. "He's my nephew. In three thousand years I've not met a direct relative until now. I—I didn't even suspect."

"I need to know where he is."

Maelea nodded. She knew all too well what would happen if Orpheus tormented Zeus with the Orb. And a part of her—the part that had believed in him the night he told her he wanted the Orb to rescue his brother from the Underworld—needed to know a soul could still overcome all that darkness. "He came down the stairs just before you. He left through there." She pointed toward the far end of the hall.

"What about the Orb?" Skyla asked.

"I—I didn't see it."

"Orpheus can flash on earth," Isadora interjected. "He won't need to tap into the Orb's energy to open a portal like the warlock did."

"Damn it," Skyla muttered, running a hand over her face. "I forgot about that."

"He doesn't need to," Maelea said. When Skyla's

head came up, she added, "He's using the Orb to give him strength. The strength he lost from his daemon."

"Where?" Skyla asked.

Maelea closed her eyes, focused on the darkness she'd felt when Orpheus had come down the stairs. It had left the colony with him, she now knew. She loosened her mind and the tendrils of awareness she so often kept locked tight.

She opened her eyes when she located it. "In the hills outside Litochoro, Greece."

"The City of Gods." Determination settled hard in Skyla's eyes, turning them to intense shards of colored glass. "Thank you."

Skyla was out the door before Maelea could think to answer. Before the queen of Argolea could stop her. Footfalls echoed from the hall, and then the great room felt ten times too small as it was suddenly flooded with too many men. Big, brawny, intimidating men.

The Argonauts.

Maelea shrank back into the shadows as quickly as she could.

The queen looked toward the dark-haired Argonaut, the one with eyes like the dead of night.

"Where?" he asked.

"Litochoro. At the base of Mount Olympus in northern Greece. The Siren's already gone to try to stop him. But, Theron..."

Her hand on his arm stopped his movement toward the door. He looked down at her. "I know, Your Highness. We won't hurt him. Not if we don't have to." He glanced over her head to the tall Argonaut beyond. "We need to go."

Low murmurs rose up in the room. The mass of male bodies moved toward the door but the tall Argonaut lingered, waited for the others to leave, then crossed to the queen and kissed her before following the others out.

And in the silence, seeing something Maelea knew she'd never find no matter how long she looked, she felt more alone than she had before. Alone and very much aware of the darkness still hovering in some hidden part of the colony. Darkness that had nothing to do with the Orb.

A darkness that called to her and taunted her to find it.

Chapter 26

THE COOL WIND WHIPPED THROUGH THE MOUNTAINS. A chill Orpheus barely registered because revenge burned hot, heating him from the inside out.

The trees were different, the mountaintops more weathered than he remembered. Though humans called the city at the base of the majestic Mount Olympus the City of Gods, it wasn't. On earth, this wasn't anything more than rock and soil. The metaphysical Mount Olympus where the gods actually lived was a different place entirely. But he didn't need to recognize the landmarks to tell him he was in the right place. The Orb grew hotter against his chest the closer he got, and memories of the last time he'd been here flickered through his mind like a steady stream of color.

There was one similarity in the two very different lives he'd led. Then, as now, his only goal had been to see justice served. The gods—those mystical beings who were nothing more than fallen angels—had one weakness. The same weakness that was responsible for their fall from grace so long ago. They were enamored of humanity. And they meddled in that which they couldn't understand and could never replicate.

The temple was nothing but crumbled rock and broken columns. A thrill of victory slinked through him as he stepped from one massive boulder to the next. Destroyed. Just as Olympus would soon be destroyed.

He located what would have been the altar area of the temple—the temple to Zeus, no irony there—and called on the power of the Orb as he conjured a spell to clear a space. When the mountain of stone had been sufficiently moved out of the way, he crawled down into the pit that remained and stared at the marble altar now broken in two, the iconic lightning bolt, the symbol of the King of the Gods, cut right down the middle.

He stepped around behind the slabs of marble and reached underneath the right side to the hidden compartment in the base. The one that held the small wooden box he'd left there so many years ago.

The Orb grew warmer. The box was lodged in the broken marble. He grimaced as he fished around inside, found the bronze latch and flipped it up, his fingers closing around a small teardrop-shaped glass.

His skin grew red-hot. He pulled his hand free and stared at the swirling cloud of gas inside the container marked with the symbol of the Titans. The mixture found in heaven and on earth and even in the Underworld. That which made life possible. Power and strength surged in the palm of his hand, shot up his arm, gathered in his chest. And he felt a stark tug where the Orb lay beneath his shirt, as if the medallion were calling the element home.

He pushed to his feet. Reached for the chain around his neck. Stopped when he heard movement behind him. Slowly, he turned and stared into eyes as old as the sun.

"Be sure of this move, hero."

Lachesis. The wrinkled and petite Fate had warned him off the air element once before. Had told him stealing it would bring a wrath he'd never understand. And looking back, he knew that it had. But then he hadn't had the Orb and the earth element. Now he did. Now he had what everyone wanted.

"It's too late for theatrics, old woman. I've already reached my quota for this lifetime, *and* the last. And I'm no hero."

He climbed out of the pit, started down the hill away from the ruins with the air element in his palm. Lachesis appeared on the path, stopping his feet.

"You were destined for something greater than this, Orpheus. Greater than thievery and vengeance, and much greater than ignorance. Do not fall into the trappings of the gods. For it makes you no better than them."

He ground his teeth. "Look close, Fate. I am no better than them. The fact I was born part daemon proves that loud and clear."

He pushed past her, nothing but a gust of wind hitting him where her solid flesh should be. He was done with people telling him what to do. His father Perseus had tried. Zeus had ordered. This Fate had even cajoled long ago. And in this life? Isadora, the Argonauts, even Skyla…they were all trying to make him into something he wasn't.

Thoughts of Skyla flittered through his mind, followed by memories of when they'd first met so many years ago. When he was a man wanting more. When he'd known she was sent by Zeus to seduce the element out from under him. When he'd turned the tide on her and seduced her right back, just to torment the god.

"You are not a daemon, hero," the Fate called after him. "Not anymore. You earned your soul back, just as I knew you would."

So he'd been right. His daemon really was gone.

And that fullness he'd felt in his chest…that had been his soul. A soul he'd come to believe he just didn't have. Not that it made a difference. It didn't change who he was inside. The same man he'd been over two thousand years ago. One who cared for nothing but what he was due.

"Vengeance will do you no good," the Fate added. "And a great many will suffer if you fail this time."

"That's where you're wrong, Fate. Retribution's the only thing that'll make all the shit I've been through worth it." What he'd done, what Skyla had done, what had happened in the long lonely years since.

"You—"

"And the nice thing about revenge," he added, "it means I'm not in hell anymore."

"There's more than one kind of hell in this life, Orpheus. There's the hell that Hades can subject you to, and then there's the living hell. The kind you create for yourself. The kind that's impossible to break free from. Ask Skyla about that hell. Ask her how many lovers she's taken since your death or why she stayed with the Sirens for so long. You are not the only one who sacrificed and suffered. You are simply the one who got a second chance."

His feet stilled on the sodden grass. He didn't want to hear about Skyla or what she'd been through. He didn't want to think about the consequences of what he'd done. He just wanted to hold on to his anger as he'd done for so long. To blame the gods for the fucking hand of fate he'd been dealt. He just wanted…

What? What did he want?

I choose you. Daemon or no daemon. Argonaut or

not. Zeus and Athena are wrong about you, Orpheus.
You're not evil.

How can you be so sure?

Because I watched you with your brother. An evil
soul can't love like that.

I don't have a soul—

Yes, you do. One that deserves so much more than
you've been given.

The air felt as if it shot out of his lungs, tightening
his chest to painful levels. He wanted *that*. He wanted
to feel the way he had in *that* moment. When the past
and future, when gods and wars and who had done what
to whom didn't matter. When he'd only known content-
ment and peace and…love.

He turned to glare at the Fate, only she was already gone.

He looked around the rubble of the temple, half expecting her to pop out from behind a broken column, only
she didn't. He was alone. And the Orb that had moments
ago felt so hot against his chest was now cold and flat.

"Bloody Fate," he muttered. "Bloody conscience." He
looked up at the sky, a swirling gray threatening—what
else?—rain. "I'm not supposed to have a conscience!"

Only he did. He always had, even when his daemon
had been with him. A conscience that now told him Skyla
wasn't entirely to blame for what had happened to him.

He looked down at the air element in his hand. It too
was cold. Just like the rain beginning to fall in big fat
droplets around him.

"Orpheus."

He turned on the path to find Skyla feet from him.
She was dressed in the same get-up she always wore,
and with her blond hair flying back from the wind and

the rain drizzling down around her, she looked powerful and formidable. How he imagined Athena would look before taking down a target.

Her gaze shot to the air element in his hand. The one she'd suspected him of taking. The one they'd argued about that last day. The one he'd told her had nothing to do with her and was none of her business. "You found it."

He heard the accusation in her voice and told himself to be careful. She was still a Siren, no matter what she'd said to him last night. And no matter where he went from here, he wasn't going to be the fool again. He closed his hand around the element, blocking it from her view. "I did."

"What do you plan to do with it?"

"Does it matter?"

A long beat of silence drew out between them. And then she said, "No."

She stared at him head-on. And in her amethyst eyes he couldn't read her thoughts. Couldn't tell if it didn't matter because she believed in him or because she was finally going to kill him.

The rain increased. Water slid down his cheek. A lifetime—two lifetimes—of things left unsaid hovered between them.

She took half a step toward him. "Orpheus—"

Movement behind her drew his attention. Five figures approached. Five females, all dressed in the same femme-fatale fighter gear, bows drawn, arrows ready.

"Good job, Skyla," the tall Siren with multicolored hair said. The one Orpheus recognized from the woods outside the colony. "You led us right to him."

Skyla's spine stiffened. Her panicked eyes held on Orpheus. "I didn't. I swear."

He wanted to believe her, but history told him otherwise.

"Step aside, Skyla," the tall one said.

Six against one. Even with the Orb, this wouldn't be easy to fight his way out of. But then he didn't have to fight, did he? The one gift his lineage had bestowed on him was the ability to flash on earth.

"Sappheire," Skyla said, turning to face her sisters. "This doesn't concern you."

"It concerns the order," the tall Siren answered. "It concerns me. Now step aside."

Orpheus was just about to get the hell out when Skyla stepped fully in front of him, blocking him with her body. "No."

"If you want him," Skyla added, "you'll have to fight me too."

His heart leaped. Right there with five arrows pointed at his chest, ready to kill. She was protecting him. Standing up for him, even though he'd just proven Zeus's claims true.

"Skyla—" he started.

"Is there a problem here, ladies?"

The male voice at the edge of the clearing caused the Sirens to shift sideways, arrows at the ready. Theron and the rest of the Argonauts appeared from the trees.

"Argonauts," the dark-haired Siren on the right hissed.

Orpheus blinked twice, barely able to believe what he was seeing.

"Yes, we are," Theron said as Zander and Titus took up the flank on his left and Phin, Cerek, and Demetrius did the same on his right. "And he's one of ours, so if you'll kindly lower your weapons, we'll get to the bottom of whatever disagreement you're all having."

"There's no disagreement," the dark-haired Siren said, shifting her bow from Orpheus to Theron. "And you'll move back."

Titus had his blade at the Siren's throat before she even saw him move. "I wouldn't advise that, missy." Her eyes grew wide. "Now lower your weapon before anyone accidentally gets hurt."

"Lower it, Daphne," Sappheire said.

The Sirens brought their bows down, but tension still crackled in the air. Even Orpheus could tell this was no surrender. It was a lull before the battle. The battle over him and the Orb.

Snarls and wolflike howls erupted from the trees around them.

The Argonauts stepped back, in line with the Sirens, and together the group of would-be enemies glanced from tree to tree.

"Hellhounds," Sappheire snapped, shooting Skyla a glare behind her. "Now do you see how this concerns the order? Fan out, Sirens."

Whatever prejudices they held against each other were forgotten as the Argonauts and Sirens took up space, blades drawn, bows at the ready. Skyla turned and pushed Orpheus back three steps. "Go. Get out of here before Hades shows up."

Panic closed in when she reached for the bow from her boot, pressed the button, and the weapon unfurled.

"Not without you."

Their eyes met for the briefest of seconds before she shoved her hand hard into his chest. "He doesn't want me. He wants the Orb. Now go!"

He stumbled back as she raced to the line with the

others and drew her weapon. The tree branches and foliage swayed. And then monsters from the Underworld broke free and charged.

Blades clashed against bone and muscle. Howls and snaps echoed through the small clearing. The whisk of arrow after arrow being released echoed through the air.

The Orb warmed against Orpheus's chest, but without all four elements it wasn't any help as a weapon. He could use his witchcraft to harness the powers of each element, though.

He looked up at the sky as the battle raged in front of him, clasped the air element in his hand, and called up a storm spell. Thunder echoed above. Black clouds swirled and a bolt of lightning shot down from the sky.

It struck a hellhound about to devour one of the Sirens to Orpheus's right. She grunted and kicked the beast away. Another bolt struck the soil with a snap and singe and billow of black smoke.

They were holding their own, but the sound of hooves or feet or claws thumping the ground from ahead told Orpheus they were about to be overrun by something else. Something worse. Something…*Oh, shit*.

Ahead, through the swirling mist of rain and smoke, Hades approached, the image of imminent death. And on each side, a Minotaur. The legendary man-eating creatures with the bodies of men and the heads of bulls, snorting red plumes of smoke as they zeroed in on the battle in the meadow.

Okay, playtime was over. Orpheus tore down the hill after Skyla. All around him, Argonauts and Sirens battled hellhounds. He grasped Skyla's arm just as she let go of an arrow. "Come on. It's time to go."

"What? I can't go anywhere. I—" She whipped around, saw Hades and the Minotaurs. "Holy hell."

"Pretty much. Let's go, Siren. Can you flash?"

"Yes, but…" She looked at her sisters. "The others…"

Orpheus's gaze followed. To the Argonauts. Battling back hell's underlings. For him. The only way for them to escape was through a portal back to Argolea, and they'd never risk opening one with hellhounds that close.

"Damn sonofabitch fucking conscience," Orpheus muttered, glancing up at the sky. "I didn't ask for this!"

"What are you doing?" Skyla's eyes grew wide as he pulled the Orb from beneath his shirt and shoved the air element into place.

"Trying to give us all a fucking chance. Stand back."

She stepped in front of him, blocking him from the battle, lifted her bow, and took aim at a charging hellhound. Orpheus closed his eyes and drew a deep breath, focusing his energy on both the Orb and the mother of all protection spells, pulling on the two elements as much as he could. Against his shirt, the Orb grew hot.

The ground rumbled. The wind picked up, tossing his hair away from his face. The chant grew in his mind and spilled from his lips, and as it did he imagined a protective barrier all around the meadow. It wouldn't save them from the hellhounds already in the circle, but if it held, it would shield them from Hades and the next wave the evil god had planned.

"Orpheus!"

He heard his name called just before the barrier was in place. Felt some sort of energy siphon through, like water through cheesecloth. But then the barrier solidified, holding a tight, careful perimeter.

He opened his eyes. Caught Hades's furious glare on the other side of the barrier. Around him the battle between Argonauts and hellhounds and Sirens waged on.

A scream echoed from ahead. He looked that direction just as Skyla's body jerked as if she'd just been hit with a bolt of lightning.

"Skyla?"

A gurgling sound echoed. She dropped to the ground at his feet with a thud. From her chest, the long curved blade and black wooden handle of a scythe protruded, surrounded by blood already welling around the blade to seep through her clothing and spill into the ground.

"No. Oh, shit. *No*. Skyla?" Panic beat a drum line to his heart as he fell to his knees. He reached for the handle of the scythe marked with the image of a three-headed dog.

"No," Skyla rasped, her shaking hand lifting to try to stop him from pulling it out. "No, don't…"

He jerked the blade free and dropped it on the wet grass at his side. She groaned in pain, her eyes rolled back in her head, but all he could see was the blood gushing out of the wound in her chest. So much blood.

Oh, gods…He had to stop the bleeding. He needed a healing spell. Couldn't think. Frantic, he tore the Orb from around his neck and pressed it to her chest, knowing it had some kind of healing element to it. "Demetrius!"

"Don't," Skyla rasped again. "It's…too late."

He looked down at her pale face and his heart clenched. Tight. So tight he felt as if he'd been stabbed with that blade. Reality, and a future, one that didn't include her, ran out like a carpet of red before him.

"It's too late," she rasped. "Let me—"

Her hand closed over his bloody one atop the Orb. But her eyes never left his. Amethyst eyes that were even now glazing over.

"Orpheus…" A ghost of a smile tugged on her mouth. "I think of you as Orpheus now. Not as Cyn—"

She coughed. Her body shook. Blood pooled at the corners of her mouth. Gushed from her chest.

No, no, no, no, no. This wasn't happening. Not when he'd just realized she was the only thing that mattered.

Tears blurred his vision as he leaned over her. The battle continued around them. Shouts and clashes of blades and teeth and arrows winging through the air. "Listen to me, Siren. Don't give up. Do you hear me? You hold on. I'm going to get you out of here. Just…just don't let go. Skyla?"

Her eyes slid closed and she drew a deep, shuddering breath. A breath he felt all the way in his soul. "Don't let Zeus have it. Or Hades. Don't let…any of the gods have it. P-promise."

"They won't. I promise." He flipped his hand over and squeezed her bloody fingers. Rain ran down his face. Why wasn't the Orb working? And where the fuck was Demetrius? "Stupid, stupid Siren." Tears lodged in his throat. "What were you thinking, stepping in front of that scythe? I don't need you protecting me, damn it. I need you alive. I need—"

"Was thinking…of…you…" Her voice grew weak. "You were…meant for something…greater. Be greater, Orpheus."

Her hand softened against his.

No, gods, no. He wrapped both arms around her

and pulled her into his lap, pressed one hand against the wound. Her head lolled against his arm. The Orb pressed between them, covered in her blood and his tears. "*Skyla?* Stay with me. Stay with me, damn it."

Please, Dimiourgos. Don't take her from me. Don't…

He looked up again, searching through watery vision for Demetrius, the pain in his chest so sharp he could barely breathe.

A figure moved toward him. A figure that looked like Demetrius at a dead run. Screaming…his name.

"I—" she started.

"Shh…" Hope leaped in his chest. He pressed his lips against the wet hair plastered to her forehead. "Help is coming. Just hold on a little longer, okay, baby? Don't let go."

"Never…did." Her hand slid down his chest to clasp his again. And through his tears he looked at their bloody fingers, entwined over her heart. Over his heart. And he knew in that moment that was exactly what she was. What she'd always been: his heart. Only he'd been so consumed with anger and jealousy and vengeance, he hadn't seen it. Not the first time. Not the second. Not until now, when it was too late.

"Never forgot…you," she whispered. "Not…once."

Demetrius skidded to a stop at his side. "*Skata.* O?"

Her breathing slowed, and even before Demetrius dropped to his knees to help him, alarm raced through Orpheus's body. He grasped her chin with his bloody hand, tipped her face up. "Skyla?"

She didn't move.

"No." He gripped both sides of her face, willed her to open her eyes. "Skyla? Dammit, *Skyla?*"

"O," Demetrius said, "let me…"

Demetrius took her from his arms, laid her out on the ground, and leaned over to listen for her breath, then felt for her pulse. His body went still, then his gaze roamed over the gaping wound in her chest. And before he could stop it, every muscle in Orpheus's body went rigid with disbelief.

"No!" He knocked Demetrius back and away from her. Demetrius hit the ground on his ass. Orpheus leaned over Skyla and grasped both of her shoulders. "Wake up, *damn it!* It's not time for you to go! Do you hear me? It's not time…"

Hands landed on his shoulders, pulling him back. Around him he saw boots—heavy, rugged ones worn by the Argonauts and platform kick-ass, knee-high ones worn by Sirens. Silence descended, seemed so out of place all of a sudden. No more battle sounds. No more roaring monsters. Just the empty, gut-wrenching silence that told him it was already too late.

He thought he'd known pain before. He was wrong. Two thousand years of torture in the Underworld hadn't prepared him for the agony that ripped through his heart and soul.

He watched through blurry vision as Sappheire dropped to one knee next to Skyla, her face drawn and somber as she ran her hand over Skyla's brow, muttering in a language Orpheus didn't understand.

Skyla's lifeless body jerked. And for a second, hope resurged. Then she dissolved into nothing right before his eyes. The Orb landed with a soft thud against the wet ground.

"What the fuck did you do?" Orpheus cried.

Sappheire pushed to stand. "I sent her home." She turned to Theron. "We need to talk."

Home.

Thoughts, plans, options raced through Orpheus's mind as the Sirens and Argonauts came to some understanding. An understanding Orpheus couldn't care less about. There was only one chance now. One bargain left to make. He eyed the Orb on the ground and, before he could change his mind, picked it up.

"Orpheus?"

Voices echoed around him. But he ignored them. Instead he closed his eyes and pictured what once had been Skyla's home.

And prayed he wasn't too late.

Chapter 27

"LET ME GET THIS STRAIGHT," THE KING OF THE GODS said, turning from the window where he'd been gazing out at Olympus. "You want to make a deal. The Siren's life for the Orb."

"And the air element." Orpheus stood rigid in the center of Zeus's temple, legs apart, arms at his sides, gaze fixed on Zeus while his heart pounded hard against his chest. A heart he now knew he *did* have. Because of Skyla.

The King of the Gods didn't look all that intimidating from his vantage point. Close-cut dark hair, a youthful face with only a handful of lines around his deep-set blue eyes, clean-shaven skin, and the body of an athlete. Definitely not the white-haired, white-bearded grand-fatherly figure humans pictured him as.

The King of the Gods eyed Orpheus suspiciously. He wanted what Orpheus had too much to jeopardize getting it now. And since he couldn't take the Orb outright—no god could take something without it being offered—that meant Zeus had to deal.

Take the deal. Take the fucking deal.

"The air element already belongs to me, son," Zeus pointed out.

"Grandson," Orpheus corrected. "And you can cut the familial term of endearment. We both know it means nothing. The way I see it, possession trumps ownership ties every time."

Zeus's jaw tightened. He turned and placed a hand on his throne, decked out in ostentatious gold. "You have surprised me. Not many do. When I branded you a troublemaker all those years ago, I had no idea I'd still be dealing with you now."

"I'm thrilled I've amused you. Now do we have a deal or not?"

Zeus considered for a moment. "Not quite. I have an addendum."

Orpheus's chest deflated. An addendum meant only one thing. "You can't bring her back."

"Oh, I can bring her back. She'll just be…different."

"Define different."

"Same body…different soul."

Orpheus's eyes narrowed. "What about Skyla's soul?"

"That belongs to the Fates."

The Fates. He needed to find Lachesis. Deal with her. Forget Zeus and this stupid addendum. Her soul was what he loved about her. Not that Barbie-doll body Zeus had given her.

"Won't work," Zeus said, interrupting his thoughts. "The Fates don't deal. Not with mortals. And the Siren was mortal. Death is part of every mortal's life, regardless of the service."

Orpheus glared across the room. "I was mortal too, and they brought me back."

Zeus barked out a laugh. "You weren't brought back because you were deserving. You were brought back because of guilt. Lachesis foresaw that you would be important to the Argolean's war against Atalanta. And when the Sirens killed you the first time— justifiably, I might add—she stepped in and made a deal with Hades to bring you back. But don't fool yourself into thinking she did so because you *deserved* a second chance. She did it because she felt guilty over Atalanta's creation in the first place. You see, Lachesis encouraged the first heroes not to include Atalanta in the order of the Argonauts. From there...Atalanta chose her own path, made her own deals, and became the pain-in-the-ass goddess she is today. But make no mistake. The Fates are using you to right a wrong they are responsible for. Nothing more, *grandson*."

Orpheus thought back to his run-in with Lachesis in the mountains. *You were destined for something greater than this, Orpheus. Greater than thievery and vengeance, and much greater than ignorance.*

He had no idea what he was meant for. He only knew what he needed. Panic swamped his chest. How was he going to get her back?

He turned for the temple doors, his mind spinning.

"If you leave here without giving me what's mine," Zeus announced, "you cut all ties with me. And the courtesy I have shown you as one of my own will cease to exist. I didn't have to tell you about her soul, Orpheus. I could have made the deal and deceived you. I didn't out of compassion."

Orpheus turned to face Zeus. "What compassion? You had me killed."

"That was never my first choice. You brought that justice on yourself. But know this. If you repeat history, my retribution will be swift. So think long and hard about this move. Your decision here could bring war or peace to the Argolean realm."

War was already upon the Argolean realm. War with

Atalanta's daemons and now with Hades, who had made it perfectly clear in that forest that he wasn't backing down.

No god could have the Orb. Not if the world was meant to go on.

Be greater, Orpheus.

He felt Skyla's hand against his chest, warm and solid and real, encouraging him. And his life—both lives—spun out before him, twisting and intersecting and finally condensing into this one moment. To choosing what he wanted to be versus what he was meant to be.

He looked down at the Argonaut markings on his arms. The markings that he'd acquired when Gryphon's soul had been sent to Tartarus. The markings that were still there, even though Gryphon was home.

Be greater.

Maybe he really was meant for something greater than himself. Maybe...after all his long, lonely years of searching...this was it.

He looked up and knew even if there was no way to bring Skyla back, he was doing the right thing.

Finally.

"Someone advised me not to give it to you." He reached for the door handle. "And this time, *gramps*, I'm listening."

For the second time in only a matter of hours, Orpheus was standing before royalty. This royalty wasn't nearly as intimidating as the last, though.

Isadora stared down at the Orb in her hands, with the two elements nestled in their chambers, her face awash with awe and surprise. Behind her, Theron and Demetrius looked on with *no way in hell* expressions. Orpheus ignored the Argonauts and focused on the queen. And when her brown eyes lifted to his, he saw...relief.

Man, he'd been such a bastard to her. He doubted a smart-ass, scheming personality like his could totally change. From what he remembered of his years as Cynurus, he'd been a sonofabitch then too. But at least his heart had changed. And his intentions.

"I knew you'd bring the earth element back," she said. "I didn't expect the rest."

"Figured they belonged together." He frowned as he stuffed his hands into the clean jeans he'd changed into when he'd come back to Argolea and made this deci-sion. "Besides, I've lost my taste for power."

A warm smile cut across her face. She turned and handed the Orb to Theron, who stared at the thing as if it might jump out and bite him, then shifted back. "Thank you."

"I only have one requirement."

"Anything."

"The Orb can't be destroyed until all four elements are in place. I know it's tempting to keep it, but once we find the other two elements...I want you to promise me we'll destroy the damn thing."

Isadora's smile widened. "We?"

Orpheus clenched his jaw, because, yeah, being a son-ofabitch was easy. Being heroic...that was a hell of a lot of work. "Yeah, 'we.' I'll take Gryphon's place with the Argonauts. Until," he added, cutting off Isadora's burst of excitement, "Gryphon's ready to come back."

Isadora stepped away from the desk in her father's old office in the castle at Tiyrns. "Orpheus, you are

welcome to stay on with the Argonauts for however
long you want." She placed her hand on his forearm.
Right over the ancient Greek text. "You don't need the
markings of the gods to do that."

"These markings don't come from the gods," he said,
looking down at her. Still stunned that she'd been able
to see the good in him before anyone else.

She squeezed his arm. "I think you might be right."

He nodded toward the Orb in Theron's hands. "What
about that?"

"That," Isadora answered, "will be locked up safe and
sound. And when we have the other two elements, it will
be destroyed. Just like you want. It won't fall into the
wrong hands."

Orpheus nodded. Glanced from Theron to Demetrius.
Neither said anything, but the fatherly grin on Theron's
face and the humor in Demetrius's eyes told him they
were both relieved. And thankful.

And *skata*…he needed to get gone before they did
something stupid. Like congratulate him or try to hug
him or some shit like that. He definitely couldn't handle
any male bonding right now.

He turned for the door, then stopped. "There's one
more thing. I'll serve with the Argonauts whenever they
need me. But I won't live here in Argolea."

Isadora's sad smile said she could still see right
through him. "I think it's smart you stay at the colony
with Gryphon. Your brother needs you there."

Orpheus wasn't so sure of that. He'd gone to see
Gryphon first, before coming back to Argolea, and
though his brother had awoken from the sedatives Callia
had given him and seemed calm, he was but a shell of

what Orpheus remembered. Gone was the easygoing, strong, and confident Argonaut who'd forever been trying to set Orpheus on the right path. In his place lurked a haunted and broken man who did nothing but stare out the window with vacant eyes, shake his head as if he was hearing voices, and twitch.

Gryphon's time in the Underworld was too fresh. Orpheus had to hold on to hope that time and distance would bring back the brother he remembered.

He nodded once more and left the room, heading down the hall for the front of the castle. There were a few things he wanted to pick up from his store on the other side of town. A few things he hoped might cheer his brother up.

"Orpheus, wait."

His feet stilled and he looked back to see Isadora rushing after him. "What now, Isa?"

"I just…" She took a breath, and when she looked up it wasn't gratitude in her eyes, nor surprise. It was worry. "Are you okay?"

He thought of Skyla—as he had every minute since she'd left him—and his attempt to bring her back. The Fates weren't listening though, and while he could access just about any realm with his magic, the land of the Fates was closed to him. They made contact when they wanted, not when others summoned them.

A thrumming pain radiated outward from his chest. Knowing she was gone and never coming back was something he was just going to have to get used to. But it hurt. More than he'd ever thought possible. The only thing that kept him going was the thought that one day, if he cleaned up his act enough, he just might see her again.

Be greater.

He was working on it. But damn, it was hard.

"Yeah," he said, drawing a deep breath that eased the ache just a touch. "I'm okay. For the first time in a long time, Isa, I'm exactly what I'm supposed to be."

~~~

"You hesitate, child. Is there a problem?"

Skyla paused at the steps of the white ship. The one with big billowing green sails that would take her to the Isles of the Blessed, where the souls of the heroes and those who had proven themselves in life dwelt in harmony.

A bright light shone far off in the distance, casting a sparkle over the water like a million tiny diamonds. She wanted to go. Felt the pull all the way to her toes. But something held her back.

She faced the Fate standing at her side—Atropos, she'd heard her called—the one with salt-and-pepper hair and a long, flowing white robe. "I—I feel like I'm forgetting something. Something I'm not supposed to forget."

Atropos frowned and looked at her sister. The white-haired Lachesis. "This is your fault, hag."

"Not mine." Lachesis grinned. "Blame Hera. She's responsible for the soul-mate curse."

Skyla had no idea what they were talking about. She looked from weathered face to weathered face and knew only one thing: The hole in her heart hurt. A pain she shouldn't have. Not when she was about to sail off to paradise.

"If you do this," Atropos said with a scowl, "you do so without my blessing."

"Now, sister hag." Lachesis cut her a look. "Have I ever needed your blessing before?"

Atropos harrumphed. "It is because of you this problem exists."

"And I will set it right." Lachesis turned to Skyla. "What if you could go back?"

"Go back?" Skyla's brow dropped. "I don't under—"

"To the human realm."

The human realm. Skyla's mind spun. Yes. She'd been human, hadn't she?

"Not everyone gets this choice—"

"*No one* gets this choice," Atropos mumbled, arms crossed over her chest.

"—but you are special." Lachesis darted a glare at her sister before refocusing on Skyla. "You sacrificed your life for another."

"I did?" Skyla couldn't remember. "Who?"

"That you can't tell her," Atropos snapped. "If she goes back, she has to make the choice not knowing what she's going back to."

Lachesis sighed. "She's right. There are rules. Rules even I can't break. You have to make the decision not knowing the life you led before."

"Or what's waiting for you," Atropos added. "Could be a child molester or a rapist you're missing."

Lachesis frowned at her sister again. "Or it could be a king."

Atropos harrumphed. "Kings are useless."

"Regardless," Lachesis said, looking at Skyla again, "you have to make the decision based on what's before you." She held out her arm. "The Isles of the Blessed, or what you are afraid to forget."

The sparkling light on the horizon called to Skyla. But the Fates' options…How could she make that decision? She tried to rationalize it and came up with only one scenario that made sense. "If I'm here, then it means I led a good life."

"Not necessarily," Lachesis answered. "But one can redeem herself in her last moment and counteract all the wrong she did before."

"Stupid loophole," Atropos muttered.

"By saving a life." The emptiness in Skyla's chest grew larger. Until she was afraid it would swallow her whole. "If I go on the ship…"

"Then the pain you feel will disappear," Atropos said. "And you'll be free—mind, body, and soul. No more suffering, no more loneliness, no more hurting. The Isles of the Blessed are Elysium. Heaven."

"But I'll forget," Skyla clarified.

"Yes," Lachesis said before Atropos could answer. "You will forget."

"And if I go back…?"

Atropos frowned.

Skyla looked at Lachesis. The white-haired Fate's eyes softened. "The pain you feel will also disappear. And you'll remember."

"Would I ever have the chance to come back here?"

"That depends on you, child," Lachesis said. "On the life you choose to lead in the human realm. Only you can make that decision."

Skyla looked back out over the water. The light consumed her, and the urge to climb on that sparkling ship was so strong it tugged at the center of her being. Slowly, ever so slowly, closing the hole in her chest, filling it with peace. A peace that, for some reason, she was sure she'd never really had before.

A peace that made her forget just what it was that was holding her back.

"Time's up," Atropos announced. "What's your decision, child?"

Chapter 28

ORPHEUS WAS PRETTY SURE HE'D NEVER BEEN SO TIRED.

He'd spent all day with Nick and his scouts, searching for daemon signs. A few new reports had come in that indicated what was left of Atalanta's scattered army was on the move. That meant two things: either someone else was gathering daemons to build a new army, or Atalanta had found her way back from the Underworld.

The last thought left Orpheus more uneasy than he liked. Gryphon's ramblings that Atalanta was "out there" suddenly didn't sound like the delusions of a crazy man.

He'd spent the evening in Gryphon's room, just as he'd done every night for the last week, talking to his brother, playing cards with him, trying to coax him out of the comatose state he seemed to inhabit. Nothing helped, though. Gryphon refused to leave his room. He only barely showed interest in the cards. And the twitching and head shakes were getting worse.

Orpheus rubbed his forehead with two fingers while Gryphon tossed and turned in the big bed. The bedside light was on and the curtains were open, allowing in enough moonlight to illuminate the entire suite. But it still wasn't enough for Gryphon. The big, tough Argonaut who'd never been afraid of anything was now scared of the dark.

He stayed with Gryphon until his brother dozed off,

then pulled the cover up to his chin and stared down at his sleeping face. Relaxed, Gryphon's forehead smoothed and the stress he carried with him seemed to evaporate. And for a moment, as he studied his brother's blond hair and the long dark lashes against his skin, it was like looking at the old Gryphon. The younger brother who'd never done anything but be a hero.

Quietly, he turned off the bedside lamp and crossed to the door. One last glance back confirmed Gryphon was still asleep, so he left, closing the door softly behind him.

He headed for the stairs. It was late, close to midnight, and he knew he could take the elevator and cross to the southern wing, but he didn't want to wake anyone. And he needed fresh air.

He headed down three flights and pushed the door to the courtyard open, heading across the garden toward the south entrance. When he spotted Maelea walking alone near the fountain, he hesitated and ducked into the shadows. The female seemed to be acclimating to life in the colony—or so Nick told him—but she kept to herself. And the only time anyone saw her venture out of her rooms was late at night.

She was an anomaly in every way possible. The daughter of Zeus and Persephone, the embodiment of light and dark. And every time Orpheus saw her, he remembered the scars on her arms. The ones he knew she'd put there herself.

She's growing on me, daemon. The more I'm around her, the more I sort of like her.

Skyla's words came back to him at unexpected times. But he was thankful. Because in a way it felt like she was still here. And on this he had to agree. Maelea was growing on him too.

But not tonight. Tonight he wasn't in the mood to talk to anyone.

The female sat on the stone bench surrounding the fountain and looked down into the gurgling water. As if something had caught her attention, she glanced up and around, then turned and faced the castle. For a moment Orpheus thought she'd heard him, then he realized she was staring at a window three stories above.

For a heartbeat she didn't move. Then she gathered her skirts and briskly crossed the courtyard, disappearing into the shadowed building on the other side.

Curious, Orpheus stepped out of the shadows and looked up. And caught sight of his brother standing at the window of his room, looking down with that same blank stare that had been on his face since returning from the Underworld.

Gryphon held Orpheus's gaze for several seconds, then turned away from the window.

And alone, surrounded by darkness and nothing but the bubble of water in the fountain behind him, Orpheus knew he should go back up there. Try to console Gryphon. Make sure he was okay. But he didn't want to. The last week was catching up with him. And the hollow ache in his chest was growing. The one he'd been struggling with since Skyla's death.

He closed his eyes and pictured his room. Seconds later he was standing in his tower, staring at the sanctuary Skyla had created for him.

That ache intensified. He crossed to the bed and dropped onto his back, one leg on the mattress, the other hanging over the side. He didn't bother to kick off his boots, didn't bother with a light or even to pull the covers back. He simply stared up at the high-beamed ceiling and breathed, in the hope that if he thought of nothing, the ache might eventually ease so he could sleep.

The irony of his destiny wasn't lost on him. After nearly three hundred years alone, purposely avoiding any kind of contact that would leave him vulnerable, even though he was surrounded at every turn by colonists, Nick, his brother, and the Argonauts, he'd never felt as lonely as he did now.

He swiped his forearm across his face, called himself a pussy when his arm came away wet. He'd kill himself if he thought it would do any good, but he knew it wouldn't. He had to hang on and do the right thing so that one day he'd see her again. And Skyla's last words, telling him to *be greater*, wouldn't allow him to take the easy route out. Not anymore.

He closed his eyes, drew three deep breaths, but the flash of light that erupted outside dragged at his attention.

He sat up. Stared out the wall of windows to the dark balcony beyond.

Lightning, he told himself. Or a meteor of some kind. But he pushed to his feet anyway, thankful for any kind of distraction. He crossed to the glass door and pulled it open. A figure draped in a black cloak with the hood pulled up stood in the moonlight facing the dark water below.

His jaw clenched. He so wasn't in the mood for company right now. He swiped at his eyes again with his shoulder and cleared his throat, putting as much intimidation into his voice as he could. "You wandered into the wrong tower. Head back where you came from."

The figure turned, her wrinkled hands reaching up to lower the hood.

The blood drained from his face. "Lachesis."

The Fate smiled. A light breeze ruffled the black cloak that he now saw had concealed her white robes. "Finally, someone remembers me."

His heart sped up. And words…pleas…lodged in his throat as he tried to figure out what to say. How to beg. Would dropping to his knees and groveling be too much? Was there even any point, this long after the fact?

That hole in his chest opened wider. He took a shaky step toward her. "I—"

"No, hero, you do not have to beg. But you do have to promise me one thing. This time, live up to your destiny."

She held her hand out to the side, and his gaze followed the sweep of her arm. To the figure across the stone balcony, standing in the shadows, also wearing a black cloak.

He squinted to see more clearly as the figure reached up with pale, feminine hands and lowered the hood. And was sure his heart jumped right out of his chest when the face he'd been dreaming of for the last week stared back at him.

"Skyla."

If he was dreaming, he didn't want to know. He was across the balcony in two leaps, his hands on her arms, pulling her into him. His mouth lowering to take hers as her warm and real and *alive* body brushed up against his.

"I remember you," she whispered against his lips, her delicate fingers landing on his chest as he kissed her. Again. And again. And again. Just because he could. Until he was light-headed and breathless and she was smiling as if he was a giant fool.

"I guess that means you remember me too," she said softly.

He could barely believe she was real. Her hair was different. Shorter. Just barely to her shoulders and more dark blond than golden. Though her face was the same, the heavy, perfect makeup was gone. A spray of freckles ran across the bridge of her nose, and he didn't remember that small scar near her left temple.

"How…? Why…?" Still unable to believe she was real, he pulled the robe she wore open, pressed a hand against her chest where the wound had been. Nothing but flesh under his touch. And a heartbeat. A strong, rapid heartbeat beneath the thin white T-shirt she wore over slim jeans.

"They gave me a choice."

He had to be dreaming. He didn't want to be dreaming. *Please don't let me be dreaming*. "Who?"

"The Fates."

He turned to look back at Lachesis, but she was already gone.

Skyla's finger tugged his chin back to her. And the emotions in her eyes cut right to the heart of him. The heart she'd reawakened. The heart that had been tattered and broken since her death. "I'm so sorry. For all of it. For everything. I should have told you who I was, who you were. I should have…" Tears swam in her eyes. "I should have trusted you all those years ago. I should have known you'd never—"

His lips met hers, cutting off her words. Gods, she was real. He still couldn't believe it. But he wasn't wasting any more time. Not on things that didn't even matter anymore. "Shh. Don't." He cupped her cheek. So smooth. So warm. So *real*. "No more apologies."

"But—"

"I've remembered a lot more about my first life since that night. And honestly, I'm surprised you didn't kill me yourself. Skyla, I did steal the air element from Zeus, and I did hide it. And not for any honorable reason like protecting the world or keeping it out of the hands of the gods. I stole it because I knew it would piss him off. I also knew what you were when we met. So I set out to seduce you right back. And piss Zeus off even more in the process."

"Are you saying—?"

"I'm saying there was nothing noble about my intentions. Not from the start. Not even at the end. The one thing I just didn't count on was falling in love with you."

Her eyes searched his. Searching, he knew, for the truth. A truth he should have told her so many times, so long ago.

Emotion tightened his throat. "Can *you* ever forgive *me*? Not just for that but for the way I reacted when I finally remembered? I shouldn't have grabbed you like that. I shouldn't have…" He brushed his hand against her soft, slim throat, closed his eyes, the memory of the way he'd treated her, the guilt from that hitting him right in the solar plexus.

Her soft hand brushed his cheek, brought his eyes open. "You didn't hurt me. And there's no forgiveness needed. In fact…" A smile turned up the corners of her lips, lips that weren't quite as plump and perfect as he remembered. "I wouldn't have blamed you if you'd killed me that night. I deserved it."

"No more killing," he whispered. "My heart can't take it. My heart can't take anything but you."

"Do you mean that? Because if you don't…" She closed her eyes, opened them. "If you don't want me anymore, I—"

He lowered his mouth to hers and kissed her with everything he had in him. All the loss and heartache and emptiness he'd been carrying with him his whole life. The emptiness he hadn't known was there because he was missing her.

"I want you," he said, bringing both hands up to frame her face, feeling her silky hair slide between his fingers. "I've always wanted you."

Her arms wound around his back and she moved into him, the heat from her body warming him all the way to his toes. She buried her head against his chest as he held her. Yeah, she was definitely shorter. And so damn perfect.

She sniffled. "I couldn't go on the ship. It was so pretty, and the light called to me. I wanted to go, but…I couldn't. I couldn't get on."

Her voice wavered. And as he pushed back and looked down, he realized just what she was talking about. "The Isles of the Blessed. You were on your way to Elysium. And you came back here? To me?"

She nodded.

He brought his hands back up to her face as disbelief rippled through him. "Why would you do that?"

"Because…I didn't want to forget. I had this ache inside me, and it was growing. And I knew it would go away if I just got on the ship, but I…I couldn't. I promised myself a long time ago that I'd never forget. I couldn't let that go."

The enormity of her sacrifice, of what she'd given up for him, nearly brought him to his knees. "Skyla…"

Her hands landed on his forearms. "I'm different, Orpheus. I know you can see it in my face, but I'm different...everywhere. It's still me, it's just...me before the Siren transformation. I know it's not what you remember. It's—"

"*Oraios*." Beautiful.

"Really? But won't you miss—?"

"Not for a second. Skyla, I'd want you even if you had a completely different body. Even if that body was part daemon."

Emotions filled her eyes. Eyes that weren't amethyst anymore but a soft, mottled green. Her natural eyes were green. As his daemon's eyes had been.

"Your daemon's gone," she whispered.

"Thanks to you."

"No, Orpheus." Her hands tightened around his arms. "Thanks to you."

Be greater. Her last words echoed in his head. He was. And with her, he could be even more.

"I can't go back to the Sirens," she whispered. "And when Zeus finds out the Fates sent me back, he won't be happy."

"I have a feeling Zeus is already unhappy. And news flash, female, you're not going anywhere. You're staying here with me."

"Here?"

"Here." He nodded to the glass windows. "Home."

The darkening of her eyes told him she liked that. But when he moved in to kiss her once more, she stopped him with her fingers against his lips. "The Fates said I would have a blessed life, but my soul isn't guaranteed a repeat ride on the white ship. Not unless I prove it again."

It was his turn to grin. "Something tells me that won't be a problem. Not this time."

He leaned in, but she eased back once more. "And they said something about a curse. A soul-mate curse. You don't know what they were talking about, do you?"

He froze millimeters from her mouth, glanced at the Argonaut markings on his forearms, and then chuckled. "That sneaky Fate. No wonder."

When her brow lowered, he ran his thumb over her lips. Her sweet and tender lips. Lips he planned to sample and taste and lose himself in this and every night from here until their days' ended—when they'd *both* be sailing on those white ships toward lands unknown, together. "Yeah, I might know. And trust me, it's the best damn curse any scheming god ever came up with."

She let him draw her face back to his. And in the cool wind, with the world dark around them and the fate of his brother, the Argonauts, and the future uncertain, one thing remained constant.

Her.

Through both his lives, through all the agonizing time in between, she was worth fighting for. She'd been worth dying for. She was the best thing in this world or the next worth living for.

"Kiss me, Siren."

She lifted her mouth to his. "I thought you'd never ask, daemon."

Eternal Guardians Lexicon

adelfos. Brother

ándras; pl. *ándres.* Male Argolean

archdaemon. Head of the daemon order; has enhanced powers from Atalanta

Argolea. Realm established by Zeus for the blessed heroes and their descendants

Argonauts. Eternal guardian warriors who protect Argolea. In every generation, one from the original seven bloodlines (Heracles, Achilles, Jason, Odysseus, Perseus, Theseus, and Bellerophon) is chosen to continue the guardian tradition

Chosen. One Argolean, one human; two individuals who, when united, completed the Argolean Prophecy and broke Atalanta's contract with Hades, thereby ejecting her from the Underworld and ending her immortality

Council of Elders. Twelve lords of Argolea who advise the reigning monarch

daemons. Beasts who were once human, recruited from the Fields of Asphodel (purgatory) by Atalanta to join her army

Dimiourgos. Creator

doulas. Slave

élencho. Mind-control technique Argonauts use on humans

Fates. Three goddesses who control the thread of life for all mortals from birth until death

Fields of Asphodel. Purgatory

gigia. Grandmother

gynaíka; pl. *gynaíkes.* Female Argolean

Hora; pl. **Horae.** Three goddesses of balance controlling life and order

Isles of the Blessed. Heaven

ilithios. Idiot

kardia. Term of endearment: my heart

matéras. Mother

meli. Term of endearment: beloved

Misos. Half-human/half-Argolean race that lives hidden among humans

Olympians. Current ruling gods of the Greek pantheon, led by Zeus, who meddle in human life

oraios. Beautiful

Orb of Krónos. Four-chambered disk that, when filled with the four classic elements—earth, wind, fire, and water—has the power to release the Titans from Tartarus

patéras. Father

Siren Order. Zeus's elite band of personal warriors. Commanded by Athena

skata. Swearword

syzygos. Wife

Tartarus. Realm of the Underworld similar to hell

Titans. The ruling gods before the Olympians

thea. Term of endearment: goddess

yios. Son

Lessons After Dark

by Isabel Cooper

Author of *No Proper Lady,* a *Publishers Weekly* and
Library Journal Best Book of the Year

~~~

A woman with an unspeakable past

Olivia Brightmore didn't know what to expect when she
took a position to teach at Englefield School, an academy for
"gifted" children. But it wasn't having to rescue a young girl
who'd levitated to the ceiling. Or battling a dark mystery in the
surrounding woods. And nothing could have prepared her for
Dr. Gareth St. John.

A man of exceptional talent

He knew all about her history and scrutinized her every move
because of it. But there was more than suspicion lurking in
those luscious green eyes. Olivia could feel the heat in each
haughty look. She could sense the desire in every touch, a
spark that had nothing to do with the magic of his healing
abilities. Even with all the strange occurrences at the school,
the most unsettling of all is the attraction pulling her and
Gareth together with a force that cannot be denied.

~~~

For more Isabel Cooper, visit:

www.sourcebooks.com

Deliver Me from Darkness

by Tes Hilaire

Angel to vampire is a long way to fall.

A stranger in the night...

He had once been a warrior of the Light, one of the revered Paladin. A protector. But now he lives in darkness, and the shadows are his sanctuary. Every day is a struggle to overcome the bloodlust. Especially the day Karissa shows up on his doorstep.

Comes knocking on the door

She is light and bright and everything beautiful—despite her scratches and torn clothes. Every creature of the night is after her. So is every male Paladin. Because Karissa is the last female of their kind. But she is *his*. Roland may not have a soul, but he can't deny his heart.

For more Tes Hilaire, visit:

www.sourcebooks.com

King of Darkness

by Elisabeth Staab

Eternal commitment is not on her agenda...

Scorned by the vampire community for her lack of power,
Isabel Anthony lives a carefree existence masquerading as
human—although, drifting through the debauched human
nightlife, she prefers the patrons' blood to other indulgences.
But when she meets the sexy, arrogant king of the vampires,
this party girl's life turns dark and dangerous.

But time's running out for the King of Vampires

Dead-set on finding the prophesied mate who will unlock
his fiery powers, Thad Morgan must find his queen before
their race is destroyed. Their enemies are gaining ground,
and Thad needs his powers to unite his subjects. But when
his search leads him to the defiant Isabel, he wonders if fate
has gotten it seriously wrong...

For more Elisabeth Staab, visit:

www.sourcebooks.com

About the Author

A former junior high science teacher, Elisabeth Naughton traded in her red pen and test-tube set for a laptop and research books. She now writes sexy romantic adventure and paranormal novels full-time from her home in western Oregon, where she lives with her husband and three children. Her work has been nominated for numerous awards, including the prestigious RITA Awards of Romance Writers of America, the Australian Romance Reader Awards, the Golden Leaf, and the Golden Heart. When not writing, Elisabeth can be found running, hanging out at the ball park, or dreaming up new and exciting adventures. Visit her at www.elisabeth naughton.com to learn more about her and her books.